Books by Nathaniel Burt

Leopards in the Garden

LEOPARDS
IN THE
GARDEN

A novel

by Nathaniel Burt

LITTLE, BROWN AND COMPANY   *Boston • Toronto*

LIBRARY OF CONGRESS CATALOG CARD NO. 68–17268

F I R S T   E D I T I O N

*Published simultaneously in Canada
by Little, Brown & Company (Canada) Limited*

PRINTED IN THE UNITED STATES OF AMERICA

To Julia Burt Atteberry

I.

i. The wind, the harsh hot Mediterranean wind, picking up whirls of white dust from the roadside, would break them against the wall and go over and through the dry dense glitterings of green on the other side — eucalyptus, mimosa, umbrella pine — twisting them, bringing out a swirl of light in the thickness, moving the noisy shimmer across the complicated gloom to the cliffs and out over the sea. The whole great round bay would be flattened and darkened by these dry land breezes, the peacock of the water stippled, made deeper. The sky, brassy at noon, deepened by four o'clock. The sun that turned the house bone color now brought lemon and orange out of the plaster. What had been irritating and tense before became luminous and exciting.

This change in light meant for us all a change in routine. The adults responded by emerging from their various holes; Mother from her bedroom, kept as cool as possible by darkened shutters, Father from his study next to it, both of them going to swim down on the rocks. Then came the ritual of evening drinks on the terrace, with guests sometimes, passing Americans, the few Frenchmen they knew. As for the rest of us, the children, this brightness and dryness kept us at a pitch all day. The winter had been colder and grayer and wetter than Americans would be willing to accept as Riviera weather, and this pouring of blue days, endless dry brightness, went to our heads. We

3

were now out of school — to the extent that some of us had really ever been "in school"; that is, I no longer walked up the dangerous road between fig trees and dogs to M. de Guichy and his twitchy, vital tutoring, though I had to keep up my French studies and the reading of *Sans Famille*. Mlle Madeleine still sometimes worked Jane and even Ronnie in the morning, as much as they ever worked. Only the older ones, Richie and Robbie, Ellie and Nan, were really officially on vacation, from real, official schools. It must have been a difficult household for our parents.

Fortunately we were pairs. Nan and Ellie, already half grown up and all woman, busied themselves with absurd, adolescent things, gushed and fought, spent hours dressing and undressing and trying out nail polish (which they weren't allowed to wear), and fixing their hair (which was severely bobbed). Richie and Robbie on the contrary had a world purely and dangerously masculine, full of climbing up things and jumping off, escapades on bicycles, meetings with strange persons, plots against everybody.

I was left with Jane. As a boy, and older, I should have been ashamed of her and myself. I wasn't. There was no surrounding society to establish conventions; Richie and Robbie were too far above me to count. Jane and I had our world to ourselves; my world, really, in which Jane played the role of stubborn, not always adaptable helpmate. My projects — vast elaborate layouts of roads and houses on the gravel paths, explorations of paneled woodwork for secret compartments, collections of sea animals, plantings of beans and nasturtiums which never bloomed — remained always mine. Jane turned and colored them with her own peculiar, sensible, original mind, sometimes flatly refusing to play along, or even actively obstructive. Usually however we made a team, boss and help, Quixote and Panza, Adam and Eve. Ronnie, staggering about, crying, an utter nuisance, sometimes tagged along with us. We used

4

him for bit parts, for walk-ons, spear-carrying. He played The Baby, or a Sentinel, or a clumsy constructor of roads. Poor Ronnie.

We did all get together sometimes of course: meals in the too-small children's dining room in the front of the house. We had breakfast on the terrace now that it was warm, and at dinner Ellie and Nan, even sometimes all of us, were allowed to eat with the grown-ups in their dining room, unless there were formidable guests, the Lewises, the Fitzgeralds, famous wanderers along the gilded coast in its gilded age. But at lunch we were together, all seven of us, and it was bedlam. We had our jokes, wearisome, endlessly repeated; "*Celestine à la soupe*," for instance. We had seen "*Soupe à la Celestine*" on hotel menus; and Celestine was our cook. Then there were teasings; teasing Nan about her "beaux," the fat, mustached postman, the little shaved-head orphans at the institution next door. It went on endlessly.

Poor Mademoiselle did her best to keep us down, her red hair flashing with temper. But we were all rather relieved to get off and back to our pairs. Nan and Ellie would go up to talk endlessly and endlessly in a dusky room about a letter from a boy. Robbie and Richie raced out to bicycles, tearing down the long gravel path that took them, eventually and by zigzags, to the shore. Ronnie napped. Jane and I, as a substitute for such a nap, went down into a sort of darkened but wide-open cellar under the terrace, where we kept toys. There we built Chinese walls and black pagodas from a discarded Mah-Jongg set. Our dog, the family dog, the community dog Lagarde, a mild Alsatian, sometimes dozed near us, or meditatively chewed on the blocks of the Mah-Jongg set.

ii. There were however community projects which got us all together — outings, picnics, entertainments. This day was to be full of them. First the expedition to wash off the cross, instigated by the indignant Protestantism of Nan and Ellie, supported by Jane and myself, scorned by the boys. Then Uncle Dick was to arrive. And in the evening we were all to go (except Ronnie of course) to the Hotel Maritime and the dance. It was a Saturday.

The cross-washing took us up the hill along a path through pines, Ellie and Nan, Jane and I, armed with a bucket of water and various rags and brushes. We were definitely religious pilgrims, representing righteousness, cleanliness and Respect for Historic Monuments. At the top of the hill there was a little votive chapel called, like our dog, Lagarde — Notre Dame de la Garde. It was of white marble, a Mediterranean Victorianism of uncouth neo-Gothic. Inside it was dark, close and plastered every-where with naïve votive tablets, pictures of broken legs mended, fishing boats rescued, all in the most garish colors and flat designs. We despised them. Crowning insult to our feeling for fitness was a white marble cross in front of the church, covered with hundreds of devout tourist-pilgrim signatures. Brought up as we were to look on this as vandalism and immoral (defacing antiquities, bathroom scatology), the names on the cross were an insult to us. Ellie and Nan conceived the idea of washing the cross, a sort of ritual act like scrubbing the steps of an altar at Eastertide.

It turned out to be harder than we expected. The scribblings were in pencil, engrained in the marble, or in ink, or even scratched with a penknife. It didn't take very long for fervor to die down. Jane had come without a hat, in all the blazing sun. This gave Ellie and Nan a raft of righteousness to ride home on. Although Jane was quite capable of going home by herself, the big girls felt it was "dangerous." For one thing, the parents actually had given strict orders that the younger children were not to go outside the garden walls unaccompanied by elders. Then, we had all been hearing rumors about a leopard, supposed to have escaped from a circus. There were always possible tramps. Jane, who wanted to stay and finish cross-washing, was dragged off. But how easily we saw through the rationalizations of foolish Ellie and Nan. They were simply bored and hot. Why did people seem to grow more able to fool themselves as they got older?

I was left, against all parental rules, alone. I didn't think of that; in fact I was enjoying myself. Any thoroughly monotonous physical activity — raking leaves, pasting stamps into an album, painting benches — I found soothing. Meditative in the midmorning heat, I scrubbed the stone of the shaft, observing satisfactory areas of gray as they grew, scouring away Superstition. Below me, between our Villa Esperance and the church, it was all pine woods and thickets. In the other direction behind the church and each side of it spread the view, a great panorama from this jutting, sacred outcrop, of vineyards and vegetables on the flat plain, then the salt fields, squares of what looked like melting ice, then the sea again on the other side of our big peninsula; and closing the vista a bulk of mountain, bald and brown-green in this rude morning light, but glowing and majestic by late afternoon. Not a sound anywhere but the cicadas, intense, all-pervading. I could hear once in a rare while the hum of a passing car from the road to town that passed the foot of the cliff; sometimes the dim beep of an irritable French auto horn.

7

I was playing monk. We had been recently to an old ex-monastery for a picnic, and playing monk had become part of our repertoire. This consisted of devotional exercises such as incense-burning processions with much chanting, rigorous punishments and penitences (as described with relish by our old guide at the monastery), flagellations, cells and cross-washings such as this. I had broken several commandments and committed various venial and mortal sins (I had only the vaguest ideas about these). For a penance I was to wash the cross day and night, saying continual prayers to the Virgin. I was dressed in sackcloth and of course my hair was all shaved off. It was bitter cold. I had walked all the way through the snow, barefoot and bloody. I was going to die of consumption any minute now. My tears flowed both night and day for the wicked wicked things I had done. But when I got through and the cross was finally as white as the new driven snow, suddenly the Virgin was going to appear to me, right *in* the cross, and I was to be carried up to heaven and be called St. Boniface, patron saint of July 18. I had a little diary in which every day was marked as the day of some patron saint, each one with the queerest of names: Ste. Delphine, S. Gratien, Ste. Leocadie. Perhaps my name could be something more interesting than Boniface. Theophylact. I actually had an old cousin at home called Theophyl-act. . . .

I put down the scrubbing brush and straightened up. I was really getting very hot, and I had a crick in my back. I stood listening to the hum of the silence. I was very much alone. No one ever seemed to come up to the church when we were there, in spite of the evidence of votive pictures inside and name scribblings out here. I could almost hear the pulsating waves of heat swimming up out of the valley.

There was a dry startling sound in the underbrush, down in front of me toward home. Silence for a minute.

8

But something was moving there; an animal. Then the noise again, and I saw plainly, not three yards away, a big black shape, slipping from the laurels into the sun and back again. Most distinctly I saw the tail, sinuous, glossy, very large, definitely catlike. I stood stock-still as the rustling went off to my left and disappeared.

It was a long time before I dared to move. As long as I didn't twitch an eyelid, I knew I was safe. The problem was getting home; especially with the creaky bucket. No doubt the leopard was hungry and probably lying in wait for a morsel of boy. However, my excitement, my feeling of exalted privilege at having been allowed, all by myself, to actually see the escaped leopard balanced my fear. I had to get home and tell the news; besides it must be lunchtime.

As an experimental move I emptied the gray water from my pail. I clanked the handle quite a bit and waited. Nothing. Then I drummed on the bottom. This must certainly scare the leopard away. After a couple of palpitating moments I clutched the handle and my courage and walked as quickly and as silently as I could down along the path. It was dreadful in the woods. I was so frightened I couldn't even pretend it was the jungle. It really *was* the jungle. As soon as I got to the wall of the orphanage I felt safe, even though the wall was only on one side of me. The leopard had been going in that direction. He couldn't have circled and recrossed the path so quickly. I ran, without stopping, along beside the wall, around the corner of it, across the dusty road, through our gate and right into our door. Everyone was at lunch.

iii. "You're late, you're late!" I handed the bucket and brush to Celestine through the kitchen door, which faced that of our children's dining room across the narrow front hall; a fairly disreputable

9

entrance for such a pseudo-grandiose villa. "Go wash your hands," from Mademoiselle. "My hands are already washed." "He's been washing the cross, Mademoiselle." "*Washing the cross? The cross?* What cross? *Sacré nom* . . ." My hands were very dirty and I was glad to use the antique lavabo darkly nestled down the hall and under the stairs. And to get away from possible awkward discussions about cross-washing with Mademoiselle. Let Nan do the explaining, it was her idea. It was also a chance for me to catch my breath and prepare to tell my tremendous news.

When I got back, sure enough, Mademoiselle was saying, her voice heavy with grievance, ". . . All those poor people. They come from miles just to write on that cross. It gets them . . . it earns them a bit of time out of purgatory you know. Every bit counts. You've put all those poor people back in the flames — oh, I hate to think how long." "Mademoiselle!" Nan gasped at the sudden French turn from sentiment to cynicism. I took my seat quickly at the big round room-filling table and caught up on my soup as quietly as possible, waiting for my chance.

It came. "Did you wash them all off?" said Ellie to me. I shook my head. "Guess what I saw though . . ." "There's lots of names still left, Mademoiselle," Ellie tried to be consoling. "We only washed one side." I was not to be deterred. "I saw the leopard!"

"The *what?*" "The leopard; the one that escaped from the circus." "Non-sense!" cried Mademoiselle, making two words of it. "There is *no* such thing. Who told you those silly stories? There is *no* circus and no leopard. I won't have you scaring my *bébé.*" She clutched Ronnie to her. He had been, up to that time, off in dreamland, but now he came to sufficiently to whimper obligingly. "It *is* so!" said Richie with his usual overintense ferocity. "I heard it from Jacques, and he said it was in all the papers. What did it look like, Howie?" "Well, it was as big as this, and black all over, and had a long long skinny tail." "Well, then, it couldn't have been a leopard," said Ellie, "because leopards aren't black." "They are too." "They are not. They have spots." "Panthers," said Nan wearily, "are black. Leopards," she closed her eyes as she barely deigned to look across at me, "have spots." "They do not. Leopards are too black, they . . ." "They have black *spots* but they are *yellow*."

As anything that could be discussed inevitably became a matter of faction, so did the issue of the leopard. The division was more or less along lines of sex. Mademoiselle was anti-leopard because she was afraid for Ro-nee. Richie was pro-leopard to spite her; Nan and Ellie anti to spite him. Robbie and Jane kept quiet, though I felt I could count on Jane. In any case, I knew I had seen a fabulous beast, and that was enough for me.

We fought all through lunch. As soon as they'd gobbled their food, Richie said to Robbie, "Let's go look for it!" "No, no!" screamed Mademoiselle. "Well if it doesn't exist, it can't hurt us, can it?" said Robbie, his first leopard-gesture. "It does exist. I saw it," said I, pleased at their going to look for it, hurt and relieved that they hadn't asked me, miffed by Robbie. "We'll see, we'll see!" and the boys stampeded out to their bicycles and were off and out the gate in their usual splattering of gravel. "Really, how *silly*," said Nan. "It was probably just a cat." "It was not. It was as big . . . as big as Lagarde." "It was a dog," said practical Ellie. "I've seen him. There's a big black dog there on the other side of the orphanage. I've seen him dozens of times." "It was not, it was not. It was a leopard." "Panther," said haughty Nan. "It was a leopard, and *I* saw it with my own eyes and it wasn't a dog because dogs' tails don't wiggle like that." "Don't shout please at the table." Mademoiselle could assert authority now the big boys were

gone. "Finish your prunes and go down *quietly*. All this
excitement! I will have to tell your father about this. We
shall see who tells the truth. Come, Ronnie."

I stomped off, with Jane, down to our cellar refuge,
hurt by the reception of my great news, my fine adventure.
But Jane was consoling. She believed me, she listened to
me. She knew it was a leopard, not a panther, not a dog. It
would be our secret then, along with all our other secrets. I
was sorry now I'd told anyone else.

iv. We had a rather restless
time of it down there in our hideaway. We knew that
Uncle Dick was due to arrive any minute, and we had no
intention of missing a thing. Every time a car passed or
seemed to stop, one or both of us would run around the
corner and up the curving steps to take a look. We hid
behind the clump of a century plant. Nobody came.

Uncle Dick was a myth to us. We'd never seen him, at
least that we could remember. He'd been living abroad ever
since his romantic and dashing service in the war — ambulance driving, aviation, espionage, what not. He had of
course been home occasionally to see Mother, who was his
favorite sister despite her being so much older. She had
from the first treated him as her baby, and evidently the
affection remained on both sides. He was at once glorious
and shady — a high liver, a reckless driver — and all of us,
irrespective of our real kinship to him, regarded him, or at
least his reputation, as a family distinction.

Jane and I took special pride in being, along with
Robbie (and Ronnie of course, who hardly counted), his
only true blood kin. Ellie and Nan belonged exclusively to
Father, children of a remote, beloved first wife early dead.
Robbie belonged, equally exclusively, to Mother and her
first husband, also dead, but not quite so beloved. There

had been a divorce, despite the issue of his Irish Catholicism; he had remarried, and Richie was the orphan of this remarriage. So that he too was not related to Uncle Dick. But we, Jane and I, we were. We (and of course Ronnie) were children of *both* Mother and Father, and it was the source of our pride and strength, and our trump card, so to speak, in the game-battles of family life. Part of our resentment against Ronnie was just that he too shared the honor, but couldn't appreciate it.

Thus Uncle Dick was *our* uncle, and though we had no idea even what he looked like, we were willing to admire. So when at last, finally, he did arrive, and a fabulous Hispano-Suiza, all made of what looked like silver, polished in little circles, did drive up and stop, and we did run up and were in fact there to see it all — well, Uncle Dick was frankly a disappointment. For one thing he was so young. He looked like a boy, and that was no recommendation. Mother was of course aged beyond all thought, over forty. Dick must have been about thirty. He looked at first sight not more than twenty. Where were the mustache, the pirate glance, the elegant suit and cane and panama hat? The tall rakishness, the swagger we naturally expected? He hopped over the closed door of his open two-seater with disgusting agility, dressed — of all things — like a French sailor, tight white sailor pants and blue-striped, bare-armed sailor's jersey. He had a nasty little beret on. Silly. That was what Jane was saying to herself, and I certainly agreed. He leaned back into the car, honking a horn, then yanked out his big suitcase and jauntily heaved it and himself through the ironwork gate.

Before he got to the house, Mother came rushing out and they fell on each other. She seemed to be taller than he was, though perhaps it was only her irreconcilably unbobbed hair, piled up messily. As for his hair, when he snatched off his beret, it too was a disappointment. Where were the carefully curling black locks, streaked with experienced gray? His hair was cut short almost like a convict's and it was the color of cinnamon toast. This of course was pretty much Mother's hair coloring too, but though we accepted and even admired it on her, it was absurd on a man. A young man too, to be so . . . well gray all right, but such an undistinguished gray. And the haircut! Almost like those of the poor boys at the orphanage who had all their heads shaved. (For *lice*, whispered Mademoiselle. We didn't know what lice were.) We had never seen a "crew cut," at that time a purely German idea. We thought it was silly.

Father came out, and his hair was bushy and wavy and iron-gray the way the hair of fathers and uncles, if they had any hair, was meant to be. Father grinned and his startling eyebrows went out and up with pleasure, and Uncle Dick bent over backward, with gestures, telling them a story we couldn't hear. We didn't like the stagy way he moved, a sort of Douglas Fairbanks staginess, hopping over the car door, swinging his great bag around, bending acrobatically over backward that way, as he raised his bare brown arms. His voice, what we could hear of it from our hiding place, was clear, forceful but high-pitched. He talked with some kind of an accent. Actorish. That was silly too.

Then he saw us, shiny-eyed but unsmiling back of our century plant. He crouched a bit, and pointed and then slapped his knees, laughing. He overdid it, we thought. But we had to come out shamefaced while the three of them laughed and laughed at us. Dick squatted down to look at us, and we looked at him. He gave us each a hand. His hands were very clean and very brown and very strong. His face was very bare and brown too, with pale funny-looking eyes in it that seemed artificial like his voice. His smile was a neat box.

"Well, you two! Niece and nephew!" He looked from one to the other, then turned back up and said, "They don't look like anybody. A pity. Nobody looks like me." "Robbie looks a bit like you," said Mother. And Father said, "Why don't you have some of your own then? I mean legally." Mother gave him what everybody in the family called "one of her looks."

Our parents were so transparent. Father was always saying things that Mother thought he shouldn't say in front of us. He obviously did it on purpose. But we would never have noticed, except for those "looks." Mother would frown slightly and press her lips together and turn to him; and then we would pay attention and try to understand whatever it was he had said. This time, as usual, we failed. How could Uncle Dick have children if he weren't married? We knew at least that one had to have a mother to have children, and Uncle Dick was a famous bachelor.

He squatted, looking from one to the other of us, but since he got no response from us, not even a smile, he rose. "Serious little beggars," he said. That was a silly phrase, "little beggars," and we didn't like it. He turned and the three of them went into the house, carrying the big suitcase between them and talking hilariously.

Mother called back at us, "Go on downstairs, children." We stood out in the sun on the gravel, crushed, yet still rather soberly gratified. Uncle Dick was certainly not what we had hoped for. But the fact that unanimously, without saying anything, we recognized him as silly gave us a superior satisfaction. What grown-ups thought of as being so wonderful frequently was silly; and silly, a word primarily of Jane's usage, was the worst thing anyone or anything could be.

This area of the silly was the one area in which Jane showed a distinct, natural, unquestionable superiority over me. If Jane thought something was silly, it was silly, and no arguments or feelings on my part had any effect. The judgment was final, brutal and always justifiable. Her standards of what was and was not silly were absolute. I knew, and she knew I knew that Uncle Dick — his sailor pants, his beret and haircut, his jumping about, his youngness, his square smile — were all silly. And that was that.

Only his car wasn't silly. We stared at it for a while through the iron bars of the gate, then went slowly back downstairs to the dark cave under the terrace and played languidly with blocks. Disappointed, superior, gratified.

v. But we hoped to have a good look at that car. This was the one facet of Uncle Dick we could not criticize. Our attitudes toward Frenchified clothes and Anglified accents might be uncompromisingly American; but cars were different. Though not then or now ever in the least mechanical, I was an avid spectator of the glorious world of the automobile, so rich at that time in variety, so full of excitement and dash. I kept a catalogue or checklist of cars seen; not a bird but a car watcher. Such common ones as Renault and Citroën had countless check lines after them: ⊬⊬ ⊬⊬-⊬⊬-⊬⊬ ⊬⊬ /// . (In any collection there must always be the Great Commoners: the ordinary red two-cent stamps, then, or, in a bottle-top collection I had at home, the caps of Whistle and Sarsaparilla.) But even here on the Riviera, Hispano-Suizas were not for every day. This one was right outside the gate.

We would naturally have climbed right into it immediately, as soon as Dick got out of it. But since we were so absolutely forbidden to go outside the gates alone, for any reason, at any time unless escorted, we didn't dare. It was the one thing denied us in our garden. We could break our necks from any branch or off any cliff inside our walls, but we could not go outside them. The road there was after all a highway that cut through between house and garage without even enough footpath way. Cars were not many, but dashed with French abandon. We usually respected that law religiously.

As soon as our time down in our cellar was done (we simply guessed by instinct and the quality of light; if we came up too soon we were sent back again), we ran up the stairs. The car was gone. Uncle Dick had evidently left his bag and then disappeared again, and we hadn't heard or noticed. We went slowly to the gate and clung to the bars heartbroken. We felt we might never get such a chance at a Hispano-Suiza again.

The routine of the afternoon swim, down on the sea-weed- and barnacle-covered yellow rocks, off the wave-mangled old stone pier, drove the disappointment out of our heads. When, somewhat later, as the daily transformation of later afternoon took place, we came up and dressed and appeared on the terrace for a postponed *goûter* of lemonade and cookies, Uncle Dick was there again. The car had been stuck in the great ex-stable garage across the road, so we hadn't noticed it. Dick was still dressed *en matelot*, and sat slouching back in one of the ironwork chairs of the porch with one white duck leg hooked and dangling over the arm of it. Mother and Father were having tea as was usual with them. Dick drank our lemonade.

Ronnie was there too, but he was sitting in a far corner of the terrace doing something childish with a little boat. Dick smiled at us mechanically, we were polite, got our lemonade and cookies and left, going into the cavernous gloom of the *salon*. Already our positions as not-favorite-uncle and not-favorite-niece-and-nephew were established.

Our antagonism, not any feeling of being crowded, forced us in. The terrace was certainly large enough for us all. That terrace, really a covered balcony, where Uncle

17

Dick rather insolently lounged (if any of us had dared to cock a leg over a chair arm like that!) had in fact become our summer living room. It ran the whole length of the seaward side of the house. The Villa Esperance was sensibly designed to take advantage of its view of garden and Mediterranean. That was however the only sensible thing about it. It lay wedged, flat and narrow, between the road on the north side and the sea view to the south. The road ran right beyond the heavily barred windows of the first floor, which on that side contained the kitchen, the stairs, bathrooms and various obscure housekeeping holes. The front door was thus squeezed into the narrow end of the wedge. It gave into a hall, which, after its humiliating progress between kitchen and children's dining room, led on past the dark state dining room and then past this great *salon* which took up most of the downstairs space.

What a fantastic room it was. On one side it was all glass doors leading out onto the porch. The other side was all false doors, leading nowhere, but made of mirrors. Everywhere, all up and down the false mirrored doors, or on the narrow mirrored strips between the real glass doors, there were painted climbing roses. Not so much painted as applied, for each rose was a big glob, a clump of appallingly not-realistic plaster, pink, at once shiny and dusty. Up to the ceiling clambered this inspiration, and then illusion carried the imaginary bower further in a simulacrum of a Roman (*ca.* 1880) atrium — a fresco of yellow plaster balustrades covered with those clambering pink roses, and then above a blue blue sky with swallows skimming across it. We children thought it was just lovely.

At the far end was a massive never used fireplace. On top of it a great gilt-framed Victorian mirror, and in front of that a huge leprous antique amphora, dug up from sea bottom. This was held in place by grim iron braces. At the other end of the long room was an equally impressive black imitation carved Renaissance highboy, which we suspected of being full of secret compartments. Over it, to balance mirror and amphora, loomed a black imitation Spanish Renaissance portrait — some pseudo-Velásquez king. Furniture consisted of a red brocade curly sofa and two curly chairs. And that was that. The parents had made feeble efforts at filling the vacuum with a nice tan Chinese rug with big white cranes flying across it and various odd chairs brought from other parts of the house. There was a battered grand piano in the front corner next to a terrace door. The floor was not red tile like the rest of the house, but elaborate parquet, breaking up under the slidings and runnings to which it was subjected by us on rainy days. Rainy days could be pretty awful.

But on lovely evenings such as this we usually sat outside and watched the breeze run through pine, mimosa, eucalyptus and a few ragged palms, watched the glow of sea grow deeper and the west more mellow. We could play the piano inside, or have our own circles outside without too much interference with our parents and their guests, and altogether it made up for that *salon*.

Tonight Jane and I resented being driven off the terrace by the presence of Uncle Dick; but then it was fun, too, pretending to have a grown-up party. We copied in a mocking way the "serious conversation" of the people outside. The satire was wasted on the grown-ups.

They were talking about Father's book. "The point," Father was saying, "is that the south of France is not the cradle of Catholic civilization people might think, but actually the cradle of Protestant civilization." He stopped and we could imagine him pulling his nose, with his eyebrows going up and down like wild gray butterflies. "You know that Provence was even a sort of center of Quakerism. Hard to believe."

Dick laughed. "So I suppose *that's* why you're here.

19

Damnedest reason for coming to the Riviera I ever heard of." "Well, not really," said Father. "But there is a connection." Over Dick's renewed laughter (he laughed so *loud*), Father protested. "No, I really mean it. I want to see where I get tracing Quakerism back to the Vaudois and the Cathars. . . ." We would easily close our ears to Father's conversation along these lines. We admired his work tremendously of course, but made no bones about our total lack of interest in it. He never gave our total lack of interest a thought. He talked about the Cathars and the Albigensian Crusade and the courts of love and the Quakers whether we were listening or not, so long as there was somebody, even only Mother, even only *us* to listen to him. This was as it should be. Father was obviously very important, and people ought to listen to him. Older people, that is.

Our satire and their discussion were both interrupted by the late, clumping, breathless entrance of the boys. They'd been out somewhere, too far, on their bicycles. To the Websters' to start with, it seemed. The parents were not pleased. We trailed out in their wake. Dick gave them a look over his shoulder, without changing his negligent position, and then each a hand. "Hi," he said. First Robbie then Richie ducked in a little bow and smirked. Young gentlemen. They were flushed and still panting from their hurry, and their voices were husky. Uncle Dick looked back at them from over his shoulder, since they seemed afraid to come forward properly. "Beautiful," he said, turning to the parents. He was obviously referring only to Robbie. Nobody could ever have called Richie that. Father raised his eyebrows; Mother, embarrassed, said, "Oh, come now, Dick, that's just because I said he looked like you." "We don't want him to get above himself," added Father in his sarcastic voice. Robbie flushed. Dick looked around at him again, taking his leg down off the chair arm. "Well, he's got the hair anyway."

The reddish hair was a trademark, a family trait — not real red, like Mademoiselle's, but sort of rust-colored. In Mother faded, in Dick salted prematurely with gray, in Robbie it was darker, almost auburn-chestnut. But as for being beautiful! We were almost as shocked as Father, if for different reasons. It was not only that people didn't use such a word about boys; it was that people shouldn't think of the word in such a connection. Girls, it was true, even grown-up ladies, could be called beautiful as a special dispensation. This meant they were all dressed up and full of airs and graces. Otherwise, and certainly to us, "beauty" meant natural phenomena. Flowers were beautiful, sunsets and the sea. The moon and the nightingales we heard here in the garden were beautiful. The present moment, the musical light of an afternoon not yet evening — these Jane and I both recognized and indeed strongly felt as beautiful. But Robbie! This was the very climax of Dick's silliness.

Robbie was almost as big and strong as a man now, but he still had, much to his utter shame, the complexion and eyelashes of a girl, not to mention the hair. Perhaps on a girl these might be misnamed "beautiful." But to Robbie, and to the rest of us, far from being considered beautiful, they were shameful. This prettiness was his cross. He bore it, but it had long made his life miserable. In earlier years he had compensated for it by ferocity and daring and an assertion of masculinity. Lately he had grown so and become so expert and powerful and agile and able to beat everyone at everything, king of his school class, athlete of our family, that he could afford to relax, to be magnanimous, to dismiss his failing as incurable but really negligible.

Mother and Father evidently agreed with us about Uncle Dick's silliness; at least they told the boys to take their lemonades and clear out. But Robbie wanted to swim.

"Isn't it too late? Haven't you been swimming already at the Websters'?" "Swim!" said Dick. "I wondered what was missing. I'm afraid I'll have to go with them. Do you mind? If I don't swim once a day my skin shrinks. Let's go." Dick stood up. "My bathing suit's upstairs," said Richie. "Oh, who needs bathing suits," said Uncle Dick. "No, they have to have them. All beaches in France are public you know." A sudden gloom fell over Robbie's face. "I left mine at the Websters'." "Oh, Robbie!" sighed Mother.

"Come on, Mary," said Dick, "don't be such a prude. Let's go, boys. We'll only be a minute. I'll be responsible. C'mon." Before the parents could say a word they trooped out, stumbling over themselves in eagerness. Father pulled his nose. "I wonder if your brother is going to be a good influence?" Mother shrugged and sighed again. "I suppose it really is foolish. After all it is our property . . ." Jane and I left the argument and ran out to see the boys take off.

"Thanks, old chap," Uncle Dick was saying, as he clapped Richie on his bony shoulder and climbed aboard Richie's bike. He had evidently requisitioned it, for he and Robbie dashed off, racing down the wide gentle slope of the main path into the garden. Lagarde followed barking. Richie stood, left behind, watching them, his thin mouth working in the grimaces that meant he was hurt and angry. We discreetly ducked back into the hall before he could take it out on us. Richie turned toward the shortcut and ran to beat the bicyclers to the beach, his thin awkward legs flying.

vi. So now we had nothing to do. We wandered idly upstairs, Jane to her room on the second floor, I to mine on the third. I was going to play with my stamps and watch the sun slowly move toward setting. I had bought some new stamps last time in town at the tiny novelty store there, and now was my chance to put them in my album and gloat over them. They were big exotic productions from Togo, and had scenes of native life on them. Now *there* was beauty for you! After that I stood at my window and watched the day get more golden. My room was at the top of the house, much too large and good for mere me, and I had it all to myself. It seemed to consist mostly of floor, red tile, smooth, deliciously cool in summer, horridly cold in winter. There was a bed made of wrought iron, all black curlicues and little bright-colored rosettes representing flowers. Over it, down from the high ceiling, swept the great, necessary folds of mosquito netting; already the mosquitoes were coming out as the sun dipped. For decor I had only my view west out of the big windows: hills that grew black against the evening, a few beautifully placed cypresses, an open prospect down the white road; over on the other side the density of the garden and the wide bay. When not occupied by natural beauty and deep thoughts (I wrote poems from up there: "Night comes on her enchanted way . . . ") I could enjoy the human activity out in front of the house.

For instance, here came Robbie and Dick (no Richie) up the path from their too-prolonged swim, pushing their bicycles slowly, deep in conversation. Dick had on only his sailor pants, with his striped jersey slung over his shoulder. At the same time, here came Mrs. Webster. You could catch her perky bright red little Citroën from far off as it came down the road. It arrived, it stopped, disgorging not only Mrs. Webster but also Nan and Ellie. Those two raced in to greet Uncle Dick, full of useless female exuberance. They knew him, remembered him from their childhood, had been the ones to cultivate most assiduously the Uncle Dick myth. He wouldn't kiss them, being too wet and messy from his swim, but they stood around him, hopping and bobbing in that way they had. They introduced him to Mrs. Webster who came up afterward.

If either Uncle Dick or Mrs. Webster were embarrassed by his being half naked, they neither of them showed it. Mrs. Webster took one of those deep breaths — what Nan called "pouting," that is, like a pouter pigeon — and got right up close to Uncle Dick and began sparkling at him. She had black curls and black eyes and a high staccato English voice and was all animation. Dick leaned against his bicycle in boyishly graceful poses, and didn't seem to be bothered in the least by the cold evening breezes on his glossy brown skin. One by one the children drifted off. Mrs. Webster flipped Robbie his bathing suit as he left, but she and Uncle Dick stayed there talking and talking.

This would make Nan furious I knew. For some reason she hated Mrs. Webster, and was always giving her nicknames like "the little red hen" from the color of her car, or "Mrs. Lobster" from the frequent color of her sunburn, or "pouter pigeon." Mrs. Webster was as nice to Nan as to the rest of us, which was very nice indeed. She lived alone, a divorcée, in a white pretty villa a mile down the shore, with two pretty daughters, Pamela and Miranda. She was a great favorite with the parents. Pam and Miranda were the only girls considered remotely human by Richie and Robbie, since they were, as Jocelyn Webster was the first to point out, "jolly good sports" and just as daring on bicycles as the boys. We all spent a lot of time there.

I got bored watching Mrs. Webster and Uncle Dick long before they got bored talking, and I returned to my stamps.

vii. A Gala Evening. That was the description used by the Hotel Maritime for their Saturday nights, and that is how we felt about them. The word "gala" in itself suggested the kind of exotic merriment that went on when big ocean liners induced their passengers to put on paper hats and throw things about — little varicolored cotton balls. In America, somehow, no evening could be quite "gala." It was a purely continental mood.

The gala-ness of it began at home with a big formal dinner for all of us — all except little Ronnie — in the darkness of the dining room. This in itself was sufficiently gala, for Jane and I were not often allowed to eat in there, even on the occasions (frequent) when Nan and Ellie or (less frequent) Robbie and Richie were.

It was a formal, not to say formidable room. It was wainscoted a good way up in ebony black, heavily carved, neo-Renaissance paneling, full of knobs and pilasters and grotesque little faces. Above this the wall was covered with purple burlap, on which were hung, rather effectively, black Piranesi prints of dungeons and ruins. About the long glossy refectory table, lit by big candles in ornate church candlesticks, sat the gang of us. Father was at the far end, presiding. On his right sat Nan, who was cast as the star of this particular occasion, all dressed up in a shiny shimmery white and gold dress, gauzy, knee-length, Parisian. Her naturally wavy gold hair was unnaturally wavier, a process that had been going on full blast next to me all the time I had been playing with my stamps upstairs, and she really looked rosy-and-golden, and, even I had to admit, "beautiful." For Nan, that is.

Uncle Dick, as her escort, sat next to her. He too was gala. Not evening dress like Father's white shirt, black bow tie and red velvet old coat, but dapper in a white suit (silk, made in Shanghai, he had said), a dark, dungaree-blue shirt and an orange tie. It made his bronzed face seem very sun-smitten and athletic. Ellie, sensible, her hair just as usual in a severe black Dutch bob, her dress nothing special, seemed resigned, just as usual, to her role as Nan's second fiddle. At least she had Dick's right side. Then I came, then Jane, and at the other end of the table, queen of below the salt, Miranda Webster, sly, long-eyed, full of sibilant mischief under a mask of manners.

Down the other side went, next to Father, Mrs. Webster, bosomy and blatant in scarlet, Mother in the turquoise green that so well became her reddish piled-up hair, Robbie decently tied and coated, Pamela blond, curling, bouncy, tanned, and then hungry Richie. A full house.

Gala too was the presence of the occasional waitress Leone, a lithe, long-faced, gypsy-like young woman whose finesse and dash about the table were mitigated only by her intense interest in what was going on there. She thought nothing of stopping to join right in, in bad but fluent English or atrocious French. She was a Niçoise of enormous local patriotism, and despised the French. She and the sternly Breton Celestine, who didn't really think much of the French either, had continual battle royals in the kitchen. They abused each other with abandoned ferocity, and admired each other considerably.

Just being there in the dining room was exciting enough for me, even dressed as I was in the First Communion suit (the only remotely formal clothes my parents could find for me) that I so hated, with its wide sissified Eton collar and ridiculous short pants. But actually during the soup nothing very interesting happened. A sort of chain reaction of smothered, senseless hilarity ran up and down the line from Miranda through Richie and Pam to the unusually subdued Robbie: nudgings, whisperings, sudden guffaws or giggles (Pam was great at these), scowlings, threats by Richie, slinky looks by Miranda. Among the grown-ups decorum reigned, Dick concentrating on Nan, so that Ellie, Jane and I were marooned as onlookers.

What we looked for was some grand grown-up argument. Father believed, and we knew he believed, in having children listen in on and even participate in uninhibited discussions of general ideas — morality, religion, politics, even sex. He felt it was part of our education, and it was. Mother could never be quite sure. Things would get really going, Father in particular would get really going, then would come one of Mother's Looks. Jocelyn Webster tended to encourage Father. But nothing seemed to be happening tonight.

An interlude broke things up temporarily: the specially planned entrance of Ronnie, all ready for bed, in fact for sleep. He was done up by Mademoiselle to look his most deceptively angelic, his brilliant curls washed and fluffed, his face scrubbed to rosiness, regally miniature in his tiny bathrobe and slippers. He made a sensation, if more among the old than the young. He circled the table, guided and coached by clucking Mademoiselle, in a daze of drowsy glory, shaking hands solemnly with all the guests. Nan, showing off, insisted on kissing him. The rest of us snickered, knowing perfectly well that she did it for effect. Under ordinary circumstances she brushed him off as a nuisance. Pam was more sincere in her admiration and kept exclaiming, "Oh, isn't he love-ly! Oh, the dear!" — suddenly deserting her role of tomboy for maternalism. For as long as Ronnie circled the table, a visitor from a golden slumberland, we were entertained. When he left, the dinner relapsed.

Then apropos of something I had missed, Mrs. Webster leaned across Mother to Robbie. "And just what *were* you doing beating about in the bushes all afternoon, may I ask?"

"Oh, nothing." "Exploring," added Miranda from her end. "Exploring?" said her mother. "You know those woods like the palm of your hand. Too well." "We were looking for something." Smothered laughter and sly glances all round. "Treasure, I suppose," said Mrs. Webster. "If you find any bring it straight back to me. I hope that's what you were looking for." "No," said Pam daringly, "we were looking for leopards."

"Leopards? Leopards?" said all the grown-ups with satisfactory emphasis. This was my chance. Summoning up all my courage and breaking in, too loudly, I shouted, "I saw the leopard. The one that escaped from the circus."

Consternation! Leone stopped on her way to the kitchen, behind Dick, wide-eyed. Exclamations and questions; Nan, bored, said, "Oh honestly, it's just that big black dog down there beyond the orphanage." "It was *not*," I yelled. "It had a tail like this," and I demonstrated sinuousness with one hand, "and it was too big. It was a leopard." "Well, it wasn't a leopard anyway. Leopards aren't black." "Don't shout so, Howie, we all believe you," said Father consolingly. "*I* don't," said Nan. "Eet's true. There's a beast from the *ménagerie*. In the *journal*," put in Leone. Everybody was excited, and no Mademoiselle to defend her Ro-nee. "Anyway it couldn't possibly be a leopard, because leopards . . . " "Ah, my dear beautiful niece," Dick shook his head at Nan, "don't be so sure. You must learn in life there are always exceptions. Even black leopards." "Oh, Uncle Dick," said Nan, all big eyes now, "you don't believe he saw it, do you?" "Well, why not? Leone believes it. Don't you?" he said, turning to her. "C'est vrai, hein?" "Mais certainement," and suddenly Leone and Dick were off into a rapid-fire exchange in what sounded like either French or Italian or neither. Leone was so pleased and excited, she forgot all about what she was doing and edged up behind Dick, nearly dropping the dishes on Nan. Meanwhile Pam and Robbie were telling Mother all about it, while Mother anxiously kept an eye on Leone and her drooping plates. Father sat back in his seat shaking with laughter. "Well, Howie, your leopard certainly livened up this party. Did you really see it?" "Yes, I really did." "Whereabouts were you?" At this point Leone suddenly gasped and gulped, gave Dick one last barrage and hurried off to the kitchen. Dick sat grinning, his face turned to follow her out the dining room door.

I answered Father, without thinking of consequences. "It was when I was up washing the cross, by the church. He came out of the bushes just — just as close as over there," pointing to the other side of the room. "He was black as black and all shiny, and his tail wiggled. Like a cat's." "Didn't anyone else see it?" "Nobody else was there."

Dick still sat looking after Leone, his grin reduced to a small mischievous smile. Nan said something to Father I couldn't hear because at the same time Mother interrupted. "Were you up there alone?" I realized suddenly then the enormity of it all. That law, that basic law that I, Jane and Ronnie were never, never to be outside the garden by ourselves. I was silent. All around me the hubbub of the leopard business still circled. Nan was arguing with Father, Mrs. Webster probably supporting him (and me), Ellie leaning across Dick to support Nan. Pam, Richie, Miranda and Jane were all busy with their own versions. At last my news was a success. Only I, caught with Mother in guilt, was left out of it; and Dick, still looking absentmindedly after Leone. Robbie too seemed to be abstracted. He sat brooding and insulated, his dark eyes half veiled, staring at Dick's bronzed neat profile, completely removed from all of us.

"You know you shouldn't have been there alone." Mother pursued the subject relentlessly. "I couldn't help it.

They all left me." Ellie became aware. "We had to take Jane home, Mother. She had a sunstroke." "I did not!" cried Jane stoutly. "What were you *doing* there?" asked Mother. Ellie and Nan answered her together: "Washing the cross."

Dick came to and swung about. Robbie dropped his eyes to his plate. "Washing *what?*" said Dick. "The cross," Nan appealed to him abjectly. "It was all covered with nasty names." She turned to Mother. "You know, the marble cross in front of the church up there." "How very odd," said Jocelyn Webster. "You were doing what to it?" "Washing it." "Whatever for?"

Ellie, full of righteousness and eager to distract Mother, put in her bit. "It was disgusting, all scribbled over. Honestly, a *cross!* So Nan and I thought we'd wash it off and make it look decent." "Do you think it's a mistake?" Nan appealed to Uncle Dick again; at every opportunity, it would seem. "Mademoiselle says we've sent all those poor pilgrims back into purgatory again." Dick threw himself back laughing. "Oh yes, oh yes. You most certainly have." "Nonsense," said Mother, "don't give them ideas." "But it's true. We'll ask Leone," who was coming back in again with the casserole. "Ah, Dick! Please," begged Mother. Father cut in, "What is it you talk with her? Qu'est-ce-que c'est cette langue que vous parlez avec Monsieur, Leone?" What bad French Father did speak too, despite all that study! Leone set down the hot dish with firm daintiness, then screamed with delight. Mother frowned and sighed. "Oh-oh, that is my patois!" "She's from Nice you know," said Dick. Mother caught Leone's eye, and she exclaimed and rushed off. She meant always to be proper.

"What an accomplished fellow you are, Dick," said Father. "I didn't know you spoke Niçois, or whatever it is." "My, yes," said Dick, "I speak it much too well. I've gotten into bad trouble. I'll get a knife stuck in me if I ever

30

go back there again." "Good heavens, how romantic," said Jocelyn. "I believe you're just boasting." "No, it's true. I got involved." "Let's hope," said Father, coughing discreetly, "you don't get involved with your — uh — proficiency in Niçois around here." Dick laughed and laughed.

Leone came back with the vegetables and in the process of serving, the grown-ups forgot leopards and, fortunately, related subjects. But not for long. Nan turned big eyes on Dick. "You don't really believe in all that about the pilgrims and the cross and purgatory, do you, Uncle Dick?"

"It's not what *I* believe. No, I certainly don't believe it. But it's all part of Catholic Arithmetic. You see, you rack up a certain amount of sin over here," he gestured with his right hand, "and each sin costs so much. Then you buy it back over here," left hand, "with prayers, pilgrimages, money, penances. If it balances out at the end, pop, into heaven you go. If there's enough surplus you might even make saint. If there's a deficit, you pay it off in purgatory. Of course, if the sins are too expensive you go bankrupt and there's hell to pay. It's very simple and satisfactory. Those signatures on the cross were proof that a pilgrimage had been made. How else would God know?" "How silly," said Nan. But Dick countered, "Well, at least you know where you stand. None of this feeling guilty over nothing, and Protestant moaning and groaning."

"None of this Protestant Christianity, either," said Father tartly.

"No doubt, no doubt," said Dick. "As a devout pagan I wouldn't know. Seems to me if you're going to play the game you ought to have fixed rules."

"I suppose if you're a 'devout pagan' — what a silly phrase — you don't have to bother with rules."

"Nonsense. And it's not a silly phrase. I mean what I say. There are plenty of rules. You don't worship Apollo and Venus without laws. Perfection in Beauty and Love requires great discipline. Very strict rules."

"Which you make up yourself?" Father's scorn was modified by his smile.

"Not at all." Dick was quite offended. "The Greeks and Romans, who had a civilization far more intelligently organized than ours, worked some things out. Then one has to adjust to modern conditions. It's a damn hard job reconciling Love and Beauty."

"My, how Pre-Raphaelite," said Jocelyn Webster. "Do you burn with a hard gemlike flame?"

"I try. A hard flame back of a hard belly. That's the ideal." Jocelyn lowered her eyes, a bit embarrassed.

"You see, I'm an idler. A no-good dissolute rake. When people ask me what I do, I have to tell them I Live and Love, which of course means I Do Nothing. The fact is I'm busy every moment. I have to keep in training like a ballet dancer. Loving just by itself is a full-time job, a real profession."

"But about those rules," said Father. Dick thought awhile, very serious. "Aptness covers it, I suppose. Appropriateness. For each form of love there is a possible perfect form of style or conduct, of beauty. To be beautiful, the act of love must not only be skillful and graceful, but true to its nature, like a dance or a drama. The Ancients divided their drama into categories, such as Tragic and Comic, and the same must be true of a well-conducted love affair."

"How *very* cold-blooded!" said Jocelyn. "Classicism always seems cold-blooded to the bloody Romantic," said Dick. "Northerners hate to apply intelligence and experience to their feelings. That's why we've all stayed barbarians. The Latins properly believe that anything that isn't beautiful is meaningless, worthless. To achieve beauty takes skill, intelligence, experience, a knowledge of materials and techniques. One doesn't just pick up these things by instinct. One studies examples, one practices like a pianist. Living and Loving require just as much patience as piano playing, if not more. Only in that way can love become really beautiful and so really moving, really meaningful. But the most important of the rules are those of appropriateness. That's where most of us go wrong. To be beautiful a flirtation musn't be confused with a grand passion, or a grand passion with true love. Or a nonsexual love with a sexual one. Do you see what I mean? I ought to love you, Mary, in a brotherly way, which would be quite different from the way I might love — hm — let's say Leone." Mother looked about wildly, but fortunately Leone wasn't in the room. "Each love must have its own proper character."

"Oh, but how is it possible?" broke in Jocelyn, rather disturbed. "I mean, one can't just control one's loves like that." She grew quite passionate. "If I love someone desperately and he loves me lightly — what *is* one to do?"

"Exactly. Control. That's what I mean when I say love's a profession. It's tremendously difficult to get it right. One goes wrong all the time. Not only difficult, but dangerous. The knife in the back in Nice. Carmen gets tired of Don José, but Don José doesn't get tired of Carmen. To manage a light love affair successfully is as difficult as a good soufflé. A serious love is as difficult as the Fifth Symphony. More difficult. Takes even more control. Beethoven had nine symphonies. Most of us can only count on two or three real loves."

"You mean," said Father, somewhat awed, "you really truly devote yourself to this sort of . . . sort of Don Juan controlled research? Exclusively, seriously?"

"Well, I do eat. And enjoy myself. And keep healthy. And even read and write sometimes. One must relax. But, yes, on the whole, I'd say I devote myself to that sort of research, seriously."

"Don't you recognize any sort of moral standards?" said Father.

"You mean by that, don't I recognize *your* moral standards. I consider my standards far more moral or ethical or philosophically justifiable than . . . than non-sensical dogmas and autocratic, unreasonable orders from on high." "Come, those are not *my* standards as you perfectly well know." "I'm not sure I do," said Dick. "What *are* your standards?" Father laughed and demurred. "Well, that's rather a large order. As a Quaker they're based on obedience to the inner voice, keeping the channels pure and open, tolerance for the conscience of others. . . . " "Even pagans?" "I said *conscience*, not just taste. Conscience, guidance, inner voice. Above all, not 'control' in your sense; rather, giving oneself up to God's control."

Father paused, ruminative, and Jocelyn, growing restive, interjected, pouting across the table at Dick, "I can't wait to hear about some of your research, professor." "I'll tell you everything I know. But not now." "Not even about Nice?" "Especially not about Nice. Not at the family table." Mother looked relieved. We were disappointed, hoping for some sort of startling story. But it seemed not. In fact the conversation went off into Nice and what it was like in general and who Dick knew there. He knew, it seemed, everybody.

viii. Then after dinner we were all off to the Maritime — dancing, driving in cars, staying up late; definitely gala. As Girl of the Evening, Nan was to drive over with Dick, Ellie beside her on the front seat. Jane and I were privileged to take up the rumble, probably because we wouldn't mind being windswept. We were overwhelmed by the honor. The others came in the red Webster Citroën and our lumbering, dark green, sharp-nosed Renault. Nan was thrilled, we were thrilled. We dashed through the warm night of cicadas and pine smells, Uncle Dick at the helm. The upholstery in the rumble was bright red leather too, like the front seat.

As we came along the shore road to the Maritime, where the little surf lapped on the narrow sand beach, a great dull orange moon popped up out of the sea. The hotel was all lit up like an excursion boat. Inside there was music in the ballroom, white and mirrored and chandeliered, with little gilt chairs all around the edge. The band played *le jazz Américain:* "Valencia" and "Who" and "Whispering."

We took over one far corner as our own, and then advanced out into the hostile territory of the dance floor. There, along with grown-ups, were various other children, strangers, enemies. Jane and I, living our secluded lives, knew none of them, but those who had been to schools, Robbie and Richie in particular, did. Whereas we young fry had to be content with an occasional "dance" with our parents (Mrs. Webster danced once with me, Dick once with Jane, a gentle process of sliding back and forth), Richie and Robbie, Pam and Miranda, made adventurous forays out into that alien world. Obviously anyone as well grown and handsome as Robbie would be a welcome partner anywhere, and a few bashful strangers, English and French girls (we seemed to be the only Americans there) with bobs and marcels and in flapperish dresses made awkwardly decent by the addition of short sleeves and slightly lowered skirts, were pranced about the floor by our boys, to our pride and amusement.

We looked on Robbie in particular as our Champion, and in various obscure intrigues he upheld the honor of the family; although we hadn't the slightest idea what all the whispering and sniggering and consulting and running about could possibly mean. There seemed to be two groups

35

— our side, led by Robbie, officered by Richie, but complemented by a few of their internationally flavored schoolmates and with the Webster girls as active camp followers, and another more strictly Maritime Hotel group of boys, nasty Latin types all of them. The idea seemed to be to corner the market in available pretty hotel girls and prevent, by organized cutting in and other ruses, the Enemy from getting at them. There were also sinister trips outside (cigarettes?) and other mysteries.

In all this Robbie was motivated, it would seem, entirely by leadership, *esprit de corps* and adventurousness, not sex. The girls themselves did not interest him in the least, no matter how interested they might be in him. He still insisted on being loyal to the codes of an earlier boyhood, in which girls were merely objects of scorn or even jealous hatred. He seemed bent on refusing to accept the new world of adolescence which obviously, in changing voice and growing virility, threatened him. The Websters in their happy tomboyishness did little toward changing his attitudes.

Nan and Ellie were above all this, and were included for the night among the grown-ups. They danced sedately with Father and Dick, he being particularly attentive to Nan, and with an occasional grown-up friend of the parents. Neither of the girls knew any of the Maritime boys, and disdained them all impartially. And indeed they were a weedy lot. Whereas the rest of us drank our lemonade sitting on the chairs about the dance floor, Nan and Ellie joined the adults in the sun room, a large, semicircular glass-enclosed bay giving off the ballroom, where there were tables and real drinks, and Japanese lanterns and paper geraniums crawling up trellises. There the adults sat watching through the open doors, sometimes emerging to dance themselves. It was really quite boring.

Scuffing our heels under the gilt chairs, we were only

too happy to see the parents, with Dick and Nan ahead of them, leave the sun room toward the moonlit out of doors. Jane and I scrambled up and joined them uninvited, following out and down the circular driveway of the hotel, bordered by beds of salvias black in the moonlight and some scruffy little palms.

The grown-ups walked along the concrete promenade, Uncle Dick arm in arm with Nan, then the parents flanking Mrs. Webster. We caracoled and curveted on the sand itself, doing our own version of a moon dance. By now the moon was high, full and white. The little ripples rustled on the beach more like the lapping of a lake than of a sea. It was very calm and warm and the air full of insect sounds. Back of the hotel were groves of flat-headed pine, down the coast each way lay dark but moon-emphasized headlands. We rushed about making silly noises.

The parents and Mrs. Webster stopped to look at moon and glittering water.

" 'With what sad steps, O moon, thou climb'st the sky,' " misquoted Father. " 'How silently and with how wan a face.' " After a short pause, and as though considering the proposition, Jocelyn Webster said, "Nonsense. Never looked less wan. She's as jolly and full of life as . . . as Nan there." "Downright adolescent." "Yes. Isn't she? A young girl at a dance. Brimming over." Jocelyn looked after Dick and Nan, who were still strolling down the strand. "And with a Mysterious Cavalier for an escort, too."

"Who happens to be her uncle," said Father dryly.

"Oh, why not?" said Jocelyn. "She's having such a whirl."

Father spoke across her to Mother. "I'm afraid your brother is really a naughty fellow."

We had stopped our careering about and now squatted

on the beach, oblivious of our party clothes, making sand houses, carefully within earshot.

"Oh, come now," said Jocelyn, "he isn't really her uncle. Although I suspect the situation is carefully covered somewhere in the back of the Book of Common Prayer." She paused. "Perhaps it's time he came to stay with me. Don't you think?"

Father laughed. "Well, he's only been with us a few hours. But it's between you two of course. Won't People Talk?"

"What people? The great advantage of living abroad is that there *are* no people to talk. And the girls do love having a man about."

"I rather suspect ours won't want him to leave. But perhaps . . ." "Mother ended uncertainly. Then she noticed us. "Children! Get up out of that sand. What do you think you're doing!" We all moved down the beach again, the parents out of our hearing. Dick and Nan were far ahead, still closely arm in arm.

We went back to the hotel with the parents and Mrs. Webster. The other two came in later. Nan looked all radiant, and as we kicked our heels again under our ballroom chairs, she and Dick danced slowly to "The Bells of Saint Mary's," which was Nan's absolutely favorite song. She liked to play it on the piano and sing it over and over. The boys and the Webster girls had disappeared, with their gang, and we had trouble finding them. They were found racing up and down the corridors upstairs, no doubt to the fury of guests. When they had been collected it was time to go home. The gala evening, the giddy day of adventure was over. Jane and I traveled somnolent in the Renault this time, leaning up against our parents, suddenly dead. Dick took our big girls as before, but this time it was Robbie and Richie in the rumble. The Websters went home by themselves.

I began to drift off as soon as we started back, nestling against Mother on the back seat while Father drove with Jane in front. As I drifted off I said to Mother, "I did see that leopard though. And it wasn't a dog." "You shouldn't have been up there alone." "Well, maybe. But I wouldn't have seen it with all those noisy girls around. And I did see it." "Those noisy girls shouldn't have left you there. We'll tend to them tomorrow." "Hmmm," I murmured, full of satisfaction at the thought of their wrongdoing, and the thought of my leopard.

ix. But by the time I got home, I was quite rested. We all disembarked with jubilant and overtired talking. Mrs. Webster drove up without her children for a nightcap with the parents. After we had all been forced to bed, I was wide awake again. Wide awake and exuberant; I couldn't stay in bed. Braving the mosquitoes, which in any case weren't bad tonight for some reason, for all the warmth and calm, I slipped from under the netting and over to my window. Behind me, one of the reasons I hadn't been able to sleep, I could hear the bubbling murmurs of Nan and Ellie from their room next door, a spate of jollity and giggles. What was it all about? I never could exactly make out their words, however hard I listened. Only one significant bit, shouted by Nan: "Well, he isn't my uncle, and I don't care. . . . "

Outside in any case was far more interesting to me, everything rapt, turned to marble under the glare of moon, like people enchanted in fairy stories. I held my breath looking at it, and realized I was going to write a poem. It was more proper to say that I seized the inspiration than that inspiration seized me. Given the proper occasion, and this was certainly one, I could easily put myself into the proper state, full-bosomed, melancholy, greatly moved.

The poem ought to begin "O Moon," and exemplify some-how Mrs. Webster's contention that its face was *not* wan. I stood there swimming in a deliciousness of feelings and moon trance. A nightingale, sure enough, was trickling silence down somewhere in the garden. "The nightingale all hushed among the eucalyptus trees. . . . "

I could not however make such good use of Nan and Ellie, still burbling romance, or whatever it was, among giggles. Nor, down below there, of Uncle Dick and Jocelyn Webster, strolling out the door and down the path, cigarettes glowing, both of them very subdued and close together. They too, presumably, were full of moon and attentive to the nightingale. But they were talking too, talking, talking, very steadily but quietly, with none of their usual yelps of sharp laughter. I watched them go down the slope of the broad path till I lost sight of them behind the trees.

"O Moon that smilest on the sleeping sea," I thought, "and makest everything to silver turn." No, that last part wouldn't do. Yet I couldn't just say, "that makes every-thing turn to silver." How to get from my moon to my nightingale? Far off I heard it again. Nan and Ellie fell silent for a while. I slapped a mosquito.

> *O Moon*
> *That smilest on the sleeping sea,*
> *Making the world turn silver,*
> *Thou art not wan*
> *But brimming full of love. The nightingale*
> *All hushed among the eucalyptus trees . . .*

How sad, how sad and true, how rich it was and mournful.

2.

i. As on any brilliant morn-
ing, and all the mornings had been brilliant lately, we had
breakfast on the terrace. Most of us were late because of
last evening's gala and because, in any case, it was Sunday.
When I came down, the parents were lingering over the
remains of coffee. To them breakfast was a delicious interlude of lazy talk; to most of us merely an irksome prelude
to exciting play. Already the boys, with Lagarde tagging
after them, had raced through their food and were out and
gone. Uncle Dick too, it seemed. The girls, on the other
hand, were still upstairs. Ronnie and Mademoiselle sat in a
far sunny corner, babbling to one another. Jane was busy
with toast and honey. I had nothing to say for myself
except "Good morning." Already I was full of plans for
the day. Unlike yesterday which had been occupied by
strange and special excitements, today was an "ordinary
day," and Jane and I were returned to our enclosed garden
life. We had a golden morning all for ourselves, interrupted
only by a welcome *goûter* of bread and milk, and after that
a not so welcome Sunday observance — a sort of family
Quaker Meeting that Father insisted we hold, twenty minutes or so of sitting in silence, with an occasional short
word or two from him. We were used to it, but it would
be too much to say we really enjoyed it.

This morning was one of an especial and intense brightness. There was perhaps something forewarning in the

brilliance, as though it were to be the last of this particular hot spell. The ocean glittered unruffled out there, tempting and deep; the leaves of the trees and plants shone nearer at hand. We could hear a faint, high French screaming as the orphanage children were let out in some more lenient phase of their jail routine. It was still early enough for various birds, different from any we knew at home, to be chirping about in the lushness. The garden lay one long bosky intricate enticement, an elaborate stage for each one of our separate dramas, the imaginary histories that involved Jane and me, the more real forays of Robbie and his cohorts (which today, our parents informed us, were to include Pam and Miranda again), and of course the meaningless mild strolls and sittings and talkings of the grown-ups, who didn't really know what to *do* with a garden. Only to Nan and Ellie, avid for outside glamor, did it seem something of a prison.

"Did you have a good time last night?" said Father. "Oh yes!" we answered together. Actually of course, in detail, it had been pretty tiresome, but as a total event it was certainly — well, an event. "Did you do any dancing?" Mother asked Jane, who shook her head rather morosely. "You really ought to try and meet some people." Those present, Mother and Jane in particular, knew how profitless this line of conversation was. "Don't you get tired of just playing with each other?" We sniggered and Jane shook her head again. She liked the way the pointed ends of her square bob tasseled her cheek, so she shook her head rather violently. "If they're happy in their Eden, leave them be," said Father. "They'll have more than enough chance to 'know people' before they're done." "I suppose so," sighed Mother. There were all sorts of things that Mother rather halfheartedly considered to be her duties toward us, generally and severally. She pursued these duties with a sort of dim persistence, but never got anywhere with most of them since we knew that the slightest talkiness on our part would make her drop the projects. Over here abroad she thought it a duty to have us "meet some nice children to play with." We never did. But she never failed to keep on at us about it.

Luckily at this moment Nan and Ellie flounced in, still fizzing from their last night's shake-up. They had evidently resumed their last night's chatter too, and the calm morning was soon full of it. "Did you *see?* . . ." such-and-such and wasn't so-and-so ". . . a *scream*, honestly." Mother and Father were indulgently amused. We ate silently so as to get away to more serious doings. But here came Duty again. Mother said, "I hate to put a damper on all this merriment; but why did you two leave Howie all alone up there by the church? Suppose there really *had* been a dangerous animal and he'd been attacked? How would you have felt then? And don't tell me Jane had a 'sunstroke' because she didn't." The girls were, for once, speechless. "For punishment you're to stay *inside* the place all today. No going off in the car with Dick, no trips to the Maritime beach. Understand?" They understood. Since actually nothing of the sort had been planned, they also understood that the punishment was really only formal and nominal. Of course if something wonderful turned up, then it would be *ghastly*. . . . They lowered their faces and assented mutely with a few moments of silent and proper respect. Then they were off again.

When Uncle Dick appeared down below, sauntering up from the beach, they were in full bounce and rushed over to the rail of the veranda to greet him. They leaned over, waving and shouting. Their short dresses pulled up to expose their big browned thighs. They said, "Hello, hello," and asked him if he'd been swimming. Silly creatures, what else could he have been doing, with his queer hair all dark and wet, and a towel over his shoulder? He stood astraddle, grinning and squinting up at them, very tanned and fit. Today he had on a pair of rust-red fisherman's pants and a faded blue jersey. They exchanged nonsense so loudly the parents told the girls to hush, and insisted Dick come back up for coffee, though he'd breakfasted long ago. He said he would. But the badinage continued. It was all like some academic picture of Old Spain, travestied: the serenading cavalier, the flashing señoritas on the balcony.

Obviously it was time for us to get out. We scampered into the gloom of the *salon*, headed for Our World. "Be careful," said Mother automatically. Careful indeed. *We* weren't the ones who did wild things. That was Robbie and Richie. Our dangers were all imaginary.

ii. So Real Life began for us.

Real life consisted, at that particular time, of an immense empire called Amuria. This was made up of three things. One: my discovery that there was an Amur River, lost up on the boundary between China and Siberia, impossibly remote. Two: a vivid remembrance of the oriental villain in Douglas Fairbanks' *Thief of Bagdad* who boiled people in great basins of hot oil, and had retainers in batlike beautiful oriental armor. Three: extensive perusal of a set of French history-postcards, which gave pictures and brief biographies of royal personages from Charlemagne on, complete with cardinals and mistresses.

Our story followed in endless epic the history of the Amurian Empire from earliest H. G. Wells *Outline of History* times up to (perhaps someday) the present. The Empire had a physical as well as temporal dimension. Not only were there many maps of it, its boundaries constantly being redrawn and re-erased (like the recent boundaries of postwar Europe), but there were also delicately detailed drawings of Amurian cities, built up and then sacked; and

Amuria as well had an actual location in our garden, covering the big space alongside the cellar-under-the-porch, where we "rested," with roads and constructions, going out in every possible direction to colonies, especially up to the front of the house (where unfortunately things had to be smoothed out after every day's work to keep the place looking decent), and from there down the path to the pond.

Religion, literature and the drama were not neglected. There were temples, elaborate ceremonies, bloody sacrifices, fancy priesthoods, a pantheon of odd gods. There were legends and poems to go with all this, and an Amurian language. I was even "translating" the chief national romance, an Amuriad (but I didn't call it that) into English. I didn't get very far with this. There were events, bloody actions in endless sequel, loves, assassinations, revolutions, poisonings, carryings on of all sorts. We acted these events out, sometimes dressed up, Jane and I taking all the parts. We drew pictures, portraits of the dramatis personae, renderings of the palaces and temples. It kept us awfully busy; and yet we continually varied this program with totally unrelated interludes having nothing to do with Amuria.

We occasionally showed some artifact to Mother, or told her about it; but we had learned to keep the whole business from all the rest of the family. Father was kindly but not really interested. The others were actively hostile, made fun of us, tried to break up the Empire. Though we played dress-up games with them too, especially Nan and Ellie, these always had to be *their* games, not ours; and never Amuria.

We had reached a crucial point in history, the death of Liu (Lee-oo; if the French could have Loo-ee, we could have Liu) the Great. Under him the Empire had achieved its greatest expansion, the last roads and watchtowers going way down the front path to the pond. Liu had died on

47

Thursday, and what with one thing and another we hadn't yet got around to burying him. So that was the first order of business.

His funeral was to be held in the Great Temple. The Great Temple was in the capital, Amur Wa, located under the terrace and made mostly of Mah-Jongg blocks. There were several ways we could act out a drama. This one was to be in minature — a Mah-Jongg block for the funeral car, and various pebbles and sticks for the cortege. These Jane and I pushed along the winding streets of the city to the Great Temple, with funeral noises of gongs and horns. There we had to shift, and enact the ceremonies in our proper persons. The cellar thus became the vault of the temple. We had a box of dress-up things we kept down there for just such emergencies. An old wooden bench became the bier, loaded with rich stuffs.

Jane was corpse. We'd had an argument about that, and she was a rebellious corpse. She lay on the bench covered with an old curtain, her eyes closed and her hands stiff in prayer. She wriggled a good deal. I was the high priest, also swathed in a curtain, and carrying a gong — an old pot lid. I banged the gong and chanted hideously, circling the bier, kneeling, bowing, celebrating the greatness of Liu. Jane started to join in. "Shut up," I ordered. "You're supposed to be dead." Jane pursed her lips and frowned. "Well, hurry up," she said. I made a few more rounds. "Okay; now the funeral." Jane leaped up happily. She got a gong for herself, the bottom of the tin box where we stowed our Mah-Jongg pieces, and we both stalked up and down the temple, making an ungodly racket. "O Li-ooo, great Li-ooo!" we hollered and gonged rhythmically. Occasionally I interjected horn calls and flutes. Finally we moved in slow procession out into the sun toward our flower bed, where the grave was to be. "Stop that *horrible* noise!" screamed Nan, leaning over the edge of the veranda. "What in the world are you doing?" Jane merely turned and stuck out her tongue. I paid no attention. "Leave them be," said Dick, coming to the rail and looking down at us with amusement. "It's a solemn moment." "Well, *I* can't stand it," and Nan flounced off into the *salon.*

It annoyed us exceedingly to have people watch us; but we had learned that if we paid no attention at all, people usually went away. Not Dick. He insisted on standing there, an unwanted spectator at the final rites of Liu the Great. We soon forgot him. With much banging of tin we knelt by the grave. There was another long prayer, this all in Amurian ("Wee a wa wa! Wong ee poo, papa no wanny wa!"). We bowed our heads to the dust for a moment of awed silence. Dick broke into applause. We still ignored him.

Then we changed roles again and began to dig the grave with our hands. We made a fine clean hole and inside laid one of our most preciously decorated Mah-Jongg blocks. We put a tiny piece of torn brocade on it, then surrounded it with bits of stick, representing slain slaves, and pebbles and objects from trees, representing treasure. A few mimosa flowers completed the ensemble. We piled the dirt on top of it, and made a mound, patted smooth, elaborately inset with pebbles. We got blocks from our cellar and built a charming tower of three stories on top of the mound. When it was done, we stood back to admire it from every side, then got down and laid our faces on the ground to achieve a proper human perspective on it. Jane left to go to the bathroom. I stayed to admire awhile, then gathered up the curtains and gongs and returned to the city.

iii. When Jane came back we proceeded with the coronation of Liu the Sixth, known as the Handsome. He was the elder of two sons of Liu the Great, and a paragon in every way. He was eighteen and not only handsome, as his nickname might indicate, but brave, generous, noble, and All Around. He had distinguished himself as a boy hero in the conquest of the land of the Wa Hus, the barbarians of the West (their country was the front path), as well as in tournaments and sports of all kinds. He was also a brilliant student. His great fault was (like Robbie) his rashness. But everyone loved and admired him, especially the Populace, *except* his wicked younger brother Agragor. Even he *pretended* to love him.

His good looks were of the peculiarly Amurian sort. The Amurians of course were orientals, but big Mongolian out-of-doors orientals, descendants of the virile nomadic Wa Hus, not of the effete little Koreans to the East. But a large invasion of Vikings during the early Middle Ages had influenced the race, particularly the royal family, so that though Liu had the smooth golden skin of the East, the rather flat nose and turned-up eyes, these eyes were blue, and he had a mane of bright yellow hair. He was very tall and of course very strong with bulging muscles. Altogether he looked much like a lion.

His coronation was thus an occasion of wild rejoicing, for though his father was revered, he had been a stern, cruel man, and besides had gotten very old and doddering these last years, and the Empire had begun to go to rack and ruin.

Since we'd already had one ceremony, not too much was to be made of the actual coronation. The bench became a throne, and I (who else?) was Liu. This time Jane was the priesthood, and, as I sat stiffly holding my stick-scepter, Jane circled about me with the usual ululations and eventually put a crown on my head, the frame of an old lampshade, with strips of cloth wound around it. After that, feasting and dancing. Since young Liu himself was of course the best dancer in Amuria, he participated, crown and all. It was hard to keep that crown on. Somehow, Javanese dancing and its attitudes had percolated to us, and so the Amurians moved about with bent knees and upturned fingertips, wiggling their heads from side to side while their eyes stood still. That was the idea anyway. Music was nasal, pentatonic, falsetto; gongs at random. The dance grew wilder, the crown fell off. We hoped the girls upstairs could hear us and were suffering acutely. Finally, after a last spasm of heady madness, we sank to the ground exhausted. We then gathered around the bench, feasting, drinking, whooping it up, and at last lay prostrate in stupor, sleeping off our excesses. It was the best party that palace had ever had.

Now the real business of the morning began: the re-subduing and resettlement of the land of the Wa Hus. Though of course that had been conquered and colonized by Liu the Great, it had reverted in his last days to savagery. On Friday, one of the days when the Italian gardeners came, all the gravel had been neatly raked and all our disfiguring roads, towns and watchtowers destroyed, except for a few way down by the pool. So the barbarians, supposedly subject to the Emperor of Amuria, but really quite independent, had taken over again, and the savage hordes were roaming the once fertile fields. Liu the Handsome intended as the first move of his reign to put a stop to all that.

We went up to the front of the house and began a morning-long bout of construction and disfigurement. Roads came first, and an immense highway, almost six inches wide, was scooped out, the white pebbly gravel pushed by our dirty hands to each side, exposing the hard dusty earth. It went all the way down the hill and joined up with the faint remains of old roads made under Liu the Great. We slaved at putting back into working condition the watchtowers, stones piled on top of each other as high as they could be made to stay, and the border camps, squares of cleared dirt with low walls of gravel around them and huts represented by eucalyptus nuts. We moved back up toward the house, making a chain of these watchtowers. The distance between them was determined by sighting from the top of one to the top of the other. They followed the wavering route of the Great Road.

We were nearly done when Robbie and Richie came sauntering up the path. The Webster girls were due to arrive, and they wanted to be on hand to meet them. Richie amused himself by kicking over our watchtowers. We rushed at him screaming. In the scuffle a section of the Great Road was demolished. Robbie laughed at us and rather brusquely called Richie off. They ran up pursued by Lagarde and by us. We didn't really mind at all; this represented perfectly a barbarian attack and victory over same by the brave Amurians. We restored the road and some of the watchtowers. We had further plans for side roads, colonial outposts, thriving new cities and such. Already traffic crowded up and down the road. All was prosperous and gay under the beneficent rule of Liu the Handsome.

iv. We were interrupted by Celestine calling out the kitchen window for us. It was time for our midmorning refreshment of milk, French bread and honey. Since we were covered with dust we had to wash up first. Then we tumbled out on the terrace, where Richie and Robbie already sat, sulky because the Websters hadn't shown up after all. We sat there munching and sucking our milk. I insisted on having mine in a pottery bowl. I thought it was more picturesque and peasant-like that way, and it tasted better. Leone, who had stayed overnight with us in one of the spare rooms over the garage, where Dick and the boys also lived, brought us our milk and tried unsuccessfully to get a word out of us. She shrugged, annoyed at our silence, and was about to leave us when she saw Dick down below. He planned to come to our First Day Meeting. Leone went to the rail, and like the girls at breakfast time, had a conversational rally in Niçois. We couldn't understand it; but it was animated.

When we had done eating and Leone had retired with the dishes, we automatically set about arranging the chairs in rows, facing westward. Two armchairs, facing east, were prepared for the Elders, that is, Mother and Father. Dick appeared as we finished. We five sat, Dick in the front row with the boys, Jane and I behind. Then the girls came in whispering, for the atmosphere had become churchlike. Mother and Father appeared to take their seats. Without more ado, and in silence, Meeting began.

We all sat there for a few minutes, resigned, uncomfortable. Only Dick was wholly at ease, legs crossed, one arm along across the back of the neighboring chair. Father cleared his throat and gave us, as was customary, a text, subject, something to think about.

"On a morning like this perhaps it would be a good idea to think about . . . uh, beauty. We talk about a 'beautiful day' or this as a 'beautiful place.' What does that really mean? What do we really feel? Do we feel grateful to God? Are we conscious enough of all this beauty as being a reflection of God? Let's put our minds to it for a while."

We sat and put our minds to it. My mind had material on beauty ready at hand — last night's poem. With my eyes closed it was easy to resurrect the beauty of the

53

moonlight, the nightingale. How did my poem go? "O Moon . . ."

> O Moon
> That smilest on the sleeping sea,
> Making the world turn silver,
> Thou art not wan
> But brimming full of love. The nightingale
> All hushed among the eucalyptus trees . . .

Then what? A last line had come to me, "So to soft music love walks through the dusk" (Uncle Dick and Jocelyn Webster?). But the problems were: that last repetition of the word "love," and a verb for the nightingale.

"Pours out his roundelay." That would do for the nightingale. Then, just cut out the "full of love" (why not?) and we had:

> O Moon
> That smilest on the sleeping sea,
> Making the world turn silver,
> Thou art not wan
> But brimming to the full. The nightingale
> All hushed among the eucalyptus trees
> Pours out his roundelay;
> So to soft music love walks through the dusk.

This of course took me quite a while of solid concentration. I had trouble enough remembering what I'd already finished. Then came the problem of remembering the completed version. Dare I get up and go for a pencil and paper? No. It made me fidgety. I went over the poem many times to fix it. "O Moon . . ." It was certainly beautiful.

But I was done with that, and my contemplation of beauty in the abstract could go no further. I watched the others; they seemed to have different things in mind. Nan, for instance, who sat alongside me, was staring with cow eyes, sorrowfully, soulfully at Dick, who lounged in front of her. His neat profile was turned, with an expression of amused irony, directly on Robbie, two chairs away. Robbie, aware of this, was scrunched in embarrassment, head down, face red, arms thrust between his knees with hands clenched. Richie looked about in his nervous way, wriggling, unaware, inattentive. Jane had her mind on something inside, eyes closed. Mother looked out to sea. Nan in particular irritated me, so I too shut my eyes and rehearsed my poem a few more times. There was a scraping of chairs. Father had turned to Mother to shake her hand as a sign the Meeting was over. I shook Jane's. We jumped up. Nan and Richie both started talking immediately. "Very rewarding," said Dick to the parents. "I had a delicious contemplation." He was being sarcastic again, I could tell; about what? Father seemed pleased, and unaware of any sarcasm. We went to shake hands with him as was our custom after the service. Then we raced out again as we had raced out from breakfast. Into the sun!

But first I had to go all the way upstairs to write my poem. "I'll be right down," I said to Jane, who was annoyed. She supposed I had to go to the bathroom. Actually somebody else was already locked in the hall toilet, so I had a perfectly good excuse to go upstairs. I did not confide my poetry to Jane, as unsympathetic about that as others were about Amuria.

v. In Amuria, once we got back down to it, there was a Triumph over the barbarian Wa Hus. In the procession, hands chained behind her back, beautiful and defiant, strode Nu Wa, daughter of the chief of the barbarians. She had dashed into battle alongside her father, her long black hair flying in the wind, dressed in the leather trousers of a Wa Hu warrior. Now she walked head up, hair down, scornful in her subjection. She was a girl after Jane's own heart.

She had been personally captured by Liu himself, and though when brought before his throne she was forced to bow her head to the dust, Liu himself stepped forward graciously, lifted her up, and with courteous words promised her every comfort while she remained his prisoner. On the sidelines stood Agragor, surly but handsome, Liu's rebellious younger brother. A sultry glance passed between Agragor and the fair prisoner; and he was a goner. But not only was she a barbarian and a captive, thus an unsuitable bride, but Agragor had already been betrothed to Wa Nee Ta, the daughter of wily Wa Fung, premier, advisor of Liu the Great, tutor of Liu the Handsome. However, this was purely a match of state, arranged by Wa Fung for his family's advancement. (The repetition of "Wa" in everything was by descent from the Wa Hus. Every Wa Hu or his descendants had to have his "Wa" as a clan patronymic.)

Liu meanwhile was to marry Chin Lee, child daughter of the Emperor of Korea. This was another state match, and also arranged by Wa Fung. Entrance of Chin Lee, toddly on bound feet, with her retainers bearing costly presents clustered about her. Chin velly demure and Chinee. Jane liked to play Chin Lee almost as much as Nu Wa.

Diplomatic formalities and greetings; Chin Lee dances for Liu, with fan. Nasal music. Party; and finally great double wedding with processions and gongs, Liu to Chin Lee, Agragor to Wa Nee Ta. Not that we weren't getting a bit tired of Amurian ceremonies and music. Rejoicing; special wedding palace built of Mah-Jongg blocks.

Lunch.

Ellie strolled by to tell us to come up and wash. We hadn't finished the palace. We said, "Yes" and didn't come.

Ellie scolded and left. Robbie and Richie yelled at us. Mother leaned down over the edge of the porch and called firmly. We came.

We were in no hurry since we knew that lunch was cold, a picnic laid out on the porch. Leone and Celestine were off for the day, but in again this evening for a special, important dinner for special important guests. The Webster girls seemed to have been dropped at our house while we were playing. When we came up, everyone was standing in front of the gate watching Dick back his car out of the garage across the road. In the car was Leone, sitting close to Dick in front and all dressed up. Much whispering and laughter took place between Celestine and Mademoiselle, dressed in black and waiting for the parents to drive them to the bus stop. Nan and Ellie however were glum prisoners as they watched their hero leave them, and with Leone alongside too. The parents appeared in time to see Dick turn and drive off, both he and Leone waving and shouting gaily. All the younger children waved and shouted back. But not the parents. They stood for a moment of silent disapprobation, then told us all to go inside for lunch. Ellie and Nan were to clean up afterward. The parents would be right back after they'd deposited Celestine. We filed chattering in and fell on the sandwiches like starlings, eating any old way in the parents' absence. Since the Websters were there the boys were no longer morose, and for a while it was a riot, with Nan trying to assert authority. Then the parents came in; we quieted down a bit and finished up as quickly as we could. Great games were planned by the Robbie-Webster group, but fortunately we had to "rest"; so we could develop the drama of Amuria, now moving toward conflict and climax.

vi. Chin Lee caught sobbing quietly in her golden chambers by Liu. Despite all the jeweled trees and precious mechanical toys, she's unhappy. Liu approaches her tenderly.

LIU: What's the matter, my little bird?

CHIN: Oh, nothing, Great Lord.

LIU: But you are crying! Tell me what's wrong. There, there! Has someone been rude to you? We'll have his head cut off! No one must hurt my little precious.

CHIN: O Great Lord, I am not happy here.

LIU: Why not? Tell me what I can do to make you happy.

CHIN: Let me go back to see my honorable father. If I do not see honorable father, Chin Lee will die.

LIU: Now, now, we must wait awhile. Then you can make a visit.

CHIN: No, I cannot stay here. I will die if I stay here. I velly sad. You velly kind, velly noble, but I cannot live here. I must go live at home. (*kneels*) Please, honorable husband, do not let poor Chin to die. Look how pale I am.

LIU: That's true, you look very pale.

CHIN: Honorable father velly old. Soon he die. Then I come back here.

LIU: Honorable father will think I am cruel to you. Nobody will understand.

CHIN: Oh no, no. You velly kind. . . .

And so forth. It was a most pathetical scene, played to the hilt by Jane. She did her best to make the tears come.

The upshot was that Liu made his first mistake and allowed Chin to go home. The Emperor of Korea did *not* understand and was furious. He thought Liu had mistreated her, then rejected her. Rumors were spread by conspirators that Liu was trying to get rid of Chin for someone else. Now these conspirators were Agragor and the wily Wa Fung, who hoped to assassinate Liu (Liu wouldn't do what he wanted anyway) and set up Agragor as his minion and his own daughter on the throne, with the real power in his own hands! He didn't know of Agragor's secret infatuation with Nu Wa. Plotting scenes: Agragor (me), Wa Fung (Jane). Then Agragor (me) and Nu Wa (Jane). "When I come to the throne, then I shall get rid of that sappy Wa Nee Ta and marry thee, my beloved! We shall be Emperor and Empress of Amuria! We shall ravage Korea and take all its riches for ourselves, helped by your valiant tribes. The Wa Hus and the Amurians shall be one. HA, HA!" said wicked Agragor, embracing Nu Wa fiercely.

Together the three plan another great invasion by Wa Hus, to be combined with a revolt from within led by Wa Fung, Agragor and Nu Wa. The barbarians make such a sudden attack that they reach the very walls of the capital itself. They despoil the tomb of Liu the Great! (Fun. We kicked the tower and tumulus down, even unburied the coffin.) They sack the new wedding palace! Shrieks and alarms. Liu battles for his life. Agragor, disguised, is leading rebellious Amurian troops. But Wa Fung sees that things are beginning to go badly for the invaders, so to save his own skin he betrays the Amurian conspirators. Nu Wa escapes with the retreating Wa Hus. Agragor is captured and bound, brought spitting and writhing before the throne. (I played this part; Jane was Liu for once.) Liu sentences Agragor to death as a traitor. How he screams and curses!

The wedding palace is rebuilt. Liu begs Chin to come back. Emperor of Korea refuses. Threatens war.

Wa Fung greatly honored for help in crushing rebellion. But Wa Nee Ta, his beautiful daughter, is distraught. Egged on by her father (who still hasn't given up his original plans), she comes to plead for the life of her husband Agragor; more in duty however than in love. She kneels, fair and melancholy, at the feet of Liu. Liu at first is adamant. Agragor must die. Wa Nee Ta argues however that Agragor did it all because of a temporary infatuation with Nu Wa. But Nu Wa is gone now, back to her barbarians. Agragor, says his wife, is repentant and reconciled. Wa Fung joins in the pleading. Liu finally gives in, moved by the loveliness of Wa Nee Ta, and Agragor is saved.

But meanwhile Liu and Wa Nee Ta have fallen desperately in love. Scene afterward in which Agragor reviles and beats up his wife because she is the daughter of that treacherous rascal Wa Fung. Tells her he loves only Nu Wa. Wa Nee Ta grovels weeping on the ground while Agragor struts and sneers and kicks her about. We enjoyed that scene.

Liu comes along and raises the weeping bride to her feet. "Why weepest thou, lovely one?" "O sire, I cannot tell thee." "Come, most beautiful, you can tell me anything." "No! [sob] No! No!" "Thou hast a black eye! Someone hast hit thee!" She dissolves in his arms (The black eye struck Jane as funny however, so she was more giggly than tearful. She hated Wa Nee Ta anyway, whom she thought definitely silly, and was pleased to have her beaten up.). "Is it that wicked Agragor? Has he mistreated thee? Answer up! I'll have his eyes torn out! I'll boil him in oil!" "No, no, no!" sobs loyal Wa Nee Ta. But the fat is in the fire. They kiss and carry on.

Meanwhile Chin Lee is sent back from Korea to Liu; but it is too late. Now he is determined to have Wa Nee Ta. In defiance of the pleas of Wa Nee Ta herself, and the advice of everybody, he exercises his royal power and dissolves marriages all round. He officially takes the happy but dubious Wa Nee Ta as his Queen. Chin Lee, also radiant, is sent home for good. But the Emperor of Korea, still in secret cahoots with wicked Wa Fung, declares war. The Wa Hus declare war. Everybody invades. Liu says a tearful farewell to his new bride.

Out we rushed to the front path for the big battle. It was late enough in the afternoon by now for us to be allowed up there. Jane of course was Nu Wa. She gleefully started destroying all the watchtowers and the road. They had to be all gone by dinnertime anyway. Jane always loved destroying artifacts. A great battle between Liu and the barbarians was in progress. We rushed about screaming. My pot lid was my shield. Richie and Miranda appeared with Lagarde and started rushing about too, noisy and ignorant but more than willing to help muck things up. We were delighted too, for this helped represent the base betrayal and revolt of the once-pardoned Agragor and all his troops.

Then Richie and Miranda loped off, called into their own world and the depths of the garden by the others. Nan, Ellie and Ronnie, the big girls having to act as nursemaids today, appeared on the front steps, alarmed and disgusted by our dirty carryings on. They were going for a walk, dull creatures. As for us, we scampered down the steps to our cellar again (Liu pursued by Nu Wa and Agragor).

The whole province of the Wa Hus has been desolated. Not one stone stands there upon another. All the roads, camps, watchtowers, villages are utterly ravaged. Liu, victorious up to the moment of Agragor's betrayal, is now forced back, dusty and bleeding, to the home counties. The Emperor of Korea joins the attack. All the outlying suburbs are destroyed. Nothing is left to Liu but the city of Amur Wa itself. There, joined by the faithful Wa Nee Ta, he is besieged.

We built up the wall around the city and acted out the siege. Boom boom went the siege guns, dropping stones in on the Mah-Jongg temples and palaces of the capital. Liu rushes out to dispel the besiegers, inflicting heavy casualties. Wa Nee Ta cheers him on from the walls, waving handkerchiefs, while Agragor grinds his teeth. But there are too many besiegers — all Korea, all the Wa Hus, all the traitors under Agragor.

The siege however could have gone on indefinitely; but it was time our tragic story drew to its lugubrious close. Just as the besiegers were giving up, the Emperor of Korea having already retired, and just as Agragor was about to go off to the land of the barbarians with Nu Wa, Wa Fung betrays the city! He opens the gates secretly, the enemy rushes in toward the palace.

Liu and Wa Nee Ta, dressed in crown and robes, stand in the throne room, deserted by all but a few faithful retainers. A messenger (Jane) staggers in, dying of wounds. "O Lord, the enemy approaches. All is lost!" He falls, gurgles and dies. Liu embraces his beloved (Jane, up again). "The time has come. Oh, farewell, lovely Wa Nee Ta. Live to be happy with another. This is the end of your miserable Liu," and, jerking a jeweled bodkin from his waist, he plunges it into his beautiful self. Agh, urgh! He falls kicking and writhing in prolonged death throes to the dirt. He's an unconscionable time a-dying. Wa Nee Ta kneels over him, keening and tearing her hair. Last dying embrace. At the same moment in come the traitors, leading their troops as they sack the palace. Wa Nee Ta rises as Agragor, Nu Wa and Wa Fung stand in the door (imaginary; I remain on the floor as the corpse of Liu the Handsome). "Daughter, come to me. You are free," says deluded Wa Fung. (I have to do that bit, corpse or no, still lying down of course.) "Yes, Father," says Wa Nee Ta, drawing herself to her full height, "I am free!" And, snatching the bloody bodkin from the wound of her lover, she plunges it into her own rare bosom and gracefully collapses over Liu.

Curtain. THE END.

vii. We put the scarves and lampshades and other props into our costume chest. All our works, the entire city of Amur Wa, had been destroyed in that last orgy, so we collected the Mah-Jongg blocks, dusted them off, and stacked them neatly in their tin box. Then we conscientiously went up and started to smooth out the gravel of the front path so it would look neat for the dinner party. It had certainly been a glorious play.

We were comparatively silent, still beglamorized by the grandeurs and tragedies of Amuria; for the bare facts of the plot were merely a framework for the splendors that clothed it in our imagination, as an opera libretto is for its music: the gorgeous brocaded cloths and costumes, splotched with jewels, the gilded armor, Japanese in style, the pillars and domes of the palaces and temples, half oriental, half Renaissance, those gongs and fifes, the beauties of Liu and Wa Nee Ta and Nu Wa and Chin Lee and even Agragor. What we actually did, our playacting and our buildings, were recognized by us, even sometimes with cynical amusement, to be no more than a symbolic sketch of what we had in mind, the reality of Amuria. The old curtains and the pot lid and the Mah-Jongg blocks were never themselves believed to be more than instruments that stood for other things. We were quite aware of the inadequacy of these things, of our own dramatic impersonations. We differed from grown-ups only in being satisfied with so much less elaborate and detailed a working out of our imaginations. Lots of the story, for instance, was not dramatized; we merely told each other what was happening, a sort of narrative dialogue. "Now he gets on his horse and we go out to the battle . . ." or "Wa Fung and Agragor and all come in just as Liu is dying. . . ." We had to be historian, director and stage manager while we were being actor and audience. Though later adult aesthetic and dramatic experience might be more poignant, none could be more totally absorbing. No wonder all the rest of our garden life, for all its pleasures, seemed comparatively banal and unreal.

Nothing in this outer life was more banal and unreal than the pleasures and absorptions of the rest of our family. Robbie and Richie in particular were always getting us into things they thought wonderful and we thought stupid and disagreeable. While we were busy with our tidying up, using our feet to smooth out the gravel — it would have been so much more sensible if we'd had rakes, but the grim gardeners jealously brought all their tools with them and jealously took them away again — Robbie, Richie, Pam, Miranda all came up to "help us." We were suspicious of their kind offices, and we were right. Their real purpose was to inveigle us into one of their dumb daredevil stunts. Someone — Pam, it seemed — had discovered a perfectly ripping place to slide down the cliffs, a sort of natural chute. Robbie and all the others were palpitating to try it, and were generously willing to let us in on it. That's what they pretended anyway. They knew perfectly well we wouldn't like it, and they really just wanted to see how scared we'd be and then gloat over our scaredness.

This was a permanent, inescapable part of our relations with what we thought of as Robbie's world, just as being snubbed and scolded was part of what we thought of as Nan's world. Though Robbie never descended to actual bullying or meanness like Richie, he had no fear or timidity himself, liked anything dashing and daring, and had no feeling for anyone else's timidities except contempt. He felt everyone ought to enjoy escapades as he did, and if by chance any of us didn't, we were just yellow-bellies and sissies who must be made to try anyway, for the good of our souls. Of course if anybody actually got hurt, he was genuinely sorry and sympathetic, especially if they bore it with a stiff upper lip. But for initial reluctance he had no sympathy at all.

Our only real excuse for not joining in the slide was that we must finish our job of straightening the gravel. Since all the other four were very efficiently doing it with us, that excuse wouldn't hold out for long. We moved down toward the pool, lustily scraping and smoothing, and when we got to the bottom, the very borders of the province of Wa Hu, we were done for.

It was the borderline of our particular playland. From here on it was in our fancy the barbarian world where the free tribes still lived; in fact it was the equally barbarian world of Robbie. It was a far more exotic section of the garden, sure enough, but less useful for the purposes of Amuria. The pool, for instance, which we did sometimes use for naval battles (Amuria vs. Korea) held a very different aspect for Robbie's gang. It was a water-lily-choked affair, the shape of an elongated bean, with sedgy things growing up in it here and there. In the middle stood on one tiptoe a reproduction of famous naked Mercury in a helmet, carrying messages. If one turned a certain handle hidden along the pool's edge, a meek little fountain would spurt up around him. We children were absolutely forbidden to play with this, but sometimes we had a surreptitious fling at it. Back of Mercury were banked mimosas, whose gray branches arched out over the pool. The great sport was to jump from these branches across the pool onto the gravel. Both I and Jane had grimly done our duty by this. In front of the pool the gravel widened out into a sort of little plaza. One would expect a café or a bandstand. In fact there was a tin table with an umbrella hole in it (no umbrella) and two tin chairs, thickly encrusted with years of green paint. Nobody had ever been known to actually use them. We, or rather the Group, had long ago pushed them to one side, and the plaza was now consecrated to games like Prisoner's Base.

Water ran through a conduit from the pool, under the plaza, and came trickling out the other side. Thence it fell into a Romantic Chasm, a little canyon all made of imitation rocks. They looked like papier-mâché, but were concrete, painted brown, very hideous but providing a series of tiny cascades that eventually trickled about a concrete green alligator with his tail lashing the air. The whole was surrounded by bamboo to give a jungle effect, and was dark in the shadow of pines and laurel. This artificial gorge descended to a V-shaped opening in the real cliffs, and there the water from it seeped down to the shore. Here we could scramble up and down. On each side of the V, the yellow cliffs, half rock, half dirt, extended all the way along our shoreline, protecting us. An iron grill placed over the outlet of the rivulet theoretically protected us too, but any agile child could squeeze through, as we did. No outsider ever seemed to try it however.

A path, mostly steps, came down from the plaza alongside the gorge, in a peek-a-boo fashion, and at the end turned steeply to the beach through a rusty gate. Halfway a flight of steps went up from the path to a tower, a round turret that looked over the sea, with crenellations in its parapet.

All this Mediterranean fancy provided of course the most wonderful settings for us all; but it was understood that as the area immediately around the house was for us and Amuria, this was for Robbie's derring-do.

The new slide, latest fruit of derring-do, was down along the beach, beyond the tower lookout. We had to push our way to it through bushes and pine growth, for this further area of garden, except for a rather ill-kept path covered with pine needles that ran parallel at some distance to the cliff edge, was deserted woods, a no-man's-land.

The slide looked very terrifying, a twisty, slippery line of dirt that seemed to go straight down to the rocks on the beach below. Lead settled in my stomach and my face shut in a stoic mask. Pam, as discoverer, had first chance. Down she zipped with no hesitation, screeching joyously. She seemed to go awfully fast. Next came Captain Robbie. Miranda squealed with fright and pleasure, twisting over on her stomach at the end, a daring maneuver. Richie went in a high state of excitement. Pam had to do it again. And Miranda.

Glumly Jane and I stood like Indian captives, waiting to run the gauntlet. "Come on, Howie, down you go!" said Richie, jubilant and sneering. I felt he was secretly a bit scared himself, and was hoping I would funk it so he could take it out on me. Gingerly I sat down at the beginning, slightly dizzy with vertigo and thoroughly terrified. Before I was quite ready, Richie gave me such a push I felt I would topple over frontward. But instead I zipped down blind with speed, and landed breathless, shaken but unhurt at the bottom. I couldn't say I'd enjoyed it, but at least I'd done it. It was almost as fearful trying to scramble up the steep slippery cliff again. Richie at the top was trying to nag Jane into coming down. She flatly refused, not saying a word, just shaking her head; but the others, still eager to do it again and again, flushed and yelling, pushed in ahead.

I took my time climbing up, while Pam, Miranda, Robbie flashed by me. Of my own accord, while Richie was below on the beach so he couldn't have the satisfaction, I sat myself down and gently let myself go. I went down much more slowly this time, and was really quite pleased with myself. Robbie came zipping down after me. Jane, I noticed, still stood grim and obstinate at the top.

"Let's go back by the steps," said Robbie, pink and glorious and panting. "Quicker that way." And he ran ahead of me, dodging and leaping over the rocks like a wild animal. I followed as best I could, not particularly anxious to make the giddy, crumbling climb up those cliffs again. When we came to the beginning of the steps, there ahead of us was Uncle Dick, sunbathing on the stone dock that went out into the water. He was, to me, rather shockingly naked. He had on brief wool trunks, striped horizontally white and blue, such as only the crudest of French beach athletes then wore. Respectable men, especially respectable Americans, wore white wool jerseys and dark blue, rather baggy flannel shorts with belts. Anyway all the men of our family, including me, did. Dick reared up on his elbows, his powerful mahogany shoulders glistening, and smiled up at us. "Why don't you come swimming?" Robbie stopped dead. After a longish pause he said suddenly, "Okay," and turned to me. "Tell the others," he said, and dashed up the steps toward the house to get into his bathing suit (white jersey and dark blue pants).

I took the opportunity to dawdle. The only thing that kept me moving at all was the fear of being caught by Robbie on his way back down. Besides, there was poor Jane. But I certainly wasn't going to hurry. I took as long as I dared.

When I finally got to the slide, a nasty tableau met me. Jane was at the top of the slide, on her stomach, her legs dangling over the edge, hanging on for dear life to a root. Richie was trying to break her grip, jeering at her meanwhile, "Yellow-belly, yellow-belly!" and the two girls stood by, urging him on. It was a very medieval scene, a martyrdom if ever there was one. Jane clung to the root, speechless, her eyes squinched shut. To my credit, I ran up and pushed the squatting Richie, so that he fell over backward, yelling, "You let her alone!" But having done the slide myself I couldn't resist trying to persuade Jane to do it too. "Come on, Jane, it's easy. It doesn't hurt a bit," I said to her, also trying to loosen her grip. Pam and Miranda joined in the refrain. Richie jumped up and in turn pushed me over backward. He then stepped across me, his face contorted, and began to stamp on her fingers, grinding his teeth and snarling. Pam said, "Oh, Richie, do stop!" and just then Robbie appeared, rather like the U.S. Cavalry, St. George dressed in his bathing suit, carrying a towel.

"Hey! Richie!" he said in surprise. Richie stopped and turned around. Jane hung there, tears seeping through her closed eyelids, racked by inaudible sobs. "What's going on?" said St. Robbie. It was obvious what was going on, but I started to explain anyway, shrill and indignant. Especially since I had really helped myself. Robbie went over to Jane and tried to get her up. She still clung blindly to her root. "It's all right, come on. I won't hurt you," and she finally gave in. Robbie pulled her up and, without a word to the others, supported her offstage. Jane was actively crying now. Richie was left behind, ignored, his face twitching. I hurried off in the wake of Robbie's protection. The girls scornfully pushed by Richie, Miranda whispering some snakelike remark; and Richie, deserted and disgraced, stayed there muttering. I made up my mind to keep as far away from *him* as I could.

Robbie handed Jane over to me when we reached the steps, and he and the girls went on down to the beach. I steered Jane up to the house so she could wash herself off, and rest awhile in her room before we both went down again. We tacitly assumed that nobody would breathe a word to the parents about all this.

viii. And now it was swimming time. The evening miracle, the change of light from harsh to luminous was already taking place over the garden and the sea. It was time for our parents to emerge into family life from their seclusions. With that in mind, Jane insisted on taking the shortcut, with her towel over her head like a fuzzy hood, so that her swollen eyelids couldn't be noticed. The shortcut went from the space in front of our cellar, down steps to a tucked-away opening where a stone bench nestled in the greenery. Then it turned into the brush, an unofficial child-made trail, to strike the canyon and alligator on the opposite bank from the path. After that, one was on one's own. We found it difficult in bathing dress; scratchy. But secrecy was important. Explanations of why Jane had been crying were too appallingly involved.

When we got down to the dock, Jane simply had to face the music, getting into the water as unobtrusively as she could. This was not difficult. Everybody was there before us, the parents finished with their dip and sitting on towels, the others all jumping into the water, clambering out of the water, laughing, snorting, screaming. Nan held Ronnie up by the arms and dunked him, delighted and terrified, off the edge of the dock. He shrieked with each immersion, his eyes tight shut. He was supremely happy.

Jane was in the water and dog-paddling industriously out to sea. She still refused to swim any other way, but she made good time. Nobody had noticed her tearstains at all. Nobody noticed either the wonderful glow about us of sea and sky. The sun was going behind the cliffs and pines (just a bit earlier each day) so that a black shadow inched out toward our sunny dock. The dead-calm water, not even stippled this breathless evening with land breezes, dozed white-surfaced all about us. The two headlands, on the east the St. Roque peninsula where we sometimes went for picnics, and far in the west the cape that hid us from Toulon, glowed in full sun. Across the mouth of the bay a string of mysterious small rocky islands made a rather oriental silhouette. How we longed to go to these islands; but nobody seemed to have ever heard of sailing there, and nobody could even remember their names. We invested them with all sorts of implausible magic qualities: pirates still lived there, spies landed there in the dead of moonless nights, there were secret installations of the French Navy, protected by hidden machine guns. And in fact this molten evening, as nearly always, we could see the hazy outline of a destroyer patrolling along the horizon back out beyond.

Tonight especially that combination of rising excitement and releasing luxuriance which characterized the Riviera evening seemed emphasized. The unusual windlessness, the heat, the richness of the light all seemed to promise and threaten something at once beautiful and disturbing. We children leaped and screamed and splashed and pushed each other in response to this hidden excitement, this preternatural silence around us.

No one more so than Uncle Dick and the boys. Dick was showing off a not unexpected acrobatic talent to the awe of Richie and Robbie. His sleek skin glistening with water, his muscles superbly under control, he was performing various dives from the end of the dock into the deep water there. The level was too low for him to display any real form, though he just managed to finish off a jackknife by jumping high in the air. But more spectacular and appropriate were his somersaults. He somersaulted forward, he somersaulted backward, always landing clean in the water. He somersaulted twice in the air, he somersaulted over the crouching Robbie, the crouching Richie, the Webster girls. He stood on his hands, tense and perfect, and landed still tense and perfect, head down, cleaving the water every time with precision. In between all this he tried to instruct the boys. Robbie especially worked at it, fearless, but, for once, inept. Even Jane and I made voluntary stabs at a somersault, landing all awry, flop and splash, but pleased with ourselves. Father and Mother were immensely amused, but a bit worried. Nan deserted Ronnie to watch in adoration. Jane and I had to admit that at this sort of thing Dick was not silly.

The only disturbing note was the overanxiety of both the boys to copy their expert uncle. Robbie's goal was the back somersault, Richie kept trying to stand on his hands. He slipped once and scraped his shin rather severely going down on the edge of the dock, a bloody-looking surface wound. Mother then put an end to the whole business. Richie, who had already suffered disgrace once this afternoon, seemed suddenly to lose all bravado. Close to tears, he came to Mother like a stray dog for comfort and solace. She examined his leg, which was certainly not really badly hurt, and, rare sight, let him lean against her, wet and slimy though he was, as she brushed the dank hair off his forehead. We were embarrassed by the incident — at least during the few moments we took to notice it. Then we went right back to our screaming and splashing and swimming. Robbie was in earnest discussion with Dick, squatting on his heels while Dick lay prone and panting. Robbie, I could see, was going to learn the back somersault or bust.

The shadow of the cliffs crept forward. Already the beach rocks were dark. Soon the parents would call us in. The water and sun seemed especially precious tonight. Perhaps in our weather bones we felt a change coming. When at last the coolness reached the towels where our parents sat, gradually took in the end of the dock, they rose. The time had come. They spoke, we protested, they were firm, we were rebellious. Dick rose and Robbie rose with him and at last we all straggled together, hair stringy and dribbling, towels cloaked over our shoulders, up the steps and into the gloom, leaving the evening beach behind us.

                                        ix. Supper was a simple, confused affair. Everyone's interest was concentrated on our parents' big formal dinner to come. There were to be Famous Guests — a literary pair — and our French Count, and Nan was to be allowed to eat with the grown-ups again as Dick's lady. The rest of us, including the Websters and Ellie, jammed ourselves about the round brown table, a tight fit, where we squabbled and gobbled. We were to get dressed afterward and be presented, as at court, during the cocktail hour; then there would be a feast of some sort just for us and, after that, up to our rooms for the rest of the evening so as not to be in the way.

"I saw your 'leopard,'" said Ellie scornfully to me. She was sour at not being included in the adult world tonight, and took it out on us all, very superior. "He ran out and barked at me. It's that farm on the corner where the road turns toward town." "Leone says she read all about it in the papers," countered Richie, an unexpected ally. "The circus was going from Cannes to Toulon and the leopard escaped right along here somewhere." "So ha!" said Jane suddenly. Ellie laughed, dégagée. "Did the paper say what color it was?" I suddenly found I wasn't really very interested. I let the two argue about it, Pam Webster adding that she was sure they saw tracks in the woods, etc. What was important was that as far as I was concerned, I had seen my fabulous beast, my unicorn. Facts were not really to the point. Perhaps, like my cross-washer's vision of the

73

Virgin, it *was* an illusion, nonetheless important. A vision after all was even more exotic than a leopard. It had been for me an experience, no matter what; the intrusion into life of real, sinister excitement, something from outside, exterior, rather than just another fabrication of my own imagination, like Amuria.

In any case, they were all fighting about something else by the time dessert — ugh, tapioca! — came along. I ran up as soon as I could to put on my communion suit, slightly stale seeming from last night. Then we all gathered down below, whispering in the hall. The guests had come, and were out on the terrace in the dusk drinking.

Finally Nan opened the door and let us, like conspirators, into the *salon*. We were to wait there *quietly* until Mother called to us. Nan was of course very officious about the whole thing, and swept back grandly to the grown-up group. We shuffled about, probably making lots of noise. The *salon* was half dark, the blue ceiling almost invisible, the Spanish highboy very tall and ominous. But we noticed a handsome guitar leaning by the fireplace. Whose? Uncle Dick's, it seemed. We couldn't resist it, touching the strings, crouching about it. Beyond us we could hear snatches of adult conversation: an affected woman's voice saying things like "My dear!" and "It was ex-*cruc*-iating," and a man who laughed very loud. Not Dick. This man laughed even louder and longer, presumably at his own jokes.

Our suspense was ended and Mother at last called us out. We bunched ourselves in the center window, then gradually emerged onto the terrace. The Comte de Tessières we knew already, in his very English dinner jacket, with his bristly tan mustache and monocle. He loved us all dearly, especially the girls. The other two guests had, sure enough, that look which we recognized as being Famous — a sort of special protuberance of the personality. The man was slumped in his chair, nakedly bald, with the face of a boyish skull. He looked at us leering and sardonic. The woman sat up very straight and was very handsome and in the extreme of fashion. Her dark dress went straight from armpit to just above the knee, and was richly, obscurely brocaded, with things at the hipline. Her hair swooped forward duskily over the cheeks, just below the prominent cheekbones, and her mouth was very big and red, her eyes very big and black. When she turned about, which she did constantly, swiveling graceful and upright from left to right, gesturing posily with her red-nailed hands, we could see that her back was bare to the sacroiliac. Big pearls, tight about her long neck, hung way down that back in a glossy strand.

Mother presented us chronologically, as we huddled back of the group. "This is Ellie, that's Robbie. . . ." "No, no, their *real* names," said Mrs. Famous; so Mother obeyed. "Anna you know," she indicated Nan this time. "Oh, my yes!" interpolated the guest. "Elise, Robert and Richard. . . ." "Two pretty men. Isn't that it? 'Robert and Richard were two pretty men.'" "Then Howard," pointing to me. "'Scots wa' ha' wi' Howard bled.'" "*Wal*lace, Wallace!" snarled her husband. "Of *course* dear, I *know*." "And Jane . . ." "'A bumpety ride in a wagon of hay.'" "She's known as the Female Bartlett." Every thing Mr. Famous said was weighted with a savage scorn, especially when he spoke to his wife. She didn't seem to mind, but she said, good-humoredly, "Oh, do shut up." ". . . and Ronald you've seen." Ronnie had evidently been presented earlier.

"Your jewels!" exclaimed Mrs. Famous, flinging out her arms theatrically. Everyone guffawed. "Aren't they beautiful!" she continued. Now her hand was splayed stylishly on her chest. "Look at that one," as she indicated Robbie, "and you," she turned on poor Richie, "you're the

75

int'resting one, aren't you?" "That's my boy," muttered Mr. Famous.

"Oh, but *that's* the one *I* love!" It was Jane's turn now. "So *serious*! Look, darling, just look. She sees through us all, doesn't she; all our poses, all our pretensions. You'll hate me, but you've got to come over here and let me hug you. Blushing! I don't blame you a bit. Come along." Jane by now really was blushing and smirking. "Adorable!" She kissed Jane and squeezed her. "Yum! Now that's over." She turned to Mother. "They *are* worth seeing. But I think they better go away. . . ." "Before they sink through the floor with shame," interrupted her husband, each word weighted with malice. "Especially that one there, the '*in*-t'resting' one," he continued relentlessly. "How he does hate us all. Don't you, boy? That's me all over at his age. Wetting my pants, jealous of all the pretty ones. Zowie, I'm glad I'm grown up." His wife turned on him. "Honest to God, darling, you do go too far!" "Of course, of course. That's the secret of my success. Why the hell am I the toast of two continents? Because I go too far. They love it."

We were filing out, smothering our giggles, Richie perfectly delighted of course, Robbie slapping him on the shoulder, Jane whispering to me. It was a lark; so much more entertaining than we could ever have expected.

When we got back indoors, we let loose a bit. Pam and Miranda and their mother came in, the girls having been taken back after supper to get dressed up. They had to be presented too, while we peeked around corners. Nothing spectacular happened to them however. Then they came in and joined us, while we all tried to tell them our riotous experiences. The treat was laid out for us on a card table in front of the fireplace — lemonade and a cake. We fell to.

On the terrace the conversation had long ago left us. We could hear Mr. Guest's heavily sarcastic remarks, Mrs.

Guest's high-toned foolishness. She was talking to the Count. "You, you live for your mustache, and I for my back," we heard her say. Everyone seemed to be having a hilarious time, Jocelyn yapping, Dick guffawing. We were pretty hilarious ourselves. Nan had to come in, pleased as she could be, to shut us off.

But soon the cake was done, the grown-ups appeared on their way to a late, late dinner. It was the signal for us to move upstairs. Pam and Miranda with Ellie, I to my room alone. Once there I could hear the three girls carrying on next to me. Like last night, I was restless. But it was not a night for poetry. Outside the moon wasn't up yet, and the sky was, I noticed, suddenly cloudy. I turned on my light, illegally, and looked at stamps. Then I was overcome with sleep, turned off the light, crept under the mosquito netting and into my bed. As I went off, completely, thoughtlessly, I heard a distant singing. The guitar. It was Uncle Dick chanting something nasal and Spanish-sounding.

3.

i. A moody, muddy-looking day; a break in our long-continued spell of glory, and a poor omen for all the new excitements broached by our parents at breakfast — breakfast held for once in the gloom of the purple dining room, under the Piranesis. It seemed our Count had asked the girls, Nan and Ellie both, to visit him for a few days at his château. They were wild with joy (and joy was so often wild with them). They loved the Count, they admired his mustache and monocle (Jane of course found these silly). They loved his "château," a very carefully and beautifully restored Provençal country manor with thick pink walls, old carved chests inside and cactus out on the terrace in big terra-cotta tubs. They above all loved his daughter, who seemed to them ineffably romantic. She was a pretty, pale dark girl, a crippled victim of polio who lived like a remote princess with her widowed father in his lovely but lonely house. All their capacities for sympathy and sentimentalism were stirred by her prettiness and her plight, and the thought of a visit there filled them with rapture. In fact it would be very quiet and very dull, but they didn't think about that, all caught up as they were with their visions of titled grandeur and hopes of bringing cheer into a poor invalid's life.

As for the rest of us, we had plans too it seemed. We were to take a trip to Malhaut. Malhaut was a famous ruin on which our father had historical designs. It was a scene of Albigensian heresy, Provençal courts of love, Renaissance Protestantism and everything juicy, besides being picturesque to the last degree. Father, Mother, Uncle Dick, the boys, Jane and I were all to go. Jocelyn Webster too, though her girls it seemed were previously involved with some other nearby English children. The boys were disappointed that the girls couldn't come, but nobody else seemed to be, including Mrs. Webster. Three cars, our gloomy Renault, Dick's gorgeous Hispano and Jocelyn's little red Citroën, were to make up our convoy. We were to start tomorrow, rain or shine.

What turmoil. The girls shrieking upstairs to pack in a maximum of exclamatory caprice and running consultation with Mother about what to wear. To-do about meals — a picnic for all on the first day; Father on the telephone, with all the attendant French hazards and delays, arranging hotel rooms for the night. It was a grand happy flurry, and took our minds off the lack of sunshine and the blustery hot wind that made swimming unpleasant, but not impossible. Robbie and Richie still insisted on practicing dives under Dick's occasional direction, but the rest of us ran to the beach and ran back. The leopard and Amuria and the slide and all the events of the past week were totally obliterated.

Next morning we started off. Jocelyn bustled over for breakfast with us, again in the dining room, for the weather was even more unpleasant, and it had actually rained during the night; our first rain in months, it seemed to us. The great question was: who was to go with whom? Should we all wait for the Count to come and claim Nan and Ellie? Was everyone properly packed? Last-minute screams from Nan and Ellie who had forgotten vital things like nail files.

At last it was arranged. The boys and Jocelyn were to go with Dick; Jane and I with our parents. The Webster car was to be left in our garage, after all. We took off, waving and cheering out our windows to Nan and Ellie, still unfetched, Mademoiselle and Ronnie, deserted, Celestine in black and about to go on a holiday, all of them waving and cheering too. Off on a trip! What exhilaration, even if the sky was dun and the Riviera looked its worst, the land a sort of pale clay color with black accents of pine and cypress, the sea a stormy slate.

The road hugged the shore for a way, and passed by the Websters' white villa in its rocky garden of cactus. Dick had gone ahead of us, and his car was parked in front of the house. We honked our horn and waved and shouted, hoping for a glimpse of Pam and Miranda. But no one answered back.

The road led on to the next town, not our usual shopping center, but a larger, stranger place. The road turned from the sea through flat, busy farms and then between long walls topped, like ours, with broken glass. The street was edged with lines of plane trees. At a small square in the middle of the town Mother had to stop for something, a drug or a cosmetic. We were allowed to get out and stretch, so long as we stayed in sight of Father and the car. The little square about its moss-dribbled fountain was as gay as a scene in a musical comedy. The sun came out in patches, and there was no gustiness in the shelter of the tall plaster houses. The market stalls were animated, children were about, boys with incredibly long bare knobby legs in incredibly short trousers, sailors looking like chorus boys in their jaunty uniforms and caps with pompoms, black and white dogs, the inevitable crew of somber widows. We spent our time examining the stock of a stationer's store, which like the one in our town, where I usually went, sold stamps and souvenirs. How I salivated at the sight of more big French Colonial stamps, like mine from Togo: miniature visions of romance in Madagascar, Mauritius, Morocco, each with its own cachet and character and native accent. The street scene meant little to me by comparison, but Jane looked about her, bored by stamps, full of scorn and amusement at the silliness of the French, who of all people most nearly answered her definition of silliness. Sailors with pompoms indeed! Dogs called Kiki!

Then Mother was done, the horn honked, we climbed aboard and headed this time northwest and inland through a desolate and no longer Riviera world of bare yellowish cliffs and gorges, naked gray villages perched up on impossible summits. Who would live there and why? Above all, how? One in particular struck us, when Father pointed it out to us. It was so steeply up from the road we could see nothing of it but a gray square church tower and a few remnants of medieval town wall. It was Saint-something now, but had once been Heliopolis, city of the sun, stuck up where it got the first and last rays of its god. Before the Greeks came it had been a holy place, and then a temple, a famous temple all through antiquity. According to Father, who had once taken the trouble to scrabble up there, the church was built about Roman columns.

We liked Heliopolis, at least the idea of it; but our next stop pleased us considerably less. The road had taken us through the hills now, and we came out into a rather bare vine-clad valley, and into a very bare brown village. Here we stopped to wait for Dick, and to examine under his guidance a church called St. Juste. It too was evidently much admired. At least, when Dick did come whirling up in a silver glitter, and he and Jocelyn Webster and the boys all piled noisily out, the grown-ups appeared to admire it excessively. The boys refused even to come inside, and roughhoused around the worn steps. We went into the cool darkness, illuminated by a few thin windows with plain dirty glass in them. The church, according to Dick, was the most perfect example of Romanesque in those parts, and we thought it pretty drab. Severe round arches,

84

everything gray stone, no nice Gothic fancy, and in fact few signs of use or decor to speak of except cheap altar furniture and some bones in dingy glass cases, relics of Juste himself. The grown-ups however professed delight. We trailed around after them trying to find something amusing. We failed. We were glad to get back to the car and the comparative warmth of the half sun. The town as we drove out of it was as grim as the church and seemed exclusively populated by those black-clad widows — no dogs, children and sailors.

ii. It wasn't long after St. Juste before we came to our monastery. We drove up a long rocky lift of the land and then steeply down the flanks of a cliff into a green valley where the ruinous building sat among great trees. We had been here more than once before. It was a favorite spot, and our experiences there had been transmuted into our own cross-washing, playing at monk, etc. It represented to us more than any other place in our experience Catholicism, medievalism and all that aspect of the old world exotic.

Jane and I jumped out of the back seat of the Renault and ran to the grassy spot where we always had picnicked. It was a lawn kept green by the influence of a spring that came out of the stern monastery wall into an old fountain, a snub-nosed lion's head with grinning spouting mouth. The water was very cold and could be presumed, even here in the south of France, to be pure. It was only a trickle now after the long drought, but still the round worn basin was mossy and the grass about it, cropped by herds, comparatively vivid. The great trees over us made a gloom. There was only occasional sun. We helped spread out the steamer rugs and dispose the picnic things neatly. By the time we were done, Dick drove up and the grove became animated with Dick and Jocelyn's noisy chatter and the boys whooping about. The four grown-ups disposed themselves in a circle. Jane, feeling obviously a bit subdued with her customary carsickness, sat by me and slowly munched on a hard-boiled egg. Nobody else was about and no traffic passed by us on the road.

Jane and I secretly hoped we might have some chance to see the monastery again; but obviously there wouldn't be time. After all, we'd already had one exhaustive, exhausting tour, stopping to look at each moldering object and collapsed chamber under the garrulous guidance of the caretaker. The caves, the sacred caves up there in the cliff, were out of the question too. Though there were several of them, one was a particular object of veneration. Mary Magdalene, it seemed, in some obscure latter part of her biography, had come there to settle and pray. The Angel Gabriel had visited her, and left his footprint on a rock as a souvenir. The cave therefore was much worked over in a sacred way. An iron paling with a gate closed it in, and this paling was almost solidly hung with offerings — rosaries, hearts and tin wreaths. The long zigzag shallow stairway up the ascent was usually, at least on bright holidays, thick with pilgrims, and several ogreish old women made a killing at the top sitting back of broad trays and selling tiny medals. Jane and I each cherished one. It was a most spectacular exhibition for us of Popish superstition, and all this, plus the dank, dark mysteriousness of the cave itself, with its Virgin, its Gabriel, its Mary Magdalene in cheap plaster surrounded by candles and votive offerings, thrilled us with a sense of the supernatural and of Protestant superiority. The indentation on the rock outside the cave, Gabriel's mark, surrounded also by an iron fence, did in fact look remarkably like an awkward print. Heavy-footed fellow, that Gabriel.

This time there were to be no such expeditions, but we

did wander about along the silent walls and in through the trees. The boys had completely disappeared, after gobbling a few sandwiches. Dick had a bottle of wine, and he and Jocelyn were hilarious over it, laughing and laughing at jokes that made no sense to us, when we bothered to listen. Jane proved a languid explorer, however, so we soon returned and were allowed a sip of wine and spring water. Father by this time was holding forth, and Dick and Jocelyn had calmed down a bit listening to him. "Such layers of religious experience!" he was saying. "Those caves up there must have known every religion known to Western man. Neolithic fire worshipers, sun worshipers, classic oracles, Mithraism. This monastery of course was founded by Dominicans here to stamp out Catharism. It was the local center of the Inquisition. Lots of nice burnings round about. Then the other side had its innings. The place was sacked by Protestants during the civil wars, and the monks dispossessed. It was finally liquidated in the Revolution. Catholicism blooming up there in the caves and secular decay down here."

"Secular decay is obviously more peaceful and in better taste," said Dick. "Yes," said Father thoughtfully. "Yes, religion and politics and industry all seem to be rather ugly when they're actually going on, don't they?"

"Oh, but think of Chartres!" said Jocelyn.

"Oh, but think of all those roasting heretics!" countered Dick. "That can't have been very pretty."

"No doubt very satisfactory and decent to good church people at the time," said Father. "After all we still tend to relish the execution of a good sound murderer. Or a traitor. Nobody pities a traitor or a spy. Their just deserts, we say."

"Rules of the game," said Dick. "If I'd been caught I'd been shot." He was referring to his mysterious wartime activities about which he wouldn't talk as a rule.

"What *were* you doing?" Jocelyn leaned up eagerly toward him. "You never say." "No," said Dick, meditative. "I don't talk about that." He brooded for a minute. "But I certainly deserved to be shot," and he brightened up and laughed. "I suppose what's true for politics is true for religion. Heretics are traitors. Don't you agree?" He leered at Father.

Father looked at him from under his eyebrows. "Incredibly frivolous, you pagans! After all, you ancients had your burnings too. Invented the idea."

"Yes. That was politics, though, not religion. Fealty to the Emperor! Salute the flag! Or get crucified. Rules of the Game. Take your choice."

"You always come back to 'rules of the game,' don't you? That sounds more English to me than pagan. What rules of what game? Or doesn't it make any difference? But do you really think the kind old monks who lived in this quaint old monastery were justified in burning men — that is, having them burned — because of rules of the game? Of course I know you don't; but even for the sake of argument. . . . "

"Hm. Hm." Dick squinted up at the trees and let the cigarette smoke drift out of his nostrils. "I suppose, theoretically, I have to subscribe to the proposition that one ought to obey the rules of whatever game one subscribes to. For instance, if you're a good Protestant Christian you're bound to observe the Protestant Christian code of sexual morality, right?" "Yes, indeed," said Father rather meaningfully. "And therefore, from your point of view, since you consider this code God-given, you have a right to burn anybody who breaks the rules, don't you?" "Burn? That's rather severe. Disapprove certainly."

"Now with us pagans it's quite the other way. . . . " Mother interrupted: "But suppose one of the 'rules of the game' is tolerance? Tolerance of other people's rules?"

Father turned toward her. "Ah, there's the rub! There's the rub! You can't burn people out of tolerance, can you? Do I tolerate murderers?" "Do you tolerate spies? Or the Cathars' nasty sexual habits?" said Dick, and Jocelyn said, "*What* sexual habits?" "*No* sexual habits," said Father sternly. "That was lying Romish propaganda." "Just the way that was all propaganda about the Beastly Huns chopping off babies' arms," said Jocelyn, and they were all off on a conversation about the war and propaganda. But we were distracted when the boys came back and squatted near us telling about their discoveries.

iii. Then it was time to set off again.

There was a consultation and it was decided to shift about for variety and health. Mother thought Jane might be happier in Dick's open rumble seat. So Mother and I were to go with him now, the boys and Jocelyn with Father.

For a while it worked, and we were exhilarated by the air and openness, though shielded from too much wind by a special rumble seat windshield. Then Jane began to feel badly again, so Dick stopped and put the windshield down. The rush of air helped. We could also hear what Dick and Mother were saying. This provided a relief from rather boring scenery — first low, rocky hills, then an increasing flatness. The sun was out a good deal now, but that sort of pervasive dun-colored glare made things look even uglier. There was also a certain amount of dust. Evidently our rain had not fallen here. We tried counting different makes of cars, but there wasn't enough traffic on this road to make it worthwhile.

"I never seem to see you alone," Mother said to Dick; and they began talking family, which wasn't very interesting either. They had brothers and sisters, aunts and uncles whom we knew slightly but seldom saw. There was a chill of some sort, never explained.

"Have you seen the McClanahans?" said Dick, and this was more interesting. McClanahan was the name of Mother's first husband, and Richie's and Robbie's real last name, though they were now officially adopted as Carruthers. We knew there was a McClanahan uncle, fabulously rich, very fashionable. "Yes. I went around with the boys one day. I thought he ought to know they exist." "Does he care?" "Not much. He has it in for me of course; and Robbie too. He seemed to rather favor Richie." "He damn well ought to favor at least one of them. Who else has he got to leave that money to? Unless he gets freakish and gives it to the cat. But I can't see Richie as a yachtsman somehow, can you?" "We'll cross that bridge when we come to it," said Mother rather stiffly. "In any case, we don't want him to have ideas. Or the children either. Nothing will probably come of it anyway." And they dropped that conversation; but not before we had this startling glimpse of Richie as an Heir. This added a surprising note of glamor to our picture of him though it was of course vague. However, a certain vista opened up of Richie in a yachting cap, smoking a big cigar on a deck as he steamed out of New York harbor. It was implausible; much easier to think of Robbie that way. Now *he* had all the makings of an Heir.

After a while even the battering rush unbroken by windshield ceased to have a proper effect on Jane. She became steadily more pale, more listless. We were going through a great level plain. The road was straight as an arrow, a Roman road, as Dick broke the silence to point out. On each side there were endless bare fields, truck gardens mostly, with bare low hills about in the distance.

Jane at last, looking rather green, leaned forward and whispered to Mother. Mother looked back concerned and spoke to Dick, who said, "Well, I don't see much hope right now. I'll keep my eyes open." Jane relapsed miserably and we drove across the remorseless, shelterless flatland.

"How about this?" said Dick, suddenly slowing, pulling off to the side and stopping. "They ought to have something." It was the first house we'd passed that was right on the road, and it was a sort of station. The railroad crossed through here, evidently from the look of it with double tracks and all, a main line. There was a crossing barrier, a signal, and on the two-story yellow plaster house a sign saying "Côte D'Arnville." Presumably a station ought to have a bathroom in it; though it looked far more like a private house than a station.

Mother and Jane got out and opened an iron gate in a low yellow plastered wall. I followed aimlessly. A concrete path went straight to the house door, which was flanked by potted geraniums. In front of the house was a big vegetable garden. Mother and Jane hurried to the door and rang. After a wait a large gray woman opened it and looked at them sternly with her hands on her big hips. When she heard the story she relented and rather cordially asked them in. I stood dawdling near the gate.

A big powerful boy of sixteen or so had been digging in the garden, bare to the waist. When he saw us drive up he stopped frozen, with one foot on his spade, first staring at Mother and Jane, then staring at the car and Dick. Dick slowly got out, looking about and then over at the boy. He began to stretch very elaborately, his arms above his head, one hand gripping the wrist of the other till the muscles of his bare arms twitched, wriggling his hips and twisting about with his eyes closed. The boy watched him, then took his foot off his spade, went to the wall and picked up a ragged blue shirt without arms and put it on. He stood awkwardly looking over the wall at Dick, obviously dying to get closer to that vision of a car.

Dick lit a cigarette, leaned back against the car, crossed his legs and smiled at the boy. Pretty soon remarks were passed. The boy vaulted easily over the wall, holding with one hand the straw hat, or rather cap; for nothing was left of it but the crown. I could see as he passed by the gate, outside, paying no attention to me, how remarkably handsome he was, except perhaps for the solid black bar of eyebrow that went across his face above blue eyes and sun-black regular features.

He and Dick were soon in conversation, Dick leaning against the car, the boy shifting about with his thumbs in his belt line, the old shirt flapping in the hot wind. I turned and wandered along the concrete path, past the door and beside the railroad tracks till I came to the opposite wall. There was something pleasingly melancholy and quiet about the great hot fertile country, almost treeless, the railway glistening off into the distance. Inside I could hear voices, Mother and the woman of the house. I sauntered around the garden admiring the cabbages and salads. At the back was a little orchard of six trees with green fruit on them.

When I had circled round to the gate again Dick was showing the boy the car engine, the boy leaning over, Dick more or less on top of him, one hand pointing out objects, the other spread out on the boy's sweaty-shirted back. I would have thought the boy would have been repulsively smelly and dirty, but this wasn't bothering democratic Dick.

However, they did not provide much entertainment for me. I looked back down the track, and shortly observed with excitement the far far distant signs of a train. Just then the woman came out and asked me smiling if I'd like to come in. Jane and Mother were having a tisane with her it seemed. I refused as graciously as I could, and pointed to the coming train. The woman reared back and nodded with great understanding. A grizzly, guimpy man, her husband no doubt, emerged and began to close the barrier gates with a crank mechanism. The train was gradually visible. Its white smoke plume blew sideways over the fields in the wind; it gave its disappointing high French scream, so unlike the virile deep melancholy of American train whistles. And finally here it was, larger and larger and then rushing by, a terribly fast, terribly stylish passenger express, thundering and glistening. Even Dick and the boy turned up to look at this, Dick's hand still on the boy's shoulder.

The old man cranked open the gate, Jane and Mother came out the door, Jane looking pleased and refreshed, Mother and the lady of the house in a spate of compliments. The boy stepped back, his face radiant with enthusiasm. He and Dick shook hands long and vigorously, a tableau that looked somehow like a statue for the rapprochement of labor and capital, with the linkage of Dick's strong lighter brown arm and the boy's big black one. I moved to the car, rather sorry to leave this queer remote place, and we all got in, waving and smiling.

iv. From there on, till we reached the hotel about four, there was very little of interest. Jane drifted off to sleep, huddled in her corner. For a while we went up a river along a main highway, so there were plenty of cars to keep me busy. Dick every now and then pointed off at sights — a distant famous city we were not to visit, a Roman remain.

Finally we came to the Hôtel du Golf. Father had

arrived first and had us all billeted in our various rooms. He was waiting on the porch for us, he and Jocelyn together. Dick's car exerted the usual fascination and more bellboys than necessary ran out to see it and us. We in turn admired the hotel, a huge very new building in cocoa-colored plaster, crinkly with bay windows and gray cement protuberances. It was not designed for Anglo-Saxon tourists and had nothing about it either Victorian or picturesque. It was chic, French and sportive. The interior was very spacious, clean, dazzling and nondescript. Brisk elevators took us up to our spacious, clean, nondescript rooms, with large windows looking over the undulant golf course, studded with pines, for which the hotel was named, and which gave it a reason for being.

We hurried about looking at all the other family rooms. Jane and I were together, next to the parents. They had a bathroom, but we had only a basin. Jocelyn was opposite a few doors off. Dick and the boys were both considerably further along. Jane and I ran up and down the brown-carpeted corridors, then got permission to go below and run up and down in the *salons* and the terraces covered with tables and umbrellas and the new, bleak gardens of geranium and mimosa.

The tea hour was important at the hotel. The clientele came in from their games of golf and tennis and sat on that long terrace under those umbrellas and had *apéritifs* or even tea. Our grown-ups did what was proper. We joined them, munched a stale macaroon or two, watched all the brown-skinned people with admiration — smart Lenglen-like ladies in short white pleated dresses with white bands over their foreheads, men in white plus-fours or flannels, with gay scarves at the neck. It was all like the advertisements in *L'Illustration*, and a great lift above the tepid provincialism of the Maritime, the only other hotel in our lives; or the great decaying hotels in our vicinity inhabited solely by English widows and their dogs. Here at the Hôtel du Golf we were cosmopolitan but not tourist; South Americans, Germans, but few English or Americans, and lots of rich bouncy French people.

We were all scrubbed and brushed and dressed up for dinner, which was an excitement of glaring chandeliers and waiters dashing about and headwaiters commanding them and indigestible courses and a sip of wine or two. We looked and felt very distinguished and spent all our time picking out garish oddities at the surrounding tables. Everyone was very dressed up, women in scarlet or purple with Spanish shawls and men in blazers or *le smoking*. We were overtired and overexuberant and Mother had a hard time getting Jane and me to a reluctant early bed, while it was still light outside, and the terrace a few stories below our window was beginning to cackle with people.

Of course, for all our tiredness, we couldn't sleep. We whispered to each other and got up and down to fetch glasses of water. The pale light gradually faded over the golf course and the cutout of velvet hills; and the mosquitoes began. The Hôtel du Golf was much too modern to go in for mosquito nettings over the bed, the inevitable miranda. On the other hand, they hadn't yet thought of screens for the big windows. The mosquitoes, bred no doubt in the water hazards of the golf course, had a fiesta. It was still too hot, especially here on the southwestward side of the hotel, to close the windows. The mosquitoes made it impossible for us to sleep. Jane wanted to call Mummy. I told her she couldn't. She whimpered and rustled around in her bed and finally got completely under a sheet like a tent. I tried, but it didn't work. I found it suffocating. I sighed and thrashed and became particularly annoyed when I found Jane had been able to go fast asleep.

It was way after midnight, or so I assumed, when I finally got an idea. I was sweaty and desperately tired. I got up and groped my way to the bureau to get the room key (the doors were efficiently automatic) and a towel; then out into the ghostly corridor and across to the public bath. There I filled the big tub to the top with tepid water and lay with only my nose showing. I could easily have drowned of course by going to sleep, and in fact did find myself slipping off and down a couple of times. I may have been there a half hour before I felt relaxed and cool enough. Deliciously clean and sleepy now, I started out toward the hall again. I was in fact just opening the bathroom door when I saw Dick also coming out of a door. It was Jocelyn Webster's room. I could tell by her shoes outside. Dick was dressed only in a short dressing gown, or jacket really, that came no lower than his upper thighs. His big brown legs were bare, and his feet too. He came out rather stealthily, looked up and down (I only opened the door a crack), then turned and very gently pulled back on the knob. His shoulders were shaking in a curious way, and his face was down. I thought he must be crying; then as he straightened up and went with lithe swiftness down the hall, I could see he was silently laughing. I waited till he'd disappeared before I returned, mystified but somnolent, to my own room. It was almost cold there now. The mosquitoes weren't in evidence. I went right off to sleep.

v. We had planned to have a very early breakfast and get to Malhaut in good time. The result was that when we did all gather, a bit too late, everyone was sleepy and grumpy. Sleepy at least. Dick and Jocelyn were anything but grumpy. They seemed subdued but sharing some delicious joke that made them chuckle at odd moments. The boys had slept well enough, but had been morose all through the trip anyway.

A good solid Americanized breakfast of eggs and toast and *café au lait* set us up and woke us, and we actually were able to get off by nine. The plan was to see Malhaut by morning before the heat settled down, have our picnic lunch there in the ruins, then go straight back all the way home, stopping for supper somewhere along the road.

Malhaut was only about an hour from the hotel. The day, which had begun nicely, though rather cloudy and windy, became increasingly unpleasant. By the time we came into the hills, the blue sky was obscured, but a good deal of that rather disagreeable sunlight filtered through. The road, after a long stretch of flat fields, went through a desolate canyon and then turned suddenly northward into a small valley surrounded everywhere by grotesquely carved yellow rocks in bulbous pillars and shattered ridges. At the very head of the valley, higher than anything else, loomed Malhaut. It was impossible to tell from a distance what was natural cliff and what was broken castle. Under the beige glare of the morning it looked totally deserted and thoroughly sinister.

When we got closer, through the meager farms, we discovered that there was an inhabited part, a village at the foot of the promontory, which still housed living people. We even passed a few small modern plaster villas, and came through a narrow short street to a town square. It was very sad, with an ugly gray Napoleonic church on one side, a dead cast-iron fountain in the middle and a depressing town hall and police station on the opposite side. It all seemed terribly silent and moribund, though there was a flyblown café and some miserable stores.

Here we had to leave our thoroughly locked-up cars, the only ones visible, and walk the rest of the way. An alley just wide enough for two of us abreast led up from the square by shallow worn dirty steps to the old town and castle. The stone houses leaned over us, smelling of urine

97

and neglect. Jane and I let the boys go first, having already had some difficult encounters with the nasty little dogs of this kind of neighborhood.

The approach to Malhaut was certainly not encouraging. We came out of the decaying houses of the "new town" and turned sharply right toward a frowning gate in a battlement. A precarious causeway carried us across a gulf, on one side a terraced draw, on the other a sharp drop into a tangle of rocks and olive trees. An old man, almost the first person we'd seen, nodded blearily at us from his canvas seat by the gate and took our centimes of admission. Inside the wall everything was in ruins. Jane and I both became excited by the thought of the whole town open for exploration like this, as though we were being let loose in a great attic. Malhaut had been incongruously prosperous in the Renaissance, and the substantial remains of the mansions of bourgeois and nobleman towered with empty square windows, richly framed, and luxurious hooded fireplaces up in floorless rooms. The parents wouldn't allow us to go inside, for fear of falling masonry; but the crooked street arched over by supports, the constant vistas through vacant doorways and down side alleys were interesting enough for us.

Then there was another town square, much handsomer than the one below. It too had its church, its dead fountain, its wonderfully decorated shell of a *hôtel de ville*. The church was the only building still usable. It had been restored (ghastly job, according to Dick) and reconsecrated. It was beyond belief old, the original small nave built by the first Visigothic converts, various wings added on at odd angles, including a most elegant late Gothic chapel. Here, Father informed us, Protestant services had been held, the ruling family (no longer Malhauts) by then having become Huguenots. Such a crannied, curious dark place, of many levels, full of marred tombs and noseless statues; it suited us perfectly. *This* was more the idea! To hell with perfect examples of the Romanesque. We poked about into every dingy corner.

There was more town up above the square, the narrow passageway always going steeply toward the visible heights of the castle. Here was another great gate, and another old caretaker. We were obviously the day's only visitors, and he was very glad to see us. Father managed to persuade him not to escort us, much to his chagrin. Father knew the place well himself, had studied it in detail and visited it before in time past.

"First let's go down to the caves, while we still have energy." "*What* energy?" said Jocelyn. "Then we can come back up to the castle and have lunch." Jocelyn sighed again as we turned along inside the walls and came to a steep narrow stairway down the side of the cliffs. It looked quite scary. "Oh dear," said Jocelyn, "do we really have to go down that? And come up again!" But of course she had to be a sport. We scrambled down first, the boys recklessly, Jane hugging the iron banister. At the bottom was a platform, and there in the cliffside a most thoroughly black narrow cave. We waited till the grown-ups arrived and went in. It was deep and clammy. There were tombs. Water dripped down the walls. The cave went far back into the dark, but a high barrier restrained us.

"This was the famous Cave of the Sorcerer. Mistral wrote it all up." "It does have a rather nasty smell," observed Jocelyn. "It's supposed to be romantic," said Dick, "not smelly" "Oh well, same thing," said Jocelyn and they both laughed and laughed as though they'd been very witty. Their good humor had persisted all through the exploration of the town and church. We plodded up the stairs again, vaguely depressed.

The castle was more satisfactory however. It had been enormous and very tall. In some places we looked up into towers five or six stories high, with vacant windows and chimney pieces way above us. Through an occasional hole we could look down into dungeons as far below; crooked spiral staircases, ending as abruptly as the near-fatal one in *Kidnapped*, oubliettes, chapels, great roofless halls, everything silent and everything that dog-yellow of the cliffs. Jane and I stuck our heads into each opening, clambered everywhere we were allowed by the vigilance of Mother. The boys of course were even more reckless and had to be called down from horrible places by angry Father.

vi. We decided the church and castle made all the rest of it worthwhile, and when we finally reached the climax, a terrace at the tip of the promontory, the very highest spot, we were quite happy and exhausted and fulfilled.

Here we were to have our lunch at last. It was well after noon by now. Jocelyn, as she repeatedly declared, was quite dead. Mother obviously too, though she merely sank down on a rug in our chosen spot and closed her eyes and leaned her head back against the yellow ruinous wall. Dick and Father, who'd been carrying all the picnic stuff, a considerable burden, laid it out, and we began to eat ravenously.

The situation was dramatic enough to have distracted us, if we hadn't all been so hungry. A flat flagged terrace, in good repair, covered the whole area, like a deck at the prow of a ship. Several round ruinous towers framed an enormous view looking miles away over the grotesque hills to a plain and then the sea. Eastward were blue tops of real mountains. Only westward, in the direction of the loud hot wind was the vista blocked off by dry heights.

We had fixed ourselves in a shallow alcove, which caught what sun came through the thin, scudding cloud cover, but sheltered us from drafts. Over to our left was a famous exhibit of this famous place, a small graceful gazebo of stone, the Pavilion d'Amour, one of the more remarkable of twelfth-century remains in being neither sacred nor utilitarian, but a summer house consecrated by Provençal courts of love to odd ceremonies of dalliance and song. Various famous ladies of the house of Malhaut, with names like Blanchette and Adelasie, Laurette and Briande, had sat in there and been serenaded by troubadours called Guilhem and Arnaut. Two of the most famous, Blanchette de Malhaut and Arnaut de Besonjaires, had indeed overdone it. The pavilion had been built by Blanchette's husband, but when he found out what was going on within, he had had Arnaut slaughtered, cut out his heart and served it up to Blanchette, who promptly went off to a nunnery. This bit of indigestive lore did not seem to prevent it from being used in exactly the same way by later Malhaut ladies and their minstrels. It struck even us children that it was all very hard on the poor lords and husbands, who had to maintain the pavilion, but still weren't allowed to play.

Dick and Father brought all this out as we munched cold chicken. Then came figs and wine and cheese, lemonade from a thermos with cookies for us, and we were all very happy.

Jocelyn gathered some grasses and meager yellow flowers and started making a wreath. Considering her materials she did very well. "Go put it on and sit in the pavilion and I'll sing you a song in three hundred and seventy well-turned verses," said Dick. "Oh, you wouldn't!" countered Jocelyn in mock modesty. "Besides you didn't bring your lute. Why didn't you bring your guitar?" "Sing without it," said Mother. "You must know some Provençal songs." And sure enough Dick did, and sang a perfectly good twelfth-century song in a nasal and rather monotonous triple rhythm. He leaned over toward

Jocelyn and pretended to be strumming to her. "Derek Webster would have your heart out for that," said Jocelyn. "If he were here; which, thank God, he isn't." It was the first time we'd ever heard her mention the missing Mr. Webster, and we were intrigued. But Dick stopped singing and the conversation went along in duller channels. Richie insisted on telling me all about the pieces of skeleton he'd found in the Cave of the Sorcerer. I began to get awfully sleepy, especially after several sips of the parents' wine. So I snuggled up against Mother on one side, and Jane took the other and we observed the grown-ups through a film of contentment. The wall we leaned on was smooth and warm, but not too warm. The west wind rushing overhead, or whining through nearby crevasses, was melancholy but soothing.

Jocelyn had finished her wreath and held it up to be admired. She put it on Dick's head. It gave him a sort of ribald, Bacchic air, and then of course everybody had to try it on: Father looking like a laureled philosopher, Richie like a Roman, hungry Cassius perhaps, Jane very innocent, a Boutet de Manvel illustration. I, it seems, was funny and everyone laughed. Only Robbie refused the crown, like Caesar.

vii. Father interrupted the silliness by starting to read from his guidebook. This had been understood as an inevitable conclusion to the day; for afterward we were to pack up our gear, go straight back to the car and head for home.

" 'No locality in the ancient country of the Langue d'Oc has been more starred by the upsets and shocks of history than has the ancient city and castle of the Lords of Malhaut,' " he began, translating freely from the flowery original of 1893. " 'Nor are the evidences of the past, be they religious or secular, found anywhere in more riotous abundance than they are here upon this desolate promontory.' And so forth for several pages."

"Do skip it," said Jocelyn.

Father flipped a leaf. "Geology anyone? '. . . a calciferous mass of the *néocomien*,' whatever that may be. I think we can skip that too."

"Get on to the blood and tortures," suggested Dick.

" 'Many remains of the Neolithic period indicate that from times most remote the formidable defensive advantages of the promontory of Malhaut have been appreciated. Before the records of history can be said to begin, the place was a fortified and populated center. Remains of walls of a construction that argues a pre-classical origin were incorporated into later defenses, notably those at the base of the southeast corner of the château, visible only from the approaches of the lower road. Archaeological excavation has revealed many notable artifacts, some of which are in exhibit at the small museum in the Mairie of the new town; the majority however have been removed to the archaeological collection at Arles. Among the more interesting discoveries has been that of a skeleton of a young man, victim perhaps of some sacrificial rite, his skull pierced, his head crowned, his remains profusely decorated with primitive jewelry and evidences of burnt offerings in a circle about his tomb. This conspicuous object was discovered under the rubble of millenniums in one of the posterior grottoes of the famous Cave of the Sorcerers. . . .' " Here Richie excitedly tried to interject his own skeletal discoveries, but despite some encouragement from Jocelyn, was frowned down by Father, who continued: " 'The remains have been tentatively dated as from 10,000 B.C. and indicate that the site has been used as a place of worship since prehistoric times. Archaeologists infer that some sort of primitive fire cult was no doubt here involved. A more detailed description of Neolithic artifacts which here follows . . .' " Father stopped and looked about at us with raised eyebrows. "No! No!" said Dick, Jocelyn and Mother all together.

" 'The inhabitants recorded as being first in possession during classical times were a tribe of the Ligurians. Feeling themselves secure upon this rugged height, they seem to have been conspicuous for their friendliness and readiness to receive all the novelties introduced by Phoenician, Greek and finally Roman colonists and traders. Innumerable bits of ancient jewelry, pottery and weapons have been unearthed and added to the collection at Arles. Not until the later Roman Empire did actual new construction seem to eventuate. Sometime under the Antonines, Malhaut was converted into a powerful military outpost. Superimposed upon the walls of the primitives, rude if strong, were massively regular stone courses of a Roman fortress. If there were previous classical buildings, they were destroyed at that time. In its turn, the Roman remains were totally obliterated in later periods by barbaric hands, except for the foundation and a few significant monuments. One was a Mithraic sanctuary built into a cave (now referred to as the "Cave of the Mysteries") which was later converted into an early Christian chapel; and there exist the scanty fragments of one of the numerous shrines dedicated by the infatuated Hadrian to his favorite Antinoüs. Another classic relic is the Roman grave stele decorated with a relief of three female figures and known popularly as the "Three Marys." . . .' "

"This doesn't seem to get on very fast, does it?" Father looked through several pages. "Visigoths. Spelled with a W. Wisigoths. Totally destroyed Roman fortress. First Lords of Malhaut of Wisigothic extraction; direct descendants of Alaric. Probably took possession *circa* 800. Castle already there by 947 when the first Lord of record, Hugues de Malhaut, died. 'From that time until the extinction of the line in 1426 the Lords of Malhaut were conspicuous in the history and culture of the Midi.' Battles. They fought with the Prince of Barcelona, which seems farfetched. Courts of love. Troubadours and ladies." Father jerked his thumb toward the pavilion in back of him. "Hearts being eaten. Ah, here we have it! 'Though removed eastward from the main seats of the heresy in Toulouse, the Lords of Malhaut were early patrons of the sect known as the Cathars, against whom was directed the Albigensian Crusade of the thirteenth century. Here as elsewhere the record of persecution and massacre is abominable. Raymond III de Malhaut alone among the members of his family actually received the *consolamentum*, or Cathar confirmation. The castle was besieged, and in 1228 capitulated. One hundred and seventy-five Cathars were burned at the stake in an arena especially constructed for the occasion, on the site of the present square of the new town. Among the victims were Raymond de Malhaut himself, his wife and his three infant children. The castle then passed into the hands of his brother Roger, who had remained true to the Catholic faith and participated in the siege. After that Malhaut continued a center of orthodoxy until the Protestant flowering of the Renaissance.' "

"Perhaps this might be a good time to describe the Cathars?" "Yes indeed! Who *were* the Cathars and what? I've been hearing you talk about them for weeks," said Jocelyn, "but I never dared ask." "They had a bad reputation," said Dick. Father frowned at him, then proceeded. "They were the first really effective Protestants. I brought along something I wrote myself. Just in case. Less flowery than M. Benoît I'm afraid."

" 'Catharism,' " he began, reading from a typewritten sheet he'd been carrying folded in the Benoît guide, " 'was

not so much a sect of Christianity as it was a separate, though still Christian, religion that spread through southern Europe sometime during the Dark Ages. It probably originated much earlier in Asia Minor, as one offshoot of Gnosticism, and is closely related to the various other heresies of Paulicianism and Priscillianism, and especially to Manicheanism. It moved to the Balkans, where it was adopted as the religion of local kings. Here it acquired the Bulgarian tinge afterward associated with it; traces of this still remain in modern European languages in such shady words as the French "bougre" or the English "bugger" and "bogeyman." These terms were derived from the Roman church's generally defamatory and *unjust* propaganda.' "
Father looked over sternly at Dick.

" 'Catharism flourished in the Po Valley, then spread to the south of France. There it became almost the established religion, especially around Toulouse, where the Counts of Toulouse were intermittent patrons and converts, and in such neighboring towns as Albi (hence "Albigensian"). Though many nobles embraced or encouraged the faith, it remained predominantly a middle-class religion of burghers and artisans. Catharism was especially influential during the twelfth century (the so-called "age of faith") and several local quasi-Protestant movements, such as that of the Waldensians of Lyons, paralleled and supported it.

" 'The Cathar religion combined elements of the Persian, Hindu and Christian traditions; that is, the Persian concept of a permanent opposition between two great spirits, one of Light, one of Darkness; the Hindu idea of reincarnation; and the Christian belief in redemption through Christ. The Cathars believed the whole visible world, the earth, our bodies, to be the creation of the Devil, the Spirit of Darkness. (The Old Testament, incidentally, was thought to be the Devil's own scriptures.) Human souls were actually all the essences of fallen angels, who had been trapped by the Devil in prisons of flesh. Though these angel-spirits were immortal, they could not escape from fleshly imprisonment, but were continually reborn, reincarnated unless they redeemed themselves. Redemption could only be achieved through the Cathar religion. In order to achieve salvation, one had to accept the Cathar confirmation, the so-called *consolamentum*, a ceremony of laying on of hands. After that one was expected to lead a "perfect life" according to Cathar precepts. This "perfect life" consisted of a total renunciation of the goods and desires of the world — property, lust, appetites, a complete sexual and dietary asceticism. Nonviolence was also enjoined. Those who were qualified to lead such a life were known as Perfecti. They constituted the priesthood of the Cathar faith, and wandered about, usually in pairs, proselytizing, entertained and supported by the laity. Both men and women could be Perfecti and even travel about in pairs together. There were both monasteries and nunneries of such Perfecti. The laity were not expected to live up to the standards of the Perfecti, and so presumably had to face the prospect of reincarnation. However, their efforts in this incarnation would no doubt be rewarded in the next, when they could presumably hope then to be Perfecti.

" 'The Cathar Perfecti seem in fact to have been quite perfect — absolutely Christian in their abstinence, loving-kindness and non-violence. They made a most striking contrast to the power-mad, greedy and cruel representatives of Rome in the Provence of that time. The Roman Church was considered by the Cathars to be the church of the Devil. If trees can be judged by their fruit, then certainly Catholicism, as it expressed itself in Provence, was devilish enough. Beginning about A.D. 1000 persecution increased, culminating in the Albigensian Crusades of the thirteenth century. These were inspired by Popes, but led by Kings of France from the north, much to their own political and territorial advantage. Thousands of Cathars were burned alive, and thousands of others, including many non-Cathars, were butchered in sieges and battles. The Inquisition was now first formally established in the Midi to further the persecution of Cathars; and so were introduced those methods of terror, physical and mental, which have been the desolation of Europe ever since. The prosperous and elegant civilization of Provence with its troubadour poetry and music, then advanced in sophistication beyond anything else in the Western world, was destroyed. The Midi was added by force to the territory of the Kings of France. Catharism itself was finally obliterated about 1250, and never reborn. Protestantism however, as evidenced in such related heresies as that of the Waldensians, continued to exist and to grow, culminating in the final outbreaks of the Renaissance. Within the Roman Church itself a "counterreformation" seems to have inspired the creation of the Franciscans, in obvious imitation of the Cathar Perfecti devoted to a life of purity, poverty and wandering proselytism, and the foundation of the Dominicans, who became the chief administrators of the Inquisition.

" 'It is probable that the conscience of French Catholicism has never fully recovered from the horrors of this Crusade, the only one ever conducted by Christians against Christians, and the bloodiest and cruelest of them all. The later popularity of the Huguenots and of the French Revolution in the Midi may well have been the result of memories of this earlier conquest, which had its local patriotic as well as religious aspects. The destruction by France of the independence of Provence and of the beautiful Langue d'Oc has never been quite forgiven.

" 'Catharism flourished in the Midi for nearly three hundred years, before it was forcibly destroyed, from about

950 to 1250. Three hundred years later, true Protestantism appeared there. Less than three hundred years later than that, the Revolution destroyed the secular power of the Church. Even nowadays Bolshevism, the present-day vehicle of anti-clericalism, is popular in cities such as Marseilles. Provence may now appear to be the most Catholic of provinces; but it can in fact be called the cradle of anti-Catholicism, if not of Protestantism.' "

He stopped.

viii. "Well, I'm so happy to know," said Jocelyn. "They sound quite sweet, poor things. I mean the Cathars of course. I'm so glad I'm a Protestant, aren't you? Though we did our bit of burning too." "As a Friend," said Father, "I have my reservations about any Established Church, especially yours." "Oh dear, I suppose so," said Jocelyn. "Why can't people just be *nice* to each other!" "They wouldn't be human," said Dick. "That," said Father, "is the whole point of Christianity, isn't it: to make people less human — and more 'nice.' " "Or of Catharism." "Or of Catharism. Of anything almost it would seem except Catholicism. Which is, God knows, 'human' enough."

"Not Paganism though." Dick was pensive. "Or at least Paganism as I understand it. The philosophers just wanted people to be human consciously, at their best. *Je m'en fiche* with Cathars, Quakers and Catholics too; the whole lot who try to pretend that humans shouldn't be humans."

Father chose not to pursue that argument. "There's quite a bit of Malhaut to cover, if you're still interested. We've only got up to about 1250." I had been, I must say, rather generally disappointed in what had been unrolled of the saga of Malhaut so far. Except perhaps for the burning of Cathars and the eating of the troubadour's heart, it had all been a lot less thrilling than my own history of Amuria. But then perhaps Father had really skipped all the good details. He now proceeded to sketch in from 1250 to the present.

The original family of Malhaut became extinct in the fifteenth century. When the last lady of the castle lay dying, a star appeared in the heavens and descended to the topmost tower of the castle, going out just as this final Malhaut drew her last breath. The Kings of France gave the place to this family and that. For inexplicable reasons, Malhaut was very prosperous during the Renaissance. It was then that the fine mansions in the old town were built, and the feudal lords of that period lived down there rather than in their gloomy castle. They turned Protestant and fought with Catholics about it. Finally Louis XIV ousted them, had the castle dismantled, and that was more or less the end of prosperity, Protestantism and Malhaut. The place declined steadily, the castle went to ruins, the old town was depopulated by plague, the final feudal family was dispossessed in the Revolution. Archaeological interest began in the middle of the nineteenth century; the church was badly restored, a New York millionaire bought one of the finest of the Renaissance fireplaces and carted it away to Fifth Avenue. Finally a descendant of the last owning family grew interested, helped preserve and restore what was left of the castle. It was made an official National Historic Monument; and here we were.

"So that's what M. Benoît has to say about Malhaut," and Father slapped the thin book shut. "Of course there's a lot more about the three sorcerers who kept a golden goat down in a cave, and the magic bell sunk in a cistern that rang whenever danger threatened and folk festivals honoring the Abbot of Youth. Very picturesque." "Didn't anybody get murdered?" put in Jane, unexpectedly, and everybody laughed. "There's always that poor troubadour. Actually M. Benoît doesn't go into those little matters. And I suppose you could consider the hundred and seventy-five Cathars to have been murdered."

"Oh no!" said Dick, always willing to take another side. "They were *executed*. That's hardly the same thing. Besides they deserved it, acting the way they did, being perfect, showing up the local bishops. Can't have that sort of thing going on. Bad as the Quakers. One thing you don't dare permit if you're a good churchman is having a lot of real Christians about."

Father laughed. "Well! For once we agree. But surely you can think of something contradictory!"

"Glad to oblige!" said Dick. "Glad to oblige: for instance — suppose the Cathars had really been guilty of the things they were accused of? One thing especially. I mean, suppose they practiced and propagandized it deliberately as part of the Cathar creed? Mortification of the flesh. After all they couldn't have looked on procreation very favorably, since it just meant more reincarnations for fallen angels."

Mother was disturbed at the turn of the talk, and Father hesitated. "I doubt if it would have made the slightest difference," he said. "And none of that was true anyway."

"Yes, but suppose it was?" Dick persisted. "Do you think we really ought to discuss it?" broke in Mother. Since we had no idea what was being discussed and cared less, Mother's objections, presumably for our benefit, were not for the first time superfluous. I at least was perfectly content to lie, still snuggling and half asleep, and let the talk of the elders and the rushing of the wind comfort me like forest murmurs. Jane was as somnolent as I was; Robbie had wandered away to examine ruins. Only Richie seemed to be paying any real attention.

Dick went on, regardless. "What's your honest opinion? Granted of course medieval attitudes, and that burning alive was an acceptable practice then. As acceptable as hanging is now."

Father seemed more interested in the subject than in bothering about Mother's scruples and our innocence. He gave the matter a moment of consideration. Jocelyn reached about, gathering material for another wreath, the first one having become rather disorganized when it was passed about.

"In other words, can I as a Quaker condone secular, legal punishment for moral offenses?" "Exactly," said Dick. "Basically no," said Father. "A real Christian ought to be a sort of anarchist. God punishes, God rewards. The only true, lasting punishment is being cut off from God. Mere physical suffering on this earth is comparatively negligible. Real Christians need no other punishment. The rest are more or less damned anyway, either through not knowing God's love, or through ignoring it. On the other hand, Christians are certainly enjoined to obey the secular law of the land except when it directly conflicts with religious conscience or laws. Yet certainly Christians have a duty to condemn, and the privilege of excommunication among themselves. Lord knows the Quakers did and do put people out of Meeting all the time for what they consider moral lapses. I'm only in myself on sufferance. My grandfather was suspended for owning a piano, which was considered a moral offense. But hanging and burning and putting in irons — that's something else. Quakers had enough of that sort of approach. They can hardly approve of it."

"But that's just a matter of degree," said Dick. "Excommunication was just a step from burning, at least in those days. Besides the Cathars weren't 'in Meeting' so they couldn't be put out." Dick had been lying on his stomach, his head propped up on his fists, while Jocelyn occasionally tried her wreath on his head for size. Now he swung about, sitting upright and facing us, cross-legged.

"The point is: if you really believe in Christianity and love thy neighbor and judge not and turn the other cheek and nonviolence and all that rot, like the Cathars — and look what happened to the Cathars — can you sincerely believe in punishment of anybody for anything? Especially for — well, Catharist tastes? Much less for just not being a Catholic. And especially if you're a Quaker, where nonviolence is obligatory."

"I suppose the answer is we're citizens first and Christians after. I was in the war, though I had a good excuse not to be. I'd certainly turn in a murderer or a rapist" ("But not a papist," interjected Dick.) "and expect him to be punished. Executed too. On the other hand, as an American citizen, as well as a Friend, I can afford to be unalterably opposed to persecuting people for their religious beliefs. Up to the point where those beliefs seriously go against the law. Quakers were thrown in jail for refusing to take oath in court, you know, just as much as for their beliefs."

"Would you approve of that? Obviously not."

"Obviously not. But that's a small matter. Like refusing to salute the flag or burn incense to the Emperor."

"But how about the Mormons? And polygamy? What's sauce for the goose is sauce for the gander. If bigamy is punishable by law, why not — hum, buggery?"

Jocelyn broke in, "Yes, I've never understood *why* the Mormons weren't allowed to have as many wives as they chose. As long as the wives didn't mind. I gather it was quite jolly — sharing the housework, always someone around to help with the children. It was just mid-Victorian prejudice if you ask me."

"Well, I'm not so sure," said Father. "I don't like to disagree with such estimable tolerance, but in fact I do begin to draw lines right about there. I think we have to accept the Decalogue as God-given and absolute. Otherwise you've got no . . . no channel markers at all. Killing, stealing, adultery . . ."

"Image-making, Sabbath-breaking, coveting asses," continued Dick mockingly. "Besides, the Mormons just precisely weren't commiting adultery. They were all together in holy wedlock."

"That's true," Father admitted. "I suppose the Jews were just as plural too. I guess it's the contract of marriage that counts rather than the number involved. I've always been inclined to be pro-Mormon on this issue."

"The fact is," Jocelyn said, "if polygamy really worked in modern days we'd have it. Then the men would find some moral excuse for it the way the Mormons did. The reason murder and burglary and bigamy are punished, and adultery isn't, is just practical. The Ten Commandments are window-dressing." Father smiled. "The eternal feminine, all right." "Why not? *Some*body has to be sensible."

"But back to our Cathars," said Dick. "*If* they had believed in practicing what in fact they didn't, as a really serious sacred rite of their religion, for instance, *would* you oppose punishing them? Or at least enforcing laws against them?"

"Condemning them, certainly. And excommunicating them, for whatever that would be worth; not much in this case. Surely this involves a pretty direct violation of the Decalogue, no matter how 'religious' they might think they were being. As for actually punishing them . . . no, I suppose not. I don't think adultery should be punished, no matter how severely condemned. But perhaps the old Victorian social ostracism wouldn't be a bad idea. At least it shows that people care."

Jocelyn shivered in disgust. "Revolting! I've seen *that* in action, and of all the sickening, hypocritical . . . All they cared about was whether or not you were caught!" Dick laughed and turned over on his back to look up at the still troubled sky, and at Jocelyn. "Thank God — or Zeus or Apollo — that I'm not involved in any of that. How people do work at making themselves and everyone else miserable! I'm sorry the Cathars didn't in fact have the courage of those peculiar convictions. The Greeks did, and they were certainly a good deal more civilized all round than the Cathars or the Catholics. Or the Quakers either for that matter. If you have real moral convictions and believe in God-given absolutes you *can't* be tolerant. You're basically on the side of the Cathar burners."

Mother came to the defense. "That's not true at all, Dick! Disapproving is one thing and burning people alive is completely different and you know it. The whole point of tolerance is that you grant the right of other people to hold convictions you think absolutely wicked. Just because you don't persecute them doesn't mean you have to approve of them. Basically it means that you have to leave final judgment up to God. The most you can hope to do is persuade or convert."

"Criminals? Bulgarians? Pagans like me? Bigamists? Rapists? It seems to me if you really believe that God the Father left instructions to his children to do this and not do that, the Church as God's Nurse has a right to spank the children."

"Oh, children; that's different!" said Mother. "We're talking about grown-ups."

"Don't quibble. You know perfectly well what I mean by 'children.' The Catholic Church looks on all the laity as children. Nobody's really grown up below a Cardinal."

Dick looked at Father. "And wouldn't you consider it your duty to punish *your* children? For their own good of course."

"Yes, I suppose so. But Protestantism, like Democracy, is a declaration of adulthood."

ix. "As for me, I don't see how anybody can pretend to be grown up and be a Christian at all," said Dick. Father was now obviously getting offended and without answering began to look up something in the old guidebook. Mother too was irritated. I could tell from the way she stiffened and twitched as I leaned against her. Dick seemed utterly unconcerned. He hiked up his knees and dangled one leg over the other in a rather annoyingly *dégagé* fashion. But just then Robbie sauntered back from his exploration, and Jocelyn called to him, holding out her finished new wreath.

"Robbie, you've got to try this one on. You're the only one who hasn't." Robbie sidled away, grinning and sheepish. But Dick sat up. "Come on, boy!" Then he stood up, took the wreath from the still sitting Jocelyn and plunked it on Robbie's head. Robbie ducked and flinched. Everyone laughed, glad of the distraction.

"There," said Dick, and stood back for the effect. It made Robbie look rather sacrificial.

"Yes," said Dick, appraising him with head cocked, "we've got to dedicate him. An offering to Apollo. A brief ceremony."

"I want to see Richie again," Jocelyn broke in. She was busy mending her first wreath, and now she said, "Come along. I'll dedicate you too." She had a way of trying to bring Richie forward, in little ways, to balance Robbie, to redress the unfairness of their opportunities. So Richie too put the wreath on again, looking again a lean and hungry Latin.

"Not to Apollo but to the Republic, or the Genius of Rome or something," said Dick, looking at him critically. "But first the Greeks. We'll do things in proper chronological order."

He moved picnic things off one of our rugs, a light, colorful Italiante blanket, shook off the dust and draped it over Robbie's unwilling shoulders. He tilted the wreath rakishly. "There. Now for an oblation," and he squatted to fill one of the paper cups with wine. "Let us proceed to the sanctuary." He propelled his snickering initiate to the edge of the cliff where there was a small raised platform. The wind billowed the blanket out backward and Robbie had to hold on to his wreath.

"O Lord Apollo, God of brightness and of truth," Dick began to intone. "All-seeing, all-fathering, nurser of arts and of joys, thou in whose face nothing can exist that is mean, unclear or fearful, in whom all true brightness and skill reside — accept this youth to thy service, that he may use his beauty and strength to none but honorable ends, that his mind may be sane, his hand graceful and deft, his success creditable to you. Grant him courage, resourcefulness and modesty, may his victories always be crowned with mercy and his defeats with dignity; and to these ends we pour out to you this unworthy libation. . . ." And Dick threw the wine out over the edge of the cliff. We were all sitting up and laughing, Robbie clutching at his wreath and blanket and laughing too. But it was hard to see just what happened.

Evidently the wine blew up into Robbie's eyes, he let go the wreath to wipe them, and the wreath blew off backward. He turned around to grab it, caught it and clapped it on his head sideways, but tangled in the blanket, stumbled and fell backward off the edge of the platform.

He disappeared. Dick jumped after him. Mother screamed and scrambled up, running toward the edge. We all followed; then Father yelled to us to stay back.

Dick's head immediately reappeared over the edge. Father ran to him and wordlessly they heaved the inert Robbie over the parapet. He was unconscious. The wreath was still on his head, over one eye, but under it was a bloody gash on the left side of his forehead. He'd evidently landed on a ledge just below, striking the rocks. Dick scrambled up holding the blanket. Mother was down beside Robbie, dabbing blood with her handkerchief. The rest of us were too surprised to say or do anything. Dick lifted Robbie up easily and carried him over to our sheltered alcove. He hung in Dick's arms totally relaxed, graceful as a statue, one hand dangling down, his head lolling, his lips parted, the blood almost purple-dark on his temple. Mother had taken off the silly wreath. Dick laid him down very carefully so that he rested sitting against the wall. We stood around and watched as Robbie suddenly opened his eyes, saw Dick, and smiled radiantly.

"Are you all right?" said Mother, crying by now. "Are you all right?" Robbie murmured something and closed his eyes again, still smiling. Dick held him away from the wall and gave him a sip of wine. He came to abruptly and immediately tried to get up, but was held down. Jocelyn had made a bandage for his head and skillfully tied it on. He looked around and asked what had happened and we all tried to tell him till Father shut us up and made us move further back.

After a short while he insisted on rising, muttering, "No, I'm all right, I'm all right." Leaning on Dick, the only one whose help he seemed to want, he started slowly across the terrace. The party was over. We all did our bit, gathering the remains of our picnic, and painfully afraid Robbie might fall, holding our breath and subdued, we went the long way back down to the car.

Robbie gradually recovered as he went. He finally shook off Dick's help and insisted on going by himself, on his own. The wind increased, and a spatter of rain hit us as we crossed the bridge into the new town. Father explained the accident to the first old caretaker, who was full of voluble curiosity and disapproval, afraid that it might get him into some sort of official trouble. Father worked hard to reassure him. Robbie in fact seemed quite well by now.

The drive home was melancholy and tiring. Jane and I were with the parents again in the Renault. Robbie rode in the front seat of Dick's car. Nobody said anything much in ours as we drove. We had a moody supper in a café en route; I was almost too sleepy to know what I was supposed to be eating. The rain started soon after we left Malhaut and continued with us all the way into darkness, the road glistening in the headlights.

As I leaned against Mother in the back seat, I murmured to her, "What is biggery?" Mother started from her reverie. "*What?*" "Biggery. What they were talking about at lunch." "Oh. That," said Mother. "It's just something grown-ups do. You wouldn't be interested." And in fact I wasn't.

4.

i. I came down with a cold. The weather got worse, and I was really perfectly happy to lie in bed and listen to the intermittent pouring of rain and play with my stamps and daydream. Of course my nose was a nuisance, and I had trouble sleeping and the sheets got rumpled and sweaty, for it was a muggy, tropical sort of rain. Still, Jane did come up sometimes to sit on the tile floor and talk with me, and I could hear the comforting rumors of the house — plumbing, footsteps running up and down stairs, the boys yelling outside or Ronnie crying inside. I was on the whole contented; and as I recuperated, after a touch of fever, how good the food brought up to me by Mother tasted! She would stay and read to me a bit. Even Father stopped in once.

I came down for lunch on Saturday, rather feeble. Dick and the girls returned that afternoon from their visit. After Malhaut, Dick had joined them at the Count's house, and now he brought them back with him. The house seemed twice as full, and Nan and Ellie both made sporadic appearances in my room, full of vague clamor and medical advice. In the evening I wandered about in a bathrobe, and I sat a bit on the girls' ruffled beds, hearing about their dull adventures.

Next day, Sunday, I was up for breakfast and for good. It was still pouring. The children's dining room seemed crowded and noisy and steamy. The rain was pelting down outside. A leak in the gutter, right in front of the dining room window and close to the front door, let down a hard narrow waterfall, rather exciting to all of us. We'd get up from our cereal to watch it battering the gravel. We wanted to go out and play in it, but of course I was forbidden to go out at all. Jane however put on her yellow slicker (each of us had one in a different size) and her sou'wester hat and she and Nan and Ellie all tramped about in the wilderness a bit. I was rather at loose ends.

I drifted into the *salon*. The parents were still over their breakfast in the black dining room. I tinkered about on the piano. I hadn't touched it for weeks, ever since my lessons with Mme de Guichy stopped when she went away for her trip to Africa. I tried some of my pieces, but didn't feel up to really practicing. Richie was arguing with Robbie, and trying to persuade him to do something. Ronnie ran round and round the room yelling while Mademoiselle sewed and watched him indulgently from her chair. It was going to be one of those dreadful days with all of us cooped up and restless.

I was about to go to my room and play with stamps when in came the girls, full of energy, shaking off the water from their slickers. They had been down to watch a yellow flood swirling through the artificial canyon and around the fake alligator; and now they had a plan to put on a show. Costumes. Music. Rehearsals. They were so full of it that the lukewarm reactions of the rest of us didn't bother them much. I was willing enough, if weak. What else to do? Richie snarled and complained. Ronnie eagerly got in everyone's way. The parents approved and removed themselves hastily.

Only Robbie, who had refused to be involved with Richie, refused to be involved with us. He lounged about dressed in his shabbiest clothes — a pair of tight filthy white American sailor pants and a loose filthy paint-stained sweatshirt. He was reading, in a morose sort of way, Conrad's *Victory*. Father had given him a whole set of Conrad for Christmas. There was nothing particularly wrong with all this; and it was not really to be expected that he would join us in our dramatics. He didn't like anything of that sort. But there was something awfully unlike him in this deliberate sloppiness and moodiness. Robbie was the only one in the family who was naturally neat. Ellie made a show of bustling orderliness; Jane was precise. But Robbie was nearly always in a condition that could be called "shipshape" — clothes crisp and in order, face and hands scrubbed, hair sleek. It was all part of his natural superiority. But now his hair was down over his face. He was wearing glasses, which he never did except for intensive study. And besides looking disreputable, his slack attitudes and slothful grunts and sighs made him seem even more of a disgrace. It was almost as though he were inviting someone, someone else, to take hold of him and shake it out of him. Shake what? Not at all like himself.

When Ellie went over and insisted he join us (foolish girl) he yelled at her and turned his chair around away from her, and sat sprawled out on his backbone. He was hopeless today. We proceeded with our opera, for that, it seems, is what it was turning out to be.

Stacks of dress-up material had been brought down-stairs and dumped on the floor. Jane, much to my dis-pleasure, had contributed some of our Amuria gear too. Ronnie sat in the middle of the pile tangling up scarves and himself. Everything was to be decided by Nan and Ellie. Jane and I did what we were told. Richie argued and got nowhere.

Actually, beyond the idea that it was to be an opera, and very much costumed, the girls seemed to have little in the way of plot or planning. One thing was certain: Nan was the heroine, and the heroine was the central figure.

And the heroine was going to have a stunning getup for herself if it took all morning. Beyond this, everything was confusion. Robbie had been cast, naturally, as hero; but since he absolutely refused to play with us, Ellie was nominated for that ungrateful secondary role. She balked. She wanted a lesser but very romantic female part of some kind, the heroine's best friend or rival or both. No, she had to be the hero. But why not Richie? Richie had to be the villain. *He* wanted to be the hero — for a change. "Why do I always have to be the bad guy?" He went around whining and snarling. Ellie and Nan were both firmly decided on his villainy however. What they said went. Jane, in turn, wanted desperately to be the villain. She was hooted at. She had to take the part Ellie wanted, the heroine's confidante. I was left over, the supernumerary, listless from my sickness, and amused and bored by the opera anyway. I didn't care.

Besides, all the girls really seemed to be interested in was those silly costumes. Nan and Ellie and even Jane fussed and looked at themselves in the rose-splotched mirrors and argued and criticized each other and put unbecoming hats on Richie and every now and then draped something over me and then snatched it away again. I spent a good deal of time at the piano, sometimes making up appropriate opera music. Robbie continued to read and sprawl. Ronnie ran about. Outside it rained and rained.

What blocked all efforts at progress was the fact that Ellie absolutely refused to dress in men's clothes. This almost came to tears, and did come to screams. Finally, a solution appeared: the hero would be disguised as a woman. Like Shakespeare. Why not? This seemed to particularly infuriate Richie as a sort of general aspersion on the masculine. He went over to Robbie again and tried to enlist his support, for the honor of the sex; but Robbie was as surly to him as to Ellie, and finally made Richie so angry that he exploded and quit the cast altogether, stamping out into the hall, into his raincoat and finally out into the rain. So now no villain. I had to take the part. Jane, I insisted, must be my villainess. The opera was actually beginning to have a shape.

Nan by now was done up in shawls and headdresses and hair combs, vaguely Spanish, with lace trains and a fan and earrings, so that she could barely move. Ellie's costume was curiously mixed — a pair of Father's old slippers and baggy trousers to indicate masculinity, under a voluminous skirt, and a great picture hat of Mother's to "disguise" her in femininity. I had, naturally, a cloak. I liked that. Ellie had a sword (a cane) hidden in her skirt, and so did I, under my cloak. Jane was possessed of a fiendish dagger and a slinky beaded dress, which tended to mollify her considerably. We were getting happier and happier when back came Richie. He was now furious at being ousted from his role of villain, so I had to make a place for him as Captain Bombardo, leader of my minions. That meant that now we had more bad people than good. But no matter.

We still needed a scenario, and the morning was half gone. Obviously the rudiments were there. Ellie, man-disguised-as-woman, was in love with Nan. Their fathers were deadly enemies, so they couldn't get together publicly. Nan (Esterilla) had been left by her voyaging parent a virtual prisoner in the palace. Ellie (Diego) had therefore disguised himself to be near her. But Esterilla and Diego had only seen each other once (this was enough), so now Esterilla did not recognize Diego in her confidante and guest "Carolina."

The villain (me) Don Squaracho was also in love with Esterilla. To make it more complicated we decided that Squaracho should be the *twin brother* of Diego, but mean! He wanted to abduct Esterilla, with the help of Captain Bombardo (Richie) and his wicked wife Poisonella (Jane), who happened to be Esterilla's lady-in-waiting. It was hard to say just how serious we were about the whole thing.

"Do we have to *sing* all the time?" said Ellie. "Of course. It's an opera." Nan could sing of course, so she didn't mind. "Great, great!" complained Richie in his raucous croak. He couldn't sing a note or carry a tune. "Well," relented Nan, "not everything I guess. I'll come out first and have a scene by myself with a real aria." Nan had been studying voice and knew all about things like arias. The rest of us didn't. "Then after that we can just talk." "Good!" "But we do have to sing a lot of it. Who's going to play the piano?" "The *piano?*" "Of course. We have to have some accompaniment. Howie can play for me and Ellie, and I'll play for the others. Something like that." "It's all so *com*plicated," sighed Ellie. She refused to be consoled in her transvestite compromise. She did *not* want to be the hero.

It certainly was complicated. The general action had been sketched for the first two scenes anyway. Nan was to come out all dressed up, tell the situation — her imprisonment, with Carolina (Diego) as her only friend. Then her opening aria. After that she was to go on about her love for the mysterious stranger she met riding in the woods (Diego). Ellie then enters as friend Carolina (Diego). Duet. Exit Esterilla. Ellie throws off her disguise, confesses love for Esterilla. Aria, interrupted by Poisonella (Jane), the wicked lady-in-waiting, who recognizes Diego. She loves him. She says she won't reveal his disguise if he will love her. What about husband Captain Bombardo? She'll take care of *that;* trust Poisonella.

This took lots of organizing. I had to play the accompaniment for Nan's opening aria. It was pretty simple, just a series of C minor chords, while Nan sang her sad song: "I'm all alo-one, I'm all alo-one and there is nobody to help me. I'm all alone, I'm all alone and there is nobody to love me." We rehearsed that very first bit.

Then out came Nan, fluttering her fan and tripping over her train so that Jane and I had a hard time to keep from laughing. Recitative (unaccompanied): "O cruel father! Why did you leave me here shut up by myself? I'm just a prisoner! But what have I done? Nothing! No one is here with me except my dear friend Carolina; and that dreadful lady-in-waiting Poisonella. Ugh! She spies on me, I know that!" (Much flapping about and earring tossing.) "I'm so miserable!" Aria (accompanied): "I'm all alo-one . . ."; a descending C minor scale, stately and Spanishy, in triple rhythm. "But I have hope! I saw a man riding in the woods the other day. So handsome! So romantic! He looked at me. I know he loves me, and I love him. He will come to rescue me, I'm sure. But I dare not tell anyone, even my dear Carolina. Here she comes!"

Ellie strode in, a ludicrous figure in her skirt, baggy pants, veils and flopping hat. "Dear Esterilla!" "Dear Carolina!" They embraced. "I've got to get rid of this awful hat," said Ellie and threw it on the floor. "I'll just wear a scarf." The duet that followed was a mess. Richie began to boo and hold his nose with one hand while he waved them away with the other. "Oh well, we'll work that out later. This is just a rehearsal," said Nan cheerfully. "Now I go out. Can't you keep that hat on till now though, Ellie? You're supposed to throw it off as soon as I'm gone." Ellie picked up the hat grumpily. Nan then left the stage (that is, the center of the room) very coyly. Ellie threw her hat on the floor again, saying (not singing), "Alone at last!"

               ii. We had to stop at this point to create an aria for Ellie. Nan took over at the piano. The rest of us, in our tacky, fussy costumes, were getting awfully tired and cross. I'd joined Jane on the floor. We were playing cards, Double Canfield. Richie had been trying to talk with Robbie again, who had now assumed an impossible posture, doubled over the arm of the sofa, bottom up, head and book on the seat, legs astraddle and trailing, toes turned in. How could anybody stay, much less read, in such a position? All Richie could get out of him was grunts. He came back and shouted, "I'm sick of this," and started to tear off his costume once more. "Now, Richie!" said Nan in her most soothing and reasonable manner. "Honestly! Can't you just wait a *few* minutes?" Ellie thought they ought to skip her aria and get on with the plot. "Poisonella is supposed to come," she said, "and find me. Then I go out and in comes Richie and they plot, and all that. You know I don't think we'll *ever* get through. It's time for *goûter* already." It was.

Mademoiselle had taken Ronnie away after a while. Now she came in and told us our milk and bread waited in our dining room, on the table. I was awfully glad to get out of my itchy cloak and the big *salon*, so full of disorganization and noise and muggy dampness and the roar of the rain. Nan and Ellie of course were too wrapped up, both in costumes and in the opera, to join us. It was a perfect chance for them to work out their duet and Ellie's aria.

When we came back they were full of new and repugnant ideas. Ellie now insisted on being Poisonella. *I* was to be the hero; after all as Don Squaracho (or whatever my name as villain was to be) I was supposed to be a twin of Don Diego, so why not play both roles? This eminently sensible rearrangement made Jane furious. I was furious. All of Jane's obstinacy emerged. No, she would not be ousted from the role of Poisonella (what could she be then, in any case?) and that was that. The three girls began to screech and rave and Richie began to laugh and laugh; even Robbie looked up from his solitude and grinned. He was now on the floor, his knees doubled under him, his head down between his elbows, a froglike effect.

Eventually Ellie had to give in. Jane would continue as Poisonella, temporarily at least. Ellie and Nan really thought of this as a month-long project, so they were inclined to be indulgent now. I knew better. Since Ellie had already rehearsed the various Poisonella entrances in the first scene, we proceeded directly to Act II: a mountain cave. Nan at the piano preluded with some melancholy but exciting gypsy music, a ballet of brigands. Then the villains were supposed to get together and plot. Hark! Comes Poisonella, disguised.

We were just about to start plotting when in fact entered Dick and the parents. It was drawing near to the time for Sunday (First Day) Meeting, which was to be held today in the dining room.

The three looked about them in amusement and consternation. The *salon* was certainly in a mess. Costumes were all over the floor and nearly every piece of furniture had been moved (except of course for such objects as the great pseudo-Renaissance chest under the portrait — so appropriate a prop for our Spanish melodrama). We three villains squatted about a campfire of piled-up books. Ellie, miffed at not being allowed to be Poisonella, was fiddling about with her costume, posing in front of a mirror. Nan, still all swathed, was at the piano. And Robbie, removed from us all, had assumed still another of his fantastic positions. Now he was draped backward over a footstool, one of the more useless relics of the previous owner's taste, in what must surely have been unbearable discomfort. His crotch thrust upward by the stool, his legs straddled out one way and his shoulders flat on the floor out the other direction, he was attempting to read straight upward. The loose sweatshirt had slipped upward to expose a foot of slim brown stomach, and he presented altogether the effect of a sort of beachcomber abandon, a giving in to some personal tropics.

He didn't observe the entrance of the parents, having long ago insulated himself from outer distractions. Nor did they at first notice him. The rest of us left our places and came over to the grown-ups, demanding attention, explaining, asking for praise. Everyone laughed; Nan insisted they watch. She was going to play music for our ballet, the gypsy dance (Ellie and Jane) by the brigands' campfire. The parents somehow found places to sit, Dick cross-legged on the floor, and Nan started playing. This had not been rehearsed and was, to put it charitably, a scene still in its infancy. Richie thought it terribly funny, and indeed it was. But the grown-ups, though they laughed, applauded and Dick shouted "Olé! Olé!" and then abruptly stood up. "Wait," he said and hurried out of the room.

In no time he was back with his guitar, which he evidently still kept somewhere handily nearby. "Now, let's do it again. You dance this time, Nan, and I'll make the music." So we had another gypsy dance, much more exciting, with Dick really Spanish on his guitar, singing snatches of nasal flamenco, and Nan and Ellie and even Jane swirling about quite expertly and everyone else clapping and shouting "Olé!"

It would have seemed impossible for Robbie not to be distracted and attracted by this; but all he did was flop over on his face, so that now it was his behind which stuck up over the stool; his head rested on folded arms, his book on the floor.

Nan explained the plot (as far as it went) and sang parts of her aria; so Dick volunteered an accompaniment for that too. "I'm all alone, I'm all alone, and there is nobody to help me," Nan sang with deep feeling, down the C minor scale; and instead of just the clumping repetitive chords I'd been playing, Dick improvised various and intricate harmonies, and it was really expressive. Nan had quite a lovely voice. There was lots of applause, and Richie stopped being derisive.

"It's about time for Meeting now," said Mother. "Are you coming, Dick?"

"I'm afraid not. I've got to be packing." Dick stood holding his guitar and looked over at Robbie, still face downward over the stool. "What's got into him?" he said. "Robbie!" said Mother. No answer. "Robbie, wake up!" Robbie turned around on one elbow, still shrouded in his fog. Mother turned to Dick. "He's been this way all morning. I hope it isn't his head. Concussion's supposed to make you drowsy." Dick snorted. "I doubt if it's his head. Just adolescence. I'd say he was in love. But who can it be?" Mother laughed and frowned. "Oh, Dick, really! Robbie, pull yourself together and go up and make yourself decent for Meeting. A shirt and tie and coat, anyway." Robbie struggled and sighed and slowly reassembled himself and eventually stood up, a bit ashamed at being caught so off his usual balance, yet angry at being disturbed. He slouched sullenly past us, giving only Dick a shy, up-from-under look and a subdued "Hi!" As he left, Mother said, "I've never seen him that way before. I do hope . . ." Dick encouraged her. "Don't worry about him. Worry because he *hasn't* been that way before."

Father had been in the dining room, trying to move furniture about. We were all ordered to take off our costumes, and wash our hands and "get decent." Dick left, his guitar slung across him, waving back through the door. Nan sighed, still full of high feelings about Dick and opera, and reluctantly began to untangle herself. I was very glad to be out of it all.

iii. It took a long time for us
to get properly settled, Nan and Ellie morose at having to
put off their costumes, Robbie still sulky, but "decent," at
least above the waist. We sat around the long table, turned
toward Mother and Father at the end. As I faced them I
could see beyond them into the *salon*, through the open
door — the fireplace with its mirror and amphora, the mess
of our costume materials all over the parquet. Outside the
rain still poured down, thrumming on the roof of the
veranda, rattling in the palms and on the gravel. After a
pause, filled with rain and with our fidgetings, Father
began to talk to us. "Last time we met it was a beautiful
day and I said . . . I thought we might . . . ah, think
about what 'beautiful' really means. What it means,
should mean, to us. Do we truly understand it as a reflection of God's glory? Today's different," and he stopped a
minute; we could hear the beating of the rain. "We can't
expect, mustn't even hope that we'll have good weather all
the time. It's the nature of the world and of humanity that
clouds should come up. Not only bad outside weather,
sickness, bad luck, but bad inside weather, depressions,
grief, things that we can't control, or things that we can
control, like the bad things we do to make ourselves unhappy and cut ourselves off from God's light." Father
stopped again and sat tapping his fingers on the edge of the
dark table. The purple and black room was lit only by a
few dim side brackets. Nan was twitching about, obviously
full only of her opera. Robbie slumped in a remote gloom.
Even Mother did not seem to be paying much attention.
"What we must remember is that back of the clouds the
sun is there, and back of our grief and pain or sin, back of
our temporary bad weather, God's sunshine and glory are

permanent. In bad weather we must use our imagination to feel the warmth of that sun. . . ."

But I wasn't really listening. Far from wanting to feel the warmth of the sun, I was totally absorbed, my eyes closed, in listening to the rain. It wrapped me in a cocoon of warmth and darkness: outside the rain through the garden, then the dark house, and finally this mysterious room. I could imagine a secret door opening out of it on to a descending passage. At the end of this passage would be a low vault, stifling with velvet, candles and incense. There would be a tremendous treasure of fantastic objects glittering in the dusk — artificial birds of gold with diamond eyes, Chinese crystal balls sitting on jade waves, chests full of rubies and amethysts. I actually saw all this exciting, dangerous display, this wonderful discovery, there back of my closed eyelids; and so missed the end of Father's sermon. I spent the following silence entirely in my imagination, in my hidden chamber, with my jewelry.

Chair scrapings and whisperings brought me to. Meeting was over; there was the usual handshaking all round. I felt a slight guilt at not having followed Father's line of thought. Nan and Ellie hurried back into the *salon* to begin their opera again, calling to us all to rejoin them. Richie, grinning and whispering to Robbie, punching him in the shoulder, had finally persuaded him out of his brown study and into some mutual project at last. "Let's go!" he said jubilantly — that characteristic signal of theirs for an exit — and off they went. The front door slammed after them. Before they left Nan stuck her head through the door and told them to be sure to ask Dick to come back with his guitar. The boys paid no attention to her. She flounced away, already half costumed, in exasperation. The parents, after a quiet confabulation, withdrew. Jane and I stayed in the dining room.

I was most reluctant to leave. My vision of treasures,

of a snug womblike chamber, stayed with me; the dining room was part of it. I began to study the Piranesi dungeons, still in my trance. Jane squatted and began to finger the complicated carving of the wainscoting, the little faces, each different, the knobs and bulbs and pilasters and panels. I knew what she was doing. She was looking for a secret compartment. We had tried this many times, here and on the big chest in the *salon*, but never very thoroughly or systematically. This was obviously the moment. Without further ado or comment I too knelt beside her. "You take the other side," she said, and totally absorbed we began to punch and pull and feel and wiggle. It seemed an endless if pleasantly enticing process.

Out in the *salon* Nan and Ellie were in full cry. They had to reconstruct their costumes and rerehearse their music. After one attempt to bully us back into it, they got thoroughly absorbed in their piece and forgot about everyone else. We were allowed to pursue our mysterious quest in silence, punctuated by occasional exclamations and false alarms when we thought we'd found something, hypnotized by hope and the roar of the rain.

Nan, at the piano, started working over her "I'm alone" aria, so Ellie, for the moment at loose ends, wandered into the dining room again to annoy us. "What on earth are you doing?" Jane merely snorted. I said, "Looking." "Looking? Looking? For *secrets*, I suppose. Such childishness. Listen, please come in and rehearse. We'll never get going." Jane grinned and shook her head. Ellie squatted down by her, a ludicrous figure in her baggy pants and big skirt. "Does anything move?" she said, and she too began to punch and feel, more and more absorbed. "El-*leee!*" screamed Nan from the next room. Ellie jumped up, guilty, and left us.

We stayed at it for quite a while until abruptly, just in one moment, all my strength left me. I'd forgotten completely about my sickness and convalescence. I was so tired suddenly that my bones seemed brittle, like those of a small dead animal. I lay down on the floor with my eyes closed, almost crying with exhaustion. Jane paid no attention. I liked lying there, drifting off, rather cold, very sad and surrounded by rain and darkness. I could hear Nan and Ellie quarreling in the next room. Ellie stamped her foot and shouted, "No, no, no!"

Mademoiselle, with Ronnie by the hand, looked in. "Howie! Are you all right?" "Oh yes," I lied, sitting up. "Well, get washed for lunch," and she moved along the hall to the *salon* to inform the girls. I heaved myself up and toward the bathroom, stopping in the hall to look at myself in the mirror there, a fantastically decorated Venetian glass baroque piece with elaborate dirty gold frame and white Chinese figures etched on the glass itself. I hoped to have significantly dark rings under my eyes and other signs of invalidism. I was not disappointed. I looked very peaked indeed. The bathroom, a closet of the utmost dinginess under the stairs and next to the *salon* at the end of the hall, was delightfully dank. Through the one high barred window giving out on the road I could hear the rain pummeling the asphalt. A car passed by with a loud swish. A great old bathtub on claws stood raised on a slatted platform. It was attached to its own heat-making gas stove, fraught with handles and directions for operation marked "A" and "B," all in technical French of course. Nobody ever dared try to use it. I scrubbed and scrubbed my hands with the big square chunk of smelly yellow soap, and felt I might like to retire to this obscure corner permanently, as to a hermitage, washing away, brooding on melancholy, listening to the rain.

But in fact it was lunchtime; fetid, noisy. And after that I was ordered by Mademoiselle to go up and really rest, and I did. In fact I slept deeply, and had dreams.

iv. I woke up to hear sounds outside, yelling and laughing and the slamming of the front door. The rain seemed to have stopped. I jumped up and looked out the window. The whole group, Nan and Ellie and Jane and Mademoiselle and Ronnie, were dressed in raincoats and heading out across the road. So I shouted down at them and finally caught their attention and they all waved for me to come along with them.

They were going to the garage to see Dick off. He was leaving us to visit the Websters. This farewell delegation was a device to get us out of the house. I caught up just as everyone entered the cavern of the former stable where all the cars were kept: our Renault, Dick's Hispano-Suiza, room for several others. Lagarde, exiled over there on rainy days, greeted us ecstatically. The building had been a carriage house, very large and black and run down, two stories high and incongruously Gothic. A peaked clock tower dominated a peaked roof full of little useless peaked gables, and when we'd first taken the villa, the clock still worked, striking the hours with ghoulish and incorrect clangs. But it had long stopped and we'd never bothered to fix it. Now the great high spaces of carriage house and stalls were used for cars and storage. Upstairs, on each side of the two-storied central chamber and along the back, were bedrooms, makeshift affairs but good enough for Robbie and Richie, good enough for Celestine and good enough for Dick. There were extra ones too for people like Leone when she spent the night, or occasionally the Webster girls.

It was a grand place to play; yet we seldom went there. For one thing of course it was out of bounds for us, across the road. For another, we were slightly scared of it. It was dark even on the brightest day, and we felt there were lurking dangers of loose boards, trapdoors, poisonous spiders and scorpions. Today however we ran all over. We were supposed to be "helping" Dick in some vague way. The boys really did. They carried down his big bag between them and Nan brought the guitar, the precious operatic accompaniment, Ellie various coats and parcels. He protested laughing, but everyone insisted. It was evidence of how much everyone, everyone but Jane and I, admired him, would miss him. There was a fuss putting things in the car. Jane and I were playing hooky. We were scurrying along an open gallery that ran across the back of the garage at the second-story level, spying on the people below, so we had to be called down. Altogether the gang of us must have delayed Dick considerably. Not to mention Lagarde hopping about and barking.

The two of us really looked on this all as an occasion for prying into rooms. The boys' room was very dull. Just a couple of beds and bureaus. Richie had a sort of study closet next door where he owned a desk and kept his obscure treasures; but he caught us snooping and ostentatiously locked the door of it. How he loved his secrets.

Celestine's room, around the corner in the back, was nicer. It was small but prettified with many family photographs and some religious pictures, neat frilly curtains and a large gilded mirror. (Why would Celestine ever want to look at herself?) Leone's room was empty. Dick's of course was now stripped. We felt rather cheated, as though there must be something in this place that was enticingly hidden away; Richie's closet of course, but still . . . We poked about and poked about.

At last Dick really was leaving. We were called down, and off he actually started, backing the great glittering wonderful car slowly out. But at the very last minute, before he got out onto the road, the boys decided to go with him, clambering into the rumble seat and then heaving up happy Lagarde beside them. So then Nan too decided to go with him, and, before anyone could say or do a thing, jumped into the front seat, dragging Jane along with her. Why Jane? Jane hung back a bit, then obeyed.

Ellie stood there glowering, tapping her foot, her hands on her hips. Obviously Nan wanted to sit next to Dick without competition from Ellie. Jane was a fill-in. Ellie was furious. Mademoiselle disapproved and protested. Ronnie jumped up and down and kept yelling good-byes. The cavernous garage echoed with them. Lagarde, sitting alert in the rumble seat, cocking his sharp pointed ears about, yapped too. The car finally pulled away and there we were left, Ellie and I, surprised and chagrined.

I didn't really care, but obviously Ellie did. Nan would suffer for this when *she* got home! I enjoyed the prospect of being all by myself. What should I do? Explore the garage? Mademoiselle, with Ronnie in hand, made cautious preparations for crossing the road, looking up and down both ways, then scuttling. "Come along, Howie! You must come with me." Ellie crossed too. There wasn't really much point in my staying here anyway. I'd rather go back to the dining room and continue explorations there.

v. "You don't really think you're going to *find* anything, do you?" said Ellie, sneering over me as I squatted in the dining room. I grunted and went on probing. Ellie had been primly straightening up the *salon* after operatic devastations; but she couldn't resist trying to interfere with me. "Look! That one moved!" she yelled, and she plumped down beside me and began shoving a little face. It was true, the face had gotten loose and did move. But nothing else happened. "Oh dear," said Ellie and kept sitting there, right in my way, her hands still busy and her arms interfering with mine.

When I told her to go away she got cross. So I suggested she start at the other end and move back toward me, and she did. We worked away silently. The rain began again, intermittently. "Something's moving! Something's moving!" cried Ellie. But it was just another false alarm. It was easy to imagine success as all these carved moldings were glued or tacked to the paneling and quite a few were loose, and budged when touched.

We gradually closed in on each other, and were about to give up that side, the sea side of the dining room, when suddenly, without warning, a small door swung open; and there was our secret compartment! Ellie screamed with excitement and we both scrambled to look inside, arguing about just which one of us had actually touched just which actual button. Inside the compartment were a few rolls of heavy paper. We took them over to the dining room table in a frenzy of eagerness and spread them out. Plans. Blueprints. Unbelievable! Plans and blueprints of World War battleships and cruisers. Ellie was so excited she could hardly contain herself. She hopped up and down and screamed and jabbered.

"Spies, Howie! There must have been *spies!* Right here in this house. Look, they were probably giving these to the Germans. We've got to show them to Father at *once* and get the police!" We rolled up the dusty tough papers and, leaving our compartment door wide open, rushed up the stairs to Father's study. He was at work, slow to answer. "Hurry! Hurry!"

"Well, what's wrong?" said Father, looking astonished but quizzical. He was always skeptical of the girls' excitements and general flurries, which we called "ducks and chickens." We showed him our plans and told him our theories, Ellie doing most of the showing and telling. I put in my oar as best I could. After all it was really *my* discovery. Father looked the stuff over. "Hm. Curious."

"Shouldn't we call the police?" "Police? What for?" "Spies!" "Oh. It's a bit late now, isn't it? The war's over and the spies are all gone. If they were spies." "If they weren't spies, why would they hide things like that?" "Well, maybe to keep them *away* from spies." But obviously no reasonableness was going to convince us that the Villa Esperance had not been — perhaps still was! — the headquarters of a desperate international ring. Ellie insisted that Father come right down and look at our cubbyhole. We rushed down first and closed it; then had a terrible time trying to find the right knob to open it again, as a demonstration for Father. He couldn't help laughing at our excitement.

"It's certainly very romantic," he said. "We'll have to get your mother down." We hadn't dared wake her from her sacred nap; but now we rushed up and Father slowly followed. He was only halfway up as we rushed down again, dragging Mother after us.

When we got down to the hall, Nan and Jane burst in through the front door, dripping and soaked and expostulating. Mother's interest was totally diverted to them. "What *have* you been doing! Just look at you!" Despite their raincoats and hats they were both drowned rats. Complete confusion resulted as Mother tried to hustle them out of their gear and upstairs for a change of clothes, while I and Ellie still tried to get Mother interested in our spy scare. There was so much noise that Celestine came out of the kitchen to see what was happening and then began scolding Nan and Jane in French. Nan tried to excuse herself; it hadn't been raining when they'd started back from the Websters'. Then Mother began attacking the Websters for letting the girls walk.

Into the hubbub came Richie, followed by Lagarde. He seemed to have been running all the way home, panting, red and soaked to the skin, for he and Robbie had gone without even their raincoats. "Where's Robbie?" said Nan, expecting some disaster. Richie laughed breathlessly and jerked his thumb over his shoulder. "Out there. Hah!" Celestine secured Lagarde and dragged him into the kitchen.

We pressed to the door to see what "Out there, hah" might mean, while Mother tried to chivvy the girls upstairs. Father, we were glad to observe, escaped to the dining room to look over our discoveries.

Robbie too it seemed had run all the way back from the Websters, dressed again in his dirty sailor pants and dirty sweatshirt. Now he presented a fantastic spectacle. He'd thrown the sodden sweatshirt off onto the ground, and was taking a sort of impromptu shower bath in the leak from the gutter that came down so forcefully just outside the window of the children's dining room. In a most un-Robbie-like orgy of abandon he postured and posed, sticking out his rump so that the powerful jetting of the water splashed off it, or bending over backward till the full impact of it caught him on his bare brown belly. He wiggled his hips and flexed his muscles, with his eyes closed. His shouting and writhing gave a very good imitation of a savage dance. Richie clapped and crowed from the front door, egging him on.

Then Father appeared. Robbie stopped abruptly as Father barked at him. He stepped out of his fountain and, picking up his degraded sweatshirt, came slouching and surly toward the house. His hair was all in streaks over his face, his bare torso shone, his trousers were plastered to him transparently. He mumbled about being "all wet anyway, so what's the difference" and he and Richie were ordered off to their room. They trailed abjectly across the road.

Everybody was in disgrace; except of course Ellie and I. The rain was coming down more furiously than ever.

vi. When we finally gathered for an early and informal supper — all of us, even the parents, in the children's dining room — we were a sullen, restless lot. Everyone was cross with everyone. It began by Mother attacking Nan. "Why on earth didn't you phone us and have somebody come and get you? You'll all catch colds and be sick for weeks." "Really, Mother, it *wasn't* raining. A little rain never hurt anyone anyway." "You'll feel hurt enough when you're in bed coughing and sneezing. Jane's sniffling already." "I am not!" "Don't you dare talk to your mother that way," said Father. "I'll send you away from the table." Jane's sniffles might now be either a cold or hurt feelings.

"I can't understand how Jocelyn could be so careless as to let them go off like that," Mother continued. "I'm really furious with her. There's no reason why she or Dick couldn't have brought you all home. . . . " Nan bore the brunt of all this, which did not improve her temper in the least. "That was lots of fun, running back in the rain," said Richie in hoarse conspiracy to Robbie, who smiled, but perhaps more absently than Richie could have wished. He seemed still to be in a daze, but a less sullen one, more mild and amiable. "*You* made a spectacle of yourself all right," said Ellie to him. "Dancing around in that disgusting way. What did you think you were doing?" Robbie looked shamefaced, but still smiling. He shrugged. "Oh, I dunno, I was all wet anyway. . . ." "That was a neat idea!" Richie broke in, "I wish I'd done it too." And so now he and Ellie began to quarrel, sitting next to each other by mischance.

Jane was on the other side of me, silent and sniffly. I hoped to console her. "Did you see what we found?" I tried as an opener. But I soon saw my mistake. She gave me a dreadful look, with her lips tight. "What's the matter?" "You could have waited till I got home. Now you've spoiled everything!" "Well, you didn't have to go to the Websters', did you?" "Yes, I *did!* Nan made me go, you saw her. I didn't want to go and I didn't want to walk back and now I've got a cold and you went and spoiled everything." She was really tearful now. So we added our bit to the general distress.

Ellie left off quarreling with Richie and introduced our discovery as a distraction. "Did you *see* what we found, Mother? All those plans and things! It must have been spies. Do you think it was spies?" "I haven't really had a chance yet . . . " began Mother, and Father interrupted. "It really may have been spies, you know. The Baron was a very suspicious character. I'll see what I can find out." The Baron de Berg, who had owned the house during the war, was an exotic person it seemed. There were all sorts of stories about him, many of which we were not allowed to hear. Everybody welcomed this subject, except of course Jane who scowled at me and sulked over her food. Unlike my leopard, this discovery pleased all, notably Richie, who began to discuss fantastic possibilities. "They probably had a German submarine come up to the dock and gave all the French secrets to them. . . . " Robbie looked over at me and gave me one of his more radiant smiles. "You certainly have all the luck, Howie! First that leopard and now all these plans. You ought to be a detective." Praise from Robbie was praise indeed. He was not one to flatter. I blushed with pride at the accolade. Ellie of course bridled. She was taking charge of this event as her very own. "Well, after all, I had something to do with it too, Robbie." "Oh, don't be so conceited, Ellie," snapped Nan. "Besides I bet it wasn't any more spies than it was a leopard. Or a panther. Or whatever." "Father said it was, didn't you, Father? . . . "

"Oh dear," sighed Mother, "can't you stop quarreling!" Richie now ignored Ellie and was eagerly discussing plans for future spy hunts with Robbie, who after his one generous nod to me had lost interest. He looked at Richie amiably but absentmindedly; dreaming, dreaming again. Dreaming of *what?* Mademoiselle removed Ronnie with much bustle and disapproval and with many remarks to Mother, who promised to come up and kiss him when in bed. Jane moved her chair away from me, very ostentatiously, edging it closer to Father in the spaces vacated by Ronnie's bedgoing. I should care. I had my spies and plans and secret compartment.

Robbie's notable vagueness all through dinner continued to worry Mother. She leaned over Nan toward him. "Are you sure you're all right, dear? Do you feel drowsy or anything? Does your head hurt? You've been so strange today." Robbie looked as though he'd just come awake. "Have I? I'm fine." A smile seemed the summit of his social response tonight. He was especially lavish with them, gentle, luminous smiles, not in his usual aggressively cheerful fashion. "You worry me," said Mother.

"That idiotic Dick and his Greek nonsense. Absurd," said Father crossly. "After all, he did save Robbie's life," Mother rather angrily sprang to her brother's defense. "I suppose that makes him a hero." "Well, he did, Dad," put in Robbie. "He also nearly killed you." "That was the wind." Like Mother, Robbie too was earnestly defending him. He obviously thought of Dick only as of someone who had "saved him." Mother said, "I don't see how you can really say it was Dick's fault. . . . " "Well, who else? Who else started all the silliness in the first place?" And now it was Mother and Father. Robbie watched them, hurt and concerned. They got madder and madder. I could tell from the way they lowered their voices so we couldn't overhear them. When Mother suddenly broke out with, "I think thee is being very unfair!" I knew they must be really angry. They never used the Quaker "thee" to each other unless the discussion was awfully serious and acrimonious. It was a sort of signal they had to warn each other against loss of temper. Father glowered and shut up. Mother rose. "I've got to see Ronnie to bed. I won't be back for dessert. I've got a headache." This as a parting shot for Father's benefit. Nan offered to go with her. Mother refused. Richie and Ellie too were bickering again.

Father suddenly slapped his hand on the table, a loud frightening noise. "That's enough of that!" He glowered over at Ellie and Richie. "If you can't be pleasant, keep quiet! God preserve us from rainy days!"

The rest of the meal was subdued enough, and we left the table gladly. Jane wouldn't talk to me, Nan wouldn't talk to Ellie and Robbie was obviously less than interested in Richie's whispered plots and secrets. He gently but definitely disengaged himself. Richie finally snarled at him, as Robbie went out the front door, and then insisted on having me show him personally my discoveries, the cubbyhole, the blueprints. This was something that really excited him.

He started going all over the paneling again to look for some other secret hideaway. I told him we'd covered the situation already, but he was caught up in the fever. Finally I just left him there by himself, squatting and probing, and went up to my room alone to play with stamps.

I was depressed by the unhappy atmosphere of the house, and I suddenly felt desperately tired from my sickness again, another of those bouts of feebleness that had bothered me all day. I crawled into bed early, all alone, without anyone to tell me goodnight.

Ellie and Nan were quarreling in the next room. I lay awake listening to the rain, now fitful and quieter, out there in the dark. It was not cozy and soothing to me tonight, as it usually was. Something chilly and sad had got into it and into me. Nan began to cry, heartbroken sobs. Ellie seemed to be scolding her.

I fell into a canyon of despondency and thought, "Perhaps I'm dying." Weak tears of self-pity started from each eye. As though for the very first time in my life, I tried to comprehend what "dying" really meant, as though I were visualizing it, black and empty in the empty blackness of my cold bedroom. Death. Death. I would die and Nan would die and even Mother and Father would die. How could that be possible? I couldn't imagine the condition of not being alive, not being, not imagining. How was it possible to just go out like a light? What happened to a light when it went out? Nothing left but a bare box of somberness, like this room, shelterless from the wet rain, everybody weeping around my grave, as Nan was weeping now. It was a long time before I could get to sleep, staring out into the night, hearing Nan's indistinct complaints and Ellie's answers, hearing the faint sorrowful rain.

5.

PART ONE

i. Father was disgusted with us all, and decided to do something about it. Next day, the day after the big rain, he called us together for a midmorning meeting in the *salon,* after *goûter.* The weather was bad, but it had turned colder, windier, drier. There were intermittent showers and leaden skies, but no actual downpours. Yet we still couldn't swim or play safely out of doors. I still felt weak from my cold. Nan and Ellie, deserted by the rest of us, still went on with their opera.

Father proposed to organize our time. Instead of drifting about at random, playing our own games, getting into rainy day squabbles, we were to be set tasks, rain or shine, jobs appropriate to our ages and genders. Basically, the girls were to help Mother with a great program of sewing and mending — curtains, clothes, ripped sheets, dressmaking, a mountain of half-finished odds and ends — and the boys were to do clean-up work, mostly for the Websters, who had lost their gardener. Nan and I had special dispensations; as the musical ones, we were to return to Mme de Guichy for piano lessons, and to practice religiously every day. Nan was to continue with her singing too; she went to a voluble Italian in town. And I was to go on with a mixed course of study with equally voluble M. de Guichy.

We were all very happy to be so firmly organized. Nan relished her aloof and aesthetic role. Full of obscure melancholy and hauteur, she was all for her art. I too was quite

151

ready for scales and Grieg (or whatever) and looked forward to going back to the excitable hours in the De Guichy farmhouse, jumping about like a badly trained flea all over the field of human knowledge under De Guichy's scatterbrained French guidance. I had previously been covering with him Latin, Greek, history, literature, zoology, botany, astronomy, arithmetic, algebra and geometry; all in French. It was good for my French.

Most of us responded with enthusiasm to Father's idea. Robbie in particular, shedding his incongruous and incomprehensible beachcomber role, came to the meeting crisp and clean, hair brushed, a bright white shirt, and could hardly be restrained from rushing right off on his bicycle to begin work for the Websters. There was a great deal of rock moving, path and shed clearing and weed pulling to be done there; and the agreeable prospect, of course, of the girls and newly moved-in Dick.

Only Richie hung back. Instead of following Robbie's lead as usual, he whined and groused and finally flatly refused to cooperate. He was willing enough to work, but not at the Websters'. He wouldn't say why. Wasn't there something he could do around home? Father said he'd see. After all, I was supposed to be doing outside work too, just as Nan had to help somewhat with the girls' sewing. But I couldn't be expected to go to the Websters' if I had to practice the piano. It was decided that Robbie should go alone, and Richie and I be given busywork right at Villa Esperance.

After our meeting, full of vigor in the cool weather, we all scattered off. The three girls clattered upstairs to Mother and Mademoiselle. Robbie dashed out with a reproachful word to Richie, more in sorrow than anger, and with many a brisk "aye, aye" to Father. Off to the Websters' and duty. Father took the two of us into the kitchen to consult with Celestine. She wanted a garden dug for her, it seemed; we were the ones to do it. Everyone was now settled and satisfied.

Celestine wiped her hands on her apron and took time off from her kitchen to bustle over to the garage and show us what she wanted. On rainy days we could clean up the garage itself, full of assorted junk. But her chief aim was to get help out back. A rickety door in the rear wall of the garage led to a secluded quarter acre of yard, completely cut off from the pine woods beyond by a high, glass-topped wall. In here Celestine was trying to grow vegetables, where there had been an old garden once before. Nowadays she never found time to work on it, and the yard itself was such a tangle of bushes and creepers, all viciously green from recent rain, that her pathetic little plot battled for its life. We were to rescue it.

As soon as Richie saw this secluded, rubbishy nook, so bosky and filled with odd lumber, he grabbed my arm and said, with incomprehensible excitement, as though something wonderful promised, "Hah! Keen, hunh? I bet there's stuff in here!" I could gather as he muttered half to himself, half to me, while Celestine instructed us, while Richie looked busily about him, that he expected to find more buried evidence of spies. Spy mania had taken him over.

This day was too wet for us to do much. It began to drizzle. We spent our time mostly in the garage itself, heaving old boards about. I had to nap, because of my convalescence. But as the days went by, each one better and brighter than the one before, though still very cool, a new pattern of life emerged for all of us.

Our couples were broken up. I and Jane for instance no longer went down cellar to play Amuria after lunch. She stayed with Mother, sewing or reading; I had to be doing homework for M. de Guichy. Since Robbie was off all day at the Websters' and Nan busy all day with her music, Jane was thrown with Ellie; and I was thrown with Richie.

I can't say I liked it much. Richie certainly meant well, and he was kind and indeed confidential; but he was always an uneasy person, we really shared few enthusiasms, and his new craze for spy-hunting back of the garage (though I suppose it was originally inspired by me) just began to baffle me. Was it real or was it play? Richie seemed to have no firm ideas about the dividing line between fancy and fact. We'd be digging a plot of earth for Celestine; Richie would romance about what was supposed to be hidden there. "I've struck something!" he'd say. "I'll bet it's a box!" Then he'd uncover a stone. "A-*hah*," he'd cry, still pretending. "Jools!" We'd go on like that, thoroughly to my liking, hauling out imaginary strings of pearls from our imaginary coffer, being attacked by rival spies or pirates or whatever, defending ourselves, forgetting our work, having fun. Yet next time when I'd say, "I hear footsteps! Back of the wall there," he'd take me quite seriously, listen, then say sourly, "You're crazy. No one's out there," and be quite disagreeable. This inconsistency applied particularly to spies. Sometimes he'd be properly inventive and *play* spies; he was good at it, full of macabre invention, torture scenes, hairbreadth escapes, hiding behind things indoors and out. But at other times he seemed to be quite serious, and would be cross if I tried embroidery. He obviously had something specific in mind he was looking for. Dark hints, sneers and mutters. But he'd never tell me exactly what it all was. "You wait and see," or "It's here somewhere," and such remarks; frantic if spasmodic diggings in places other than Celestine's garden plot. "They met here, and she heard them *digging*," he'd say. Who met and who heard? He'd laugh or snarl if I asked him directly, or wink and punch my arm, conspirators. What was the conspiracy, what was the secret?

This was annoying enough. And then I didn't really like this back-of-garage enclosure much. It smelled of sewage and seepage and rotting plant material. It was claustrophobic with rubble, the broken-down remains of an inappropriate rustic log summer house at the back, a pile of immovable concrete blocks in the far corner. We did our best to order things, but it was heavy work for me. Also the place was crawling with unpleasant insects, notably scorpions. There were some of these in the garden too, but many more here. They were handsome little black lobster-like midgets, more curious than dreadful; but I'd been told that one bite caused instant and painful death, and they terrified me. When a scorpion crawled up my leg once I screamed and carried on and Richie hit me and I hit him; and so it went.

Altogether I was *not* adjusted to the new order. Richie was no fair substitute for Jane as a playmate. She remained cool to me, still offended, but I had the satisfaction of feeling that she was enjoying Ellie no more than I enjoyed Richie.

ii. A constant distraction from Richie and his febrile concerns was my life at the De Guichys'. Welcome distraction. I loved it there, and loved my odd cultural career, Music and Learning. I went three late-mornings a week, driven along the road to town usually by Mother, but sometimes by Jocelyn Webster. We went from our villa past the orphanage, along the shore a bit, where there was a wide seaweed-banked public beach. Then the road turned sharply to the left, inland. At the corner was the farm with Ellie's big black dog. After that we had pine-covered heights on one side, villas at the bottom, the chapel of Notre Dame at the top, vineyards on the other side. The road climbed a ridge, spur of the pine-covered hills, where most of the great decaying old English hotels were, and then the road dropped down again toward town. At that point I was left to make my way on foot along a narrow track to the De Guichys'.

In time past this had been a sort of terror to me. A very fierce French police dog with a nasal bark and vicious teeth used to rush out at me every single time I went by. He was behind a gate, and so safe enough; but it scared me dreadfully on each separate occasion, and the dog knew it. It was all very well for Ellie or Robbie to say that dogs could smell fear, and if you weren't afraid then they wouldn't bite you. I *was* scared, and that dog could easily smell my fear. Now, to my vast relief, the dog was gone — summer vacation, perhaps dead. I scurried up the road past grapes and fig trees and reached the De Guichys' villa unmolested.

It was a nice Provençal farmhouse with the usual plaster walls and old red roof. In front was a tile terrace with grapevines over it, and inside lots of cheap black French furniture, a grand piano, and reproductions of Botticelli's "Venus," etc. I invested all this with romance and culture, largely because of the De Guichys themselves. Like their furniture, the De Guichys were not particularly handsome or distinguished. She was thin and blond, with hair that tended to come loose, and buckteeth. He was very short with a great African bush of gray hair and a flaring mustache. They both hopped about a great deal, he more than she. They had a thin little boy named Pierre Alix Hyacinth, a name I thought terribly funny. His nickname was Pepi. He had a melodious whine, and he was usually referred to with great melancholy as the "*pauvre petit* Pepi.*" He was really a spoiled brat.

What made the De Guichys romantic was their absorption in music and science respectively, the excitement they could communicate; and then, back of this, the whispers of their history. M. de Guichy was in fact actually, it seemed, not plain Monsieur at all, but a veritable honest-to-God *ancien régime* Duc. He had deserted his wellborn Duchesse just for Madame. Hard to believe. And they had run off down here. Since the Duchesse was so terribly Catholic, they couldn't get a divorce, and they weren't really married at all! I got this in breathless gasps from the big girls, who reveled in anything so Hearst Sunday Supplement. Naturally you couldn't ask the De Guichys about it, so nobody really knew if it had any basis in fact. The girls firmly believed it, and therefore doted on the De Guichys, though their rather absurd looks and bourgeois surroundings made it a bit difficult to sustain illusions of grandeur and passion.

I had one lesson a week with Madame, who taught the *Méthode Jaël.* This had been invented, so I presume, by a languid Parisienne of the *fin de siècle* who believed in serpentine movements of the arm, very Art Nouveau, and caressings of the finger down along the piano keys. There were lots of exercises and diagrams designed to bring out these undulations and slidings, and it was no doubt very bad for my technique, such as it was. I rather enjoyed the pictures and graphs of the *Méthode,* and the wiggly exercises; I was appropriately trying to play the first Debussy Arabesque without much success.

With Monsieur I kept on looking at seaweed through the microscope, but dropped all other subjects except French — grammar, literature, history. He also put me up as a member of the Astronomical Society of France. I was duly elected and received their unreadable journal in its dingy orange cover. He did beautiful accurate little drawings of algae; I copied them. And somehow lessons of grammar, which interested neither of us, turned into lessons on astronomy, and medieval history merged into ancient. We talked in a medley of two languages, though all my reading at least was French. He seemed to believe that knowledge for its own sake was terribly exciting, an impression none of my other teachers had ever come even close to giving me.

iii. My after-lunch nap period, formerly devoted to Jane and Amuria, was now devoted to M. de Guichy's devoirs. Molière and Racine were my most inappropriate diet. They both bored me stiff. I got nothing out of them, except of course practice in the language; and actually to this area of knowledge M. de Guichy's own enthusiasms did not really extend. He told me about Love vs. Duty and classic grandeur, but his heart wasn't in it. The parallels of French classic drama to my own more disheveled imaginary play world never even occurred to me. Or perhaps not so much that; for in fact it did stir me on to thoughts of making up my own dramas. Instead of reading *Andromaque*, I began to conceive of plays of my own; but this did not make me like *Andromaque* any better. It was water through a sieve.

Sitting alone cross-legged on the red cool carpetless floor of my room, the feeble afternoon sun coming in through sluggish clouds, watching a patch of it on the white wall fade or swell as the clouds moved, I brought up stories to my mind's eye full of pageantry, bloodshed and heroic mystery. *Andromaque*, which had set me off without gaining any attraction for me, lay open and neglected on the floor at my knee. I was tempted to continue the history of Amuria; it was to be exciting under the misrule of handsome wicked Agragor. He wanted to marry Nu Wa of course, now that Wa Nee Ta was dead; but old Wa

Fung had other ideas, and was trying to force him on poor little Chin Lee. . . . No, I couldn't go through all that without Jane. That would really be betrayal. I'd have to wait till she came round again and we were allowed back to our cellar.

So I'd make up some different, forgettable story. No wind outside, despite moving clouds; inside as always faint occasional house noises. A faint revival in the garden, through the pines, of the cicadas. Somewhere, in my imaginary worlds, back of the action, was a concealed source of excitement, a magic compartment that contained — what? That gave special value to my tale-making. What was it? I could feel it, sense it, almost see it; but it — whatever it was — stayed hidden, a treasure, a mythical beast back of bushes, a grail in a forest. I felt if I just let my mind go, I might get to the magic place; a dark tower, a sacred cave. Then I would know what the secret was, and become a wizard myself perhaps. The stories streamed out, but I never caught more than a faintest glimpse of their birthplace. What was it, where was it, who lived there? I wasted my study time dreaming of it.

During the cold spell I wasn't allowed to swim. I was considered still convalescent; but not convalescent enough to get out of having to help Richie in the garage. So after my supposed study period, after my daydreaming, I'd go down and look for Richie. He was as like as not grubbing around in the garden plot.

His greetings varied from feverish excitement to surly moroseness, seldom anything relaxed or amiable. One day it would be something he thought he had found, stupid pieces of junk most likely, for the place had been long used as a dump. One of the more unattractive aspects of it was this constant digging up of nasty remnants from the steamy earth. The place seemed essentially unclean to me. In attempting to clear off some of the growth that was dragging down the decayed cedar-log summer house, Richie found items of this kind. The interior had obviously been used by somebody not too long ago. The plants and grass that grew rankly inside it had been trampled down. Richie came across a small cheap-looking coral earring; and then, with enormous glee, a dirty white circle of flimsy rubber, a horrid object which he held up before me chortling and snickering at a tremendous rate. "What's that?" I asked, disgusted by both the object and his attitude. But he refused to answer, guffawing, carefully putting both the earring and the thing in a crumpled envelope he kept in his back pocket for just such prizes. Some more items for his mysterious but boring collection — the unaccountable bits he locked away in his study room upstairs. What did they mean to him? He acted as though, a detective, he'd found a most significant clue. But in true Watson fashion, the clues made no sense to me. Besides, what was the crime? No use looking for a criminal until I knew that; but though Richie winked and leered, he'd never tell me. Something to do with spies, perhaps connected to my discovery in the dining room. Something real, not just play; in Richie's mind at least.

iv. He had a way of digging about at random in all the places not authorized by Celestine; then carefully tramping down the evidences. When I asked him why, he'd say "Hah!" mysteriously, and give me dark looks. He seldom found anything at all, though any old object was enough to send him into frenzies. One day I discovered him at work with a pitchfork along the wall on the further side of the door. I sniffed and was about to settle down to hoeing vegetables in a proper fashion when Richie gave a great cry and went down on his knees. Despite all the previous false alarms, I couldn't help running over to him. He rummaged madly in the dirt and brought out a muddy bundle, a package tied up in paper and string. He was so excited he couldn't get the wrapping off, cursing and carrying on and refusing to let me touch. At last he got it open: a bunch of old clothes, very shabby, a sort of dirty-blue French workman's outfit, shirt and trousers and cap. In the pocket of the shirt was a tiny cheap notebook. This really sent Richie into ecstasies. Kneeling in the fresh-turned mud he flipped the pages over. I got behind him to see. There was nothing in the book but series of numbers with an occasional letter, "17921384X." "It's a code, see?" said Richie. "This was his disguise. He came in and they buried it and he went out with a new disguise!" "*Who?* Whose disguise?" "Ah-*Hah!*" was all Richie would say, as usual; then crowing with joy he hopped up, waving the book around in one hand, with the clothes under his other arm. He dashed into the garage to take these prizes up to his hideout. I was thoroughly disgusted; and when he came back, full of exuberances, clapping me on the back (but still refusing to tell me anything), I turned away from him and went back to my hoeing. This made him surly. But how could he expect me to share his excitement if he wouldn't tell me anything about it? He did though. My deliberate coldness infuriated him. From this point on our relationship steadily deteriorated.

I longed to be done with it all and get back to playing with Jane. I'd wander up to the "women's quarters," either Mother's bedroom looking out over the sea, or the room in front, really the best bedroom in the house, shared by Mademoiselle and Ronnie. But I was not wanted. Ellie and Jane and Mademoiselle, usually, would be sitting busily in a pile of materials, chatting away and fussing and sewing. Nan, I noticed, never seemed to be there. Mother only once; and Jane didn't do much of the chatting. When I came in, standing in the doorway, they'd tease me. "Come along, here's a thimble. You can take that curtain." Jane refused even to look at me.

Nan and I, since we shared the piano, saw each other when our practice periods overlapped. We built up a mild companionship of suffering, both feeling obscurely outcast. What Nan's misery was based on I couldn't know, but it made her gentle and kind to me. She'd condescend to play her piece, a melancholy Chopin nocturne, for my uninformed criticism; I was flattered. Occasionally she'd practice Esterilla's aria, "I'm all alone," with me as accompanist, and this brightened us both considerably. She talked of reviving the opera, but without Ellie this was obviously hopeless.

As for Robbie, none of us ever saw him. He'd dash off to the Websters' on his bicycle, rain or shine, right after breakfast, and come back just before supper. As the weather improved, so did his air of ruddy health. He got browner and browner from working stripped in the sun, his muscles visibly bulged and his hair, sunburned too, got more fiery. He was kind and brisk to us all, but not interested. Only through Jocelyn and Dick, who told the parents, who told us, did we learn of his prodigies of energy. He was transforming the barren Webster garden. They had to stop him, make him come inside for lemonade to prevent him from having sunstroke. He got both Webster girls out helping him; even Dick, even Jocelyn. They all had an uproarious time, we gathered. Swims in between jobs, off the Webster rocks, jolly games when it actually rained, or alfresco lunches under the trellises, when Dick would play his guitar. I was so sorry now I hadn't got myself into this (not that I'd been asked) instead of my imprisonment with Richie in his nasty backyard. I noticed incidentally that Dick and the Websters never seemed to come over to us any more. We were too dreary a household for them, I suspected.

Misery. The contrast of Robbie's glow and Ellie's female self-esteem brought into relief the melancholies of the rest of us; for Jane was obviously no happier than I was, bored with sewing, bored with chatting.

PART TWO

i. At last Jane and I made peace. It came about on one of our trips to town. This was a rather special trip. It came after one of my sessions at the De Guichys'. Usually I was dropped there in midmorning, and came home for lunch. Trips to town occurred separately, in the afternoon. Today I went to the De Guichys' later, almost at noontime, and, rare thrill, had lunch with them on their terrace, after my piano practice, my slippery slidey Jaël exercises. We had bread and cheese and fruit and salad, and daringly, red wine with water in it for me and Pepi. Monsieur had just had an article published in the new Astronomical bulletin, all about the *rayon vert*, so we talked mostly about that. Of all the many things that excited him — algae, Greek, stars — this *rayon vert* excited him most, and he was an, in fact the, authority on the subject. At sunset, just as the sun goes down over the sea, as the final edge of the disc sinks under the water, if you look closely you can see a vivid green ray shooting across to you from the horizon. To make it last a fraction of a second longer, you squat quickly. This green ray is due to the sun shining through the curvature of the water — or something like that (De Guichy knew of course and told me all the various hypotheses, correct and incorrect). His paper was supposed to settle the business once and for all. He could hardly eat lunch, he was so full of it. His excitement was increased by a future expectation. We were to have an eclipse, any moment now; and during the eclipse the sun would set. If we could get to the right place, we'd be able to see not one, but two *rayons*, as the two horns of the half-sun sank into the ocean. M. de Guichy was planning a picnic. A boat would take us across our bay, and carry us all to those mysterious, Japanesy islets way out there. We'd have an unobstructed view of the sun going down into the Mediterranean, and presumably all stand in line on the rocks, squatting in unison, not once, but twice. Rare opportunity! There might never be another such in the whole astronomical history.

Naturally I was as keyed up about this as De Guichy; more because of going to those rocks, than because of his *rayons*. Actually I'd never been able to catch the *rayon vert*, though I'd peered and squatted. What I looked forward to was island exploration. Would there be machine-gun nests out there? Evidence of pirates, buried treasure even? Though I rather doubted that. We could hardly keep our minds on grammar and *Andromaque* after lunch. Inflamed by wine, I insisted on getting back to the subject of the picnic and De Guichy was just as bad. He read me his entire article, of which I understood not one word.

Afterward I strolled back down the track to the main road to meet the parents and to go with them to town. The track from the De Guichys' was too narrow for a car, and the De Guichys did without one, preferring in any case the healthful bicycle, on which they pedaled incredible distances. I walked, bicycleless as I was (only Robbie and Richie owned them in our family), past the fig tree, where real ripe figs grew for me to steal, past the wall and gate, so happily dog-free, past the vineyard and to the road.

There I sat on a big square white rock, even whiter with the dust that now covered everything, and waited for the family. The rock was flat on top and mysterious. An old milestone? A Roman remain? It had no visible inscriptions on it, but a few inticing indentations that might have meant something. Perhaps it was a gravestone. I'd examined it thoroughly in time past. Now I sat and meditated.

No cars went by, which was fortunate. For some obscure administrative reason this particular stretch of road was unpaved and terribly dusty. It was hot in the early afternoon sun, already westering behind me. The rains had finally drifted away, and by now things were back to Riviera norm — the sky brassy blue, the earth powdery and chalk-colored, or a faded tan, the pine woods all over the ridge to my right full of sharp smells and loud insects.

There was another, special quality in the bright silence which I recognized as just faintly autumnal, an added weight of stillness, an added edge to the cicadas' noisiness. Something about the smells too of drying plants and ripening grapes. Soon we'd be able to rob the vineyard, protected only by a wire fence like any American farm, of its great-hung, dirt-powdered purple bunches. The skins would break hot and ecstatic on our tongues, after we'd carefully polished each grape on our shirts till it glowed. The fact that it was illegal made it more fun, though nobody had ever stopped us.

We'd robbed this particular vineyard often, a year ago, last fall before we moved to our villa. The autumnal atmosphere, the place, the dust and the grapes all brought it back to me vividly; vividly and sadly too. Next fall we wouldn't be here, for only too soon we'd leave and sail back home; home, which I loved, school, which bored me, friends and occupations which I'd forgotten.

ii. It had been two summers and a winter in between since we'd been gone. The excitement of that embarkation, going to New York, leaving the pier with the slowly widening black water and the calling summer crowds seeing us off; the endless runnings and pokings about the passageways and decks of the ship; the warming weather as we drew southward — could anything really beat all that? Or the first glimpse at dawn out of our porthole of the Azores, a sharp-finned sail of rust red slipping along behind a stone mole, with an exotic mountain behind, lush with green, dotted with little houses painted violet and pink? Abroad! I had small precious souvenirs of the rest of the trip, a piece of rock fallen from Gibraltar itself (I trusted), a little donkey and cart from Palermo, tiny white marble doves around a yellow marble bowl from Naples. Finally Marseilles and the train trip up the Rhone, at night alas; and then Paris.

Our first summer had been rather dispersed and confused. We'd been separated part of the time. I and Jane spent a few weeks alone in the apartment of Mme de Greuze, a lady who believed strongly in Louis XV and la Pompadour, in rooms crammed to the last inch with elegant little faded chairs and breakable *objets d'art*. We were taken on solemn tours of museums by a grave young spinster, a Greuze cousin. Madame herself spent all her time on the phone, mostly complaining of the phone service. "*E*-pouvantable! *In*-croyable!" she would scream to friend or operator. The parents were off on a motor trip with companions, one of whom was Uncle Dick. The older boys and girls were here and there.

We all got together again in Brittany and played in the sand with other summer children. And then we separated again; and some of us came down here.

The parents and we youngsters spent the first weeks at the Côte d'Or, one of the English hotels, formerly frequented by Queen Victoria. It was immense and seemed quite empty, although actually haunted by any number of ancient residents, upper middle-class English relics of both sexes, who cut each other judiciously and murmured in the great dining room. There was a deserted ballroom, the chandeliers swathed in muslin (when had it last been used?), where I spent somnolent after-lunch hours at the jangling grand piano, twanging away in the echoing shadows. An equally deserted library provided bound copies of old French periodicals of the nineties, illustrated pudgily in gray.

The older children, off on their own again, had not yet arrived. First came Ellie. We three, Ellie, Jane and I, investigated this new world, easily ignoring a governess. Mademoiselle was not then Mademoiselle, but merely Ronnie's nurse and Mother's maid. We were supposed to be in the charge (clutches would be more apt) of Mme Moukina, a plump, violent Russian woman, who alternately hugged us and tortured us, driving her sharp fingernails into our palms, baring her teeth at us in fury. She regaled us with stories of her refugee relations in Bulgaria, who were *eating* each other in their starvation. She taught us set pieces in French to recite. Mine was the apostrophe from Molière's *L'Avare*, when he finds his money stolen. "On ma coupé la gorge!" I couldn't imagine anyone ever acting that way about anything, except perhaps Mme Moukina herself. She left abruptly about the time we too left the Côte d'Or. The parents couldn't stand the food there any longer, and we moved briefly but gaily to the Maritime. There the boys and Nan joined us, before finally we were all taken at last to Villa Esperance together.

Meanwhile, at the Côte d'Or, we three, Ellie, Jane and I, had fun in the woods. They smelled wonderfully, as they were smelling today, pungent in the sun, and were wide open to us as guests of the hotel. There were other hotels, their grounds also open. Sedate paths led to the graveyard where the dogs of Queen Victoria were buried in their own small enclosure with dolorous monuments. Back toward the hills, across the road (this very road) were more open woods for us to wander in. We played endless games there. Our way was finally blocked by the wall of a huge deserted villa, an imitation castle in such flawless French bad taste of papier-mâché colored stone that even we could recognize its vulgarity. It was owned, they said, by a famous Parisian couturier; but during the war (not so many years ago after all) it had been the headquarters for *spies*. So right from the beginning we had this sort of thing put into our minds. We longed to get inside the wall, but it was impregnable. Robbie and Richie of course would certainly have found some hair-raising way in. They were off on a farm in the nearby mountains, learning rude dialect and how to milk cows in French. We had to turn back from the wall defeated.

When we got back to the hotel from these woodland expeditions, responsibly on time for meals under Ellie's stern guidance, Mme Moukina would scream and rave at us. Where had we been? I would snicker at her; Jane would whimper. We were awfully glad when she left; back to her cannibal kin in Bulgaria? It was here at the Côte d'Or that I began my diary in the little brown book with the saints' names for every day (Ste. Leocadie). I recorded all events telegraphically: "Played in the woods. Found a shell. Fight with Jane. Swim at the Maritime." And I still continued this routine, right up to the present. My Trip Abroad.

There at the Maritime, where an old English gentleman professed a passion for Jane which she took as her due (old gentlemen always had passions for her), we all enjoyed beach life and the contrast to the Côte d'Or. Everything at the Maritime was so almost up to date, and the food so good. The boys arrived, brown and uncouth. Finally Nan came from her high-toned visit; and we moved to our marvelous villa. Of all the excitements of Abroad, this was

168

the most permanently satisfactory; something of our own, wholly ours to play in, to live in.

The group of us, Ronnie, Jane, Howie, Richie, Robbie, Ellie and Nan, fell on the villa as though we'd been Mme Moukina's starving relations at a banquet. It was the first home we'd had since we'd left home, and we immediately made it, in our different ways, part of us. We had a full staff of servants then; not only Celestine and recently promoted Mademoiselle, who was now theoretically our governess, but also handsome and mysterious Albert and Rose. They lived over in the garage next to Celestine in a room now vacant, and fought loudly and dreadfully all night. . . .

iii. But at this moment, along came our big green Renault down the road with a whirl of dust behind it. I stood up. Robbie was in the back seat and opened the door for me. He was all dressed up. He looked even more ruddy and glowing than usual, encased in starchy clothes that like all his clothes now seemed too small for him — white duck trousers that might split at any moment, white shirt biting into his brown neck, a regimental (school) tie and a dark green (school) blazer. He was in fact going to some sort of scholastic reunion in the garden of the English church. The clergyman doubled as headmaster; St. Eustace was the only decent educational establishment for boys in the district, and it was very English indeed. Robbie loved it; Richie hated it, and had refused to attend this party. So in fact had the parents, who were supposed to be there, Mamá presumably in gloves and garden hat. Their refusal had hurt Robbie's feelings.

I crawled over him to the middle of the seat. Jane sat scrunched up on the far side. Jane smiled tentatively, the first smile she'd given me since our fight. Robbie leaned forward and rested his arms on the back of the front seat, behind Father. He resumed his conversation with the parents. The taut arc of his body and the big legs doubled up seemed to take up all the room in the back there. I was pushed right over on top of Jane. She didn't seem to mind.

"Is he going to be in his same room?" asked Robbie. "I'm afraid so," Mother answered. "It's not very nice for a guest, but it'll have to do I suppose." "Why don't you move Howie and put Dick up there?" suggested Father. I was outraged, and was about to protest when Robbie said, "Oh, please don't. I know he likes it there and we like having him." "*We* or *you?*" said Father. "Richie doesn't seem so fond any more, does he?"

Robbie flushed and lowered his chin to his arms. He muttered something, but his mouth was hidden by his sleeve. "I can't hear you," said Father crossly. "Why doesn't he stay at the Websters' where he can be housed properly?" Father's irritation was obviously with Dick, not with Robbie.

"I don't think that's very hospitable, dear," said Mother in an injured tone. "He is my brother after all. And you didn't seem to approve much of his going to the Websters' in the first place."

"Well, the damage, such as it is, is certainly done now. I won't be inhospitable, darling. We'll welcome the Prodigal Son back with open arms, won't we?" Robbie gave a laugh. "We'll even kill a fatted calf," continued Father. "Jane here. Are you fatted enough? Or Ronnie. Now there's a nice fat little calf. We'll cook him and serve him with an apple — no, a lemon in his mouth. Won't he look cute?"

Jane was hysterical with the humor of this, though of course Mother protested mildly. But she laughed too, and the subject of Dick's return passed off in merriment. The merriment broke whatever was left of the ice between Jane and myself, and we elaborated tirelessly, tiresomely, hilariously in childish fashion on the theme of serving people up to Dick: Celestine as a fatted calf! With one of Robbie's soccer balls in *her* big mouth! She could cook herself! We were very funny to ourselves, though the others began to talk about other things, Robbie still straining his bursting bulk over across toward the front.

Town became evident, first in larger villas behind higher walls, then smaller ones with walls that showed, through spiked gates of varying sizes, neat gravel and geranium front gardens. These new houses were all of uniform and elaborate hideousness, decorated in misapplications of the plasterer's art with contrasts of nubbly brown panels against smooth cream-yellow. Much was made of little useless wrought-iron balconies.

Then began the palms, which strode up to the center of town along the Avenue Garibaldi (why Garibaldi?). These, planted when the avenue was first ruthlessly put through in the late nineteenth century, were now the pride of the municipality, and justified the addition to the town's proper name of "Les Palmiers." The Avenue Garibaldi always depressed me — dusty, bare, a predominantly dingo color, though it was really cheerful enough, with its neat newish houses. But an aroma of provincial dullness penetrated even to me. Here lived in stuffy small-scale state the local officials.

Obtrusive in the middle of this was the equally stuffy but exotic English church. Its wall, with iron-grilled partitions and yellow pilasters, its two palm trees, its gravel and geraniums were identical to the neighbors'. But back of those flanking palms was the incongruous ugliness of a gray stone English neo-Gothic chapel, with tall peaked roof and painful stained-glass windows. We were to leave Robbie off here for his fete. The grounds were already crowded with boys and parents and even a few sisters; the boys, like Robbie, all in green blazers and white pants, the mothers fussily ornamented as befitted vicarage affairs in England. It must have been very hot indeed for all of them, especially the English fathers in their uncompromisingly tailored outfits.

Another source of Robbie's grief, aside from the parents' nonattendance (they'd sooner be seen dead than at such an affair) was his trousers. Everyone else, all the *English* boys anyway, had *flannel* trousers. Baggy, expensive-looking, hot flannels. Robbie didn't have a pair with him; his pair at home was now obviously outgrown and almost ready for me, and the parents, for all his urging, refused to buy him a pair just for this occasion. Mother had toyed with the idea. Father said no. In the first place, whatever a Carruthers wore was right, no matter what, so why bother? In the second place, Father was most Quakerish in his refusal to spend a penny on worldly show, unless, un-Quakerish, he thought it picturesque or really beautiful. A pair of flannel trousers for this silly business was absurd. Mother, more inclined to convention, nonetheless let it go.

So Robbie, climbing over us, since he was on the wrong side of the car, with a great deal of damage and confusion, his big feet and legs trampling over us while we screamed, emerged full of embarrassment to face his peers. They would laugh at him. Actually the trousers were if anything rather becoming. But Robbie was still so unselfconscious that it did not occur to him that such a thing as too tight trousers would enhance rather than detract from the overwhelming effect of youth, health and strength he was bound to have on anybody, especially his boyish contemporaries. He started off rather tentatively, scrunched up as though he could somehow retract his failings into himself and invisibility, and dawdled toward the receiving line beyond the gate.

Father called to him, "Hey! How will you get up to the castle?" Robbie turned, came out of his fog of apprehension and said, "Oh. I'll borrow a bike." "Are you sure you can? You know how to get there?" Robbie just smiled and nodded, waved and turned toward his hosts. Father sighed and grumbled, "He'll make it somehow I suppose." The parents stayed to watch him go past the clergyman and his wife, a master and his wife, Robbie bowing irreproachably if quickly. "That school really did improve his manners if nothing else," said Father. Then we drove off. "He's so worried about his trousers," said Mother. "Happy youth, to have no other worries." "Oh dear! Howie!" said Mother, suddenly turning to me with her hand to her mouth. "You look awful, don't you? I forgot all about you. We're going to tea at the castle and I suppose you've got to go the way you are." "She won't mind in the least," said Father. "I can't imagine anyone who would mind more." Mother sighed. "Well, it can't be helped. Just sit quietly when you get there and don't attract attention to yourself. I'll brush you off before you go in and hope for the best. Jane looks pretty enough and Robbie will be all right if he doesn't get hot and mussed coming up. Don't you think you better go fetch him?" Father just shook his head. Mother turned to me again. "It's all my fault, Howie. I just completely forgot about it."

"About *what?*" said I, still mystified. Mother explained; tea at the castle. The castle, a veritable ancient gray crumbling medieval castle, dominated the town, and was in turn dominated by a great lady, internationally, socially, financially and, above all, intellectually famous, who was an old friend of the family. American, she'd married a French nobleman, he'd died, she'd written novels and poems and essays and pieces about furniture and snuffboxes, and had bought and restored the castle many years ago. She lived there in considerable seclusion, broken by extensive trips to the capitals of the world where she knew everybody worth knowing. I'd never met her, at least to my recollection. I was excited by the thought of the castle, but depressed by the thought of tea. Jane was excited by both, and told me what she could about the occasion. The lady had particularly wanted to see us. She'd known us as babies or something. How boring it threatened to be; except for seeing the castle from inside of course.

When we got into town, Father found a place to put the car just off the main square. We were to go to our curio shop and stay there until picked up by the shopping parents. Mother looked me over on the sidewalk, spanked the dust off my rear where I'd been sitting on the stone, tried to order my hair, sighed and gave up. We raced to our store. It was a tiny slice of one of the yellow business buildings around the square, the square with its city hall and bright-awninged cafés and hideous new war memorial with Victory holding a bronze palm above a soldier in full battle dress leaning dramatically wounded over a cannon. Real palms, new nasty little ones, surrounded this. Everybody said there'd been a pretty little cast-iron fountain there before with big old palms, and all the local people and habitual tourists took sides pro and con monument. We were pro.

The store had in it everything that the heart could desire. For Jane it had endless little shelves of china animals, cats, mice, donkeys, sheep. It had tiny chamber pots with forget-me-nots applied, it had curiosities from foreign parts, miniature Greek vases black and red with warriors fighting, Italian carts just like the one I got in Palermo. It had small picture frames of yellow varnished wood, decorated by hand. It had stationery, pads, pencils, crayons. Here I had bought my diary. And above all it had stamps. Oh, what happiness. How could anything match the glory and wonder, the appetite inspired by stamps? Passion, ecstasy, torture to stand and look over each display behind glass: sheets, packages, even a rare individual mounted all by itself, of great price. Jane had a little money, I had a little money, and we were each to buy something. But what? Jane couldn't make up her mind between a white china cat and a gray china mouse. I had my eye on a big stamp from Borneo with a gorilla on it. but it was too expensive for me. I looked for other less reckless possibilities.

Finally Jane made up her mind: the mouse. I went with her to the sour, mustached old woman behind the counter, and watched her pay for it. The woman gave us a horrible snaggle-toothed grimace, meant to be a kindly smile. We took it as such, since the beauty of her store haloed her too. Besides, we were old familiar customers. She wrapped the little mouse in tissue paper and box, and Jane paid for it. It was cheaper than the cat and I saw she had quite a bit of change left over.

I held my breath. Dared I ask her? She went back to contemplate the animals and chamber pots, now too expensive for what she had left. I finally screwed up courage. I asked her if she'd lend me enough to buy my Borneo stamp. I showed her the stamp. She didn't say anything, but silently handed me the money. I counted it; it was enough. I hugged her in jubilation. She made a face at me. I went over and got the proprietress to open up the glass cabinet. Mine, mine, all mine, that obviously terribly valuable Borneo stamp! My heart was swollen with joy and thanks to Jane for her generosity. Of course I'd have to pay her back later; but would any objects ever again mean as much to me in life as stamps did then?

iv. The parents stopped the car in front of the shop. We ran out, we were taken up the narrow street toward the castle, through the old town so gray and leaning, like Malhaut, that it didn't seem possible that it could actually be inhabited. But it was. The street turned into the zigzag ramp that led to the castle itself, barely navigable by our big car. Father fumed and fretted and changed gears. We crept along the same track no doubt once traveled by clanking knights in suitable armor with banner and lance.

Jane and I had been to various castles, but never to one actually lived in by someone we knew. We took it for granted everyone would be dressed in medieval clothes, with pages and varlets about. When we went through the frowning outer gate into a black stone courtyard, and with trepidation traveled up worn steps to a huge studded oak door, where Father yanked the big iron bell handle, we were appalled to find the door opened by an ordinary little French manservant in a sleazy black butler's jacket. Inside things were equally disappointing. True, there was a four-square hall with Gothic vaulting and a great ancient chest and iron candlesticks; but once we were up the steps beyond into the living room, formerly a Great Hall, everything was nauseatingly Louis.

If there was anything Jane and I heartily disliked and found truly silly it was French Louis-ness. Shepherds in wigs, shepherdesses with patches on their faces forsooth! So to see the original Gothic we so admired besmeared, to our thinking, with gilt and satin chairs, flowered rugs, cabinets of little things (shepherdesses), even a luster-filled big chandelier hanging from the beautiful gray groining, broke our hearts. I'd only been willing to come anyway because of the chance to see the inside. Now I resigned myself to sheer hell.

The big room was empty when we got there except for the silken ticking of little clocks. I had a chance to go to the big double-arched window and look out over the valley. This was nice; but then in came our hostess, all in lace, leaning a bit on a delicate cane, so I had to turn round and be polite.

She was certainly every inch a great lady, from white pompadourish head to satin-slippered feet hid in ruffly long skirts. No compromise on her part with the world of flapper and bob. She meant to be regal to the end.

Mother hurried across and the two women embraced. "My dears!" said our hostess, beaming grandly at us all. "I feel so guilty. Here we've been all along, and I haven't seen you. It's entirely my fault." She sat, with a good deal of awkwardness and cane business, before the elaborately silvered teakettle. "This is pretty meager. But I plead travel and health. This is the first week I've been out of bed since I got home."

Mother and Father condoled, and there followed talk about where everyone had been and whom they'd seen. I sat off as far as I dared, and, as Mother suggested, tried to be inconspicuous. It was no use. The great lady turned her relentless brilliance on us, Jane and me. "So. I haven't seen you since you were babies. Very bouncing you were then. Very nice looking now." She turned to Mother. "Aren't you fortunate. Ugly children are such a burden, especially to themselves. I was such an ugly duckling myself."

"Ah, but what a swan came of it!" said Father gallantly. The atmosphere of course demanded such gallantries.

"Old, cross, stiff-legged. I shall hope to have one swan song yet at least. But the children, what do you do with them all? Schools?" "In winter. The older girls went to Sacre Coeur." "Excellent I'm told. The good sisters. How I would have liked being a nun." "Mother Superior in no time of course."

She smiled, then looked absently and rather sadly out the window, a trick she had. "The habit, the habit of command. It would have been good for me to *obey* a bit more. But the others, where did they go?"

"The boys went to the English School. Mr. Cuthbert."

She laughed. "Our vicar! What a silly ass he is, isn't he? The flawless specimen of English foolishness. I love him for it. I have him here often, so that I can continue to have faith in Trollope. My nieces . . . no, I mean, *great*-nieces like to call him 'Mr. Custard.' And the other two?"

She turned to us in our inconspicuousness. "Well, for Jane we have a mademoiselle. At least she's learning French. And Howard's being tutored by M. de Guichy."

She laughed. "Good heavens, that must be breathless. Can you keep up with him? What does he teach you, Universal Knowledge?"

"Almost," answered Mother for me. "Let's see: geography, history (ancient and French), botany, zoology, Latin, Greek, algebra, geometry — and of course French." "You forgot astronomy," I said, grinning. "Yes indeed," Father added impressively. "Howard here is a bona fide member of the Astronomical Society of France, or something of that sort. De Guichy had him elected. He gets their journal."

Our hostess could hardly contain herself with mirth and delight. "Oh, that wonderful creature! If he didn't exist Voltaire would have had to have invented him. The noblesse of the Enlightenment. Can't you see him with Diderot and Franklin? And Voltaire himself? Nature, both scientific and Romantic. Rousseau and electricity." She paused, then added, "His wife, that is, the Duchesse, was a first cousin of my husband's, you know."

"No. I didn't know. Is she still alive?

"Very much so. Lives in great style *dans ses terres*. It's quite a thing, you know. He gave up everything to her; which is a lot. She's miserable, with all that everything; he's happy. It's a lesson to us all. But it *was* irresponsible just the

178

same; a return to childhood. He's like a schoolboy who collects frogs, with all his fads and experiments. What's his passion of the moment?" she asked me.

"The *rayon vert.*"

"Oh, the *rayon vert!* Yes, yes, that's his King Charles's Head, isn't it?" Mother read Dickens to us, but I didn't get this reference, which puzzled me enormously. "I remember standing on the beach, trying to squat, falling backward on the rocks, most awkward." Everybody laughed trying to picture her in such an unmajestic predicament.

"Then the story is true?" said Father. "I mean about running off and all that." Mother frowned at him. "Yes, yes, quite true. Tessières, who's another cousin, won't speak to him, but I dote on them both. However, De Guichy doesn't approve of *me*. I've embraced everything he's run away from, including his family. Odd how differently things look, depending on where you stand. I suppose my own terrible family would look picturesque to some who were quite outside it, coming from Iowa, say. Or yours," she said, smiling at Father.

"Oh, come, mine's not terrible! Just dull."

"Terrible enough to a young girl of aspiration and spirit; and no looks. I'll never forget a certain Carruthers Christmas dinner, on Walnut Street. Everybody there at least a cousin, except me. Neither of you present, fortunate people." She was lost a moment in reminiscence. "No, I don't regret having escaped from all that, do you?"

"We haven't escaped," said Mother, with a trace of humorous sarcasm.

"Well, you have for the time being, haven't you? And how do you get on at the Villa Esperance?" "We get on beautifully despite our lack of servants and furniture. At least *I* do. Margaret suffers a bit. This summer has been rather makeshift. One reason we haven't had you around."

"No, no, that's my fault. But I'm amazed at your lack

of furniture. Surely De Berg must have left *some* of his atrocities?"

"He did, but nothing to sit on. Just a Greek vase and a Spanish chest and so on."

"Yes, I remember both of them. In that room all crawling with paper roses." "Not paper. Plaster. Painted plaster." "Br-rr!" She made a face. "You should have seen it in its glory. Tessières took me there once for dinner. Poor fellow, he was so shocked and ashamed. Apologized to me all the way home for 'exposing' me. You can't imagine the effect then, Aladdin's cave if Aladdin had been German Jewish. Chinese jars and Japanese screens and Spanish chairs and Italian mirrors. It was appallingly gorgeous. The dinner was superb, very elegant, all wrong. People I've never seen since, curiously sinister. A beautiful young man at the other end of the table — in that fearful black dining room — acting as 'hostess.' Beautiful maids too, in some sort of peasant dress. They came out and *danced* for us afterward with the beautiful young man in Spanish costume. It was really so weird. Yet De Berg himself was attractive in a diabolic way, all black and white and red like a playing card, mustache over those lips, eyes, hair, that corpselike complexion à la Dracula. I was intrigued, but of course Tessières would never take me there again. In any case the Baron disappeared. Just vanished, with his young man and Chinese jars. Unless of course they're all buried in the garden somewhere. I wouldn't be surprised. There were all sorts of rumors — murder, either he had murdered his friend or vice versa; and then spies. . . . "

"*Spies!*" I couldn't restrain myself, sitting on the edge of my chair in rapture.

"Oh, yes." She turned on me, delighted with my enthusiasm. "Spies! His family had been German originally, after all, ennobled by the last Napoleon, and everyone suspected him, living like that all through the war. Mysterious guests.

That secluded coastline, a dock; a sort of watchtower, I believe?"

Father couldn't help laughing. "Well, Howie, you may really have something. Howie discovered a secret compartment, you know, with naval plans hidden away inside, French cruisers. It does look suspicious, doesn't it?"

"How wonderful for you! You lucky boy. Did you really just come on it one rainy day? Tell me!" I stumbled out my version of the event, in which Ellie played no part, blushing, hemming and hawing, while Jane looked sadly down at her hands. She would never really forgive me.

"You do have fun there, don't you? I suppose it's a paradise for children. Now what exactly do you do there?" She fixed herself on me. How I wished she'd stop.

"Oh, we play."

"Well, of course. But what sort of play?"

"Oh — we build things. And make up stories." Mother stepped in. "He and Jane have an imaginary country. I forget what it's called. What's its name, Howie?"

"Amuria," I muttered, furious at Mother's betrayal, naked in my shame.

"Amuria, that's it. They act out its history and build cities. It's very bloody with wars and murders and ceremonies. That was an awful ceremony you had the other day. Nan complained to me about it."

I gave her a black look.

"It's a secret of course. I wouldn't have told anyone but you," and she smiled at her hostess.

"I appreciate the compliment, and will respect the confidence, Howie. I wish I could play with you. Oh Lord, how I wish I could." She turned again toward the window, that melancholy farawayness. "What does happen to our instinct for play? Why isn't our writing, our research 'play' any more? I'm sure it is for De Guichy. But not for me. Is it for you?" She looked at Father, serious and searching.

He shook his head. "No," and she looked out the window again, up into the sky growing mellow now. We'd been here an awfully long time. Waiting for stupid Robbie, I suppose.

"No, it's not play. Ought it to be? Or do we have to lose our innocence to be saved? Is it a sort of crime to be happy like De Guichy? The church would certainly say so. At least in his case." There was a long pause while nobody spoke. The westering sun now shone into the depths of the room, picking out crystals and gilding. "I whip myself till the blood comes. No fun at all. Yet when I'm done, what have I got but play for somebody else? Imaginary kingdoms much less exciting than Amuria, I'll be bound. Play for people too bored and stupid to make up their own Amurias."

"Oh, but you must . . . must feel it's worthwhile. That you *have* to do it." Mother was upset to hear someone as famous, as successful, as brilliant as this talk in such a melancholy vein.

"Yes. That's true. I suppose I have to do it. But perhaps it's only a high sort of vanity. Fame is the spur; not just the joy of doing it. I'll admit I'd feel horribly guilty *not* working. But it's work, work, not play. How I'd like to play once more. If I come to visit, will you let me into Amuria, Howie and Jane?"

We all laughed, but she knew perfectly well what a silly request that was! Not even Mother really could share it with us. And then after that, thank goodness, the conversation slipped away from us into a purely grown-up world. What had happened to other people? How could grown-ups go on and on about these "other people" so? Hardly anything really interesting did seem to happen to them. They moved here and there, they got married, they died.

I lost myself in a reverie, looking at the sunlight, now beginning to slant upward, as it glistened in the big low

chandelier. I hoped if I looked long enough into the irides-
cent rosy depth I would hypnotize myself. By moving my
head from side to side I could make the prisms sparkle and
change their iris for me. I suspect my mouth was open.

         v. I was brought to and
confounded by my hostess saying to me, "You're hypnotiz-
ing yourself, aren't you? I believe it really works." She
rang the bell, summoning the neat maid who had passed us
our tea and cake, long-consumed. She spoke to her in
French, and said at large, "This is all very amusing for us
old people, but the younger ones must be dying of boredom." The butler came in now, dark and spry, and, ad-
dressing him as Antoine, she told him to take us to the
tower.

He waved and smirked at us like a conspirator, and we
jumped up, thanking our hostess hastily. This was more
like it, and what I'd really been wanting to do all along.

The way to the tower led up a broad stone circular
stairway from the entrance hall right to the top. We
scrambled up so quickly that we soon left even the wiry
Antoine behind and he had to beg us to wait for him,
gasping and laughing. He only stopped once, flung open a
big door that showed a vaulted passageway. "Les aparte-
ments," he said. There was really nothing to see but doors,
so after a perfunctory glimpse, we went on upward again.

Even we were breathless before we reached the top, a
level platform with a balustrade of ancient crenellations.
What a view! The whole of our country spread out before
us. Jane and I, panting, stood for a moment hand in hand,
enraptured. Antoine came up after us, panting too, and
began to point out various landmarks, in an overloud and
overemphatic way, as though to deaf idiots or a baby. We

moved to the balustrade and, ignoring Antoine, began to point out our own landmarks. He fell silent.

Straight ahead of us, a bit to the left, the peninsula stuck out into the ocean. To one side, eastward, lay the bay and beach of the Maritime, with islands out beyond; larger, inhabited islands. Back of the beach were the salt flats and the plains leading up to the edge of the town right below us — the new city with its straight drab streets, the avenue of palms, the English church, the square with its war memorial, and then climbing up to us, the old town, falling apart with age and ill usage, so clumped together and narrow-alleyed.

In front of us, between here and the peninsula, lay what was more strictly our own country, the piny ridge crossed by the road to town, the just barely visible roof of the Côte d'Or, the brown pseudo-battlements of the spy villa in its pines, and very conspicuous on its point, our church, Notre Dame de la Garde, a little sharp gray-white thing from here. Our villa itself was hidden behind it. Out beyond stretched the blueness of our bay, with our little rocky islets, no longer on the horizon which lay further out all around us in late afternoon deepnesses. Far off westward were distant capes and coasts.

Everything was at its most beautiful, that magical hour of transformation. Sure enough, the wind came up back of us, the sea was darkened with it, the world glowed. Antoine was silent, thank goodness. We leaned over the edge of the battlements to look straight down the high wall and its supporting cliff. We could see a black beetle of a car coming up the road to the castle, and pointed to it.

When Antoine saw it he straightened up with an exclamation. He must go down, he told us rapidly, and we were not to leave until he came back for us. "Soyez sage," he said and popped down the stairs. We were delighted to be left alone. We went together to look out the back way. There were the jumbled roofs of the castle itself. Not much of the old castle was still usable. Ruins stretched northward with broken vaults and empty windows. Then a ragged town wall undulated along the spine of the ridge to towers, and eventually enclosed the whole back of the city in a forlorn protection. Still further were the foothills of the barren mountains, the mysterious inland country where we'd never been.

Only too soon Antoine came back up and, twitching his head, jerking his hands, forced us down into the house. We were awfully sorry to leave, taking a last turn around despite his hisses and frowns. When we got to the *salon* once more, Robbie was there. The black car must have brought him. It was Mr. Cuthbert, "Mr. Custard" himself, it seemed who had insisted on coming. Robbie had had to wait till the party was over, and that was why he was so late.

The grown-ups were making fun of the departed Cuthbert as we came in. "He'd never miss a chance to visit the castle," the lady was saying. "I represent the 'great house' for him, even though it's only a French house and I'm only an American. Still, one must make do. He's in heaven here, drinking his sherry, dropping his quotations." "Both Latin *and* Greek, I noticed," said Father.

"Odd how different from the De Guichy quotations. Cuthbert's are for show, De Guichy really means them. How does your boy here respond to the advantages of a classical education?" This of course was Robbie, sitting big and embarrassed on a too small chair in his too small trousers.

"He certainly hasn't reached the quoting stage," said Father. "But we really must go." Both Mother and Father rose and we all rose. The hostess slowly got up on her cane, with a ruffling of lace and many smiles. We came up and made our obeisances. She had a word for each of us. To me she said, "If you find any more evidence of spies, be sure to let me know!" I was pleased; but of course she didn't mean it any more than she meant it about coming to play Amuria with us.

She held Robbie's hand longest, and looked at him rather quizzically, her smile a bit withdrawn. "The unfairness of youth," she finally said, more to the parents than to him. "To make us feel so old. It's worse than a mirror. We can fool ourselves at a mirror. But not face to face with this . . . this full bloom." Robbie didn't know what to say. As he withdrew, she added, "Congratulations on your children. I wish I could see the rest of them." "Oh, you will," said Mother. "We'll have you at the Villa Esperance very soon," and we trooped out, led by Antoine.

PART THREE

i. It was the afternoon of the picnic, the trip to the island to see the eclipse and its double exposure of the *rayon vert.* Of all our expeditions — Malhaut, gala evenings at the Maritime, trips to town — this was by far the most exciting to me. As a member of the Astronomical Society I had of course to profess interest in the *rayon,* and preserve a knowing attitude; but it was getting to those islands that thrilled me. The far Japanese little silhouettes out there had fascinated me from the first. It had never occurred to me that we'd actually be able to go there, set foot on one of them, though in fantasy I'd done it many times, with remarkable results. But now we were *really* going.

Everybody was invited. All our family of course, even Mademoiselle and Ronnie. Only Celestine, overcome by an obscure Breton prejudice against setting foot in a Provençal boat, insisted on staying home with Lagarde to protect the villa. Dick came, naturally, and the three Websters; all three De Guichys. What with food and drink for everybody, it was a "formidable problem in logistics," as De Guichy observed Napoleonically. After a great deal of arranging, Father had finally found us a big enough fishing boat. Celestine, Mademoiselle and Mother had created the supper. The afternoon was half done, full as it was of disturbances, ducks and chickens on the part of womenfolk, and crises of emotion. Now, finally, just as the light began to lengthen, we were off.

The fishing boat was too big to come right into our dock. Groups of us had to be ferried out in a dinghy rowed by one of the saturnine fishermen. There were three of them, dark, dirty-looking, humorous persons of indeterminate age. One of them, the oldest, the actual owner and captain of the boat, wore a patch over his right eye, which certainly lent a wonderfully illegal air to the whole transaction. I immediately invested the three with charms of piracy, and was dying to ask them leading questions; but of course I was too shy.

The grown-ups went first, Mother, Jocelyn, Father, Mademoiselle and Ronnie. Then Dick and the rest of us in several boatloads. We were all rather subdued. Our ferryman said nothing, our piratical captain said nothing. There was, for some reason and just this day, no wind; most annoying, because we'd hoped so to be able to actually sail out there. The intense calm, the pale sleekness of the water, the creak of oars in oarlocks as the dinghy went to and fro, all made us silent; as though we were really smugglers, or escaping refugees. Jocelyn whispered loudly to Dick, "What's the matter with us all?" Dick whispered back, equally mock mysterious, "Crossing the Styx!"

Once we were all aboard, and the dinghy was tied

behind us to follow at the end of a long rope, the engine started up, fortunately a quiet one. We drew put-putting out from the shade of the cliffs, leaving a smooth swirling wake. We settled in various places, not without a good deal of restless experimentation at first, jostling, looking down into the smelly cabin (ugh, fish!), quarreling for the best places.

As we moved away, landmarks began to come up on the shore, and we grew more and more animated and noisy pointing them out to one another. Our shadowed quietness wore off. There were the cliffs of course; the dock, the brown round watchtower with its crenellations, the streak of the sliding place (I was so glad we'd never gone back to *that* again), the trees and the villa itself. The girls insisted on showing us just where their room was, as though we didn't know, up there in the corner of the third story. Below were the second-story windows of the parents' rooms and then the high roof of the balcony. The lower part of the house was hidden at first by trees, but emerged a bit as we moved out to sea. Up the coast to the right, eastward, we could see the big grotesque ex-hotel building of the orphanage; our mysterious neighbor. Over the pine woods, on the crest of the hill, perked up the white steeple of Notre Dame, just as conspicuous as it had been when viewed from the castle. And down there, as we went still further out, lay the bright speck of the Webster villa on its rocks. Everyone was terribly excited to see that.

ii. I had a wonderful panorama, not only of the shore, but of our boatload. Father and Nan were right below me. My legs dangled between them and all I could see of them were the tops of their heads. Nan, on the outside, kept complaining of my sneakers in her face. Across the curved covering of the hatchway that led into the dark cabin (one of the fisher-men stayed down there in the smelly dinginess, steer-ing the boat through glass portholes) sat Jane, her legs dangling too, with Mother and Ronnie below her. He kept untying her laces and she kept pinching his neck. Beyond Nan, on my side, ranged on boxes and improvised seats, were the De Guichy family, whining little Pierre, *le pauvre* Pepi, Madame with her hair blowing loose, M. de Guichy talking excitedly across Miranda Webster to the captain lounged in the stern. The captain smiled sardonically under his eye patch, and he, De Guichy and Dick talked know-ingly, to Miranda's rapt admiration; but I couldn't hear them. The third sailor lay alone up on the bow.

On the other side of the boat, from Dick to Made-moiselle (protectively next to Ronnie) were the rest of us: Robbie squeezed in between Dick and Richie, Jocelyn next, and on the floor at their feet Pam and Ellie. That whole side of the boat somehow gave the effect of being posed for an old-fashioned photo, deliberately informal.

They seemed to make a circle of youth and *le sport* separated from the rest of us, exclusive. Dick was dressed in the sailor costume he'd worn on arrival, the striped jersey, the white trousers, and Robbie, as he so often seemed to want to do now, imitated him as closely as possible. They were jammed in against each other, twinlike in sunburned athleticism. Pam, equally ruddy and crisp, sat leaning against Robbie's legs, and there was a great deal of tickling and punching and laughing going on between them. It was understood pretty generally these days that Pam was "Robbie's girl." Teasing took place along those lines, and both Pam and Robbie were pleasantly embarrassed by it all. The parallel pairing of Richie and Miranda had been broken up ever since the New Order, Robbie's work at the Websters', and so forth. Richie, so sallow and lanky next to Robbie's hemmed-in effulgence, sat wistfully excluded from the three others; but Jocelyn at his side and Ellie at his feet seemed bent on flattering him and coaxing him into good humor. He would listen in on the rather rough play and laughter of Robbie and Pam; then Jocelyn would speak to him, or Ellie, and he'd turn around reluctantly to them. Jocelyn was dressed in a blue costume of what would have then been called "beach pajamas," comfortable perhaps but not becoming to her plumpness. However, her hair curled and sparkled in the breeze of our motion, her eyes sparkled too, and she kept both lean Richie and stocky brown Ellie, lying with her face upturned back toward them, adequately amused.

I saw them suddenly, as by a trick of the eyesight, quite newly: strangers, people in an advertisement. They made a tableau of the "out of doors" — the casual poses, the clean sunburned arms and faces, the scanty bright clothes, the teeth and eyes in an occasional brilliance, the short hair, all colors: Dick's cinnamon, Robbie's glowing auburn, Pam's mop of gold, Richie's stringy black, Ellie's thick straight bob of dark brown, Jocelyn's jetty bobbing curls. I couldn't have known, being too young, what the group represented in the way of style, the emancipation of the twenties from cloth and starch and furbelows, conventions and parasols, which would have helped to conceal them even ten years earlier. But I was quite aware of their being "modern," of us as representing a certain kind of unostentatious chic; and I was consciously proud of the good looks and health of all, into which even the discordancy of Richie's homeliness blended without noticeable bad effect.

I saw them too, as though for the first time, as affections, relationships, personal discords. Dick was talking to the captain, paying no attention to the others; but his physical closeness, his big right arm back of Robbie, Robbie's imitation costume all indicated the teacher-pupil sort of relationship between them, Dick's earnest protectiveness and Robbie's returned hero worship. This was serious as opposed to the coltish play, half companionship, half flirtation going on between Robbie and Pam. The parents and Jocelyn I knew made jokes about this. Even now I saw Mother and Jocelyn catch each other's eyes and smile.

Then there was Richie, never leaner or hungrier than now when he was so shut off from Robbie, both by Dick and Pam. Without intention, jammed together as they all were, a distinct social cleavage split the group. Ellie paid no attention to Pam. She concentrated on Richie and Jocelyn; and both in turn seemed to want to coddle and protect Richie from what they knew was bitter isolation. He was at once grateful and restive, longing to be back as Robbie's henchman, as part of the valiant quartet with the Webster girls.

I was happy to be aloof and observing, kicking my rubber heels against the wooden bulkhead, occasionally grazing Nan's ear. I had nothing to do with all that complex, now that Jane was restored to me. My world — Jane, the parents, the De Guichys — was safe from upset. Let Jocelyn and Dick be cool to each other now as they had once been warm; let Ellie take over the burden of Richie's intense secrets and changes of mood. Not me. I already began to think of what would come next, in Amuria. Tomorrow after lunch I'd get Jane down again to our cellar. . . .

De Guichy was giving an oration, a scientific explanation to the grown-ups on the subject of wind. The customary evening offshore wind still was not blowing. On the one day required, it had failed us. M. de Guichy couldn't tell us why, but he could and did tell us about the wind itself. It was, according to him, peculiar to just this part of the coastline. It even had an odd Provençal local name, and was caused by a complication of geography, the lay of mountains, valleys, Mediterranean currents and promontories which channeled breezes from other parts of the coast through the hills and out again over our bay. This had all sorts of economic aftereffects. This part of the shoreline for instance had never become a favorite as a summer resort, like Nice and Cannes, mostly on account of the hot dryness of its afternoons. Agriculture too responded. Some things grew and some things didn't.

What, he asked our captain, was the effect on fishing? Ah, good, thought the captain. Good for those that went out at night, since one could count on an offshore wind. Usually. Every night but tonight, for example, sacred blue, etc.

Dick and M. de Guichy quizzed the captain on his profession. Did he come out toward these islands often? What was on the islands, if anything? Some islands it seemed were military. No one was allowed on those, they were guarded with wire fences. Others were depots for the fishermen; little rough docks, anchorages, places to keep gear. They had other uses too, a-ha! The captain, smirking and reluctant, told about smuggling. Right here under the noses of the Navy. It didn't take much to imagine that the patch-eye and the slight embarrassment meant that our captain was as active in this as any. He told some stories, but I had a hard time following his guttural patois and seafaring colloquialisms.

I got up courage enough to shout (I had to shout because otherwise I'd be ignored), "What about *spies?*" Everyone laughed at me; it was known to be my obsession these days. The captain had to be asked again, but only grinned and shrugged. That was the war. He'd been in service and away.

Richie broke in, "Ask Uncle Dick; *he* knows." Dick looked at him with friendly surprise. "Why should *I* know?" "Well, you're a spy. I mean you *were* a spy, weren't you?" "Not around here." Miranda, leaning forward in tense excitement, cried to him, "Oh, do tell us about it! Was it exciting?" Dick, as usual when this subject came up, drew back into aloof amused reserve. "Not very. Dangerous but drab." "But you must have had *some* adventures." "Nothing I can talk about. Don't believe all you read about spying." Jocelyn broke in, "That's enough, Miranda. The subject is taboo." "Oh dear," and she subsided.

"Poor Howie," said Nan from beneath me, and everyone put in their bit. I was disappointed but of course rather flattered by the universal attention. Conversation split up and drifted away from spying.

And then the breezes suddenly sprung up at last. The big orange-red sail creaked and filled, the boat took a slight extra lurch forward. The children all begged the captain to turn off the motor, and it was turned off. The rest of the way we drifted wind-driven.

The bay came alive, darkening as it ought. The light too performed, always now a bit earlier, its mellowing benedictions. The half-dozen islands were ahead or abreast of us, the mainland extended astern with glowing mountains and blue headlands and miniature shore landmarks. We could see a little car going along the road that led by the public beach, where tiny white objects indicated evening bathers.

Now my whole interest was in the islands. I turned around forward so I could see them — humps of black rock, quite sizable really, but without any visible signs of human use. The usual sentinel destroyer paced by, further out beyond than I'd have thought. Soon we were landing, again ferried across in the dinghy, jumping precariously on the rocks from the wobbling boat, and immediately running in all directions. Actually there was little to discover: irregularities of stone, culminating in a sort of flat lookout some dozen feet high; several tiny beaches, only one of which, looking westward, was really in any way usable; a miniature cave, into which Jane and I crawled; many rock pools, much in the way of seaweed and sea urchins and mussels and barnacles. It kept us all busy enough, while the stodgy grown-ups settled for the afternoon near or on the biggest beach under large umbrellas tipped sideways against the sun.

iii. As soon as we got ashore we stripped to our bathing suits, worn underneath, and all our various games and investigations were punctuated by dips. The rout of older children found a perfect shelf for diving into deep water; and so endless repetitions of back flips and handstands were attempted or accomplished. Jane and I had other plans. We made a city of sand from one of the tinier beaches, up along a two-foot cliff, out around a two-foot lake. The sun was low enough not to burn us, the water was delicious.

As the afternoon wore on toward evening, we became more boisterous and fidgety. Our island was too small. Richie and Robbie wanted to swim off to a neighboring rock. They were stopped. They sulked; then that group was broken up by Dick's taking Robbie off and up to the flat high point. There they were to practice an acrobatic act they proposed to give as supper entertainment. We were to eat early, forestalling eclipse and sunset, so that we could take off for home immediately afterward, before dark fell.

Jane and I grew tired of our city and arranged a cataclysm. A flood, carried leaky in our hands, gradually swept everything away. When Father hurt his foot, coming up from his leisurely swim off the biggest beach, it was a welcome distraction. He'd stepped on a sharp sea-thing, an urchin perhaps, going over the rocks to fetch a towel. We all gathered about to watch as Jocelyn nursed him in her semi-professional fashion. The cut was painful, we had no real dressing, a strip of something had to do. The rest of the day Father hobbled about with a driftwood cane. Even the acrobats stopped momentarily to see what had happened to him.

Soon we were put to work setting up for supper; lots of rugs and various baskets. This was no sandwich affair. We had come with cold meats and a salad and wine and pastries. We salivated, though some of this, the wine, the aspic, was out of our gastronomic range.

There were two groups of us, when we finally settled down; although there was never a time when some weren't up and about. The four girls sat here next to me, playing a noisy game of cards. Dick, Father and Jocelyn lined up across the picnic spread; Mother and Jane sat with their backs to the sea. Over on the beach, behind Dick and Father, we had a predominantly French-speaking group of De Guichys and Mademoiselle. It would be hard to say where Richie and Robbie belonged, as they were never in one place for more than a few minutes at a time. Father, made cross by his foot wound, barked at them to stay still; but it did no good.

We were all edgy, and ate indiscriminately and ravenously. We were allowed a little wine, and Richie in particular, as usual when the opportunity came, took too much. The girls made a fearful thing out of their card game, alternating between shrill disputes and equally shrill giggling. I could see that the parents in particular were getting exasperated.

Dick however seemed calm and even jubilant, full of jokes and tricks. He was in a sweaty glow from his acrobatic session with Robbie, and sat more or less naked in his scanty swim trunks, his body almost black now with summer sunburn. "Why don't we just live on this island?" he said, toasting it generally with an uplifted wineglass (we had *glasses* on this trip!).

"Oh jolly!" said Jocelyn, but obviously sarcastic. "Like *The Tempest.*"

"Like *The Tempest.*" He now toasted Father, sprawled in his dirty duck trousers. "Here's our Prospero. He'll need a change of costume of course; and we already have our Miranda." "And lots of sailors. Plenty of young people for the other parts."

"But where's Caliban and Ariel?" said Jocelyn. Dick frowned questioningly, with lips tightened, over at Richie, and Jocelyn, frowning too, leaned over and hit him sharply on the bare knee with her knuckles.

"No, I'm afraid we don't really have a Caliban; or an Ariel," she said. "Too bad. We'll have to give up the thought."

Dick turned away from Richie, who was leaning oblivious over Miranda's shoulder as she played cards, and said to Jocelyn, rather as though he meant more than he said, "We can't have a *Tempest* without a Caliban, can we? He's really the whole show."

"It's curious how we all secretly love him, don't we? Shakespeare certainly couldn't have intended that." Father wanted to keep things on a general plane, out of whatever obscure personalities Dick and Jocelyn had in mind.

"Calibanism," said Dick. "The curse of the modern world. The underdog is *always* right, no matter how ugly and how vicious." "Absolutely," said Jocelyn, "I'm *always* for the loser. Ever since my brothers made me read G. H. Henty. How I hated those dreadful bloody heroes! As for me, I take the wrong side every time, the criminal, the murderer in the detective story, the enemy spy. . . . "

"Cathars, Quakers," said Dick maliciously. "What I mostly object to is the glorification of ugliness. I'm with

196

Shakespeare; all on the side of beauty, and ugliness gets what it deserves."

Jocelyn looked at him a minute, and spoke coldly. "How hateful. How arrogant. How conceited. Serve you right if you got your pretty face mucked up, says I. Give me Caliban any day!"

"There's such a short step from pitying the criminal to loving the crime," continued Father, doggedly impersonal, as though he'd noticed none of this byplay; he probably hadn't. "And that's where we seem headed now. . . . " At which point a great raucous cry of triumph went up from Nan and Pam, and screams of outrage from the other two. It was impossible for anyone else to go on talking. Richie stood up, then squatted again. Robbie came back from wherever he was, Mother called to them all to be quiet, Father raised his eyebrows and sighed, "Not an atmosphere conducive to discussion on a higher plane."

"Shut up, you silly people," said Dick; but he was so amiable the girls just laughed at him. "A little music," he said, and got up. "That'll soothe 'em." He went off and returned with his guitar, which he'd hidden from us among the rocks. He was desperately secretive about his instrument, justly afraid we'd get our hands on it and ruin it.

iv. He settled down in our midst again. This time Robbie was by him, wide-eyed as usual with admiration, now for his musical virtuosity. He really was very good. He began one of his spectacular Spanish flamenco displays, with interjections of "Olé," and the girls began to clap. Then Nan and Ellie got up and started dancing about, pretending to castanets and combs.

They did a version of their bandit dance from our defunct opera. We were done eating now, and Nan pulled up one of the tablecloths (we had real tablecloths too) and wrapped it about her bathing suit. Mother threw Ellie a shawl. The dancers took over the middle of our circle, and really performed quite nicely, despite a few uncouth bumpings and stumblings. Dick's guitar rang and banged and everyone clapped and shouted. The De Guichys came over to look.

Our boat had appeared again, after being off on its own errands, and now the boatmen gathered too and guffawed sarcastically but amiably. With the three of them added to the group, the captain with his eye patch and all, the girls being so gypsy, we really did begin to look like brigands.

"*Carmen*, not *The Tempest!*" said Jocelyn. "That's more our line!" Dick threw back his head and sang fiercely and nasally till finally the girls had to stop in sheer exhaustion. Everyone clapped and cheered and it had been a great success. Dick continued on his guitar, moody and melancholy now. The Webster girls started playing cards again, Nan and Ellie rejoined them; Mother chatted quietly, till Jocelyn called over to Dick, "Oh, it is too bad we can't have a campfire. Smugglers all!"

Dick, still plucking moodily at the guitar, said, "You're not far wrong you know," and tossed his head toward the sailors, who were drifting off again toward the boat, now that the dancing was done.

"Aren't they delightfully low?" Jocelyn looked after them with admiration. "Calibanism," said Dick. "Oh yes! I *do* love the low," and Jocelyn turned to Richie, "Don't you, Richie?"

Richie, taken by surprise, was now sitting by himself, back to back with card-playing Miranda, brooding, glowering, neglected, perhaps a bit affected by his wine. "Don't I what?" he said. Jocelyn smiled at him, indulgent as always, "Don't you like the low life; smugglers and such?" "No, I don't," he said with surprising passion, as though coming out of his thoughts, but still involved with

198

them. He leaned over, and looking right at Dick, sitting with his guitar not six feet away, snarled, "Dirty low double-crossing skunks, skulking around and hiding things! I hate them! They ought to be arrested and shot!" "Good gracious, child, *who?* The poor fishermen? For doing what?" Richie sneered, but lowered his head. "*I* know who, and *what* too!" And he gave Dick another malevolent look. "Spies!" he spat out, in a hoarse whisper, then jumped up awkwardly and scrambled off like a lanky crab toward the other side of the rocks.

"Heavens," said Mother; and "Good Lord, what was that about?" from Father; all the grown-ups were amazed. I lowered my eyes, hoping someone might notice me and my effect of guilty knowledge. Of course nobody did. Dick, who'd been staring at Richie open-mouthed, snapped his teeth together and gave a savage snort. "The rewards of Calibanism," he said nastily to Jocelyn. "That's what you get for patronizing the criminal classes." He stood up without waiting for a rebuttal, and started putting away his guitar. Jocelyn was so hurt and mystified she hadn't a word to say. Dick looked at his watch. "We've got about fifteen minutes, right?" He called over to De Guichy; then, "Okay, Robbie; we're on!"

Robbie sprang to attention up top of the rocky platform and grinned. He shook his hands over his head in a prizefighter gesture. "La-dies and gen-e-num," called out Dick. "The breathless, the daring, the never-before-attempted feats of legerdemain and upholstery as practiced by the Carruthers Brothers will now be presented for your *dee*-light and edification!"

Everybody's attention swung round on him; laughter and applause. He finished snapping his guitar into its case and clambered up on the rocks alongside Robbie. He went on declaiming in his circus style; then he and Robbie bowed right and left with arms out, exaggeratedly.

They did indeed look just like brothers; a pair, an "act." Dick's trunks were blue, Robbie's red, French, unrespectable, very short and tight and woolen, horizontally white-striped, trunks that no decent American gentleman would ever wear, and Robbie had certainly never worn before. Had Father permitted this, or had Robbie just gotten them from Dick anyway? We all disapproved. The resemblance went much further than that. Seeing them both up there together, the actual similarities were obvious too. Robbie a softer, more boyish and just slightly smaller, but still accurate replica of his uncle's muscular perfection and deep sleek tan.

They then performed silently, earnestly, expertly, without too much grunting, wobbling or teetering; a sort of slow dance of heaving and balancing, with a few "hups" and springs in it. Robbie stood, jittering, on Dick's shoulders, no hands; or Dick, on his back, lifted handstanding Robbie on his own hands.

As a climax, Dick ended up with Robbie horizontal and stiff as a brown board, while Dick, standing, held him up above his head, one palm flat to his rigid body. They both teetered and grunted, Dick showed his white teeth in effort, and Mother was quite perturbed. Then Dick brought up his other hand and grasped Robbie about his bare waist. Robbie doubled his legs forward and slid down over Dick's left shoulder to the ground. They stopped and bowed low, once southward, once northward. Robbie crossed in front of Dick, and on the other side of him bowed and bowed again. We were all clapping and shouting. Even Richie, who had at first refused to bother, had found himself drawn in, and now added his shrill vulgar whistle of approval to the acclaim.

Having nothing better to do, all of us children kept clapping on and on, more restless than ever. During the act we'd been busy stowing away the picnic gear; a disconcerting audience no doubt, black bustling shadows below that platform with its two bright bodies. Now we were done, and we scrambled about in the increasing effulgence, at nervous loose ends.

At this moment De Guichy brought everyone to attention, pointing toward the sun, swollen and red and not far above the level of the water. The eclipse had begun! Sure enough, a small dark dent appeared in one edge of the disc. Haze and the obstruction of evening and sea air had dimmed the sun so that we had no trouble in looking straight at it. We all turned our faces westward.

Up on their stage Robbie and Dick were caught, frozen like everyone else in the excitement. They stood side by side, still glistening and panting from their acrobatics, with their arms about each other's waists. The rosy light transfigured them standing against the still violent but darkening blueness of sky. Both their profiles were turned together toward the eclipse, both had the same half smile, expectant and surprised, and the extraordinary resemblance of uncle and nephew stood out, not only of coinlike profiles, but of poised glowing bodies. It was impossible not to see them as classical visitants, a heavenly pair who had just tripped wing-footed over the water and were now manifested to us up on their altar.

But no one had time for them. We rushed to get a view of the odd and somewhat sinister effect, as the eclipse progressed with rather frightening speed. Those of us who were scientists and intent on getting in on the *rayon vert* hurried to the little beach, where De Guichy lined us up, with much French haste and confusion, his fuzzy hair a bush of command and electricity.

Not everyone was involved. Father of course couldn't stand about. Mother and Jocelyn kept him company. Dick and Robbie stayed up on their rock, though no longer locked in their statuesque pose. The members of the Astronomical Society, that is De Guichy and myself, naturally had the best positions in mid-beach; but all the girls noisily and unnecessarily flocked down on us.

"Attention!" shouted M. de Guichy. We waited breathless. The sun was now a broad crescent; one cusp was about to go under the horizon, thus giving us the first of two *rayons*. At a bark from De Guichy we all squatted, just as the sun crossed the line. I saw nothing. Others claimed they had. The grown-ups, Jocelyn in particular, laughed and laughed at us. Mademoiselle and Ronnie joined in, but too late, and Ronnie, thinking this was setting-up exercises, kept bobbing up and down, up and down.

It seemed an interminable wait before the next dip. The eclipse continued, so that I was afraid the whole sun might be gone, too soon. But at last, majestically, silently, the sun lowered and lowered and a final topmost point, another moonlike cusp, touched the sea. Again, "Attention!" and again, "Baissez-vous!" and down we went. This time I *did* see it! A sudden vivid point of green light at the water's edge. Everyone saw it! Everyone was thrilled! We stood there congratulating each other and ourselves. A mysterious darkness dimmed the sunset as the eclipse came to its full.

It was time to leave. We were again hustled and bustled by De Guichy to take up our picnic gear and start for the boat. The parents made us put on clothes over our damp suits, though the calm evening was as warm as daytime. With a maximum of mix-up and exclamation we trailed boatward, Father hobbling on a stick like an old king, the rest of us lugging our burdens. By the time we'd all been ferried over to the boat, it was definitely twilight, though the eclipse was over. Farewell to our island. The girls threw kisses at it, the three sailors were doubled up with mirth watching them. By now the girls and sailors seemed to have established rapport, Lord knows how, and much badinage went on between them.

Again there was no wind, so again we put-putted over the white water, back home under the powdery pink sky. Dick got out his guitar once more, and we all sang sentimentally. The effect this time was not Spanish, but Italian; a barcarolle. Happily over the sunset wave to Neapolitan harmonies were we wafted, as the increasingly dark shore came up toward us, the inland mountains still beautifully and deeply reddened. Our island rocks faded away behind us into their familiar jagged silhouettes.

"Santa Lucia" we sang, and "Funiculì, Funiculà" and it got duskier and duskier. At last we were inshore, close to our dock, under the shade of our cliffs and pines. The motor stopped. We were in sudden stillness, as we had been starting out. Everything was obscure in the early night. A star broke out over the water where our horned sun had gone down.

We were helped into the dinghy, oldsters first. Jocelyn, sitting on board just as she was about to shove off, shivered, looking at the black path going up from the dock to the garden. She clasped her arms about her. "It frightens me," she said. "So dark." Dick, next to her, whispered something, mock solemn, and she threw back her head laughing. Off they went. Our turn came soon. Father and Jocelyn had walked slowly on ahead, disappearing up into the gloom. The girls stood on the dock and waved and called at the sailors as the boat started back out onto the hushed opalescent bay. Jane and I turned up toward the house, unconsciously taking each other's hands for security.

6.

i. It was as though we had graduated, and the picnic had been a ceremony, a celebration. All of Father's rainy day schemes and dispositions collapsed. Our artificial realignments, Ellie with Jane, Richie with me, dissolved like treaties of expedience between essentially rival nations. Sewing stopped, digging in the garage yard stopped, Robbie no longer went bicycling off to the Websters'.

Like figures in a square dance we all returned to our proper places and partners. It was a great relief. Nan and Ellie for instance, estranged for the past weeks, suddenly took up again their life of confidences and emotional wallowings. Once more they wasted good hours of the day gabbling up in their room. They started their opera again too; but nobody paid any attention to them, so they went along on their own, making up characters and costumes, practicing arias and dances, just the two of them.

Ellie, true enough, did keep on sewing in a desultory way, just as Richie dug about a bit in Celestine's garden. But most of Richie's time was once more absorbed by life in quartet, with Robbie and the Webster girls. Once again the four of them roamed the garden thinking of desperate projects, laughing and screeching and bullying others when they could. They had a new toy, a camera. It was Pam's, given her on a birthday just after the picnic. Their activities centered much around this object, and they were forever posing and snapping each other in front of things, and forcing everyone else to pose with them. They were all four as much of a nuisance as ever.

There was one great exception however to the return to status quo. Richie and Robbie as a pair did not combine easily. This was really Richie's fault. Robbie, released from work at the Websters', spent most of his time now at Villa Esperance. He would persuade Richie into projects, the usual bicycle trips, the usual diving practices; but if Dick came along, either Richie would skulk away, or Robbie would drop him and go off. The antagonism between Richie and Dick was now open and flagrant. Dick simply ignored Richie; Richie hung about sneering and snarling at Dick. Robbie was much distressed.

As for Uncle Dick himself, he seemed to be deliberately avoiding all of us, as much as he could, and concentrating on the parents. As though he felt he'd been too much away from her, he now spent hours with Mother. They talked of old times, Dick drove the parents on almost daily tours of the country; and almost every day there would be guests for tea or drinks on the balcony. Each time it would be at least the parents, Dick and Jocelyn as a foursome; frequently the De Guichys or Tessières. Once our lady from the castle. We were not included.

The exception to all this — Dick's new aloofness, Robbie's return to child-life — was a sort of tutoring program, quite routine and formal, of Robbie by Dick. He was, it seems, brushing him up on his English literature in preparation for a return to school; and diving lessons were not neglected either. So frequently Dick would appear to snatch Robbie from whatever he was doing. The Webster girls would complain, Richie would curse and jerk about. Off would go Robbie, down to the dock, over to the garage, off to the Websters' where there was a really good secluded diving rock, high above safely deep water.

As far as I was concerned, what counted was the revival of our cellar life, Jane and I after lunch down there reconstructing Amuria. It seemed all the more exciting and vivid to us after our absence. We were full of zest, and went busily to work rebuilding our cities and replotting our histories.

Bad, exciting days were ahead. Things were *not* going to flourish under wicked Agragor. As usual, we made it all up piecemeal — a building project of blocks one day, an acted-out scene or ceremony the next. Essentially we saw and felt it as a movie; the kind of wide-screen, technicolor pseudo-epic talkie which had not yet been actually invented, but which we already had in our mind's eye. We were not, for instance, really thinking of things in terms of live theater — of stage and audience and lighting. Nor in truly literary terms — words and pages and writing things down. If we could, we would have realized it all cinematically, with ourselves as at once directors, actors and audience. We were very much *in* the picture, not just managing it. We were Agragor and Nu Wa and Wa Fung and Chin Lee; yet we also created them as we went along.

The story began with the long-frustrated love affair of Agragor and Nu Wa. Now that he was, thanks largely to the wiles of Wa Fung, Emperor of Amuria, he was determined to make Nu Wa his Empress. Wa Fung determined otherwise. He felt it was vital to forge links with Korea. Nu Wa was a visitor in the palace in preparation for the official engagement and wedding; but Wa Fung did everything he could to put it off and break it up. Necromancers had to pick just the right day for the wedding; Wa Fung saw to it that they picked a date far off in the future. He also hired a wicked slinky slave girl, Lilipopo. She was seen creeping in and out of Agragor's chambers, frequently by Nu Wa herself. Rumors were circulated by Wa Fung that Agragor was really tired of Nu Wa, and only interested in

Lilipopo. Nu Wa began to believe them. Why was the wedding being put off? Little insults and annoyances were arranged for Nu Wa by Wa Fung, etc., etc.

Jane and I had a fight over the name Lilipopo. I said it was silly. Jane insisted on keeping the name; largely because it *was* silly. Though she enjoyed playing the role (based largely on Sally Lung, the Eurasian leper mistress of the villain in the old De Mille *Ten Commandments*), she rather despised Lili, and the name reflected her feelings. Lilipopo it was.

Wa Fung wanted to marry Agragor off to Chin Lee, to make sure of Korea. He didn't care much about Nu Wa and her barbarian hordes. Finally, a big scene: Nu Wa confronts Agragor with her suspicions. They both being very bad-tempered people, a most awful fight takes place. Nu Wa leaps on her horse and dashes off to her own country, followed by her yelling tribesmen. Agragor, heartbroken, writes a long sobbing letter to her, begging her to come back; but Wa Fung intercepts it, and substitutes a forged note, very cold, cutting her off.

From then on Nu Wa devotes herself to Revenge.

At this point we decided to change the script a bit by fabricating a new character. It seems (we decided) that Liu the Handsome and Wa Nee Ta had had a son, also named Liu, born just a few days before their mutual deaths (the inconveniences of pregnancy during that troubled period were ignored). The boy's parents, fearing for his life, had smuggled him off to a remote mountain fastness, in charge of Liu's most devoted captain. There this son was reared in secrecy.

Meanwhile, frustrated in his love for Nu Wa, furious at the letter from her saying she will never forgive him, Agragor gives up. He obeys Wa Fung, marries Chin Lee, making no pretense at even being nice to her, and takes up with Lilipopo for real and for good. Wa Fung very happy.

ii. We were up in front of the house scraping gravel. A new order here; no longer colonial enterprises of the Amurians, but new and important battle camps of the Wa Hus. Nu Wa was biding her time, training a fierce army to invade Amuria and get hold of Agragor and torture him to death, gr-r-r.

The battle camps were round bare spaces surrounded by low circular walls with little watchtowers, and connected one to another by secret narrow trails. Inside, nothing but the usual felt tents (eucalyptus nuts) and a rude temple or two. It was fun making the winding trails and building the tiny towns and temples of white slippery pebbles.

Along came the quartet, up the path from their nether region. "Come and get took," shouted Pam. So rather unwilling to be disturbed, we left our play and went up to the front of the house with them and their camera. Actually it was fun. Each one of us was allowed to take one picture of all the rest of us. We clumped together and forced ourselves into every silly pose we could think of, tongues out, arms at strange angles with clutching fingers. The camera was a big black box of a Kodak. I was scared of it, and made more nervous by all the shouted instructions as I took my turn. Nan and Ellie came running down from their room when they saw what was afoot, and they too had to take and be taken. We got very hilarious, trying to think of still more extravagant nonsense. I was afraid my shaking hands would ruin my picture; but actually they all turned out approximately the same. No one was really recognizable. Only the immutable façade of the villa itself, fussy with steps and curved railings, came out looking like itself.

Dick drove up just then, and was greeted by an effusive chorus. "What's going on?" he said, and so of course he had to join in. "What a pity we didn't have it along on the picnic," said someone, and that started us all off on the thought of another picnic; just so we could take pictures of it, presumably. Dick made a reality of the plans. "Why not? Let's hire the boat again, and really go sailing this time. Sailing and fishing." This was a most successful thought and we all babbled about it. All except Richie, who was noticeably unenthusiastic. Dick would ask the parents and Jocelyn, Dick would make the arrangements.

Then he spoke to Rob and they were off to the Websters' for diving. Should Pam and Miranda go with them? They couldn't make up their minds. Did their mother really want them at home yet or not? Then Nan and Ellie had to go too, crowding in with chatter and laughter; and we were suddenly left behind with poor Richie, who hadn't been asked and wasn't going to go if asked anyway.

He was utterly crushed; almost crying. So sad he couldn't even be angry. Jane and I turned away from the iron bars of the fence and gate to go back to Amuria. Richie followed forlornly. We let him squat down and help us move pebbles about. He began to get interested, and bossy. He wanted grand engineering projects. We told him that wasn't the idea. Then at last he did get angry, and messing up one or two of our camps with his big feet, he stormed off aimlessly down the path into the garden. What would he do? We were sorry enough for him, for a few minutes. But then Nu Wa and her camps were so much more interesting.

The plans for Dick's sailing expedition progressed. More and more we felt we must use every day. Summer was ending. A somewhat desperate quality went into our enjoyment of each hour. The weather was more and more brilliant. As a result, we tended to overdo things. I spent too long a time in swimming one late afternoon; when the sun went down it could get cool. My sickness, cold or flu or whatever, woke up again, and I relapsed to bed. Oh gloom and horror, I was going to have to miss the sailing trip. I argued and yelled and sulked and then suddenly rather liked the idea of being left behind, all by myself.

Or almost by myself. Various people kept volunteering to stay by me, notably Richie. He was really in a state now, and wouldn't go on the picnic. He used me as an excuse. Celestine, who was to have the day off, cautiously said she might stay if nobody else could. Mademoiselle, not to be outdone, also made her offer. Mother wouldn't hear of that. *She* would stay. Jocelyn said she wouldn't go if Richie wouldn't. So the ballet of self-sacrifice, supposedly all for my benefit, went on and on. I kept saying, please, everybody go, I'll be perfectly all right alone here with Lagarde, I won't go out of the grounds. I was certainly much depressed by the thought of being left alone with Richie.

Finally it was decided: Richie, secretly much flattered by all this attention, but grousing and grumbling and surly to the last, was made to go along. Mother would stay with me. This was much better than Richie of course, really lovely. But I had secretly wanted to be absolutely *alone*. Alone at the Villa Esperance for the very first time. I couldn't say that to anyone, especially Mother.

Then at the last moment, in a dramatic move, Robbie volunteered. He insisted on staying. He had to do lots of reading, he said. This threw the group into turmoil again; but when Rob in his calm, executive way made up his mind, his mind was made up. Reluctantly everyone, even Mother, even Pam who was most disappointed, gave in. Dick, rather oddly, not only agreed but encouraged him. He did have lots of reading to do, summer reading for school that he should have done before. It was as though

Dick, in his role of tutor to the Prince, felt he must encourage Virtue. Since there seemed to be no other real motive in Robbie's offer except virtue, it was hard to argue with him. Jocelyn was much annoyed, and even called him a "silly ass." He laughed. He stayed.

As for me, I felt Robbie would at least be likely to leave me to myself, which is what I wanted. Aside from being fairly quiet, and *not* being allowed to swim, I was free: free to wander about the garden into obscure almost unexplored nooks. Free to go into everybody's rooms and look at their things! As for not swimming, it was a cool breezy day despite brilliant sun, better for sailing than bathing; and I really was a bit weak, subject again to those sudden fatigues.

iii. So off they all went, to take ship at some nearby docking place. Lagarde was tied up in the garage, where he howled occasionally. Food (cold) was left out for us on the balcony, covered with a dish towel to protect it. Rob and I ate it early, as soon as the others had left. We didn't talk to each other. We separated, me to my room, he to a chair and book. How very quiet it seemed with only the wind moving or fading in the trees of the garden.

I'd been up in my room for a long while, not napping of course, but absorbed in stamps. The door to the hall was open, despite the breezes, and the window too. It always got stuffy under the roof on a sunny day, whatever the outside temperature. Robbie appeared. He was, after all, supposed to be taking care of me. He leaned gracefully against the doorsill and said, "Hi." He drifted into the room; I went on with my stamps. He began to look about idly. "I've never been up here before," he said. I was interested in that, and much surprised. "Haven't you?" He looked over the few things I had up here; not much. My stamps and appurtenances were all about me on the floor. There were a few books and a desk and a bureau. On the bureau was my antique box, prize treasure bought in town, with little drawers full of sea shells and foreign coins.

My poem about the nightingale was lying on the desk. Father had just typed it for me, with cautious words of approval. Rob stood looking down at it, with an unaccountable interest. Poetry, and my poetry in particular, had never concerned him in the least. He picked it up and turned to me. "Can I read it?" "Sure." He'd obviously already been reading it; but let that pass.

He ambled moodily over to the window, holding the poem. There he leaned reading; then stood looking out at my view. "You see everything from up here, don't you?" He lost himself in the distance of sea, the yellow sheet of the poem still dangling in his hand. "Can you hear nightingales out there? I heard one the other night," he said. "This is like that Keats poem, isn't it"; flattering reference to mine. "It's nice." A dreamy and poetical Robbie was certainly something new. Of all unlikely people to be appreciating my poem! "I didn't know you wrote poems," he said; but I didn't offer to show him any of the few others, and he didn't ask. He returned to the view. I wanted to know since when he'd been reading Keats. Mother had read Keats aloud to me, and even given me a thin "Works" bound in golden leather. This was in fact about the only poetry I really had read; but I considered myself something of a connoisseur, and wasn't so sure I was pleased at Robbie's unlikely trespass on this territory. I presumed it was Dick in his tutoring that had led him to nightingales.

He shook himself out of a reverie and turned and stretched. "Let's go!" he said. "Where?" "Oh, out somewhere." "Let's look in the girls' room first," I said, "you've never seen it." "Who else lives up here?" "Ghosts," I said, and he thought that was very funny. We went out into the hall, and I showed him the door to the back attic. This was locked, presumably stored with the Baron's treasures (if the Baron and his treasures still existed). Another tiny room between the attic and the girls' room was used by us to keep our trunks in. I had of course been in the girls' room often enough, but never without them. I intended to poke and pry everywhere, unless inhibited by Robbie.

It was basically a pretty room, with its two views, seaward and westward, but decorated with extreme fussiness, vapid little pictures and flowery curtains and little rugs — things that didn't go at all with the Mediterranean of red tile and white plaster. A big brown wardrobe with mirrored doors took up the east wall. I opened each door and looked at the array of dresses and shoes. "Hey," said Robbie, "look at that!" I was pleased he hadn't objected to my invasion. "More junk!" he said, flipping the limp clothes disdainfully. "How can they be so stuck up?" which echoed my sentiments exactly. But when I started to go through the drawers he stopped me. "I don't think we ought to do that." I then began going over their books and pictures, but Rob was bored by then. He looked out one window, and then the other. He leaned way over the low sill, trying to see if he could touch the roof of the balcony, a story and a half below. Then he squatted, put his hands on the windowsill and, balancing there, his head out over space, he began slowly, powerfully to lift his legs, moving toward a handstand. I yelped and grabbed his feet, pulling them down. "Are you *crazy?*" I shouted. "Crazy? What's crazy?" "You could get killed!" "I could get killed falling downstairs. Besides, there's the balcony."

I went over beside him to look down onto the balcony roof. If a tall man hung by his hands to our windowsill, his feet might touch. It looked very fragile to me, made of strips of some odd composition, gray, patched with black tar. There were sharp upstanding edges between the narrow panels of it. It might break a fall, but not carry much weight.

Suddenly Rob, standing right behind me, grabbed me under the armpits, heaved me up over the sill, and dangled me out the window. He had me firmly about the wrists, but swung me to and fro. "See if you can touch the roof there," he said calmly, chuckling at my surprise. I was utterly terrified by the height, the sudden shock of it. I don't suppose I'd ever been more frightened outside of a nightmare. I closed my eyes and screamed and screamed, "Let me go! Let me go!" This was certainly the wrong thing. He stopped swinging me. "You really mean it? Let you go?" "No, no, no," I wailed and started to cry. "Pull me up!" I couldn't bear to look at the dreadful wideness of the view. Actually the balcony roof was only a few feet under me, and if it could be trusted would have been safe enough. Robbie himself would have thought nothing of landing on it, climbing down over the edge of it, and so dropping to the balcony itself. Not me. "Oh, all right," he said. "What are you so scared of?" I just continued to let out yelps like a French steam engine. Much disgusted, he yanked me up and set me down neatly inside.

I stumbled blindly over to the wardrobe and fell at the foot of it, hiding my head in my arms and sobbing. I couldn't seem to control myself, but lay shivering and gasping. Robbie, at last really worried, came over and crouched by me. "Hey, Howie, come on! You're not hurt or anything. I thought you'd like it. The way Ronnie does, in the water. I'm sorry. I didn't mean to scare you that way."

"Yes, you did." I turned on him, furious. "All you want to do is scare other people. You're a dirty bully and I'm going to tell Father. You just wait and see. You . . . you

. . . you tyrant!" This odd expletive seemed to me at the moment the worst thing I could think of. Robbie stood up and stepped back, honestly abashed. He realized that if I did tell the parents, he would certainly come out in the wrong. "Really, Howie, I didn't mean it. You were perfectly safe. How could I know you'd take on like that?"

"You never know how anybody else feels and you don't care. You just make everybody do your stupid things and you don't care about other people. You're a selfish stupid mean bully and I hate you and so does everyone else!" I didn't care what he did, this time I was really going to tell him what I thought of him.

Instead of getting angry, he just seemed astonished. He squatted down where he stood with wide eyes and half-opened mouth. It had obviously never occurred to him that he was not always and universally beloved. "You really *mean* that, Howie? You really *hate* me?" "Yes. Of course. You're always coming along and messing up our play and bossing Jane and me around and making fun of the girls and being mean to Richie. Why shouldn't we all hate you? And you think you're so great." I was already feeling much better, and laying it on as thick as I could while I had the chance.

Rob closed his eyes and shook his head, as though dizzy. "Gosh," he said, almost breathless, "I never would have thought that. You mean all these years you and Jane felt this way? Didn't I ever do anything nice for you? I always . . . I always thought . . ." He couldn't finish. He was really upset, and I was amazed and pleased to observe it. The invulnerable Robbie! Well, served him right.

"You thought wrong. I mean you're not nasty like Richie is sometimes, or . . . or sneery like Nan. But you certainly never did anything nice for me that *I* can think of. Really." I did remember his saving Jane from the ordeal of the slide; but that was Jane, not me. "Except Christmas presents and things."

"Gosh," he said again, overwhelmed it seemed by this revelation. "I guess you're right. I guess I never do think about anyone else really. I mean I just never thought you'd be as scared as all that. I would have thought it was fun, swinging about; of course if somebody strong had hold of me. But other people are different I suppose."

"You always act as if anyone that doesn't like what you like must be a coward or something. Just because you don't *feel* scared at things like heights."

"Well, that's true. It's silly to feel scared of a high place if you know what you're doing. I'd be just as safe up there on the windowsill on my hands as I would be on the floor. But I guess you don't feel that way, do you?" "I most certainly do not." I couldn't help snickering.

"I'm awfully sorry, Howie, I really am. Not just about this but about everything. I'm just stupid. It . . . it never occurred to me. . . ." He stood up and came over to me where I lay still crouching tearstained at the foot of the wardrobe. He held out his hand. "Let's make up. I'm truly sorry and swear it won't happen again. Okay?" He smiled, and there was certainly nothing synthetic or selfish about that unfairly radiant smile. I took his outstretched hand and he pulled me up gently. He patted me on the shoulder. "Feeling all right?" I sniffed and grinned, and we were friends again. Perhaps it would be more true to say friends for the first time. Neither of us had really given any thought to each other, we had just taken each other for granted as brothers and nuisances, for better or for worse.

"What do you want to do now?" he said jovially. "Explore," I answered. "All right, we'll explore. Whereabouts?" "Let's go over to *your* room," I said maliciously. He laughed. "There's nothing to see over there. I'm not like Richie, with all those secrets." "Let's go there anyway,

I'll show you our garden." "Yeah, great." As he said it this was not sarcastic; not like Richie. He really meant it. So we clattered down the two flights of stairs, our feet echoing in the empty house, and ran out into the brilliant afternoon.

I was now wildly exuberant in reaction to my former state of shock, and I romped around, talking foolishly and yelling. My sickness had made me a bit overemotional in every direction. We crossed the road, and went through the garage to my garden, not forgetting to speak to poor prisoner Lagarde on the way. He too, like me, leaped and yelped.

Celestine's garden was now green and flourishing, and I felt I could take credit for it myself. As I explained to Rob, I'd done most of the work, while Richie dug elsewhere looking for treasure. "Did he find any?" "Yes. *He* thought it was treasure," and I described his finding of the package. Robbie, who'd been amiable and indulgent up to that moment, suddenly sobered. He was obviously disturbed by the business and asked me to describe everything in detail. I told him that Richie had taken the stuff up to his hideout.

Without saying what he planned to do, Robbie, still frowning and worried, led me upstairs. His bedroom contained two plain bare bureaus. From a small box on top of Richie's bureau he took a little key. This unlocked one of the top drawers. In this, carefully hidden among layers of handkerchiefs, was another bigger key. This one unlocked the door to Richie's secret chamber.

It really was no bigger than a closet; but it had its narrow dormer window, and just room enough for a small desk, a kitchen chair and a wall of rough shelves. These shelves were covered with a miscellany — all sorts of peculiar objects that meant something no doubt to Richie. On the lowest shelf was the bundle of clothes. Robbie squatted down and looked over the dirty blue stuff. The little code book wasn't there. Another key from a pigeonhole of the desk opened the desk drawer. There, tucked away among a mass of such souvenirs, was the code book. Robbie looked it all over carefully and put it back, exactly where it had come from, without saying a word.

"Did Richie ever talk to you about this?" he asked me. "No. How about you?" He snorted. "He wouldn't tell *me!*" "It's spies," I said, "I know that. He thinks it has to do with Dick. Is Dick really a spy?" Robbie hesitated a moment. "It's what he calls 'working in intelligence' which means sort of spying; so he can't say anything to anybody." "You mean he really is a spy!" I was enthralled. "Well, you can't call it a spy exactly. I mean France isn't our enemy, is it, so I guess you can't spy on a friend. But he does something like that all right. I don't know what it is, but it's okay of course. I'm just worried about Richie and what he's got on his mind. He's got some stupid plot, that's a cinch. Suppose he told people about something that was really secret, and got Dick in trouble?" "Richie's the one that ought to be the spy."

Robbie laughed and pushed me out of the treasure room. "He'd kill us if he ever knew we'd been in here. I don't know whether I better tell Dick or not." "I think you better," I said. "And if he tells you what it's all about, promise you'll tell me." Robbie laughed again, but didn't answer. He put the two keys back carefully and by common consent we rattled downstairs, Robbie fetching along his bathing trunks. We stopped and patted Lagarde, who whined and jumped, begging to come with us; so we unsnapped his leash. Robbie hung onto his collar as we crossed the road.

iv. Robbie was going to swim. I couldn't. He undressed in our children's dining room, which he often did before swimming, and he and I and Lagarde took the shortcut down to the water. I of course had nothing to do there. Watching Robbie as he practiced his dives was a bore. Now was my chance to explore — the whole garden, mine, with nobody else in it. I planned to go from one end of it to another, pretending it really belonged to me alone. I took Lagarde along, rather unwillingly, and we scrambled up the path by the fake alligator. First to the tower; I could make out Robbie down below, standing on his hands at the end of the dock, so brown, strong and perfectly poised. How blue the sea was today, ruffled but not disturbed by the breeze. I looked for the sail of the fishing boat with its picnickers but couldn't spot it. There was the usual guardian destroyer, out beyond the islands.

Then I walked as close as I could along the very edge of the cliff westward, past the terrible slide (nobody had been down it since that last time), scrambling through thickets till I came at last to the terminal wall, with its fan of spikes out over the cliff edge and its nasty jagged broken-glass top. Everyone in France was so scared of thieves; but nobody had ever tried to break into the Villa Esperance.

I pushed my way through the undergrowth up along the wall. In the corner, at the angle, there was a big junk pile. Old logs and branches and brush. It smelled. I turned to follow the course of the wall back toward the house. An occasional car wooshed past down the road, hidden from me. I saw a scorpion at my feet. It was all rather nasty and difficult and boring, bending and squeezing my way, back of the pool and its mimosas, finally out to the gate. I did get tired quickly after I'd been sick.

I felt I'd had enough of this kind of exploring. Lagarde kept running off; I stood by the front gate calling him and calling him, while an idea grew and blossomed. When Lagarde finally came bounding up, I used him as self-justification for what I meant to do: go across the road and investigate Richie's closet for myself. I knew it was wrong in almost every way I could think of. But when would I ever have another chance? And I might find some clue to his spy mystery and to Dick's "intelligence" or whatever it was.

So I dragged poor protesting Lagarde back to his prison and snapped his collar to the tied-up leash. He jumped and barked and wagged and begged to be let loose. How sad the sight of his tail gradually drooping down as he realized I was actually going to desert him! But I was already leaping up the stairs. I remembered just where the keys were, and was most careful to notice between just which handkerchiefs the second one was hidden.

Horray! Inside the room of mystery, all by myself. It was most disappointing. I couldn't make out why in the world Richie kept all this debris. Some of it was obviously scientific, rocks and shells and dried seaweed. But why those chunks of concrete or sections of old pipe? Old clothes, old newspapers, old pieces of wood. Tin cans full of objects. Indescribable junk. I turned to the desk. The locked drawer was crammed with papers, but very neatly ordered. I'd have to be careful not to mix them up. There was the famous code book, just as baffling as ever. He'd collected quite a few letters, some addressed to Richie himself, but many more addressed to others: the parents (Richie certainly had no business with those) and a quite bulky collection of stuff which he'd obviously taken from Dick. There were letters, postcards, even a small address book. I untied the elastic that bound them, scared to death it might break, keeping an ear cocked for Robbie. Except for a few melancholy whines from Lagarde there was no sound.

In the middle of the package were some snapshots; they looked like the ones that Pam's camera made. They probably were, but they were of Robbie. He was posed on rocks against the water, and he had nothing on at all. There was one of Dick too, and he too was naked. I couldn't have said why, but I was disturbed and shocked. I could imagine the pictures being taken as a sort of joke, and indeed some of the poses were obviously meant to be humorous. The locale was no doubt that special diving place at the Websters'. I knew that the boys quite often swam there without suits, as they had that very first day of Dick's arrival. But just the same there was something upsetting about finding those pictures there, locked away in Richie's most secret files, no doubt secretly stolen by him like the rest of Dick's stuff. I put the snapshots back, I carefully arranged the desk drawer. I locked it, I locked the room door, I locked the bureau drawer and put away the first key, anxious now only to get out and get away, across the road, far from Richie and his nasty things. I felt now that I just didn't want to know anything about any of them. I paid no attention to poor Lagarde, who yapped at me pitifully as I went by. I only felt safe when the iron gate clanged behind me, and I was in our garden again.

I had planned to go into every single bedroom in the house and look about; but my appetite for prying was gone. I wandered upstairs at loose ends. Here on the second floor was Jane's little room, right over the front door, very pretty and full of her things, dolls and a lovely set of Provençal carved doll's furniture, and her set of the Librarie Rose: the girlish side of her life which we did not share. Coming slowly up the path, still far down by the pond, was Robbie. I ducked back from the window, as though it were somehow important that he shouldn't see me.

As for the big room in the corner where Mademoiselle and Ronnie slept, that offered very little of interest. It was full, as always, of sewing things and clothes to be mended or laundered. What in this whole world was more utterly boring than clothes? I was really rather put off this kind of poking about anyway by now. Richie's closet had been

224

more than enough. I just wanted to be sure to avoid seeing Robbie again before the family got back. I was afraid he might guess where I'd been. And the family was due any minute. Should I go up to my room? Rob might find me there. Or stay here? Nothing to do. I didn't dare go into the parents' rooms; they might catch me. Or perhaps I could slip downstairs and outdoors while Robbie was dressing in the dining room? I decided to try that. It was sort of exciting to see if I could get past him. I tiptoed out into the hall and started down the stairs as quietly as I could. How very silent everything was today. It was becoming oppressive.

I stopped short. There was Robbie, still in his striped bathing trunks, standing down there in the front hall. He was looking at himself in the Venetian mirror. It was a study, and examination, not a casual hairbrushing business. He was staring at himself as though for the first time. As though for the first time seeing himself as others did. He evidently liked what he saw, as of course well he might. He stuck out his chest, he made muscles, turning about, grinning sometimes at his own vanity, but then quite seriously admiring himself. In Robbie, of all people, this narcissism was startling. Nan of course could never go past a mirror without primping and smirking. She spent hours up in her room examining every single little detail of her appearance. Robbie, for all his self-confidence and self-assurance, had none of that sort of personal vanity. He kept himself neat because it was proper to do so. He'd always been ashamed of those girlish aspects of his looks, the long eyelashes, the fresh complexion. To see him now at once preening and questioning his own beauty like this, sure that he was alone, seemed to me in its way almost as odd as the hidden-away snapshots in Richie's closet. I stood awhile watching him, restraining my giggles with some difficulty. Wouldn't he be furious if he knew I'd seen him! Maybe I could black-

225

mail him in some way if he found out I'd been across the road without him. (Oh grief! I suddenly remembered Lagarde, tied up in the garage again, evidence against me!)

And just at this moment, as I was about to sneak back upstairs, overwhelmed with guilt, a car stopped outside, somebody blew a horn playfully; loud talking, the family, the picnickers were back. I ran upstairs a few steps, then came noisily down again. Rob was at the door. Here came everybody.

v. I was rather disturbed by my discoveries in Richie's closet. I couldn't imagine, for instance, why he wanted to hide away those snapshots. The pictures themselves bothered me too; but since I couldn't see any point in any of it, either the pictures or Richie's hiding of them, I dismissed it all from my mind. What Robbie had said about Dick's spying, "intelligence work" (such a queer meaning for that word!) bothered me still more. What was he doing in the garden burying clothes? What did Richie know? I really felt that Father ought to be advised. Somebody should consult him. Why not Robbie?

So I decided to speak to him; but there I was inhibited too. He was bound to realize that I'd been across the road, off the place without permission. I might get in trouble. Still, I had to talk to somebody, somebody of course except Richie, about this spy business. After lunch next day, while I was on my way down to my cellar to join Jane, while Rob was going back to his room, alone for once, I saw my chance and took it. I spoke to him, right there on the front steps.

"Does Father know about this spy stuff with Dick and all?" Robbie bit his lower lip, shook his head, and looked upset. "Shouldn't somebody tell him? Why don't you tell him?" Robbie snorted. "Me? I don't know anything. What can I tell him?" "Well then, why don't you get Dick to tell him? Hasn't he told you *any*thing?" Robbie looked down at his smooth brown hands, as though they might hold some information, written in code across the knuckles. Then he looked at me. "That's one thing Uncle Dick won't talk about. You know that. Richie thinks he's so wonderful, snooping around. He'll just get us all into terrible trouble, that's what." "Why don't you speak to *him?*" Robbie snorted again, and started to move off. The conversation made him uncomfortable. "Trouble enough already. I don't know what's wrong with Richie anyway. He's so mean, I can't talk to him about anything; much less this. Why don't *you* talk to him? You're his friend now," but he said it grinning, as though he knew it wasn't really possible. "And by the way," he said (my stomach jolted), "what were you doing across the road yesterday, when I was down swimming?" I lied glibly. "I had to tie Lagarde up, he was such a nuisance and all. And I couldn't go all the way back to the beach just to tell you. Don't say anything to Mother, please!" Robbie smiled and sauntered off. "That's all right." I was relieved; but I certainly hadn't gotten very far with the Great Spy Mystery.

When I got down to the cellar, I confided in Jane. I told her all I knew, Richie's discovery of the clothes, Robbie's tale of Dick being "in intelligence." "That's what he said. That's what they call spying I guess." "How can Dick be a spy now when there's no war on?" "Enemies spy on each other all the time. Don't be so silly." "Yes, but France isn't an enemy." "Maybe he spies on *German* spies. Or maybe he goes off to Germany and spies." "Or maybe he is a German spy!" We agreed, excited, that that was probably it. Still, it didn't seem to make much sense, at least around the Villa Esperance. Of course there were those destroyers out there, and those islands with machine guns; and Dick was always going off on picnics, and driving around in his car.

"Do you suppose he's really an enemy spy then?" said Jane, thrilled to the core. "If Richie tells on him, will they arrest him and shoot him?" She almost, but not quite, added, "I hope so." Her distaste for Dick was firmer and more uncompromising than ever. Silly he had been from the beginning, silly he remained. I found that I had weakened lately, in some way, for some reason. Perhaps it was my rapprochement with Robbie.

All this was exciting of course, but after all a mere side issue, an unimportant digression in our lives. I did not tell Jane about the nude snapshots. We had business, serious business to attend to. The events in the reign of Agragor the Wicked were building up to their juicily gruesome climax.

P A R T   T W O

i. Fifteen years had passed. For all his dissipated ways, Agragor was just as evilly handsome as ever. But everybody hated him now. He had taken up permanently with Lilipopo, who was installed in the palace as his real Queen. He couldn't divorce Chin Lee as long as Wa Fung was alive; but he had sent her back to Korea. Wa Fung was sorry he'd started the whole thing. The old Emperor of Korea finally died, Chin Lee's brother became the new Emperor, and he was just waiting to attack Agragor and revenge his sister. Poor Chin Lee lived alone in exile, velly sad.

Agragor spent all his time having parties and being cruel to people. Lilipopo encouraged him. We had many a scene in which Agragor kicked people in the face as they knelt before him, then had their heads cut off, after horrible tortures, while he and Lilipopo laughed and laughed. Meanwhile Nu Wa was in league with young Liu, the pretender. He had become a boy wonder, a daring outlaw who raided the capital and gave to the poor. Nu Wa officially adopted him as her heir, she now being chieftainess of all her people. So Liu would be the future chief of the Wa Hus, and changed his name to Liu Wa to please them. Only old Wa Fung kept things together in Amuria. He really ruled the kingdom while Agragor wasted his time. Wa Fung worked on Chin Lee not to let her brother start a war. He kept the army in shape, and tried desperately to catch Liu Wa, and kill him. But in vain.

Agragor and Chin Lee had a beautiful young daughter Kalila, their only child. One day while she was walking alone in the palace garden, neglected and sad like her faraway mother, a handsome boy of her own age hopped over the wall. He had golden hair and slanty eyes and bulgy muscles, and he was of course Liu Wa. He grabbed her before she could scream and covered her mouth. She promised not to call for help. They got into conversation, and before they knew it, they were in love. He told her his whole story, and she was horrified to hear what her papa had done. As they parted (guards were coming) she swore to be true to him, and to help him regain his rightful throne. He hopped back over the wall just in time. From then on, secret meetings and smuggled messages were the rule.

Wa Fung finally lay dying. He was not in the capital, but in his own great castle in the mountains. He refused to see Agragor or any of his minions. He secretly summoned Kalila, who summoned Liu Wa, and they were officially introduced across his deathbed. Wa Fung apologized for all the wicked things he had done. He told Kalila that a caravan awaited to take her swiftly to her mother, with a message for her uncle. Liu Wa was to return to the Wa Hus and alert them. He, Wa Fung, had himself seen to it that the Amurian generals would betray Agragor at the right time and go over to Liu Wa. Let Liu marry Kalila and live happily ever after as Emperor of Amuria and friend of Korea and the Wa Hus. "Oh, if only I had not betrayed my own dear daughter Wa Nee Ta!" were his last words. "May she forgive me."

He dies.

Agragor is carrying on in the palace, drunk as usual, torturing people, throwing jewels at Lilipopo. A messenger staggers in (we always enjoyed the messenger-staggering bit). "Wa Fung is dead! The Wa Hus and Koreans have invaded! The army is in revolt! Flee!!" Agragor in a fury chops the messenger's head off right there and then. Lilipopo screams and dashes out to save herself and her jewels. Agragor scorns flight. He seizes his broadsword and rages into the throne room. Already the armies are at the gate. Only Agragor's loyal palace guard sticks with him. The rebel forces, led by Liu Wa, Nu Wa and the young Emperor of Korea, enter the city in triumph, acclaimed by the populace, who hate Agragor. They reach the palace and batter down the door. They start massacring the palace guard.

Agragor, surrounded by his last faithful companions in arms, stands waiting in the great throne room. The army rushes in. Nu Wa is first. "Don't kill him!" she shrieks. "I want him — alive!" They butcher those still defending Agragor and disarm and bind him. Lilipopo has been captured trying to flee.

Nu Wa prepares a great basin of boiling oil. Despite the desperate pleas of Chin Lee, Liu Wa and Kalila, she will have her revenge. Stripped and tied by their hair to bamboo poles, Agragor and Lilipopo, writhing and screaming, are slowly, slowly lowered into the boiling oil. Nu Wa watches in exultation. She stands there, smiling in savage delight, through the hours it takes to finally kill them.

The remains of Agragor and Lilipopo are thrown to the dogs. Wa Fung is buried in the grand tomb he prepared for himself. After all, he is the new King's grandfather. Liu Wa is crowned in triumph with his new bride and Queen, Kalila. Nu Wa and Chin Lee make friends. Permanent peace between the three countries is declared. Bells ring, gongs sound wang-wang, flutes and pipes squeal, Hurray!

So ended this particular chapter in Amurian history. What next? We were rather at a loss to continue it.

ii. Meanwhile the last of big family events, before we all left, before we went away from Villa Esperance, was to be a Fancy Dress Ball. Jocelyn first thought of it. Mother enthusiastically accepted the idea. Everyone got caught up in it. We were to ask all our friends from round about and hire the dance band from the Hotel Maritime. The house and gardens were to be lit with lanterns, and everybody talked and talked about costumes. No one could make up his mind. Jocelyn wanted to get nearly all of us involved in a Shakespearean pageant, built about *A Midsummer Night's Dream*; but we all resisted. Nobody really liked the idea. Nan and Ellie wanted to costume the Carruthers, at least, as characters from the opera *Esterilla*. Why not go as characters from Amurian history, said Jane and I; but only to one another.

The planning and fussing totally absorbed the female element, and left the men rather out of it. Left us alone even. A great shopping spree, involving every single woman of our group — Mother and Jocelyn, Nan and

Ellie, Pamela and Miranda, Jane, Mademoiselle and even unconscious Ronnie — took them to town for the day. It certainly was quiet without them. Dick and Father, Robbie and Richie were more or less forced together, refugees of this madness. I was by myself, which always suited me well enough.

We spent a long hot afternoon down on the dock by the water. Father, still on his cane, could hobble that far, and even swim. We took sandwiches down with us, and afterward Dick tutored Robbie, while the rest of us drowsed or read. Everything was very amiable, very somnolent in the heat. Father sat like an African chief under his big umbrella. I found a nook of shade and dreamed more than I read.

Only Richie was restless. He wandered about aimlessly, throwing stones into the water, examining sea animals, pestering me at intervals, interrupting Robbie's lessons in the most insolent way by ignoring Dick completely and trying to get Robbie to join him. Dick and Robbie were both forbearing, but Father told Richie in no uncertain terms to settle down and stop annoying the rest of us. Richie sat on the end of the dock, dangling his feet in the water, tossing pebbles about, sulking.

Finally Rob and Dick moved from literature to athletics. They rose and went toward Richie. Diving again. But Richie was sitting right in their way. Rob good-naturedly nudged him with his toes and told him to clear out. Richie refused. Robbie then pushed him off into the water. It was all in fun, but Richie came up spluttering and furious, scrambled up out of the water and attacked Robbie, flailing away awkwardly at him, splashing wetness around. Robbie drew back laughing, protecting himself with his hands, until Richie by chance more than skill landed a scraping slap on Robbie's face. Robbie instantly grabbed Richie's arm and twisted it back of him. I couldn't hear what he said to him; it was quiet and grim. He let Richie go. Richie shouted something at him, hoarse and incoherent, turned up toward the house, then turned back and spat at Robbie's feet. Before Father could speak to him or stop him, he raced up the dock and into the garden.

Robbie stood looking after him, legs straddled and arms akimbo, angry and serious. Father called after Richie, but he'd gone. "Let him go, let him go," said Dick, sighing. Robbie and he turned to their diving instructions. Dick stood by Robbie, giving him points of form and style. Robbie of course by now was almost as good as Dick himself — somersaults, handstands, the whole repertoire of water acrobatics. Just doing them successfully wasn't enough however. Subtle refinements had to be taught and mastered.

After a while Dick sauntered away, leaving Rob to his practice, and squatted in front of Father, under the shade of his great bumbershoot, like a naked dark savage at the foot of his king.

"What *are* we going to do with Richie?" said Father. One gathered from the confidential tone that this wasn't the first time they'd approached the subject; and indeed there had been a noticeable drawing together of Uncle Dick and Father since Dick's return from the Websters'. Part of this was certainly due to Mother's influence; but part to a change in Dick himself. He was so much more calm and serious and kind, and, even Jane had to admit, so much less affected, provocative, show-off than he had been at first. Less silly altogether, particularly in his welcome reserve with us. No more of that spurious "little beggars" business.

Dick pondered a moment, head down, thinking over the problem, tossing fragments of yellow rock from palm to palm. "I think when I leave things'll be better. For a while anyway. Part of this is just jealousy of course." "Of course," echoed Father. "But that doesn't get at the root of it, does it? Richie's always been a lonely soul. Even when he was six, when we first took him in after his parents were killed. He resented us then, he resents us now. I don't think his parents wasted much time on him, and I don't think he's ever quite felt one of our family. And of course he isn't. Being the only one that's *nobody's* child . . ." Father lapsed into silence, and Dick too.

Robbie was down at the end of the dock, in and out of the water, and out of earshot. I wasn't. I sat in my shadowed nook of the rocks right across from the grown-ups, presumably buried in my book. I could hear them plainly.

"I suppose we've been neglectful," said Father, continuing the train of thought. "It's hard to parcel out affection equally, make sure nobody gets too much or too little. We've let Robbie take care of him, so to speak. Now when Robbie goes off on his own that leaves Richie with nobody."

"He has you." "Yes, he has Margaret at least. There's no lack of loving there. But all the rest of us are enemies, I'm afraid. Perhaps he doesn't think so consciously, but the feeling's there." Father sighed. "You're just another enemy. One of the family. I don't believe he'd have accepted you even if you hadn't drawn Robbie off. Poor Jocelyn defends him and pets him, but she doesn't get anywhere with him."

"He's really been very annoying. More than just rude and jealous. He spies on me all the time. Searches my room, steals letters."

Father sat up astonished. "What? Why didn't you tell me? We'll put a stop to that in a hurry!" "No, no, please. It doesn't really do any harm, and I suppose it gives him pleasure. He's a natural intriguer." Dick snorted. "He's the one should be in intelligence, not me. I've got colleagues like that. They love the sheer apparatus, disguises, codes.

One of them came by here a few weeks ago. You'd think we were about to go to war. Poor fellow, he's out of place in peacetime. Poor Richie too. He manufactures mystery for the hell of it."

Father, bent as usual on the abstract application, moved from the particular to the generalization. "That sort of thing does seem to be naturally attractive to the young, doesn't it? I wonder what's back of it? The appetite for mystification; very powerful human trait, the Poe in every adolescent. But that still doesn't give Richie the right to search your room. He ought to be talked to."

Dick raised his head and looked at Father for the first time. "I'd really wait if I were you. It's only a few more weeks. When he gets home he'll forget all about it. If you scold him now he'll just get worse than he is." "Well, if *you* don't mind. I suppose it would be even worse if *you* spoke to him. Or Robbie." Dick agreed to that.

"We've thought of sending him off to school. But that might be worse too. At least he's got a mother and a brother he trusts. At school he'd be lost, all on his own." "You've never sent any of them away, have you?" "I was brought up not to approve of boarding schools. Parvenu. If you were a Quaker, like the Carrutherses, naturally the best schools were right there in Philadelphia. Boarding schools were for vulgar, worldly people who went to Newport and had yachts. I've never really gotten over the prejudice myself."

"We never went to Newport or had yachts, but I certainly went away to school."

"How did you like it?" "Well, it was easy for me because I was an athlete. Good enough at studies. Got on well with people. Rich too, in those days. But I hated the damn sanctimoniousness of it, the sacredness of football; Father, Son and Holy Coach. Christianity, Sportsmanship and Bluff. There was always a false note back of it. The false note was money of course, but I didn't know it then. Behind the books and candles were Mammon and Puritanism, a gruesome combination. It was well to suffer now so you could become a good banker in afterlife. I still think it was pretty devilish."

"That's what turned you to Paganism, eh?" "Yes. Christianity and Athleticism made a poor combination I thought. I chose athletics. Of a sort. Or at least the ideal back of athletics."

"That's not going to help Richie, is it? He's neither a Christian nor an athlete." "Frankly I don't think he could do better than just stick with Robbie. He'll get all the Christianity and Athletics and Sportsmanship right there in the home, without the bluff and the Mammon." "Yes, I suppose Robbie's well cast as the Christian athlete. Now *he* would do well in any school."

"Not that the ideal is really Christian at all. Apollonian perhaps. The Christian athlete is a misbegotten mule, an attempt to reconcile Anglicanism and a classical education with devotion to the Empire in English Public Schools. Robbie would be a natural for the role though, no doubt of that." Dick paused and sighed. "When I leave, Richie can go back to him, and all will be well."

"Unless of course Richie influences Robbie. That could happen too." "Never. Robbie's incorruptible." "Come now. Nobody's incorruptible. At least we Christians know that. Just growing up is a corruption. Robbie will have to go through it like all the rest of us." "Yes, dammit. What a shame it is too. Why can't he be allowed to stay just as he is, perfect?"

"Perfect? Robbie? You idealize him. Physically perhaps, but not in other ways." "In what ways isn't he perfect? Noble, true, loyal, just, kind. . . . " "Limited, unimaginative, not too bright, anti-intellectual, intolerant, humorless, insensitive . . . I can think of lots of ways in which Master Robert could change for the better."

"Surely not insensitive. He's not a thinker, that's true. A doer. But if anything he's too sensitive." "About other people, for instance? I don't think he really knows anyone else exists." (How pleased I was to have my own criticisms echoed by such high authority!) "How does he really feel about any of us? Loyal of course. Oh yes. I'm sure he'd gladly lay down his young life for Mother, Father, Flag or Philadelphia. But does he really know anything about . . . sympathy, affection? Is he really capable yet of love?"

Dick again looked down, almost as though embarrassed. He was silent for a while.

"I wonder if you really know him?" he said at last. "If any of us know him. I think he's only too capable of love. Too sensitive. He just hasn't come to it quite yet. I'm afraid for him when he does. Too much love, too completely, to the wrong person in the wrong way."

"Perhaps. Let's hope he has some time to go yet; and after all, each of us has to have that experience, or should have it. Part of the necessary corruptions of growing up, isn't it? Except perhaps for virtuosi like you. Tell me, do you ever get into that trouble? Too much love, for the wrong person? Surely not. Control, control!"

Dick laughed. "Yes. You're right to . . . to tease me on that. I've been pretty arrogant about love, haven't I? As Jocelyn tells me so often. Perhaps I've underestimated Venus. Even Apollo has to submit to her. Perhaps a love you can control isn't really love. You have to give everything to it, even control."

"That's Pagan enough all right, if not exactly what I'd call Classical. More what we should call Romantic, shouldn't we? 'All for love.' Not Christian at least." "Why, I thought that was the essence of Christianity . . . 'with

237

all thy heart and all thy soul' and so forth. As you said, if I remember, losing control." "God, not humans." "And thy neighbor as thyself?" "But not quite in the way you mean it, I rather suspect. God definitely comes first. If there's a conflict, God wins. The control's still there, but it's God's."

"I don't make that exception. I'm just All for Love." Dick rose, easily in one bronze motion. "But duty calls. Rob takes this diving seriously." "He takes everything seriously, doesn't he? Too seriously. That's another of his faults." "You're hard on him. Appreciate him as he is, while he lasts," and Dick strolled over to the end of the dock, where Robbie waited to ask him some question of technique.

Dick stood behind him, adjusting his shoulders, then put his hands on Rob's hips as though to steady him. He moved away, as Robbie, from a presumably perfect position, made his perfect forward somersault. When he came up and heaved himself out of the water, he said, "How was that?" Dick said, "Pretty good." Robbie came up to him and put one hand on Dick's shoulder, breathing heavily, asking some question. Dick moved off, leaving the hand suspended, and Robbie, as though reprimanded, followed him humbly to the end of the dock.

I went back to my book.

PART THREE

i. The plans for the Ball, the great masquerade, grew and matured; and became more and more complicated. For all our resistances, Jocelyn's *Midsummer Night's Dream* idea began to prevail. The theme of the costuming was, after all, supposed to be "Famous Couples" and the play took care of lots of us at once, coupled and sufficiently famous. Jocelyn and Dick were to be Duke Theseus and his fiancée Hippolyta; Pam, Miranda, Rob and Richie, the mixed-up lovers. And Jane and I, Titania and Oberon. The great advantage of the plan was its costuming, a mass production of scanty classical numbers made of sheeting, or something cheap. This appealed immensely to those who would have to make them, that is, Mother and Jocelyn. Since they were the chief organizers of the whole thing, what they wanted carried a lot of weight. Even Ronnie was to be a miniature Puck or Pease-Blossom. He couldn't object, but all the rest of us could and did. Since all our ideas were very foolish and very involved (our intention for instance of being Amurians; how did Amurians dress for a dance?), we were overruled. We were going to be characters from Shakespeare and like it. Jane and I secretly decided that we'd pretend to ourselves we were really Young Liu and his bride-cousin, no matter what; but we wouldn't tell anybody. After all, even if we told people, they wouldn't know what we were talking about.

Only Nan and Ellie had been adamant from the beginning. They were going to be Diego and Esterilla from their own silly opera, and nobody was going to stop them. They flounced about very stuck on themselves. They planned to get up and sing pieces of the opera for "entertainment," so they might as well be in costume to start with. They were seriously disappointed that none of the rest of us would join them; but we hated that opera even more than we did Shakespeare.

It was a rather disgruntled group of maskers gathered about for measurings and fittings. Mother was all for simplicity; Jocelyn for beauty. She went to great lengths to devise costumes that would show off Dick, herself and her girls to best advantage. Instead of just sheets and sandals, Mother's design, there were scanty but artfully pleated white tunics. Hippolyta and Theseus had secondhand French dragoon helmets, with ostrich plumes from an old fan, and long red velvet cloaks (curtains). Jane and I had short spangly cloaks and pretty crowns, as fairy royalty. The lovers had wreaths of imitation flowers. Otherwise we all wore identical shifts that came down in a becoming V front and back, but for the boys exposed lots of thigh and chest, caught up on one shoulder, whereas the girls were more discreetly bodiced. It was immensely becoming to the beautiful ones. Pam and Robbie in particular were dazzling. Poor Richie however came off looking very lanky and undernourished indeed, a starving Athenian. Gilded sandals on our feet, broad gold belts at our waists, necklaces for the girls — and that was that. We spent stuffy miserable hours up in Mademoiselle's room being fussed over and fitted, and laughing at others, our only relief.

However, it was an excitement: our final excitement after all. This was the last, the last of excursions and parties and Abroad. In the next weeks we'd have to be packing up and cleaning up and closing up, putting away our Riviera experience for good. Uncle Dick would be leaving; the Websters were going back to England and to a new school they dreaded. Mademoiselle, Celestine would leave us (with what emotional scenes!) and we would all be returned to a life that I'd almost forgotten — the big trees and lawns and Victorian stone-and-gable darkness of our Chestnut Hill house, the athletic boredom of our Chestnut Hill schools.

ii. The night came. It was very hot and very still. We were all so grateful for Jocelyn's forethought in clothing us so lightly. How sorry

Nan and Ellie were going to be in their voluminous seven-teenth-century operatic getups (great crinoline and high hair for Nan, great hat and baggy breeches for Ellie). But they were more than willing to suffer in this cause. There was to be, later on, a great full moon. Nightingales we hoped would oblige.

Meanwhile Villa Esperance had been transformed in and out with Japanese lanterns and flowers. The lanterns, in all sorts of pale fruit colors, apricot, plum, orange and lemon, globed and glimmered all the way down the big path to the pond, where the little fountain around Mercury was turned on, and chairs and tables set out for strollers. Lanterns were hung all about the gate and the door and inside in hall and dining room. The *salon* however was brilliant with chandeliers and real roses that blended with the artificial plaster ones. Every piece of movable furniture had been cleared and there were gilt chairs from the Maritime all about. The Maritime jazz band too. Tables with candles were out on the balcony. Buckets and buckets of champagne waited with Leone and Celestine in the kitchen. Leone brought her sister, as homely as Leone was handsome. Both were dressed in some sort of dashing native costume; Celestine too had fetched up a Breton lace cap from a piece of stored luggage, and rather belligerently went into costume too. Mademoiselle of course as a proper bourgeoise had no truck with that sort of thing. She wore a vaguely Greek outfit, like the rest of us. A few raffish waiters, also from the Maritime, helped out, smoked ciga-rettes in the kitchen, and made coarse jokes to Leone, to Celestine's extreme indignation and delight.

People came.

By then we were all sick with the excitement and expectancy. We'd been costumed, recostumed and then partly uncostumed, fed a noisy, noisome supper which we couldn't eat. Everybody had quarreled. Richie and Robbie had a fight which almost came to fists. Ellie had a hysterical crying fit. Mother got a headache and had to rest. Father stayed up in his room, nursing his lame foot. Only Jocelyn and Dick were good-humored and gay. They really seemed to be enthralled with the business, active everywhere, full of last-minute ideas.

The band had been thrumming softly away at their American songs long before any guests were there to hear them. The Japanese lanterns were lit, and glowed more and more warmly as the earlier dusk came down. Nan and Ellie practiced and practiced their entertainment. First Nan's aria, then a Spanish dance accompanied by Dick on his guitar. Dick and Rob were to do their acrobatics.

The first to arrive were the Famous Couple, Adam and Eve. They had flesh-colored tights, large green hands for fig leaves, and wigs. His was red and stuck out all around. He did look dreadful, like a farmer in his winter underwear. Her wig was red too, but long and very becoming indeed; and *she* had a beautiful figure. They drove up in a rented car and chauffeur and everybody was out to welcome them, she obviously furious at being first. She would have preferred to make a somewhat shocking entrance after everyone else. But she recovered quickly, very animated as we all trooped into the *salon*. She made a game of trying to remember and identify all of us, hugged and kissed Jane, accepted the first glass of champagne and clinked glasses with Father. She and her husband danced sedately to "Alice Blue Gown" which she declared brought back memories of an unhappy youth in Sioux City, Iowa. The party was off to a start.

Mother and Father were in soberly unidentifiable floor-length monklike robes. Father carried a great staff (for his limp). Mother wore a wreath. They were, it seems, a pair of wandering Cathar Perfecti. "I'm sure the wreath is wrong," said Mother, "but I had to wear something pretty.

At least it's a cool costume, because I haven't anything on underneath, to speak of." "As for me, I itch," said Mr. Famous. "But I'm funny," he added very gloomily. "Yes, darling, you are per*fec*tion," said his wife. "I knew it, I knew it," he croaked, as though all his worst fears were confirmed.

More people arrived, and we ran out to greet each and every one; though most of them were total strangers to us. The parents and Jocelyn were bent on asking everyone who had ever been nice to them, and it was really a rather motley group. But since everyone was disguised, it made no difference whether anyone really knew anyone. The honor of making the grand late entrance went not to Adam and Eve but to a quintet of the De Guichys, the two Tessières and the Lady of the Castle, who all drove up in her great caramel-colored car with its chauffeur *and* footman, something we weren't sure we'd ever really seen before. The footman came in handy unloading Tessières's lame daughter, who had to be put into a wheelchair, unfolded from the baggage compartment. Even such a big car must have been pretty cramped for them all, for they were done up in the most hot and gorgeous of Louis XIV costumes, and represented all sorts of real, abstruse, seventeenth-century ancestors.

We heard the whole complicated story later from Nan and Ellie. Tessières and the De Guichys we already knew were cousins but enemies. Tessières felt De Guichy had let the family down. Their mutual friend, the Lady of the Castle, whose late French husband had also been a cousin, planned to bring them together on the basis of costumes for this party. Tessières already had his costume, which he always wore on such occasions: the stiffly elaborate getup of his famous ancestor the Marshal Lombert, greatest general of the Grand Monarch. It was covered with lace and medals and he had a big brown wig to go with it. Since the

Marshal had had a mustache too, Tessières didn't have to shave his, which of course was the whole point. He was to escort the Lady of the Castle in the guise of his sister, who had married none other than the contemporary Duc de Guichy, direct ancestor of Monsieur. So obviously De Guichy had to come as that Duke. Nan and Ellie told us all about the difficulties of persuading him; but finally De Guichy's love of theater overcame his anti-royalist scruples. Tessières had all the makings for another gorgeous costume. Things soon got to such a point that De Guichy trimmed *his* mustache down to the hair line proper to his ancestor; and justified it all on the basis that the Duke, as opposed to the Marshal, was as ignoble and as bad an advertisement for the *ancien régime* as Lombert was a good one. Not only was he a double-dyed traitor to the King during the Fronde, switching back and forth to his own advantage, but he had been notoriously unfaithful to his high-toned, intellectual, long-suffering, letter-writing wife. Mme de Guichy came as the most respectable of his many mistresses, Mlle de Sainte-Helleu, famous for her devotional works. Even this literary aspect of things did not make up for it all to Mme de Guichy, who was sulky with everybody, notably her husband, and almost refused to come. In contrast to the gorgeousness of the other three, she was very plain in dark gray satin, and as a result really looked quite lovely and a lot more seventeenth century, with her blond hair pulled back in ringlets, than the others did. The poor crippled daughter had to just come as herself, though an attempt was made to identify her with some obscure niece of Mlle de Sainte-Helleu.

They made an entrance. They climbed and unfolded themselves out of the glistening car, the chauffeur hopping about in his caramel uniform. They swept in, followed by the footman pushing the daughter in her wheelchair. They entered the *salon* like royalty, and the fact that they almost were (the family had numerous Bourbon connections) was lost on no one. Except perhaps for Mr. and Mrs. Famous, who didn't know what the commotion was all about.

This was remedied in short order by the parents, who arranged a Presentation; the question of course being exactly who was being presented to whom. The confrontation occured in the *salon*, after the new arrivals had their champagne in hand. A visible shock and congealment was manifested on both sides upon this introduction of the most belligerent representative of the successful New to the most entrenched and already somewhat embittered Old in American letters. Mrs. Famous searched wildly for something brilliantly provocative to say, conscious that her costume was not quite what she would have chosen for the moment. The Great Lady reared back and murmured cold clichés. Mr. Famous glowered. Only Tessières, as ignorant on his side as the Famous Couple were on theirs, merely remembered having met this dashing woman once before. He stepped in with amiable politenesses, admired Madame's costume — "Your back never showed to greater advantage," to which she responded, "And you, your mustache! The perfect setting! We were born out of our time." This dialogue carried things off, while Mother consoled Adam, and Father steered the Duchesse away, like a galleon on a port tack. Soon Tessières was telling Eve all about Lombert, the De Guichys and the modern situation; very indiscreet for him, very delightful for her. She whooped with pleasure and threw back her long red-wig hair. This was hands across the sea at least, even if two generations of American literature had failed to mesh.

People, different people, began to pay court to the Great Lady and the Famous Author, so a truce was maintained. They carefully avoided speaking to or even looking at one another for the rest of the evening. The parents must have been disappointed at their failure to crossbreed literary lions.

Merriment became pretty unconfined. With exhaustless energy we children scuttled about, getting in everybody's way, snitching forbidden swigs of champagne, eating things. On the balcony were too many tables with candles on them, and too many people drinking and smoking. Outside in the warm garden couples strolled, and we ran — down the broad path so beautifully mysterious now with its lanterns, round about the pond, water tinkling away at the feet of Mercury, people at last appropriately sitting on the little chairs at the little tables, some still with champagne glasses. Oh, it was glorious. We raced to the beach through the spooky gloom of the alligator's glen; and then, as we ran up the path again toward the illuminated noisy house, here came the moon, huge and almost sinisterly red behind pine boughs and eucalyptus; then at last sailing free and august and full over the sea. Glorious, glorious.

iii. The orchestra retired for a break and a smoke and the stage was set for our entertainments. The chandeliers were turned out in the *salon* and, illuminated by spotlights ingeniously rigged up by Dick and M. de Guichy and operated by a Dick-instructed Leone, a procession of costumes entered from the dining room. Mme de Guichy, only too pleased not to have to appear in her rather invidious light as her husband's ancestor's mistress (considering that she wasn't really married to him in fact, if what we had heard was true), played music for the March, a cleverly adapted potpourri of music from the *Midsummer Night's Dream* Overture. We paraded in a sort of vaguely chronological order. First came M. de Guichy as a sort of majordomo, very grand for all his small size, in that great wig, brocaded coat and wielding a huge gold-knobbed cane. Then followed the supposed Lombert and sister. After them came Nan and Ellie in operatic costume, of the same general period, so they looked well enough as courtiers, a page and lady in waiting. This did for the seventeenth century. The Shakespearean pageant could stand for either Renaissance or Classic. It began with Ronnie trotting out as that fairy — Puck or Pease-Blossom — all by himself, with tiny wings. He pranced and curveted to Mme de Guichy's scherzando accompaniment. This was a wild success. Next came Jane and I, with our glittering crowns and cloaks. Then, to the same statelier theme that had announced the De Guichy group, came the four lovers and Jocelyn and Dick very grand in their helmets and red velvet. We all swept out into the room and down to the end of it, and there became audience for the last comers.

I didn't know who the next four people were: an Egyptian pair (Cleopatra and escort I presumed) and then a furry cave couple. Finally, at the very end, representatives of the very beginning, came Adam and Eve, who received an ovation, based partly on their lastness, partly on everyone knowing who they really were, and partly on Mme de Guichy's tongue-in-cheek adaptation of the Wedding March. There were enough people not in the parade to create a large public for this spectacle.

Afterward we had music — Nan singing her aria "I'm all alone," Mme de Guichy, rather than Dick, accompanying her this time. Nan really did very well. We were proud of her. Then came the Spanish dance, Diego and Esterilla; and this time it was Dick on the guitar for flamenco atmosphere.

When Nan had finished her aria and was curtsying in a seventeenth-century fashion (she hoped) to the applause, very stiff and beruffed, Dick and Robbie appeared from the darkness of the audience into the spotlight. Dick carried the guitar he was going to play for the dancing; and Robbie was coming with him to be ready for the acrobatic finale. Dick had taken off his cloak and helmet, but Robbie still had his wreath, tilted rakishly over one eye. Like all of us, he'd had a sip too much champagne, and looked very flushed and bright-eyed. Their basic costumes were identical, the minimum white tunic, artfully pleated in a short V fore and aft, fastened at one shoulder, dark thighs and chests bare, gold belts around the narrow waists, gold sandals on the feet. That twinlike, or older-younger brother effect was never more remarkable, both glowing, both grinning under the sudden brightness. Dick carried his guitar, and Robbie, with the wreath over one temple, reminded me of Malhaut and his accident and Dick's "dedication" of him. A continuation, a fulfillment of that pagan rite; they ought to be about some business more important than merely their acrobatic act. The scar of Robbie's wound had disappeared now. In any case it would have been hidden by a russet lock and by the wreath itself.

They stopped for a moment, waiting while Esterilla bowed again; then came forward and stepped back into the shadow around the piano. Dick manned his guitar for the dancing, Diego and Esterilla prancing about, very foolish indeed. I thought; but at least they didn't bump into each other. This too was applauded. Then to a rattle and bang on the piano, out stepped the acrobats. Once more, as on the island picnic, they did their hauling and lifting and balancing, Robbie at the end rigidly suspended on Dick's uplifted palm, then slowly brought down over his shoulder to the floor. And once more the little business of Robbie bowing to one side, then crossing over and bowing to the other. Clapping, cries and bravos. Nan, Ellie, Mme de Guichy had to come out for credit too.

The main lights went on, champagne was circulated again, Leone shifting roles from lighting assistant to butler, and everyone congregated noisily. The band returned from the garden. "Tea for Two" brought us back to modern times.

iv. The party began to end, as parties must. Before it was all done, we had to go up to bed. Not without protests of course. First to go was Richie, who inevitably had quite a bit too much champagne, got first noisy, then bleary, and finally sick. So he was sent across to his room. Ronnie had disappeared right after the parade. We were next. Pam and Miranda were taken home by a friend of Jocelyn's. She stayed on and on. Only the older ones, Nan, Ellie, Robbie, exhilarated too, but not disgraceful, were allowed to see the very end of things. How unfair it was. I couldn't possibly sleep, so I stood at my window as usual, looking once more at the moonlit garden, listening once more for a nightingale.

The moon was certainly splendid enough. I couldn't see its face, back of me over our roof; but it flooded the garden and the court below, paling the few lanterns that still guttered down through the darkness. Final guests left; no one I knew. The De Guichy group were long gone.

Dick came out alone, breathing the silence, squinting at the moon, incongruously in his scanty Greek costume smoking a cigarette. Jocelyn came out soon afterward. He'd been waiting for her. They strolled a way down the path, murmuring; then back to the gate. He was earnest, she seemed exasperated, and at the end I could hear her voice, raised in distinct English emphasis.

"I don't care what you call it, *I* think it's rather disgusting. I don't see *how* . . ." she said, turning on him as she opened the gate.

"I didn't have to tell you about it, did I? I should think you might be flattered at the confidence." "Flattered! Oh, you're beyond belief. Good *night*. You appall me. And don't you dare hurt that child in any way, do you hear? I'll punish you with my own two hands if you do." "Hurt him? My God. You don't understand at all, do you?" "No, I do *not*." She slammed the gate, got into her little red car, slammed its door too and sputtered off.

Now what could that fight be about, I wondered. Jocelyn and Dick fought a good deal all the time about mysterious things. Then they made up and seemed as jolly as ever. But I felt it a vague duty to write another poem, or at least be poetical; so I dismissed mundane affairs, no matter how curious, and listened as hard as I could for a nightingale. There was no nightingale. How contradictory. Surely such a total moon and such a delirious occasion should have stirred one up. Perhaps they'd been frightened by the party. A pair of guests came out now and said effusive French good-byes to Dick, who lingered on in the courtyard still smoking.

I was certainly full of emotions, but no poems suggested themselves. Could it be that I was drunk, like Richie? The thought thrilled me. I had had any number of sips and so I suppose I ought to be drunk. It didn't feel very different though from just being tired and generally worked up. I certainly wasn't sick like Richie.

Robbie came out. I was surprised and annoyed that he was still allowed up. The girls were already in their room, bubbling and giggling away as usual. Robbie certainly seemed drunk. When he got out in the moonlight he flung out his arms and turned round and round. Then he did a few rather unsteady cartwheels. When he tried to stand on his hands, he fell sprawling to the gravel. Dick laughed at him; laughed and laughed in that stagy overacted way, bending over backward. When Robbie scrambled up, laughing too, Dick threw away his cigarette, cupped his hands at thigh level and shouted, "Hup!" It was their signal for part of the acrobatics. Robbie gave a yip and ran forward, leaping up so that one foot rested on Dick's clasped hands. He almost missed, and was laughing so hard he had to stop there, wavering and gasping, his knees against Dick's chest. "Concentrate!" said Dick, so Robbie sobered down, tightened up, and they were off through the last part of their act.

This ended as always, to much grunting and groaning, with Robbie being hoisted up on one of Dick's hands. He was supposed to stay there rigid and to lie perpendicular; the climax of their feats. But now he was so limp and lax that he just angled in an arc, his legs weaving, and Dick had to put up both hands to keep him from slipping off. He held him overhead by his waist and its golden belt, while Robbie deliberately swung his arms and legs about and made foolish noises.

"You're no good," said Dick, but laughing too. "Lemme down, lemme down," chanted Robbie. Dick lowered him so that he hung like a sack over his left shoulder; then, according to their routine, with his hands on the tight belt, Dick slowly drew Rob to the ground. But this time, instead of being taut and alert, bouncing to earth ready for his bow and the applause, Robbie just rolled and hung. One arm was caught behind Dick's head, around his neck. Robbie's own head swung back, then toppled over till his tangled hair, bound with the silly wreath, clouded Dick's face. Dick ejaculated "Pfui!" and with one hand tore off the wreath and threw it away toward the bushes. They stood there for a while, no longer laughing, facing the full glare of the moon. Rob's head still drooped against Dick's cheek, his arm hooked around him. Dick still had both hands tight about the narrowness of the belted waist, holding him close. Robbie seemed almost unconscious or

251

asleep; Dick stood very straight, taut and awake, looking down and sidewise at Robbie's face. They said and did nothing.

Finally Rob woke up, sighed, took his arm from around Dick, and moved away. Then he turned and they stood facing. Dick put out his hands onto Robbie's shoulders and they stared and stared into each other's eyes, not moving, not saying a word. Robbie too lifted hands, encircling Dick's wrists with his fingers, gradually running them up the brown arms till he grasped the shoulders. Like wrestlers, like a statue of wrestlers, they held this moonlit pose without seeming to breathe. Suddenly, as by common consent, still silent, they turned and strolled, arms about each other, toward the fence, out the gate, across the bone-white road, through the sharp edge of darkness into the garage and its cavernous overarch of shadows.

7.

i. Something I'd always been told by nurses when I was a baby was that if I made a face and the wind changed, the face would freeze and become permanent. Evidently face-making was a very bad thing. Now it was as though the ball had been a wind, and had frozen us in the various attitudes struck at the end of the party. In some cases it was almost as though our slight drunkennesses were to last forever. Richie for instance seemed to be in a mood of perpetual hangover, bilious, pale, incredibly morose and disagreeable. Dick and Rob on the other hand were almost feverishly glowing and exuberant. It was as though both of them were still "flushed with wine," as though the exhilaration of champagne and moonlight and their last acrobatic pantomime refused to wear off. Nan and Ellie continued to fancy themselves as divas and ballerinas, not to mention social authorities, and talked and talked about the party, about how successful they'd been, and how funny everyone else had looked. The rest of us got pretty fed up.

Especially, it would seem, the parents. Father's lameness had not been at all improved by stumping about at the party, Mother was obviously worn out by it. Jocelyn too was cross, harassed by getting ready to leave, still miffed at Dick. As for Jane and I, we were in a queer state of animation; but a suspended animation, without real object or outlet. We dreaded leaving our villa, yet were excited by the thought. We had nothing really to do, drifted about at loose ends, yet couldn't settle back to Amuria, which seemed to be finished, an epic with a happy ending.

The great exhausting processes of Packing were begun; Celestine, Mademoiselle, Mother, Nan, Ellie, like witches stirring some mammoth hell broth, destroyed the peace and security of the house, dragging trunks and bags and boxes about, dismantling things. The weather too was uncomfortable, hotter and hotter, a gray haze for a sky instead of brash blue. Altogether rather miserable yet rather stirring times.

Finally, the Websters' last day came; and simultaneously an invitation from Tessières for Nan and Ellie to come for a last visit. They were torn between horror at not being able to say proper good-byes to the Websters, and the delicious sadness of a farewell to their crippled friend. They made up their minds in public, going on and on and on about it. In the end they went to the Tessières'.

The rest of us went to the Websters', a final visit to what had been a second home for us all summer. Jane and I of course, as being too young, had always been a bit peripheral to the Webster circle. Even so we'd been over there often enough, and even to us it was saddening to think we'd never be able to go there again. The Websters were actually leaving next morning. We would miss the small sun-struck villa with its grape-arbored terraces, the rocky peninsular garden, almost as much a part of life as our own bosky Villa Esperance.

Everybody, even the parents, even Mademoiselle and Ronnie, everybody except Nan and Ellie, was there this morning, helping Jocelyn Webster put away things indoors, then romping out into the heat and down the rocks to the water. First, all of us, Father still hobbling there with a cane, swam from the regular swimming place at the end of the point, a little pebbly beach, hard on the feet. The water was oily, the air stifling, the world in general bleached. Then, led by Robbie, all of the children scrambled across the rocks westward to the cove where the famous diving rock was. It was in fact quite a scramble, and we were bruised, scratched and sweaty when we got there.

What a beautiful deep pool under its high square prominence! And though Jane refused to dive, and I was a bit scared myself, it was wonderful to drop head or feet first down into the green coolness, today as smooth as a landlocked lake. Rob gave us an exhibition of all he'd learned, real dives like the swan and jackknife, the various somersaults. Even Richie was seduced out of his gloom for a few attempts of his own. Rob as usual — he never gave up — encouraged and flattered him; Pam and Miranda too, and for a while there we were all happy together, the quartet reestablished in harmony, Jane and I in concert. We flopped in and out of the water barking like seals, screeching like seagulls.

We quieted down a bit and lay basking in the sun. It was getting close to lunchtime. Rob, who'd been sprawled in abandon on top of the diving rock next to Richie, rose, a signal to us all to think of going back to the house. He stood for a minute breathing deeply, smiling out over the sea; then he stretched, arms straight above his head, fingers of one hand linked about the wrist of the other, straining and pulling every muscle, wriggling his hips about, eyes closed and grinning in a sort of sensual ecstasy. It reminded me of something. I lifted my face off my crossed arms, observing him and remembering: that stop on the way to Malhaut, when Dick got out of his car and in exactly the same way stretched himself in the heat of the great bare plain. This then was another of Dick's mannerisms borrowed by Rob. It reminded me also, as an unpleasant afterthought, of the poses in those snapshots hidden in Richie's closet; taken I was sure on that very rock.

Richie, sitting half up on his elbow, was watching Robbie, his lips working, half amused, half, for some reason, angry. He clattered up, all bones, knees and elbows, and grinning and shouting something derisive gave Robbie a great push. Robbie turned and laughed and struck back, but he was off balance and surprised. Richie had him at a disadvantage, gave him a mighty heave and pushed him off flailing into the water. "Ha ha, that's your best dive yet!" Richie crowed, standing up on the edge of the rock looking down as Robbie came up flustered. Robbie threw water up at him, choking and laughing in good humor; and though Richie was grinning, there was something menacing and unpleasant under the horseplay. When Rob heaved up out of the water, dripping and glistening, he found he'd scraped the top of one foot going over the rock edge. Pam and Miranda both made a fuss over this; it was a rather red-looking blotch, and they accused Richie of roughness. Though Rob laughed it off and said he didn't even feel it, Richie's feelings were hurt, the girls were cross with him, the momentary concord was broken.

However, we all had to troop back now to get dressed and have lunch, and when we were finally seated out under the dapples of the grape arbor we were friends once more. This was the pretty place where Dick had entertained the Websters and hard-working Robbie with his guitar. You could see into the cool house with its thick walls and old black Mediterranean furniture, looking bare now it was stripped of the Websters' momentos. In the other direction lay the hot white garden, mostly rocks and varieties of cactus, with smooth paths and scattered black pines. Beyond lay the sea in its noonday glare. Up the coast we could just make out the tufted presence of our garden.

The grown-ups, including Mademoiselle, preferred to eat in the dining room, where it was cooler and quieter. We were noisy as could be out here, and yet sad. Pam and

Robbie were particularly boisterous, close to one another, while Miranda seemed to be soothing Richie. The grown-ups, inspired by Dick, made a point of not paying any attention to us, leaving us for this final time to enjoy ourselves by ourselves. The last, the last, the last of this black and white house and garden.

The parents came out, and we all pretended to be grief-stricken, sobbing and crying our good-byes, knowing the Websters would be coming over in an hour or two to visit us.

ii.   Our cellar, our siesta time seemed rather boring and desolate. We made halfhearted Amurian attempts. We built a bijou pleasure dome of Mah-Jongg blocks. We entertained Korean royalty in it. Jane in a perverse fit of boredom invented a typhoon which wrecked the whole thing, and I got angry with her. The truth was, Amuria didn't really interest us any more. What to do?

When the Websters came, we tried to be exuberant for them; but we were still listless. We felt obligated to tag along, while the quartet wandered up and down the garden trying to think of something. It was too early to swim, certainly. It was too oppressive for violent action. Up and down the broad gravel path from porch to pond we trailed, talking in spurts, desultory. Lagarde followed along, then disappeared and was finally taken into the kitchen by Celestine.

Later in the afternoon, instead of just a haze, there were big clouds eastward. They mounded up in satisfactory thunderheads above the flaccid eucalyptus, the dark sickle-shaped leaves hanging for once quite stirless. I would stop to lose myself for a while in those far palaces beyond the trees, then run to catch up. Pamela took a few pictures. But we'd already taken so many pictures. The cicadas were very loud today. Each individual round white pebble at our feet was hot to the touch under the baking afternoon. The quartet laughed all the time, and settled down in odd places: that little sort of alcove that neighbored our play cellar, down a step or two. Nobody ever sat there on that bench but Mademoiselle. But she kept indoors today. What to do, what to do? The boys so wanted to make something special of this last visit, the girls were full of goodwill and sorrow; but nothing seemed to happen. For once, for the first time our garden seemed empty of enchantment and suggestion. For the first time it seemed very like the prison it often was for Nan.

We were pleased when Mademoiselle appeared on the balcony and called down to us (we were still sprawled in her alcove) to come up for *goûter*. We trampled into the gloom of the house. Though things were ready for us on the balcony, we insisted on moving into the black dining room, where it was coldest and darkest. There we ate and gabbled, and when we were done, made a game of having the Webster girls try to find our secret compartment and its blueprints. With much squatting and squealing, they finally succeeded.

Then we spread the blueprints out on the refectory table and pored over them — those battleships and cruisers — full of idle speculations and wild fancies. Richie was stirred into his usual frenzy, imagining a dozen plots past and present, pointing out significant, nonexistent clues and coincidences. Finally forthright Pam turned on him. "Oh, Richie, I really do think you're so *absurd* about all this! Who cares nowadays? There's not going to be any more war." "That's what M. de Guichy says," I volunteered. "Yes, so why should anyone care about these old things?" Richie glared at her and sat for a moment building up his storm. He burst out, "Oh yeah? That's because you don't know anything. There's a spy in this house spying all the time, *right now*. . . ." Robbie cut across him roughly. "You're crazy, and you better shut up with all that stupid stuff." Robbie was flushed and furious. "Or I'll shut you up myself." Richie twitched and muttered, but he was afraid of Robbie, and simmered down. The girls were embarrassed and pretended not to notice. Jane and I exchanged one of our significant looks. "Let's get out of here," ordered Captain Rob, and so we put away the plans and shut the compartment and trailed out into the glowering afternoon.

Jane and I felt we really couldn't stand much more of this, and looked for an opportunity to sneak off. The others seemed perfectly content to wander and chatter and push and shove, and occasionally sit down, doing nothing. We waited for our proper moment and slipped off into the shrubbery. After a while our absence was noticed, and as much out of sheer idleness as any real need to have us around, the others began calling for us and looking for us.

So we evolved a kind of one-sided hide-and-seek, and it was quite fun. The idea was for us to try to vanish without being caught. As we cruised about we'd fall back, dart behind a tree together or separately, and then try to make for deeper shelter. It was difficult; when we were caught we would suffer imaginary punishments and we'd howl in imaginary torment. We were obviously (Jane and I decided) some sort of . . . well, spies. Traitors and deserters from an army, let's say. We never bothered to be clear about this, just enjoying the escapade for its own sake, the amusement of fading away like savages into the shade. It was hard too. We were always caught or found. But the others had only half a mind for us and this game.

They seemed to be having their own dreary messy sort of adolescent fun.

At one point, when we were down at that rather shrubby scrubby east end of the garden, near the orphanage wall, places where none of us ever went, Jane and I managed a real getaway. The quartet were at that moment having a furious but hilarious argument, so we slipped off. "Follow me," whispered Jane, conspiratorial. We ducked and scrambled through the dense undergrowth. Without another word she led me zigzag and crouching to a tiny open circle at the foot of a clump of pine trees, right next to the wall. It was a brand-new hiding place she'd found all by herself, and she was rightly proud of it. We could hear the calls of the hunters after us, like hounds, beating in nearby thickets; but here we were safe and sheltered, bushed thick about and overhead, a round ring of pine needles underneath us and the hot pine smell everywhere. We settled down quietly and cozily, smothering giggles as we heard the frustrated rampaging of the others. They made such a noise.

A little bell sounded, a school bell tinkling faintly from the orphanage, and then a surge of children's voices muffled by the wall and the pine trees. This was such a nice secret place; more remarkable for being brand new. I'd have thought that every possible nook of this garden had already been exploited. The hunters were closing in on us, nearer and nearer.

It took a long long time for them to find us, and they were almost ready to give up before Pam's ruddy sweaty face, framed in messy gold, came at us through the bushes. "A-HAH! There you are, my beauties!" she crowed, and then called the rest of them. How they crashed and hollered, breaking open our seclusion. We were half glad and half sorry as they tied our arms behind us with handkerchiefs and prepared to torture us. They were now the savages we supposed. At any rate, it was lots of fun, and we were renegades of some kind; we certainly deserved whatever we got.

iii. After our swim, later than usual because we were all so frivously involved in our hide-and-seek, warmer than usual under a sky now really heavy with cloud and an air totally breezeless, we got dressed up and ready for dinner. It was to be a formal celebration just for *us*, waited on by Leone, laid out on the balcony. The grown-ups, after a drink, were to go out for the last time to a favorite restaurant down the coast. Sometime later Nan and Ellie were due to come back from the Tessières', conveyed by the De Guichys; so that at the end everybody could say good-bye to everybody.

The last, the last; the last time the balcony would be filled by the yapping of Dick and Jocelyn together, the ramping energies of the Carruthers boys and the Webster girls. Everyone was indeed all dressed up, I of course in my horrid communion suit, Rob in his green blazer and tight pants, the girls in pretty dresses. They certainly did look better that way than in the bathing suits or the so-called "beach pajamas" or gym suits they usually wore.

Rob and Pamela again sat close to one another, balanced on the balcony rail. Pam had a firm grip on a stanchion. Rob however just teetered, both hands on the rail but his feet usually swinging. Mother spoke to him about it, with no effect. He was so sure of himself. They were subdued tonight, full of sidelong glances and downcast smiles. They had never looked so clean and brilliant. Dick and Jocelyn sat, also side by side, watching them, talking quietly but

263

almost inaudibly, since Richie and Miranda were making such a racket that everyone else spoke in their shadow.

But I could hear Pam and Rob, he looking down at his swinging feet. "You will write me, won't you?" Pam would be saying. "Sure. Of course." "You won't at all! I hate to write letters, don't you?" Rob, ashamed to admit that he never wrote them, just laughed. "But I do like to get them," said Pam remorselessly, "and if we don't write we'll lose touch." "Oh, I'll write," said Rob, "but you have to too." I thought to myself, I bet neither of you do. I was quite resigned to the fact that none of us would ever see any of the others as long as we lived; the Websters, the De Guichys, the Tessières would go from our lives forever.

Dick and Jocelyn meanwhile were talking too, of Pam and Rob, but quietly so as not to be overheard by them. "Now you must admit they do suit each other," said Jocelyn. "So blond and rose. Such a pity they'll never meet again, probably." "I wouldn't be too sure. I'll be around, and you can have both of us for a visit." "Rob? With you? No indeed. Separately perhaps." She turned to him impulsively, away from the couple on the railing. "It's so much better, much *prettier*, isn't it? I mean the two of them. So much more natural." "Of course, of course. Nobody would deny that; especially me! For him it's just a phase. Natural enough though. He'll forget all about it in a year or two. Forget I ever existed." "And for you?" said Jocelyn, very seriously. "For me? Ah, I don't know." He looked down, like Robbie, at his feet; but they were anchored before him, not idly dangling. Jocelyn put out her hand, again impulsively. "Oh, Dick, please, please be careful!" Dick, suddenly conscious of all of us around him, looked at her in warning. "I'm leaving in a few days, you know. They all leave soon after. I won't see them for years." She gave a great artificial sigh, smiling and pouting. "Good!" "But I'll see *you* whenever you want me to," said

264

Dick. "Even better!" "So, we're friends?" "We shall see, we shall see. But for the moment, yes."

The parents stood up, full of advice; Dick and Jocelyn stood up. They were off for dinner, leaving us by ourselves, but with trepidation. "Now do behave," said Jocelyn, kissing her daughters, and Mother kissed all of us. It was as though we were to be separated forever; a rehearsal for the real farewells when they returned. Even Dick participated. He also kissed the Webster girls, with a facetious remark or two, and gave a clap on the back to Richie, who grinned but winced. He then semi-solemnly shook hands with Robbie. "You're senior officer in charge here, Major. I expect you to do your duty." He placed one hand on Rob's shoulder. "The honor of the cavalry is in yo' keeping. God bless you!" He bowed his head, stern and sorrowful. "You and your men is all that stands between these here wimmin and chillen and them Injuns." "Oh, come on, Dick," cried Jocelyn. But half in play, oddly half in earnest, Rob and Dick lingered, shaking hands as though it really were some solemn occasion.

iv. We were left now to ourselves. The first thing Major Robbie did was request permission for us officers to take our coats off. His blazer was half down his arms as he asked. "La, sir!" said Pamela, her hands to her face, "I've never seen a gentleman in his shirt-sleeves." It was atrociously hot. Bad enough being in collar and tie (my ridiculous, infamous, wide effeminate Frenchified "Eton collar" that spread out over my shoulders!). Coats were too much.

So that when we sat down at the table on the balcony, our parents' attempt at formality was a bit dissipated by our undress. Still, there were candles, motionless in the still warmth, there was Leone bustling back of us, scolding us or teasing us, there was the damask tablecloth and the wine, given us in half glasses. Like that evening at the Maritime so long ago, it was all quite "gala."

Pam started playing up to this by imitating grown-up party mannerisms, always a favorite with us: the affected overanimation, the fluting voice, the exaggerated laughter. "You, you live for your musta-ahche, and I for my back," she quoted, bridling at Rob, next to her and at the head of the table, and soon we were all screaming about in a parody of social scintillation.

This act brought to mind that actual evening when the Famous Couple had examined us, and we went over those events with our own more genuine and raucous, unpolite laughter. Soon, appropriate to this final occasion, we were rehearsing all sorts of old events, "Remember when . . ." "Remember that time . . ." Many of the times were strange to me, memories of the quartet only. But some of our most conspicuous community events had been, in fact, mine.

"Did they ever find that leopard?" for instance; and I had the pleasure of telling my tale all over again — cross-washing, leopard-glimpsing — to a thoroughly sympathetic audience. Every one of them believed in my leopard, every single one. We mentioned trips to the Maritime, the boys told of Malhaut (Richie's skeleton, Robbie's accident). We all looked at the faint traces of the scar on Rob's temple.

Finally we got to the discovery of the secret compartment, the mysterious battleship plans. Again, since Ellie wasn't there, I got all the credit; and Jane, as expected, withdrew into injured silence. Richie, also as expected, began to seethe and bubble like a geyser about to erupt; but knowing how Rob felt about these dark plots and sinister suspicions, Richie merely wriggled in his chair and made his fierce faces. "Oh dear, nothing like that *ever* happens at home," sighed Pam. "Does it, Miranda?" "Well, we do have a ghost." "Pish-*tush!*" said Pam, an expression that sent the rest of us off into squalls of laughter.

For the moment we seemed to have avoided ugliness between Rob and Richie — the increasing quarrel that seeped like a dank undercurrent through all our family relationships, bearing a sediment of mystery and incomprehensible emotion. What was the fight about? Why was Richie so bitter, why was Rob so stern, and yet . . . well, frightened? Frightened of whatever secrets Richie thought he possessed, so afraid of Richie's letting something out of its cage. We talked breathlessly about Miranda's English ghost, of which Pam was thoroughly scornful; even by Miranda's account it was a pretty pathetic, wispy creature. But our minds were really on that other matter: spies, what Richie knew or suspected, what Robbie feared. A revelation that might send Dick to jail or even to the firing squad? The exposure of his godlike hero as some sort of vile traitor? Richie seethed with malice and indignation, Rob kept him under control, like a horse ready to bolt or to buck. We two, Jane and I, observed and conjectured and hoped, but got no inkling of what the mystery was. And everyone else, except perhaps Father in his worry about Richie's disposition, seemed quite unaware that anything was going on at all.

Pam and Miranda certainly chose to ignore the business; and since the near-crisis had been so easily passed, they went on chattering — plans, schools, the future now rather than the past. Rob entered into this with gusto. Not so Richie, permanently depressed, morose, unresponsive to Miranda's teasings and insinuations.

Finally, dinner was over. We sat about the table in the twilight, by the glimmer of candles, while Leone cleared the dessert dishes and we made noisy French conversation with her. There was the great honking of an auto horn; the De Guichys had arrived, bringing back the girls. We tumbled out to see them. After the ball, peace between the two estranged branches of that august house had been declared, and Tessières had actually asked the renegade Duke and consort over for a visit. De Guichy now brought home our sisters, and stayed to say farewells too, for he and his wife were now off for another visit, this time to her relations. It was altogether a time for emotional demonstrations. De Guichy embraced me and kissed me on alternate cheeks. How embarrassed, amused and flattered I was. The Carruthers girls told the Webster girls about their visit and then made vast implausible plans for correspondence and visits to England and America. When the parents returned we were still standing out there, milling about like a crowd in a play.

Dick and Jocelyn insisted on strolling down toward the pond; by themselves. Father insisted on having an *apéritif* with the De Guichys on the balcony. Since there was nothing arranged for the youngsters we were restless; and now really upset by the partings. When Dick and Jocelyn got back, it was time. Out we streamed again, seeing Jocelyn and Pam and Miranda into that little red car, now black-looking in this end of twilight, seeing the De Guichys into their shaky, rented sedan (I was surprised he knew how to drive; but then he knew everything). We called and waved and shouted funny remarks, and stood chattering for a long time after both cars had driven off in their opposite directions.

P A R T   T W O

i. The departure of the Websters, and the De Guichys too, left a terrible vacancy; a surprising vacancy. We had had no idea of how large a part the Websters in particular had played in our lives. We'd taken them for granted. The boys of course were especially bereft; more especially now that they were so uneasy with each other. Robbie did his best to go back to their former relationship. Even Richie seemed willing to make an effort. But Dick was still there, there was so much last-minute tutoring and diving to do.

We were thrown back too, Jane and I, on our own resources, and for once, for the first time, we didn't seem to have many. The confinement of the cellar after lunch was just that. Mah-Jongg blocks were just Mah-Jongg blocks, curtains just old curtains. Jane grew moody, and even committed the heresy of bringing down a book to read there. Creative inspiration was at a very low ebb.

Actually our new game really began that very time, while Jane was absorbed in her book. I was cross with her for reading, so I sneaked off, to see if she'd notice me, and hid around a corner. When Jane looked up, I was gone. She called. I didn't answer. She started looking for me, and it was reminiscent of the fun we had had that last day with the Webster girls. Soon we'd developed this into a full-scale dramatic series. It differed from our old Amuria in that it could be set anywhere in the Villa Esperance. We were all over the place with it, indoors and out.

Though the action was more suitable to the Renaissance — the age of say the opera *Esterilla*, the decor of Spanish chest and carved dining room paneling — we kept the scene, for the sake of continuity, in old Amuria; but our characters were no longer royalty. We were spies.

The story was now to involve two gorgeous young people, Kim Cha (Jane) and Gurandu (Howie). Kim was a Korean lady-in-waiting to the Empress of Amuria, Gurandu the captain of the royal bodyguard. She was really a spy for Korea. He was really a brother of Agragor's wicked concubine Lilipopo. He had escaped execution, changed his name and was now in league with various subversive pro-Agragor elements, plotting to slay the Emperor and seize the throne for himself. Little did anyone know!

Meanwhile of course Kim Cha and Gurandu had fallen desperately in love; but they couldn't get together because ladies-in-waiting had their heads chopped off if they fooled around. An added and welcome new complication had also been added: the Chinese. We'd never done much about the Chinese before. Now it seemed they were out to acquire Korea, Amuria and the land of the Wa Hus by devious means. They had succeeded in bribing *both* Kim Cha and Gurandu, separately. So the lovers met secretly, plotted their various plots secretly, and never knew about each other's Chinese affiliations. This all meant that we had to spend our time leaving secret messages, holding secret trysts, receiving secret instructions from China, meeting secretly with other conspirators. Jane and I slipped through the hall, skulked in the dining room, rustled behind bushes. If we'd had an arras, we would have rustled behind that.

Naturally it didn't take long before Richie got wind of our enterprises. He would intercept a message, written in a code of oriental characters, and try to force us to tell him what it meant. "Aw come on!" he'd whine, and he was such a nuisance that we finally decided to let him play too. We gave him a name, Fung Wa (cousin of Nu Wa, cousin of old Wa Fung) and made him a spy for the Wa Hus. He loved his name and went around repeating it to himself with relish, "Fung WA-A!," but aside from the fact that he was a spy and oriental, we didn't tell him a thing. He didn't really care. It was action he was after. He helped us build up our code book of oriental characters, symbols for people (Gurandu, Kim Cha) and places (the Throne Room and the Council Chamber, otherwise *salon* and dining room), and he was full of ideas about our messages — a sort of treasure hunt in which message led on to message and finally to a get-together to hatch *more* messages.

No one was safe from our spying, though when we saw Richie sneaking out of Mother's room we put a stop to that. The parents were off limits; but not Dick or Celestine or Nan and Ellie. How we hid and pried, how we tracked them through house and garden; and yet nobody knew, nobody seemed to notice us. How clever we were to be sure.

We spent much time in Jane's new secret hiding place, even allowing Richie to join us once in a while. There we hatched our plots; and (when Richie wasn't around) carried on the dim tangled story of Gurandu and Kim Cha and their love affair, which really wasn't progressing. Unlike our previous Pageant of Amuria, this new enterprise was full of miscellaneous adventure, but very low in true plot development.

The weather obliged us by providing just the right atmosphere. It grew increasingly oppressive. Each afternoon the clouds piled up, yellow, sinister. It was deadly calm, and deadly hot too — no breeze, no relief. Nights were stifling. We were obviously in for something, just as the machinations of Gurandu and Kim Cha were bound, if properly handled, to set off some fearful Amurian explosion.

ii. It was late morning, our most oppressive day so far; but a sultry sun came through veils of saffron, and a restless gusty wind disturbed the trees. I dallied in the gloom of the Council Chamber (dining room) writing notes, cogitating on ingenious uses for them. Outside there was a confused murmur of leaves, of birds and insects, but no sound of voices. The cicadas though were never louder; nobody seemed to be about. A motorboat put-putted along past our shores; most unusual. I resented the intrusion. It passed off. I planned now to steal from the Council Chamber by a window, creep along the balcony outside, close to the wall, see if anyone was in the *salon*, drop a note there, and . . . what exactly? Something slimy. The dining room windows were high up, and opened on that end of the balcony sacred to the parents. Since the terracing went all the way to the end of the house, there was one part, alongside the windowless wall of the children's dining room, that was secluded, a cul-de-sac. There Mother kept a chaise longue and a table littered with her books and sewing, and it was understood that children were not allowed. I heard no sound, so I had cautiously drawn myself up and put one leg over the windowsill before I saw that somebody was there in Mother's nook. Two people in fact.

Robbie was lying sprawled in Mother's forbidden chair. He looked as though he'd been asleep, and had just come awake, ruddy and bewildered. He wore nothing but his old sailor pants and a shirt. The pants had evidently been seized by Celestine since last wearing and washed and starched till they were crisp, if still paint-spotted. His shirt was wide open and his upper body bared. Dick sat astraddle behind him, arms crossed on a chair back, dangling in Robbie's face the gold mesh bracelet of his wristwatch. The watch had been tickling Rob's sun-peeled nose. Now Rob was looking up at Dick, reaching to catch the bracelet. Dick, still unsmiling, twitched it out of reach, as Rob lifted one hand, and smiling with sleepy radiance, let it fall to hang from the chair back. He lay there smiling and gazing at Dick, and Dick sat, now shaking with that soundless laughter of his. Robbie's hips and legs moved with small sensuous awakening stretches.

Should I go on out, or creep back in? The two had no idea I was there. I might make it. The risk of being caught added zest. On the other hand what a fool they'd think me if they did catch me, slinking like that along the wall toward the *salon*. They might laugh or ask questions. Better not take the chance. Very cautiously I pulled my leg in and left them alone on the porch.

Lunch was as noisy as the morning had been silent. We were all, for this meal, to eat in the children's dining room, most unpleasant on a day like this, enough sun outside to make it hot, and a steamy, kitchen-smelly, turbid fog inside. Why this change of routine? We were all indignant about being kicked off the porch. Nan's explanations made us feel little better.

We were packed in here because, forsooth, Dick had brought a special unexpected female guest for lunch on the balcony, and it was obvious that we were not good enough for her. Nan dilated; and who could dilate at greater length, making so much of so little? For reasons of her own she gloried in this guest, and described in detail just how beautiful, smart and rich she was. The idea was that, though Nan couldn't eat with her either, she had at least seen her, spoken to her; and had been able to understand how utterly beneath this paragon the rest of us all were.

How beautiful this woman was! Very dark, very slim, dressed all in the most chic of black with *real pearls!* And no hat! Gold cigarette case and holder and compact and purse were described lovingly, supposedly for Ellie's benefit, who responded with the proper awed enthusiasm, but really for the benefit of us all.

Dick, it seemed, was head over heels in love with her, according to Nan, but she wouldn't marry him because he didn't *do* anything. She herself of course did nothing but race around the Riviera to parties in a car just as wonderful as Dick's, driving at top speed and getting arrested all the time.

We tried to carry on conversations of our own under

this downpour of information, but it was difficult. Nan talked so hilariously, full of her subject; and we were actually so interested. Robbie had come to lunch with his arm affectionately around Richie's shoulders, discussing something dull like a get-together on the dock, later in the afternoon after Rob had done his homework. They kept on talking to each other for a while, oblivious of the rest of us; but gradually Nan's eulogy became more and more engrossing to Richie. He was all ears; while on the other hand Robbie slumped more and more despondent over his food, elbows on the table, feeding himself morosely in a very crude manner.

Dick, it seemed, was going to make one more attack on the citadel. He'd given his lady all summer to make up her mind and now he was going to make her say *yes*. How wonderful to have someone like that in the family! What a villa she had in Cannes! Goodness what gardens and fountains and dinners and balls every other minute and a huge swimming pool with columns around it!

Dick, it seemed, was to cut short his visit here to us and hustle right over to that villa and if she said no this time Nan didn't know what the poor thing would do, he would be so distracted. He might even *kill* himself!

Jane sniffed audibly at this, Ellie drank it in, Robbie ignored it. Richie sat forward grinning with sarcastic delight and muttering interjections, presumably in asides to Robbie, though he paid no attention to them at all. "Wow!" he'd say, apropos swimming pool and columns, "Hot diggity!" and other of his low catch phrases, that he thought were so up to date and rebellious and offensive to the parents (as indeed they were).

Dick, it seemed, just couldn't wait to get out of here and be gone to his lady love.

"Well, he better not *wait* or he'll be sorry." Richie growled this threat, again in Robbie's direction, just as though he really thought Robbie might be responsive. Robbie turned, gave him one stony stare, then went back to his guzzling again.

Nan interrupted her exordium long enough to correct Robbie's manners. "Honestly, the way you eat, Robbie, what an oaf!" Then she went right back to Dick and glamor. Robbie sat up very straight, pushed his plate away, and brooded with his head lowered, mouth full and sorrowful, eyes down. He looked as though he might be holding back tears. Richie grew more and more exultant. As though overcome against all judgment and compunction by his malice, he kept nudging Robbie's arm and saying, "That'll put old Jocelyn in her place, hunh?" or "What a babe. Guess she can handle Dick all right. I hope she gives him hell," until suddenly Rob stood up, stiff and powerful with anger, slammed his napkin on the table, glowered down at Richie as though he might demolish him, and then hunched out of the room.

"Heavens, what's got into him?" said Nan blithely, then went right on gabbling to Ellie about details of grandeur. Dick's guest had one hundred dresses at least. Nan, on the basis of hearsay, undertook to describe each one. Ellie did not bother to check her credentials.

As Rob got up, Richie first sat there terrified and twitching, then half rose to follow him. Finally he sagged down, appalled by what he'd done. He spent the rest of the meal rocking to and fro, groaning to himself, regretting his stupidity, afraid to run after Robbie, afraid not to. Nan remained jubilant. She'd put a spoke in Rob's wheel and paid off Jocelyn *in absentia* too. If she, Nan, could not be the apple of her uncle's eye, then at least no other member of this community, past or present, could or would be that apple.

iii. Down in our cellar Jane and I, as so often before, talked and talked it over. Could all this be true? The woman certainly existed, and was up on the balcony right now. We could hear her voice above us, throaty and full of a contagious deep laughter. We hadn't seen her, and doubted if we'd be allowed to. But suppose Dick did leave? What would Richie do with his precious secrets then? And we'd never never know what it was all about! "Can't you just *ask* Richie?" said Jane, and I made a face. "He'd never tell me." "Well, you could try, couldn't you?" Yes, I could. But when and how? Though after all we were seeing a good deal of him these days.

Which brought us back to Amuria and our truly important problems. Instead of being a full-blown, panoplied and gorgeous unity of all the arts, our play was now a shambles of disjointed fragments. There was our Gurandu-Kim Cha story, which was getting nowhere. There was our play with Richie, all those messages, which was getting monotonous. And there was Amurian history itself — all that had gone on in our cellar; our blocks, our costumes, that glorious long lurid chronicle, which was being sadly neglected.

For instance, down here after lunch there really wasn't much for us to do. We'd pretty well finished our Amurian code-message dictionary. It was hard to play at Gurandu in this restricted area; and besides, we missed mucking about with pebbles and dirt and roads. So we made up our minds. We'd get rid of Richie somehow, and then kill off Gurandu and that whole bunch. Meanwhile, Liu and Kalila, in the flush of prosperity (did they know what dire plottings and threats overshadowed them?), would launch a vast program of construction: a whole new palace in the capital, and all over the country summer lodges, each a masterpiece of this final flowering of Amurian art and architecture. For after all, in a matter of days we'd be gone; then what would happen to Amuria?

We set to with absorption on the building of the new palace. It was to be enormous. Perhaps we'd have to get new blocks to continue after our old Mah-Jongg pieces gave out. Then esplanades would lead to the edge of the gravel path out there, and another palace would stand on the site of the ravaged tomb of old grandfather Liu the Great (how long ago that had been). Then, up in front of the house . . . It was to be a sunset burst before we left forever.

We had to tear ourselves away from our new palace to meet Richie upstairs. He grew more and more eager as we grew less and less. He was in the *salon* waiting for us and he suggested a typically desperate adventure. We were each to make up a message and leave it in somebody's room — right on the bed. Then each one of us would have to go to a room and pick up someone else's message there, all without being seen or caught, either by the rest of the family, or by one another. For instance, I had to place my message in Nan's room, and pick up one in Dick's that had been dropped there by Jane. Wow! We'd never get away with that! Each message would then guide us to a separate place in the garden, where Richie would leave instructions for us all to meet together in some other place — that familiar routine. Perhaps, on second thought, the bed was too conspicuous a place for messages. . . . Time passed so quickly as we whispered and chuckled together. Richie in this mood, self-forgetful and inventive, was such a deviously delightful co-worker.

iv. He himself broke it up however by looking at his watch and remembering his date on the dock with Robbie. He mustn't be late. He and I left Jane for the children's dining room, where the boys were allowed to keep their bathing suits, if thoroughly dry, in a drawer of the hideous fumed-oak sideboard.

Robbie was already there undressing. Richie rushed up to him, as though nothing had happened between them at lunch, as though he could expect to be welcome. He clutched Robbie by the arm and still full of the exuberance of his conspiracy with us, overexuberant in fact as always, began to tell Rob all about it. "Hey, we've been having more fun . . ." I was appalled. Richie knew how dead secret this was all supposed to be.

I was about to interrupt him; but I needn't have worried. Robbie shook Rich's hand off his arm before he'd said anything damaging, and walked over to the window carrying his clothes and trunks. He said nothing, and didn't even look at us. Richie stood there in a silent frenzy, his hands clenching spasmodically. "All right!" he screamed. "All right, you can go to hell! You both can go to hell. That's where you belong and I hope you fry and sizzle." As Richie cursed him Robbie stood with his back to us, facing the window, quickly stripping off his trousers and underpants, about to put on his trunks. Richie, now roaring incoherently, flung himself across the room caroming off the furniture, and grabbed Robbie's bare shoulders. Rob turned, cut down Richie's arms, and struck him across the face. Richie fell back into a chair and sat there, holding his cheek, mouth open, eyes wide, dead white under his brown sallowness.

Rob stood naked against the window, his dangling undershirt held to his midriff as though for protection,

278

wide shoulders and slim curve of waist and hip silhouetted against the sulfureous light. "Don't touch me," he whispered, his face in the shadows very still, open-eyed and expressionless. "Don't you ever touch me again." He stooped, scrambling into his trunks and sandals, and grabbing his towel from the windowsill, raced out of the door and down toward the beach.

Richie sat stupefied, mouth still open, still holding his hand to his face. I started undressing. Richie, in a daze, speechless, followed suit.

As we walked slowly down the broad path, lingering because Richie was so afraid to meet Robbie again, I dared to break our silence. "Is that really true about Uncle Dick leaving right away?" Richie nodded absently. "No, I mean about the lady and all?" Richie merely shrugged. I screwed up my courage. "Well, if he goes, you won't be able to tell anybody about your secret, will you?" I was appalled at my audacity. Richie however was so lost in despair that he barely responded. He looked at me as though he'd half heard me. "Secret? What secret?" My God, he'd been hinting about nothing else for weeks.

"Your secret about Dick," I said, my lips dry. "What about it?" said Richie, now alert and wary. "Well, are you going to tell anybody? If it's that important you ought to tell Father, shouldn't you?" Richie laughed, discordant, disconsolate. "It's important all right!" "What are you going to do?" But Richie only shook his head and gritted his teeth. Then he gave me a look which told me pretty plainly to keep my mouth closed.

We sauntered without speaking to the pond. How oppressive the sky and air were, the wind now subsided, the sun obscured in an increasing dun cloud cover. We turned down the steps past the alligator. At the point where the path led up to the tower Richie suddenly balked, jerked his head up that way and said, "Come on." "What for?" "Aw shut up and come on." Mystified, I followed him up to the tower.

The sea lay all about us, a strange brown-black, like a taut sheet of satin, but rippled underneath by a quite sizable swell, breaking white on the rocks at the tower's base. It was wonderfully threatening, the horizon heavy and dark beyond the far little islands. I exclaimed and pointed out there to Richie, glad now he'd made me come. But he was not interested. He was looking at the dock, close enough down below us, but obscured by intervening pine branches.

We could see the end of it though clearly enough, and Dick and Robbie were there, practicing the diving as usual. Dick stood close behind Robbie checking his shoulders and stance, giving him advice inaudible to us. Robbie turned his head to look back at him, laughing, and as Dick brought his hands down to adjust Robbie's hips, Rob seized both of Dick's wrists and pulled the arms about him. Dick stood there holding Robbie tight, bending his face down to nuzzle Rob's brown neck and red-bronze hair. Otherwise both of them were as silent and taut as the sea and sky.

Richie, standing next to me livid with attention, began slowly, rhythmically to beat the heels of both hands on the parapet, baring his teeth, half crouching, making a low sound like a smothered scream. The beat of his hands grew faster and harder, hands turned to fists, he gave one hoarse shout and turned running down the steps. As I stumbled after him I saw him head not down to the beach, but flailing up the shortcut to the house.

8.

i. The storm broke after midnight. We'd had a restless bedgoing, disturbed and excited by the obvious threat in the atmosphere — offstage thunder, heavy clouds, breathless quiet. Bed itself was sticky and rumpled. I'd held off going to sleep as long as I could, hoping for the cataclysm, hopping up to look out the window. When at last the rain did come I half woke, thought of rising again, relished the roar and the crash, and involuntarily slipped back to dreams again.

When morning came the storm was still rampaging, an inexhaustible hurricane. I could scarcely see the garden out my window through the torrents, my bedroom floor was puddled. I dashed through dressing, dashed downstairs, dashed through breakfast so as to get out into it. Jane and I, Nan and Ellie, waterproofed and exuberant, went out to see. Neither of the boys had yet appeared.

The impact almost smothered us, knocked us over. We had to turn our backs and duck our faces. Then we scuttled, heads lowered, along the littered path to watch the brown turbulence about the alligator in the glen, the ocean flattened but roiling, seen from the tower, the leaves and branches down everywhere, the sudden rivulets newly grooved in the gravel of the paths. It was as satisfactory and thrilling as possible; much better, the girls all magnanimously admitted, than the last rain storm that I'd missed when I was sick.

We finally stamped back into the front hall and took off our things, leaving great splotches that Celestine had to mop up, grumbling. We found the house in almost as much turmoil as the garden, the final throes of packing. Nan and Ellie were immediately commandeered, and that was the last we saw of them. The boys were now about, heaving heavy objects. Mother and Celestine and Mademoiselle were in command, though since Ronnie was sick in bed Mademoiselle had to entertain him a good deal.

It was a mess. We were definitely peripheral. We hung about a bit, then faded away and into the somber dining room, where we began to construct oriental messages. Richie joined us. The plan was now not to leave these messages on beds, but to *hide* them; interior messages to be left and discovered during bad weather, then exterior messages to be concealed and found in the garden when the good weather came. Eventually the inevitable rendezvous for all three of us, and an account of our adventures.

While Richie was there, eager, overeager, conspiratorial as ever, it seemed like great fun. Whenever he left us, we lost enthusiasm. But now, for the moment, for the morning, we were enthralled, planning just where we'd hide our coded cards, just where in the garden we'd send our terrified recipients.

Rob wandered in. Obviously heavy work was no longer needed upstairs. Richie seized on him, obsequious and fawning. Robbie was kind enough to him, smiled vaguely, but seemed thoroughly preoccupied. Something was on his mind. When Richie immediately began to show him all our messages, all our codes, we started to protest. But then did we really care? And Robbie was so totally uninterested. He smiled perfunctorily, took none of it in, said a few words of condescending meaningless quasi-parental praise, and then wandered out again.

We were greatly relieved. Richie was crushed. Where before he'd been too excited by our game, he was now too disenchanted. He fussed about with us for a while, then stood up and said in a heartbroken voice, "What's the use? What's the use?" As though suddenly everything depended on Robbie's approval.

Fortunately at this moment we were called in to a midmorning *goûter*. Richie remained tragic and twitchy, Rob stolid and abstracted, Nan and Ellie full of their business. When we returned to the dining room Richie was not with us. We waited awhile for him. I took a small cautious dutiful tour of the downstairs looking for him. I called up the stairs. When it was clear that he wasn't going to come, we happily set aside our calligraphy and got to work on Amuria.

What was going to happen?

Fung Wa (We were certainly sorry we'd given him that name now, much as Richie liked it. We kept getting him confused with old Wa Fung) had become the intimate of our sexy connivers. In his rude way he'd fallen in love with Kim Cha, and though he knew it was hopeless, followed her about, a faithful dog. This did not prevent him from being equally enslaved to Gurandu, and willing to serve him in all things. Kim Cha even persuaded the rustic fool to play the most dangerous part in the enterprise. He agreed to assassinate the royal pair himself.

The scheme was this: Fung was to crave a special audience alone with their Majesties, supposedly to communicate most important news from his mistress Nu Wa. He was then and there to dispatch Liu and Kalila. Gurandu, as captain of the guard, was to burst in, seize the assassin and drag him off to jail. Gurandu was thereupon to declare himself Regent of the infant heir apparent (still another Liu) and make Kim his Regentess. Meanwhile, Fung was to be allowed to escape, make his way back to his tribes, overthrow Nu Wa and "make peace" with the new Gurandu regime.

But meanwhile of course Gurandu really meant to slay Fung on the spot after the assassination. Dead men tell no tales. Kim, horrified and genuinely fond of the poor fellow, pleaded with her grim lover, but to no avail. The plot must go through as planned; Liu, Kalila and Fung all three must die.

Well, that was more fun than messages, Jane and I decided, and we forgot all about Richie and Robbie and packing and even the storm as we worked this out. We played various juicy scenes of it, with the dining room doors closed against interlopers, and the lessening rain battering the balcony roof.

We had to be prodded and shouted at to get us to lunch, dull dingy lunch. We were surprised to notice that Richie did not appear at all. Rob was there, totally silent and hulking. The girls gabbled. Mademoiselle was upstairs with Ronnie, both parents too, who ate with the invalid to cheer him up. We just wanted to get back to Amuria and Life.

Nonetheless we couldn't help being aware of a strange atmosphere of disquiet; a disquiet above and beyond that of mere packing or of stormy weather. Something was certainly going on. As though we'd heard actual rumors, we sensed disturbance in the occasional whispers of the girls, followed by solemn faces, the queer hypnotic silence of Robbie, the absence of Richie. Various people had been closeted with and interviewed by Father during the morning. This much we somehow gathered. But we did not gather what the interviews were about, or who had had them. Father was upset it seemed. The girls of course told us nothing, and knew little; but apprehension seeped down to us.

When we scuttled up to my room, in lieu of our cellar, to play Amuria, we forgot all about such things. Now we must sketch out the finale of this episode. It was too complicated to improvise as we went along. We really had to make a sort of rough libretto. My room was transformed into a vaulted conference chamber, high up in the round tower of the Old Palace. The Emperor's new construction had drained the life off from this part of the great pile, and it now became suitable for the meeting of traitors, the hatching of plots. Dimly embroidered silken hangings, threadbare and tarnished, rustled in the drafts. Outside the rains beat on the small dark casements. Inside a roaring blaze warmed the three conspirators, Gurandu, Kim Cha and Fung Wa, as they developed their campaign of murder. Behind the hangings, known only to Gurandu himself, hid trusty henchmen, ready to spring out to his defense at the least sign of treachery.

All was ready. This very day Fung was to have his private meeting with the royal pair, to do his deed, and be done by. The three conspirators were to meet here in this ancient closet, firm the details of the dire deed, drink a toast to success and be off to infamy and fortune. Kim Cha was the first to enter. Dressed in a gorgeous golden robe which covered her from neck to floor and which was, she hoped, suitable to the occasion of becoming *de facto* Empress of Amuria, she billowed in, her face pale with fear and horror, clutching a ciphered missive. This contained orders, just received, from her unseen and unknown Chinese spymasters. What shocking news! The message read: "Fung Wa is your master and our chief servant. Obey him in all things or die." She paced up and down the stone-flagged room, her shadow flickering on the walls from the fire, her gestures distraught.

When Fung Wa entered she stopped, looking at him

with horror and dismay. Tremblingly she reached out the note to him. He smiled, and took it from her, smiled and returned it to her. He nodded; she bowed deeply. Was this her old Fung Wa, the simple rustic swain, her doglike devotee? Though dressed as always in his soiled leather clothes, as though he'd just ridden in from the plains with his barbarian troopers, he had completely changed. Just to look at him, one could see he was no longer clumsy slave but suave master.

"You must do as I say," he began; and outlined for her a still more dreadful variation of the plot. He was not going to assassinate Liu and Kalila at all. Instead, he was going to warn them of Gurandu's plot. They were to call in guards, primed ahead by Fung, and then pretend to be assassinated. When Gurandu rushed in he would be seized. He was then to be imprisoned, tried, condemned, tortured, executed. Fung and Kim Cha were to be chief witnesses against him!

Kim Cha reeled, sickened with shock. And what then? Fung as survivor was to demand two rewards. The first, the hand of lady-in-waiting Kim Cha as his bride; the second, the now vacant captaincy of the royal bodyguard. Fung and Kim as the most intimate imperial servants would then ingratiate themselves in royal favor. When the time came another plot was to be engineered. Liu and Kalila were to be decoyed on a hunting trip, kidnaped and held prisoner in old Wa Fung's mountain castle. Their ransom: capitulation to the Chinese. They would still retain the throne and mastery of Amuria, but they must swear allegiance to the Emperor of China. Similar and simultaneous plots would take place in both Korea and among the Wa Hus. In the end, Fung and Kim would emerge not as rulers of Amuria only, but as the Chinese viceroys of all three kingdoms.

Kim can do nothing but bow and assent. She even

pretends enthusiasm; but in her heart is hatred, and in her hand revenge!

Then Gurandu enters. He too is resplendent. He wears a skintight armor, head to foot, of jet-black glittering metal scales, like a snake's skin. Around his tiny waist coils a gold belt in the form of dragons. He carries a great gold dragon helmet. He too is ready to become Regent. He is in famous spirits. After a brief discussion, going over each point to make sure of details, he cries, "Now let us drink to our future!" Kim Cha brings out from a cabinet a golden beaker of wine and three carved golden goblets. She fills each one. The three conspirators raise their cups, clash them together, and smiling, drink.

Suddenly Fung goes rigid. He clutches his belly. A demonic grin contorts his sallow features. Kim Cha, unobserved, has slipped a deadly poison into his cup. Gurandu, appalled and totally unsuspecting, rushes forward to his aid. Fung with his last strength whips out his sword and with both hands plunges it through Gurandu's lithe body, armor and all, just above the golden belt. Gurandu falls screaming and flailing to the floor. Kim Cha rushes forward and stabs Fung Wa in the back of the neck, a *coup de grâce*, just as Gurandu's hidden retainers emerge, too late, from hiding.

They see Kim Cha standing there with a bloody dagger and move to seize her. She loses her head completely, drops the dagger and runs toward a small opening in the further wall. It leads to a staircase and to the very top of the tower. The guards follow her, grabbing her great cloak as they pound up the steps. It comes off in their hands, impeding their progress; but Kim Cha has hardly reached the open platform on top when they are after her. She backs away from them, pleading incoherently. As they advance, she comes to the edge of the platform, which is guarded only by a low parapet. She trips, she topples, she falls backward and with one long fearful shriek plummets to her death in the courtyard below.

That's how we planned it, though obviously details and actual performance would take time. We were pretty satisfied with ourselves as we went downstairs together, having decided that our naptime was up, and curious to see what might be going on below. Nothing much it seemed. Nan pushed by us, still involved on the second floor with her packing. We could hear voices murmuring in Father's study. We wondered whose. Ronnie complained loudly. Nobody was downstairs. The boys seemed to have vanished. Jane went back up to her room. I fiddled at the piano awhile, then got bored.

As I was going up the stairs again, in the rainy gloom, Dick came jouncing athletically down, bemused, upset. He went past me without a word. His face was flushed and he looked very angry. As I made the turn and emerged up toward the landing, I could see and hear the parents. They were standing outside the open door of Father's room, talking to each other in tense whispers.

Father was saying, "He *boasted* of it! He *boasted* of it!" When I got to where I could see his face, he looked furious, more furious than I could ever remember seeing him. Mother too was obviously disturbed. She put her hand on his arm and said, almost inaudibly, "Who is thee to judge?" At that point, perhaps seeing me ascend from the shadows, they both turned and reentered the study, Father slamming the door brutally behind him.

I paused, looking about the empty hall. A fight between Dick and Father; perhaps over Richie's spy secrets. I'd have to find out somehow. I wandered on up to my room. The storm, which had calmed down after lunch, now started up again. The water lashed my window. Though I knew it was wicked, I couldn't resist the urge: I flung open the halves of it and stood there, full of empathy and getting soaked to the skin. What an orgy, what delightful destruction. The rain battered in on me, outside the trees twisted, and as though for my private satisfaction a great limb of one of the eucalyptus giants crashed to the front path.

This deserved its poem just as much as the surfeited moonlit peace of the nightingales. I had one ready, the beginnings of a supposed Amurian mythological epic which began in appropriately galloping measures, "Tarantor, Tarantor, born of the mountains," tum tiddy tum tum, tum diddy tum. So I stood, getting wet, absorbed by the battle outside, intrigued by the hinted dissonances of the household inside, as I watched the earlier dusk darken the wonderful storm-battered confusion.

ii. It was Sunday before the weather cleared up again; cleared up to an unimaginable Eden freshness and glitter and benediction of sun and greenery. I was as excited by this as by the storm, and ran about the garden after breakfast again, this time to see what damage had been done. The big limb was still down on the front path. There were branches and twigs everywhere, leaves plastered to rocks, pebbles washed away in long streaks off the walkways. All our Amurian fantasies had been obliterated except for a few in the shelter of the balcony.

Since it was Sunday, we had Meeting, back on the porch again, where it was almost too cool to be comfortable. I sat right by the rail, where the sun struck me, and I was cozy enough. Everyone was there except Dick, who'd been on mysterious car trips most of the time lately. He was due to leave for good any moment now.

Father, with some apologies for it, followed his usual custom of drawing his text from the weather. This time his moral was "Forgiveness." After conflicts, he said, times of upheaval and stress, we should be sure to clear our own atmospheres by reconciliation. Those that have done wrong must be sure their repentence was real and sincere and wholehearted. Those that have been wronged must be equally wholehearted in forgiving the repentant wrongdoer. This was so obviously all for the benefit of the boys that it made the rest of us a bit uncomfortable for them. Robbie especially sat scrunched up, with his head down, his arms thrust down between his knees, symbols and expressions for him of shame. He at least was taking it very much to heart. Whatever the wrong was he had done (and he certainly acted the repentant wrongdoer) he was reacting strongly to Father's sermonizing. Richie however seemed less inclined to be forgiving — if that's the way it was. Perhaps it was really the other way round, Robbie forgiving and Richie trespassing. I couldn't be sure. Evidently Dick was just not having any of this semi-religious celebration of renewal. Peace, then, had been declared, a superficial serenity was restored. I noticed the boys were very solicitous of each other afterward, but hardly convivial. Still, they were speaking.

We returned to our cellar after lunch. The dramas of Amuria were finished, our revels ended, and all we had left now was architecture. Everything of course had to be rebuilt, all the roads and palaces and towns and hunting lodges. Liu and Kalila, reigning gloriously and forever, since we'd obviously never work out our Chinese subversion, could devote themselves to internal improvements and good works. Richie had vanished from our lives. After that first morning of the storm, he'd had nothing to do with us. Messages had not been hidden in bedrooms, messages had not been mislaid throughout the garden. A pity in a way, but what a relief it was to get rid of him. We spent our time happy with Mah-Jongg blocks and grubby hands in the gravel.

When it grew late enough, we decided to examine more remote parts of the garden for destruction, notably Jane's new hiding place. It would certainly need some housecleaning. We sauntered in that direction, admiring the debris as we went. Discussing too what had actually been going on in the house lately. Jane brought up the subject; should we try to go on with those messages? Or wait and see if Richie did come back to us? Or just decide not to fool with them any more, no matter what Richie might do? I was firm. "Let's just tell Richie we're through." "But he'll get mad and . . . and, you know, do things to us." "No, he won't. He's got other things on his mind. I'm not worried about him. Besides, he's supposed to be friendly to Robbie now. Father said so, didn't he? So he won't have any time for us." "That's just what Father says. I don't think Robbie has forgiven him for whatever it was he did." Evidently she took that view of it. "What did Richie do anyway?" she went on. I said, "He told Father about Dick being a spy and all that." "How do *you* know?" "Well, I don't *know*; but that's what I think," and I told Jane about seeing Dick coming downstairs, so angry, and Father's remark about his "boasting of it." She was impressed. "But I don't see why that bothers Robbie." "Oh, you know how he is about Dick. Thinks he's so wonderful. I guess Robbie's mad at Richie for telling Father." Jane let it go at that, but neither of us was really satisfied, and we were frustrated not to know more. But it was obvious we were never to be allowed to know more; not if Father could help it.

As we approached our hiding place we heard strange noises. We stopped, alert, petrified. It might be an animal, perhaps even a leopard! The sounds might be those of growling; certainly an odd thrashing about. Thrilled, fearful, we crept forward as stealthily as we could. Jane stepped on something that snapped and rattled. I gave her a fierce look. We waited to see what would happen. Nothing. Another queer noise. What was it? Finally we got close enough, and were able to look through the screening of branches.

It was Robbie. We were flabbergasted. In the first place, we didn't know he knew of the place. Richie must have shown him. And then, what was he doing here anyway? He was lying full length on the pine needles, rolling about as though in agony. Jane in fact thought he must be sick, and started instinctively to go help him. I stopped her. It was not physical illness that had him. He was crying. He had turned over on his back now, and lay there writhing, rocking to and fro, the tears spurting from closed eyes, biting the side of his hand as though to keep from screaming. He arched up, slammed down again, rocked to and fro, kicking his legs about. Then with a sound much like the suppressed roar of an animal, he twisted himself face down again and lay beating his head on the ground, clawing at the dirt.

We were too shocked to breathe or move. We stood for an endless minute gaping through the tangle at this appalling exhibition, till shame and decency got the better of us and we turned, tiptoeing off, trying to make ourselves silent. "Shouldn't we get somebody?" said Jane. "He might be poisoned." I shook my head. "He's not poisoned. I think we just better leave him alone."

iii. It was most uncomfortable, after all these hints and visions, to have to come together at swimming time down on the dock and pretend that nothing had happened. All of us obviously felt the constraint. Jane and I delayed going down. When we got there Ellie was sitting with a book (P. G. Wodehouse's *Leave It to Psmith*) and she'd finished her swimming. Robbie squatted next to her, talking earnestly. I noticed he no longer wore his striped French trunks, but had gone back to his two-piece American bathing suit, white top, blue bottoms. Dick, all by himself, dove from the far end of the dock and began to swim out to sea. We were ill-at-ease, and didn't quite know what to do. It was miserable to feel this way within our own family; whether we actually liked each other at any given moment was not as important as being totally at home together. Now we were strangers, well intentioned, polite, nervous.

Ellie helped us by turning from her conversation with Robbie and saying hello. We were grateful, and went up to her, standing about, making idle remarks, while Robbie looked silently down at his feet and pushed a shell about. He rose and left us, without a word, as though miffed by our interruption. We took his place by Ellie, sitting for a while, chatting, enjoying the last of the sunshine.

Then we too went into the water, setting off one side of the dock, along from where Ellie sat, as our particular preserve, jumping off, climbing back, already making up some sort of silly game involving sea monsters. Now it was Robbie who dove from the dock end, Dick being still far out in the bay. Robbie was so expert these days, compared to that first time when Dick had inspired him, and the boys, still friends, had been so awed by him. Long ago now. It had been the diving, more than any one other thing, that had split Richie off from Robbie. Robbie could somersault, Robbie could dive from a handstand, and was now doing so. He seemed indefatigable, and went through the repertoire as though training for an Olympic test. Annoyed by the constriction of his old bathing suit top, he tore off the heavy white jersey and threw it on the rocks.

When Richie came down at last, he paid no attention to

Robbie. Instead he went up to Ellie as we had done; like us he squatted and chatted. Ellie was neutral territory, still everyone's friend. Then he saw us. He came over, pushed Jane into the water, crowed over her, splashed us both, and then like Dick started to swim out into the Mediterranean, toward our rocky islands, toward Africa. He had somehow managed to break up our silly game, such as it was. Now we were just swimmers; just swimmers and a bit bored, getting a bit chilly too as the sun grew lower and the shadows crept out from the cliffs.

When Dick finally returned from his water trip, and stood up on the dock, strong and panting, Robbie greeted him shyly and walked away as though to pick up the top of his bathing suit and reassume modesty. Dick spoke to him; almost a command, but quieter. Rob turned. They stood facing each other, tense and silent.

I and Jane were sitting side by side thrashing the water with our feet, seeing who could bring up the biggest geyser. When Dick had emerged, I'd turned about to look. I was still looking back when I felt a sudden clammy grip about one ankle. It was Richie. He'd been swimming underwater and now surfaced, his lank dark hair streaming down over his face, a true enough sea monster, dragging me into the water. Jane screamed in mock terror and splashed water into his face with her feet. I managed to get my leg away from him, so he turned on Jane. Still kicking water in Richie's face, I swiveled about again to look at Robbie and Dick in their curious trance. Jane was still screaming at Richie as she inched off the dock and noisily into the water. Ellie still was serenely absorbed in her book. Richie, done with Jane and while she attacked him underwater, now grabbed both my legs. "I've got you, you slimy little bugger," he shouted, "I'll fix *you!*" As he dragged me in, and before I turned back to him, I had a final glimpse of Robbie, silently biting the side of his hand, eyes wide, staring at Dick as odd contractive spasms jerked down his body, while Dick stayed as he was, a statue.

Then I was in the water, Jane and I and Richie all in a froth, salt in our mouths and eyes, flailing and mock furious. Suddenly Richie pushed us both away from him and tried to clamber out on land. We saw what he had seen: Robbie suddenly turning, stumbling, then sprinting up the dock, past Ellie, up the steps, through the gate and into the darkness of the garden. Richie paused, arrested, crouched half erect on the dock, awkward and dripping. Ellie came out of her book and started to go after Rob.

"No," said Dick, putting out an arm to stop her. "No, leave him be. Let him go." We all stayed for a moment as we were, Jane and I in the water, Richie, Ellie, Dick caught as though playing Red Light, Still-Pond-No-More-Moving, Ellie about to run up into the garden, Richie half stooping and very bedraggled, Dick with his preventive arm out to hold them back.

Then we moved. By common consent our swim was over. Now the sun had gone back of the trees and it was cold. Richie raced off first, probably hoping to catch Rob dressing in the dining room. Then Jane and I scuttled up toward the house, our teeth chattering, through the dazzling cool glow of the evening. Ellie and Dick walked briskly behind us. "I'm so worried about Robbie," said she. There was a pause. Then Dick said, "He'll be all right," and he added, almost under his breath, "I hope." "But he seems so upset," said Ellie, solicitous. "What's the matter with him?"

Dick hesitated again, and in a rather strained voice said, "His father's been scolding him." "Scolding him? Scolding Robbie? What for?" "The way he's been treating Richie." "*Rob* treating *Richie*? I should think it would be the other way round!" "You might think so; but then Richie's a special case, isn't he?" "He certainly is!" "He depends on

Robbie so; and then when Robbie's cold to him and cuts him off, he can't take it. He complained to his father, and his father gave Rob a talking to." "Well, I still don't see why he's *that* upset." Dick paused again. He was not happy with this conversation. "Robbie's not used to being scolded you know," he said at last. "Especially by his father. It's not the normal thing. It was quite a shock for him." "I still say it's Richie's fault, and Father had no business taking it out on poor Robbie." "It's not our business either, is it?" Dick's rebuke was gentle, but pointed. Ellie was the one now to pause. "I suppose not," she muttered reluctantly. "But I *am* worried about Robbie just the same." "Aren't we all? Aren't we all?" said Dick, and they fell silent.

I couldn't honestly say I was. If anyone could take care of himself I should have thought it would be Robbie. If I had to be sorry for anyone in this, to me, rather unnecessary wrangle, it would be poor Richie. Not of course that I normally had much sympathy for him; but I knew how it felt to have a friend cut off, to find oneself really alone, even in a family. I remembered vividly what it was like being separated from Jane, having no one to confide in, no one to play with. And how much worse for Richie, who really didn't quite belong to the family anyway, than for me. Besides, I thought rather smugly, it really did serve Robbie right to be out of favor for once, to realize that other people could be right and he could be wrong. I felt Father was merely carrying on an educative process begun by me. Blasted from his unassailable position of virtue, Robbie could be made human like the rest of us, a real person rather than a Greek idol, standing up there on one strong toe, Mercury in his pond sneering down on the world from a godlike superiority.

Then it occurred to me, rather bleakly, that perhaps all this fuss, all this mystery had nothing to do with spies after all! Maybe that was just Richie's usual blowhard, windy nonsense, a screen to conceal his true feelings of pain and jealousy. No spies, no codes, nothing for the police or the government to be concerned over, nothing but a stupid, unromantic, boring family squabble, ducks and chickens. I refused to face this. What was Dick "boasting" about if not his spying? Surely just a scolding from Father about being mean to Richie would not have driven Rob to such excesses of grief, such agonies as those we'd seen in our hiding place.

iv. We came to the house. I looked into the dining room as I passed. The boys were gone. I'd undressed this time in my own room. Once up there, rather unintentionally, only half clothed with my shirt unbuttoned and one shoe off, I got absorbed in stamps. A piece of fudge saved from the day before stayed my hunger. When the room got too cold and dark I closed the window and lit the floor lamp, but still didn't bother to put on my other shoe.

In the circle of light, on the cold floor, I lost myself. I had no watch, but I did have a small brisk cream-colored alarm clock, and when I next looked up at it I saw it read seven-thirty, way past suppertime. I thought I must have missed hearing the bell, that incised Algerian bell guarded so jealously from us, hidden in the kitchen by Celestine. Supper might be all over. And suddenly I was so hungry; I hadn't noticed before.

I put on my shoe and trotted downstairs to see what was the matter, leaving my stamp material spread out on the floor, in the dark cold room under the yellow circle of light. There seemed to be a commotion downstairs, the effect of a crowd milling about in the front hall. I couldn't make out what was happening. The crowd resolved itself into only a few people, when I actually got down there, but they were all moving and talking, watching and waiting, terribly upset. No one wanted to bother with me. I asked Nan, who came in from outside, what had happened. An accident. What? Who? Where? Nan left me without answering, went outside again, and then ran in shouting, "They're here!" Who was here? Everyone else, that is Father, Mother, Ellie, Celestine, started out the door. Father turned back, saw me and said peremptorily, "Go back to your room and stay there." "But what's *happened?*" "Robbie. He fell and hurt himself. Stay in your room till suppertime. Do as I say." And he left me alone in the hall.

I slowly obeyed him, dragging up the stairs, wondering where Jane and Richie and Dick could be; then suddenly hurrying two steps at a time to get to my window. Sure enough, I could see everything from there. A big white ambulance stood by our gate in a blaze of headlights, and after an interminable wait, as the green traces of twilight subsided and it grew darker and increasingly colder, a procession emerged from the bottom of the garden. First flashlights down there, winking, throwing their beams about; then slowly a cluster of jerking black figures carrying a long pale thing; a stretcher, humped up, which came closer along the path, across to the gate, out and around and into the back of the ambulance. It was too dark to make out any of the details.

The ambulance left with a great whoosh, and a gaggle of people, only Father really distinguishable by his limp and his cane, crossed in the dusk to the garage. Then out came two cars, Dick's and ours, and streamed off toward town after the ambulance. Suddenly everything seemed deserted. I closed the window and picked up my stamps as at last the bell for supper sounded. Only Jane and I, Ellie and Mademoiselle and Ronnie were left to eat it. Ellie told us, finally, what had happened. She'd gone into the dining room, on the way up from swimming, to leave Robbie's bathing suit top there. She'd noticed his clothes, neatly folded on a chair, and was worried. He obviously had not yet come up from the beach. She wondered where he could be. So she went down there again, first climbing to the tower to look about. At first she saw nothing, but finally, looking straight below, she saw him sprawled on the rocks. When she got down to him she found him unconscious, badly hurt, all bloody. She ran to the house, told Father, the ambulance was called for, and now Robbie was in the hospital. Both parents had gone with him. They were spending the night at the castle; Nan too. Richie refused to be left behind. He and Dick had both gone to the beach, sitting by Robbie until the ambulance men came, and were both now in town too. Ellie couldn't tell us how badly Robbie was hurt; but pretty badly. He had fallen from the tower. She had no idea what he could have been doing. Probably practicing one of his crazy handstands on the parapet. But why there, and why then? It didn't make any sense. Ellie got so worked up telling us that she had to leave the table.

When she came back, red-eyed, she was composed enough, but wouldn't talk about the accident any more. Mademoiselle had hurried Ronnie through supper, distracting him so he wouldn't hear, then leaving quickly. Ellie skipped dessert. Only Jane and I stayed on, awed, depressed, excited. We went over and over it: what had he been doing, why had he done it?

v. There was a horrid sort of vacuum in the Villa Esperance next day. Jane and I rattled around in it forlornly. There was nobody to tell us what to do, except Ellie of course, and Mademoiselle if she chose; above all no safe background, no setting for us, nothing to define our role and place in the world. There being no restraints, we had no desires. Even being alone in my room was no longer a refuge. I sat on the terrace in the sun, moodily trying to concentrate on *Leave It to Psmith*, which I'd taken over from Ellie. The day was so wonderful, too. I felt guilty not to be doing something about it; the air still basically cool and crisp, but a blazing sun, an electric dryness in everything, a hot silence.

Sometime in midmorning both Father and Dick returned, but separately. Dick had to go today. In fact, he had meant to leave yesterday, driving by dark, supposedly to his lady love in Cannes, to her villa with its parties and pillared swimming pool. Ellie gave us periodic bulletins. Mother was in a state of collapse, up in the Great Lady's castle and tended by Nan as nurse. Richie had had to be dragged from the hospital. He had wanted to spend the night sleeping at the foot of Robbie's bed like a dog. As soon as he could this morning he'd gone right back to the hospital; but they wouldn't let anyone in. Robbie was still unconscious. No one seemed to know exactly how serious his condition was, but he did have a fractured skull and other broken bones. Mother sent messages for us to be good and stay out of trouble. Not very consoling. Ellie was to watch out for us. Nobody knew when Mother and Nan and Richie would be back, or how long Robbie would have to stay in the hospital. All our family plans were permanently deranged.

Our doldrums were dissipated by Ellie. She organized an expedition, just the three of us, up to the church of La Garde to pray for Robbie. It was an original idea, one that appealed to us, typical of Ellie's thoughtful sanctimoniousness. We debated whether we should take the dog Lagarde with us, then decided not to. He was handed over to Celestine; poor thing, as deserted and derelict as we were.

It was so still on the way up through the pines, so

aromatic, so bright. I listened, deliberately, for sinister sounds in the bushes, but of course there were none. When we reached the top the distance spread out shimmering before us, the mountains clear but colorless. Nobody there; but pilgrims had been, and the part of the cross I'd washed clean was already scribbled over again.

Inside it was dark and clammy. The walls, cluttered with their naïve votive pictures, received our casual, scornful inspection. Ellie led the way, kneeling with her head and hands on the back of one of the few loose chairs that served in place of pews for the occasional worshipers. We too found chairs, and followed suit.

How to pray for Robbie? Wordless petitions, or one of the perfunctory obeisances we still made every night at bedtime, "GodblessMotherandFatherandNanandEllie," the Lord's Prayer added, equally parrotlike. I tried to feel the grief and sympathy for Robbie that I should feel. He was after all a brother, a half-brother at least. I could touch nothing but a sort of horror at the realness of what had happened. He really *was* close to dying, someone I knew; that, and a feeling I tried to suppress, of being rather thrilled at the magnitude of the event.

"Please Lord make Robbie all right, and make Mother and Father feel better," was about the best I could manage, squeezing my eyes shut in the gloom, trying to *feel* the proper things. I was grateful when Ellie rose and we were allowed to go out into the wonderful warmth. She appeared to be all sad and illuminated and thoroughly satisfied with her emotional state. Dead-pan Jane gave away no secrets.

We stood for a silent moment, looking at the view, looking at the cross. I whispered, pointing out to Jane the new names there. She giggled at them, and was interested as I showed her just where the leopard had appeared, just where he had reentered the laurel thicket. Ellie fortunately paid no attention to us, lost in melancholy contemplation of the far pale bay and the pale mountains.

She pulled herself together. "Come along," she ordered, and we reluctantly followed. It would be nice to play up here, to explore. Jane even went so far as to ask Ellie if we couldn't stay. But Ellie was firm; and there was something a bit sacrilegious in the thought. We had to go away from this sunny place, significant in its associations, go back down to the empty prison of the villa. We walked through the resinous pine woods, rather sullen and resentful. We turned the corner of the wall back of the garage that contained Celestine's scorpion-filled garden. I wondered what Richie would do now with all his souvenirs; and with his secrets too. I wondered if anyone would ever know now what it was Dick had done, whether he was truly an enemy spy, say, or a traitor. All that would be wiped out of Richie's mind by the accident. Dick was probably in his garage room right now packing up to leave forever. We'd never know.

When we came to the road, Ellie, the Young Policewoman, ostentatiously stopped us, looking overcarefully both ways along the road. As we stood there, a gust of wind came down the hill from the church, hushing the pines, stirring faint tendrils of fresh dust from the roadside up against the yellow wall and through the bars of the gate. The gust died away oracular through the noon, through the shiny garden and out toward the sea. We crossed the road in the renewal of the hot dry stillness.

vi. Out of habit we went to our "nap," our play in the cellar, just as usual, just as if there was somebody to make us go there. Mademoiselle was too busy superintending Celestine and the house, fussing over Ronnie, to bother much with us. Ellie meant to be disciplinary but didn't really know our proper routine. Everyone else was still in town but Father, who secluded himself in his room, and whom we had not even glimpsed since he came home; and Dick.

We could have been doing anything; but what else would we rather have done? Amuria, palaces and roads and pavilions, and when we'd had enough of the cellar, out into the staring sun and up to the front of the house — the great plains of the Wa Hus — to build a new system of highways and camps. It was so hot out, after the damp and cool cellar, and so taut. Not a leaf moved except for a perpetual slight dangling of the eucalyptus leaves. Not even cicadas yet, since the storm and coldness. So quiet we could hear noises from inside the house, the running of a spigot from a bathroom, voices from way up in the parents' rooms, two men talking. We couldn't hear what they were saying, as we walked around the corner, but just as we turned the steps between the century plant and the oleander, we heard a sudden shout, "Unclean! Unclean!" echoing from above us. Who was that? Father? The other man's voice must be Dick's.

His car was waiting for him by the gate, packed, ready to leave, glittering silver. We settled in front of the house, in the very middle of the gravel, to create our base of operations. This was to be the Emperor Liu's principal headquarters, from which activities would radiate. We started to clear a square space for him, dot eucalyptus nuts about in ordered rows, build up gravel dikes.

The front door opened and Uncle Dick himself appeared in the black entranceway, coming slowly, slowly out of the villa onto the steps. He stopped there, totally unconscious of us, somewhat dazed. He was dressed as he had been when he first came, sailor pants, striped jersey, but no beret. He stood interminably halfway down the steps, holding the iron curve of the railing with one hand, his other hand to the left side of his face. We held our breaths, hoping he wouldn't see us, hoping to avoid the embarrassment of falsely cordial good-byes.

It was so very still, so very hot. I felt I could listen to the sun beating down, like the hum of a motor. Dick took his hand away from his face and looked at it. Across his brown cheekbone, where his hand had been, was a livid bar of purple black, mark from the blow of a stick, and I noticed for the first time a bloody patch and bruise on his left eyebrow.

He stood looking at the traces of the blood on his fingers, still not observing us, still not moving. Then very slowly, like an old man, as though his knees were creaking, he came down the steps, went stiffly to the gate. Stiffly, very slowly, he slipped into his car. He sat for a while on the red seat, with legs dangling out the open door, still dazed; then suddenly and swiftly moved over, slammed the door, roared off down the road. He had never seen us at all.

We stirred, released from our tension. The silence seemed to come alive again, and we chattered about our plans; busy once more with our play, absorbed once more and happy in our garden.